COURAGE AND HONOUR

THE TAU ROSE to meet his charge and though full-enclosing helmets obscured their faces, Uriel saw the panic in them. They had come here expecting an easy mission, but were now in a fight for their lives. A few snap shots flashed past him. Uriel's squad followed him into the fight, but this moment was his and his alone.

He hammered his boot through the chest of the next tau and smashed his sword through the armour of the warrior behind him. More tau turned their weapons on him, but he was already among them and it was too late for guns. This was a close quarters fight that required the brutal skills of a killer and there were no finer killers than the Space Marines. Uriel fought with total economy of motion as he struck the tau like a thunderbolt. No blow was wasted and each time his sword or fist clove flesh or armour, an enemy fell.

The tau were helpless against him, for he was a warrior of the Adeptus Astartes and he was fighting for more than just victory, he was fighting for the glory of his Chapter. For too long Uriel had fought for redemption or simply survival.

This fight was for the honour of the Ultramarines.

A WARHAMMER 40,000 NOVEL

COURAGE AND HONOUR

Graham McNeill

BLACK LIBRARY

To Justin and Vashti; great mates and generous hosts.

A BLACK LIBRARY PUBLICATION

First published in Great Britain in 2009.
Paperback edition published in 2010 by
BL Publishing,
Games Workshop Ltd.,
Willow Road, Nottingham,
NG7 2WS, UK.

10 9 8 7 6 5 4 3 2 1

Cover illustration by Adrian Smith.
Map by Adrian Wood.

A CIP record for this book is available from the British Library.

UK ISBN 13: 978 1 84416 722 7
US ISBN 13: 978 1 84416 723 4

See the Black Library on the Internet at
www.blacklibrary.com

Find out more about Games Workshop
and the world of Warhammer 40,000 at
www.games-workshop.com

Printed and bound in the UK.

IT IS THE 41st millennium. For more than a hundred centuries the Emperor has sat immobile on the Golden Throne of Earth. He is the master of mankind by the will of the gods, and master of a million worlds by the might of his inexhaustible armies. He is a rotting carcass writhing invisibly with power from the Dark Age of Technology. He is the Carrion Lord of the Imperium for whom a thousand souls are sacrificed every day, so that he may never truly die.

YET EVEN IN his deathless state, the Emperor continues his eternal vigilance. Mighty battlefleets cross the daemon-infested miasma of the warp, the only route between distant stars, their way lit by the Astronomican, the psychic manifestation of the Emperor's will. Vast armies give battle in His name on uncounted worlds. Greatest amongst his soldiers are the Adeptus Astartes, the Space Marines, bio-engineered super-warriors. Their comrades in arms are legion: the Imperial Guard and countless planetary defence forces, the ever-vigilant Inquisition and the tech-priests of the Adeptus Mechanicus to name only a few. But for all their multitudes, they are barely enough to hold off the ever-present threat from aliens, heretics, mutants – and worse.

TO BE A man in such times is to be one amongst untold billions. It is to live in the cruellest and most bloody regime imaginable. These are the tales of those times. Forget the power of technology and science, for so much has been forgotten, never to be re-learned. Forget the promise of progress and understanding, for in the grim dark future there is only war. There is no peace amongst the stars, only an eternity of carnage and slaughter, and the laughter of thirsting gods.

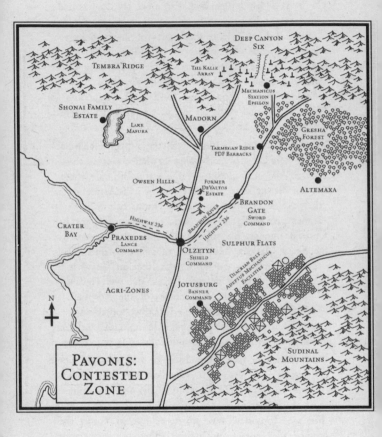

DEEP CANYON
SIX

TEMBRA RIDGE

THE KALIZ
ARRAY

MADORN

MECHANICUS
STATION
EPSILON

SHONAI FAMILY
ESTATE

LAKE
MASURA

GRESHA
FOREST

TARMEGAN RIDGE
PDF BARRACKS

OWSEN HILLS

FORMER
DEVALTOS
ESTATE

ALTEMAXA

BRANDON
GATE
SWORD
COMMAND

CRATER
BAY

HIGHWAY 236

SULPHUR FLATS

PRAXEDES
LANCE
COMMAND

HIGHWAY 236

OLZETYN
SHIELD
COMMAND

DHACRIAN BELT
ADEPTUS MECHANICUS
FACILITIES

AGRI-ZONES

JOTUSBURG
BANNER
COMMAND

N

SUDINAL
MOUNTAINS

PAVONIS:
CONTESTED
ZONE

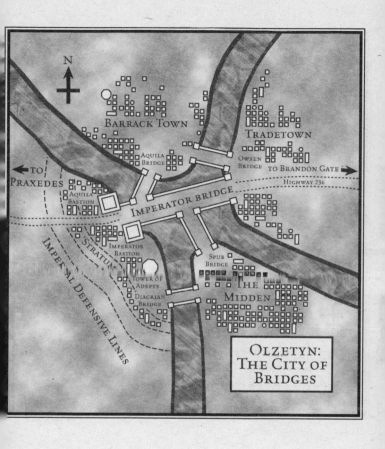

OLZETYN: THE CITY OF BRIDGES

N

BARRACK TOWN

TRADETOWN

Aquila Bridge

Owsen Bridge to BRANDON GATE

TO PRAXEDES

HIGHWAY 236

Aquila Bastion

IMPERATOR BRIDGE

STRATUM

Imperator Bastion

Spur Bridge

Tower of Adepts

THE MIDDEN

Diacrian Bridge

IMPERIAL DEFENSIVE LINES

Planetary Designation: Pavonis

Imperial Reference: AD Terra 101.01
[M/FW- Industrial World:
Ultima Segmentum]
Cross Ref: Tarsis Ultra, Taren IV, BX-998
Population: Eleven billion

Military and Governance

Aestimare: B350
Governor's Capital: Brandon Gate
Planetary Garrison: 44th Lavrentian Hussars –
Reduced Strength.
Planetary Draft: On hold, pending Administratum
review and sanction.
Prefix Inquisitoria: Pax Bellum Vigilatus.

Production

Tithe Grade: Exactis Particular
Chief Exports: Tank chassis, engines and ordnance.
Local liquor known as *Uskavar*.

Compiler's Notes:

Pavonis is a world typical of the Eastern Fringe, productive, hard-working and, previously, able to function with minimal intervention from the Administratum. However, such independence can foster a dangerously independent 'frontier spirit' that often manifests in worlds distant from Terra. Kasimir de Valtos, head of one of the planet's major industrial cartels, sought to subvert Imperial rule on Pavonis with the aid of xenos pirates, and dragged the planet into a brief but brutal civil war for reasons beyond the Inquisitorial clearance of this document to record. Only the timely intervention of my former master, Inquisitor Barzano, and Captain Uriel Ventris of the Ultramarines halted the planet's slide into anarchy. Order was restored to Pavonis, and the previous Planetary Governor, Mykola Shonai, was allowed to serve out the remainder of her term of office under the auspices of the Administratum. Imperial Guard units from the 44th Lavrentian Hussars, together with emissaries from the Adeptus Terra and Adeptus Ministorum have been put in place to bring a measure of Imperial stability to the planet. Governor Shonai's nephew, Koudelkar, now commands Pavonis, though I fear he is not the administrator his aunt was.

Lortuen Perjed – Permanent Administratum Observer to Pavonis.

PART 1
PURE OF HEART, AND STRONG OF BODY

ᚢ
ONE

A TRAITOR HAD once made his home among the tumbled slopes of the Owsen Hills. The late Kasimir de Valtos had dwelt in a lofty, marble-fronted villa, finely constructed and lavishly appointed with every amenity his wealth and position could provide. His extensive estate ran with game, servants attended to his every need, and the thousands of workers that slaved in his many weapon mills, engine assembly yards and artillery manufactorum could only dream of their master's luxurious lifestyle.

Wealth, position and power had been his, but now the traitor was dead and his estate was overgrowing, his palatial demesne little more than stumps of stonework scattered throughout waving fields of untended grass. Vengeful workers had looted his villa of anything worth stealing in the wake of the civil war that his schemes had unleashed. They had cast its walls to ruin and set fires where once he had plotted to become an immortal god.

Such were the dreams of men, grandiose and fleeting.

* * *

AN ORNAMENTAL LAKE rippled in the sunlight before the ruined villa, fed by an underground aqueduct linked to the wide river that flowed south from Tembra Ridge in the north. The river cut a path through the de Valtos estate, splitting into dozens of narrow watercourses as it threaded its way through the undulant terrain. Eventually, these smaller rivers came together and meandered southwards to join the Brandon River on its journey to the ocean in the west.

Though the de Valtos lands were abandoned, the landscape silent and the forests growing wild, they were far from empty. Scattered throughout the Owsen Hills, stealthy observers patiently kept watch on the many sharp-sided gullies and shallow valleys.

The traitor was dead, but his lands were still important.

A tremor in the grass was the first sign of movement, a barely discernible bow wave as a stealthy humanoid figure in olive-coloured armour ghosted slowly from the trees at the base of a low hill. It moved gracefully, crouched over, its every step carefully placed as its helmeted head swung back and forth, scanning the terrain with the patient eye of a hunter.

Or a scout, thought Uriel Ventris from his position of concealment in a tumbled fan of rocks on the slopes of the hill above the ruined villa.

Soon, other scouts followed the first from the trees, moving in pairs as they eased towards the fallen stones of the de Valtos villa. There were eight in total, their movements slick and professional.

Though the scouts advanced with a smooth, precise gait, there was something fundamentally wrong with their movements, something *inhuman*. Their posture was subtly different, as if their bone structure wasn't quite right or their feet were shaped differently to those of humans.

The Ultramarines had learned much of the ways of the tau and their rapidly expanding empire on the killing fields of Malbede, Praetonis V and Augura.

That experience was being put to good use here on Pavonis.

The lead scout reached the edge of the ruins, and placed a gloved hand to the side of its helmet, a tapered dome with a vox aerial on one side and a gem-like optical device on the other.

Watching the scouts spread out, Uriel saw that they had read the ground well.

Just as he had done earlier that day.

A flashing icon lit up on the inner surface of Uriel's helmet visor, an insistent urging from his senior sergeant to release the killing precision of his warriors. He ignored it for the time being. Instincts honed on a hundred battlefields were telling Uriel that the prey was not yet fully in the killing box, and the risk of their target detecting vox-traffic was too great.

No sooner had the scout finished his silent communication than a prowling vehicle with curved flanks emerged from the trees. It had the bulk of a tank, but hovered just above the ground, bending the stalks of grass as it drew close to the scouts. A rotary-barrelled cannon spun lazily below its tapered prow, and flaring dorsal engines kept it aloft with a barely audible hum.

The tank was unmistakably alien, its curved lines and silent menace putting Uriel in mind of a shark prowling the seabed.

From the intelligence files Uriel had read en route to Pavonis from Macragge, he recognised it as a Devilfish, a troop carrier analogous to the Rhino. It was fast, agile and armoured to the front, but vulnerable to attacks from the rear. Codex ambush tactics would serve them well here.

The alien tank came to a halt, and a pair of flat discs with under-slung weapon mounts detached from the vehicle's frontal fins. They hovered just above the tank, twitching sensor spines rotating on their upper surfaces.

Sniffer dogs.

Uriel glanced anxiously towards the grassy mounds spread throughout the ruins of the de Valtos villa.

Apparently satisfied that there was nothing in the immediate vicinity, the hovering discs returned to their mounts on the Devilfish, and the lead scout unsnapped a device from the rigid backpack he wore. Uriel watched as a pair of thin legs extended from the device and the scout planted it in the ground in front of him.

Lights flickered on the domed surface of the device, and Uriel's auto-senses detected a low-level pressure pulse sweep over the landscape.

Some kind of three-dimensional cartographic device? Imperial forces that had fought the tau before had christened these warriors Pathfinders, and the name was an apt one. These troops were thrown out ahead of an army to reconnoitre the ground before it and plot the best routes of advance.

The Pathfinders were working quickly, and every second Uriel delayed gave them more time to detect his warriors. The Ultramarines were in place, and, as Uriel watched the enemy scouts at work, he knew it was time to unleash them.

'Primary units, engage,' he whispered into his throat mic, knowing it was the last order he would need to issue in this engagement.

The Pathfinder's head snapped up as soon as the words left Uriel's mouth, but it was already too late for the tau.

Two Space Marines from Uriel's Devastator section rose from the rocks to the east of the ruined villa, carrying bulky missile launchers on their shoulders. The tau scattered, and the Devilfish's engines rose in pitch as the driver angled his frontal section towards the threat.

Uriel smiled grimly as the Devastators fired their weapons, the missiles *swooshing* through the air on arcing contrails of smoke.

The first detonated above a pair of Pathfinders as they sought to reach the cover of the trees, shredding their bodies into torn masses of butchered meat and shattered armour plates. The second slammed into the frontal armour of the Devilfish with a thunderous bang followed by a smeared explosion of black smoke and shrapnel.

The Devilfish rocked under the impact of the missile, but its armour remained intact. Its rotary cannon spooled up, and a burst of heavy-calibre shells blitzed from the weapon, tracing a blazing arc between the tank and its attackers. The ground above the villa exploded as the hillside disintegrated under the blizzard of impacts, but Uriel's warriors had already ducked back into cover.

The roaring of the cannon was tremendous, but Uriel still heard the metallic cough of two more missiles being launched. He glanced over to the west, where the other half of the Devastator section opened fire. The tank tried to reverse its turn, but the missiles were faster.

One punched through the rear assault ramp as the other slammed into the left engine nacelle. The back of the Devilfish exploded in a spray of red-hot fragments, scything down another Pathfinder. A secondary blast completed its destruction, and the blazing vehicle crashed to the ground.

Uriel rose from the rocks, and locked his bolter in the crook of his arm. Behind him, a ten-strong squad of blue-armoured Space Marines rose with him, matching his pace as he set off towards the killing ground.

The surviving aliens made for the cover of the villa, but Uriel knew they wouldn't reach it.

As the Pathfinders reached the ruined dwelling, the grassy mounds within its fallen walls shifted, and a combat squad of Ultramarines scouts cast off their camo-cloaks.

The scouts opened fire, bolter rounds punching through the lightly armoured Pathfinders, and hurling them from their feet. Two were killed instantly, and a third screamed in agony as the explosion of a mass-reactive shell ripped his arm from his shoulder.

The two remaining Pathfinders returned fire, their rifles spitting bright bolts among the scouts in dazzling bursts of light and sound. The aliens fired a last defiant burst before fleeing for the trees, all pretence of stealth forgotten in their desire to escape the trap that had been set for them.

Uriel dropped to one knee and swung his gleaming, eagle-plated bolter to his shoulder. The weapon's targeting mechanism was synced to his helmet, and he tracked the zigzagging pattern of an enemy warrior for a moment before pulling the trigger.

His bolter slammed back with a fearsome recoil, and the Pathfinder dropped, the bottom half of his right leg pulped by the shell's detonation. Seeing that escape wasn't an option, the last tau warrior halted and threw down his weapon. He turned, and began walking back towards the blazing wreck of the Devilfish with his hands in the air.

'You've gotten rusty with your targeting rituals,' said a voice at Uriel's side. 'You were aiming for the middle of his back, weren't you?'

Uriel turned, and slung his bolter. Then he reached up to disengage the vacuum seals at his gorget. Pressurised air hissed, and he lifted his golden-winged helm clear. He turned towards the speaker, a Space Marine in the livery of a veteran sergeant of the Ultramarines, his red helmet encircled by a white laurel wreath.

'I was,' admitted Uriel, 'and you're right about the targeting rituals, I fell out of the habit while I was away.'

'Best get back into the habit then, quickly.'

'I will,' said Uriel, surprised at the sergeant's caustic tone.

'We should get down there. The scouts are securing the prisoner,' said the sergeant before making his way downhill.

Uriel nodded and followed Learchus.

IT FELT GOOD to lead warriors in combat, even if his involvement had been minimal once the planning had been done. Smoke from the smouldering Devilfish caught in the back of Uriel's throat, the trace chemicals triggering a number of sensory impulses within him. He tasted the abrasive compounds used to etch the insignia on the vehicle's hull, the alien lubricants used on the engine mounts, and the coarse, roasted scent of the seared crew.

Uriel ran a hand over his scalp, the dark hair cut short. A band of silver had developed at his temples, though his grey, storm cloud eyes were as sharp as ever. Cut from a classical mould, Uriel's features were angular and sharp, without the distinctive flattening common to some members of the Adeptus Astartes.

His physique was lean for a Space Marine, although, cloaked in his new armour, he was as bulky and fearsome as the rest of his warriors. The sword of Idaeus was belted at Uriel's waist, and a green cloak hung from his shoulders, secured with a pin in the shape of a white rose that recalled his last journey to Pavonis.

Uriel surveyed the utter destruction of the enemy as Learchus formed the warriors of the 4th Company into a perimeter around the site of the ambush.

Two Space Marines guarded the tau prisoner, the only survivor of the ambush, who knelt facing an upright slab with his hands on his head. A pair of Rhino APCs idled on what had once been a wide gravelled driveway. Their side doors were open, and a Space Marine gunner manned the storm bolter mounted on the vehicle's forward cupola. The kill-team of scouts gathered their photo-absorptive camo-cloaks from the ruins, cloaks that ensured the first inkling most targets had of the scouts' presence was the sound of the shot that blew their head off.

Watching Learchus issue his orders, Uriel was struck by how his friend had changed since he and Pasanius had marched from the Fortress of Hera and into exile.

Learchus had promised to look after Uriel's warriors, and he had done a fine job, rebuilding the company after the losses taken on Tarsis Ultra, and leading its warriors in battle against a host of orks on Espandor. The sergeant's orders were obeyed with alacrity and respect, and, though Uriel was sure it was just his imagination, it was as though Learchus carried himself a little taller than before.

Command had been good for him, it seemed.

Uriel beckoned to Learchus, walking towards the wreckage of the Devilfish.

'Sergeant,' said Uriel as Learchus approached and snapped to attention. Learchus hammered his fist against his breastplate, and then reached up to remove his helmet.

Learchus was everything a Space Marine should be: tall and proud, with a regal countenance that was the image of the heroes carved in luminous marble upon the steps of the Temple of Correction on Macragge. His blond hair was cropped tightly to his skull, his features wide and clearly of the most illustrious lineage.

Each of the worlds of Ultramar had differing quirks of genetics that no amount of genhancement could eradicate, making it an easy matter to identify from where a warrior hailed. Learchus was unmistakably a native of Macragge, fortress-world of the Ultramarines, and a planet from which the greatest of heroes had marched onto the pages of legend.

'Captain,' said Learchus.

'Is everything all right?'

'Everything is in hand,' said Learchus. 'Sentries are in place, enemy weapons are gathered, and I have deployed long-range pickets to watch for follow on forces.'

'Very good,' said Uriel, keeping his tone light, 'but that's not what I was asking.'

'Then what were you asking?'

'Are you planning on leaving *me* anything to do?'

'Everything that needs attending to is being done,' replied Learchus. 'What orders are left to give?'

'I am the captain of this company, Learchus,' said Uriel, hating that he sounded so petulant. 'The orders are mine to give.'

Learchus was too controlled to show much in the way of emotion, but Uriel saw a shadow cross his face, and guessed the reason for his stiff formality. He decided not to press the point. The company's leaders had to be seen to display unity of purpose, especially now, so soon after Uriel's return.

'Of course, sir. Sorry, sir,' replied Learchus.

'We'll talk about this later,' said Uriel, turning and marching towards the captured Pathfinder. 'Now, let's see what our prisoner has to say for himself.'

The alien heard their approaching steps, and turned his helmeted head to face them. One of the Space Marine guards delivered a sharp blow to the alien's neck with the butt of his bolter, and it sagged against the stub of broken wall with a shrill yelp of pain.

The captive gripped the stonework, and Uriel saw that he had only four fingers on each hand.

'Get him up,' said Uriel.

Learchus reached down and hauled the prisoner to his feet, and Uriel was impressed by its defiant body language. This creature was from an alien species, a race utterly apart from humanity, yet the hostility in its posture was unmistakable.

'Take it off,' said Uriel, miming the act of lifting off a helmet.

The alien didn't move, and Uriel drew his bolt pistol, tapping the barrel against the side of the alien's helmet.

'Off,' he said.

The tau reached up, unsnapped a trio of clips and a cable-feed where it attached to his armour, and lifted clear the helmet.

Learchus snatched it from the alien, and Uriel found himself looking down at the face of the prisoner.

The creature's skin was the colour of weathered lead, grey and textured like old linen, with a sheen to it that might have been perspiration. It had a curious odour, a pungent mix of smells that Uriel found impossible to place: part animal, part burned plastic and hot spices, but wholly alien.

A glossy topknot of white hair trailed from the top of its scalp to the base of its neck, held in place by gold bands studded with gems.

The alien looked up at Uriel with eyes of dull red, set deep in a flat face without any visible indication of a nose. A curious vertical indentation, like an old surgical wound or birth scar, sat in the centre of its forehead, and the cast of its features, though alien and strange, suggested that their captive was female.

The alien's amber pupils burned with hostility.

'This is a world of the Imperium,' said Uriel. 'Why are you here?'

The alien spat a brief torrent of language, a lyrical stream of unfamiliar tones and exotic multi-part words. Uriel's enhanced cognitive faculties were able to sort the streams into word groupings, but he could make no sense of them. He hadn't expected to understand the alien's language, but had held out a vague hope that it might have had a grasp of Imperial Gothic.

'Do. You. Understand. Me?' he said, slowly and carefully enunciating each word.

Once again, the captive spoke in her singsong language, and Uriel knew that she had simply repeated the words she had already spoken.

'Do you know what it's saying?' asked Learchus.

'No,' said Uriel, 'but I don't need a translator to understand the sense of it.'

'So what's it saying?'

'It sounds like name, rank and number to me. I think she's called La'tyen.'

'She?'

'Yes,' said Uriel. 'At least, I think it's female.'

'So, what do you want done with her?'

'Cuff her and stick her in one of the Rhinos. We'll take her back to Brandon Gate and put her in the Glasshouse,' said Uriel. 'I'll have a xenolexicon servitor brought down from the *Vae Victus* to enable an interrogation. We need to find out how many more of her kind are on Pavonis.'

'You think there are more?'

'Probably,' said Uriel, moving away from the prisoner. 'Brandon Gate is only sixty kilometres to the east over flat and open terrain. These hills are a logical spot for an enemy force to scout with a view to attacking. Pathfinders are the eyes and ears of a tau battle force, and I'd be surprised if her unit was operating alone.'

'If there are other units, we'll find them,' said Learchus. 'The after-action telemetry from the Zeist Campaign helped us find this one, and if this battle is anything to go by, we shouldn't have much trouble finishing them off.'

'This wasn't a battle,' said Uriel.

'No?' asked Learchus, marching in step with Uriel. 'What was it then?'

'For all my adrenal system reacted once we engaged, it might as well have been a training exercise,' said Uriel. 'Everything about this fight was textbook, from the diversionary shot to the concealed kill-team and the fire support group.'

'And that is a bad thing?' asked Learchus. 'We executed a perfect Codex-pattern ambush; the tau were caught completely off guard. We fooled their tank crew into making a rudimentary manoeuvring error, and then we gunned down the survivors. Would that all engagements were fought with such precision.'

'I agree, but the Pathfinders were incredibly lax in their advance. From what I've heard of the battles the Chapter has fought against the tau over the last few years, it's a trait I'm surprised to find in warriors with such a reputation for being careful.'

'Perhaps they were new troops, yet to be tested in combat,' suggested Learchus.

'That's certainly possible,' conceded Uriel. 'Although it still feels strange that we destroyed them so easily.'

'We fight with the Codex Astartes as our guide precisely because the order it brings to our battles makes them seem easy to those who are not schooled in its ways.'

'I know that, Learchus. You don't need to remind me.'

'Don't I?' asked Learchus. 'You were exiled once already because you failed to heed its teachings.'

'Aye, and I saw the error of my ways on Medrengard,' said Uriel, fighting down his irritation at Learchus's words, even though he knew they were justified.

'I hope that is true.'

'I swear to you it is, my friend,' said Uriel. 'I suppose it's been so long since I fought with such sublime warriors under my command, I'd almost forgotten what it is to have the advantage in a tactical situation. For so long it was just Pasanius and myself against impossible odds.'

'Clearly not *that* impossible,' noted Learchus. 'After all, you both made it back.'

THE FORTRESS OF Hera. Uriel had not dared believe he would once again stand before its glittering, marble immensity for fear that the more he wanted it the more if would fade away.

Soaring walls of purest white towered above them, crowned by majestic towers capped with golden weapon-domes and lined with adamantine siege hoardings that were as beautiful as they were deadly. Like a living structure of indescribably beautiful coral, the fortress appeared to grow out of the very rock of the mountains, a mighty edifice conceived by the genius of the Ultramarines primarch in a long-forgotten age.

It stood on the mightiest chain of mountains, a testament to one man's genius and legendary vision. As wondrous and colossal a structure as it was, the Fortress of Hera was no monument to arrogance. Rather, it was a masterpiece of design and construction that lifted the soul and reminded all who looked upon it that they could aspire to great things. It was a creation of visual poetry and magnificence that spoke to the heart and not the ego.

Uriel and Pasanius stood alone in the wide, statue-lined plaza at the end of the Via Fortissimus, the grand processional road that wound from the lower reaches of the mountains all the way to the Porta Guilliman. The great gate of the fortress was a towering golden slab engraved with the ten thousand deeds of Roboute Guilliman, and Uriel vividly remembered the awful sound of it closing behind him.

The dolorous crash of adamantium had sounded like the final sound at the end of all things, and now, as the gate slowly began to open, the illumination that shone from within was like the first light at the dawn of creation.

Behind them, the hull of the Thunderhawk that had brought them from the Grey Knight vessel in orbit creaked and popped as it cooled after its rapid descent through the atmosphere. Lifter-servitors were already unloading the power armour of the Sons of Guilliman they had brought back from Salinas, and, within moments, the gunship would depart for the cold dark of space once more.

'We're home,' said Pasanius, but Uriel was too choked with emotion to reply.

His closest friend and battle-brother was crying, tears of joy falling unashamedly from his eyes as he swept his gaze over the high walls and glittering ramparts of the fortress.

Uriel reached up and touched his face, not at all surprised to find that he too was weeping with the sheer, boundless sense of homecoming that threatened to unman him with its intensity.

'Home,' he said, as though afraid to give voice to the idea.

'Did you ever think we'd see it again?' asked Pasanius, his voice wavering and brittle.

'I always hoped we would,' said Uriel, 'but I tried not to think about it too much. I knew that if I dwelt on what we'd lost I wouldn't have the strength to go on.'

'I thought about home all the time,' confessed Pasanius. 'I don't think I'd have made it back without the hope we'd see it again.'

Uriel turned to Pasanius and placed his hand on his friend's shoulder guard. Pasanius was a giant of a Space Marine, by far the biggest Uriel had ever known, and, fully armoured, he towered over Uriel. Pasanius's right arm ended abruptly at the elbow, the limb shorn from him beneath the surface of another world by a creature from the dawn of time.

His armour had been repaired and renewed by the artificers of the Grey Knights, and, with its restoration, a piece of Pasanius's soul that had been rent asunder by his exile was made whole once more.

'We each hold on to what keeps us going, my friend,' said Uriel. 'For you it was the idea of home, for me it was the quest itself. Without that balance between us, I don't think either of us would be standing here now.'

Pasanius nodded, and swept Uriel into a crushing, one-armed bear hug. The big warrior's emotions were raw and wounded, but they were healing. They had shared adventures and horrors on their journey, and, to come through it alive, let alone whole in spirit, was a miracle of which both were suddenly and acutely aware.

Uriel felt Pasanius's massive strength and laughed.

'You're crushing the life out of me, you fool!' he gasped.

Uriel's armour had been destroyed on their quest for redemption, and he wore a simple chiton of pale blue with the sword his former captain had entrusted to him belted at his waist. Pasanius joined Uriel's laughter, the last of the darkness that had cloaked his soul banished by the bright sun of Macragge and the gift of friendship freely given.

Pasanius released Uriel as the Porta Guilliman opened further and the light from within the fortress grew in intensity.

Both warriors stood proudly to attention, their backs ramrod straight and heads held high.

They had endured their quest into the darkness at the heart of the galaxy and within the souls of men, each trial bringing them closer to this final redemption. The end of that quest was at hand, and Uriel felt his heart pound within his ribless torso as it would at the moment of battle.

Three warriors stepped from the dazzling brightness of the fortress, three giants who lived in the legends of the Ultramarines, and whose names stood for courage and honour the length and breadth of the Imperium.

Leading the trio, resplendent in the vast and terrible Armour of Antilochus, and bearing the Gauntlets of Ultramar, was Marneus Calgar, Chapter Master of the Ultramarines. A warrior without peer and strategist beyond compare, Calgar was the epitome of what it meant to be a commander of the Adeptus Astartes.

At Calgar's side marched a towering warrior clad in lustrous blue armour, his head haloed with a crystalline hood. This was Varro Tigurius, Chief Librarian of the Ultramarines, and Uriel felt the power of the mighty warrior's gaze upon them, a bright light that would seek out any darkness and expunge it without mercy.

To Calgar's right was the most venerable member of the Ultramarines still on active duty, Chaplain Ortan Cassius, the Master of Sanctity and keeper of the Chapter's soul. Unlike his battle-brothers, Cassius wore armour of deepest black, and where his comrades were warriors of fair countenance, the Chaplain's face was a nightmarish patchwork of scarred flesh and bionics.

As these incredible, legendary warriors marched towards them, Uriel and Pasanius dropped to their knees, their heads bowed. To stand in the presence of one of these warriors would have been an honour unmatched, but to be greeted by three such giants amongst the Astartes was truly incredible.

'You return to us, Uriel Ventris,' said Lord Calgar, and Uriel's heart soared to hear the welcome and respect in his voice. 'I had not thought to ever lay eyes on you again.'

Uriel looked up into Lord Calgar's face, revelling in the sight of so perfect a warrior. Marneus Calgar's features were as hard as granite hewn from the deepest quarry, yet there was wisdom and nobility within them, his eyes cold as steel and yet filled with humanity.

'Nor I you, my lord,' said Uriel, unable to keep his tears from falling.

'Varro here said we would see you again, but I didn't believe him,' said Calgar. 'I should have known better.'

'Yes,' agreed Tigurius, 'you should have. Did I not say the Sentinel of the Tower would fight alongside us when the Thrice Born is clad in flesh once more?'

'Aye, that you did, Varro,' said Calgar, 'and one day you will explain what that means.'

Calgar turned from his Chief Librarian, and placed the open palm of his heavy gauntlet upon Uriel's head.

The Chapter Master's grip could crush the hardest metal, yet could cradle the most delicate glass sculpture without fear of its destruction. Uriel's life was in his lord and master's hand, yet he could think of no one to whom he would more gladly entrust his fate.

'What say you, Uriel?' asked Calgar. 'Do you return to us in glory?'

'We return to our Chapter having completed our Death Oath,' replied Uriel.

'Then you will be welcomed,' said Calgar.

'The creatures I saw in my vision,' said Tigurius, and Uriel sensed his words were laden with meaning beyond his understanding. 'The daemonic brood creatures... you found them?'

'We did, my lord,' confirmed Uriel, 'on a world taken by the Ruinous Powers. We found them and destroyed them. Our journey has been long and hard, and we have seen much that is terrible, but also much that is glorious and inspirational. I have seen men become monsters, and monsters that became heroes.'

'And you will stand with this, Pasanius?' asked Cassius with a grimace that appeared sardonic, but which was simply a fact of the hideous scars he bore. 'You did so once before, and were cast from your Chapter. That must have been a wound as grievous as the loss of your arm.'

Pasanius shrugged. 'I am whole within, my Lord Chaplain.'

'That remains to be seen,' said Tigurius, addressing them both. 'You have returned to us as brothers, but you have trodden the soil and breathed the air of a damned world. Brother Leodegarius of the Grey Knights vouches for the purity of your flesh, and his word is all that allowed you to descend to the surface of Macragge alive.'

Tigurius loomed over Uriel and Pasanius, the crystalline matrix of his hood leaping with shimmering wych fire.

'You will tell me all that occurred on your journey,' stated Tigurius, the dark pupils of his eyes crackling with the light of ancient powers, 'and woe betide you if I discover any taint in your souls.'

Ʊ
TWO

THE ENFORCERS WERE closing in on her, and she didn't have many places left to run. Her legs were tired, the air burned in her lungs, and her shoulder-length blonde hair was damp with sweat. She'd been on the run for nearly three hours, but Jenna Sharben wasn't going to be brought down without a fight.

She blinked dust from her eyes, wishing she hadn't lost her helmet in that tussle with the slab of muscle who'd tried to pin her to the wall with a net-caster. Jenna had dodged the projectile net and busted her pursuer's ribs with two quick blows of her shock maul. She'd put his lights out with a swift blow to the throat. Amateur.

Their orders were to take her alive, and that gave her the advantage.

The black of her armour was grey with dust, and she pressed herself flat against a tumbled wall as she heard a pair of enforcers run past the roofless portion of the collapsed structure she was sheltering in.

This had once been the Imperial Armoury and Arbites Precinct, but little survived save for crumbling ruins, fallen slabs of rockcrete, and precariously balanced walls and twisted gantries.

Jenna shifted into position beside the doorway and reached down to grab a handful of rock chippings. She skidded them across the ruptured floor timbers. Instantly, she heard the enforcers turn and make their way back towards her hiding place.

Jenna heard the clicking of their micro-bead vox and waited.

A grey-uniformed figure darted through the doorway, and Jenna let him go. The second enforcer immediately followed the first, and she surged to her feet, slamming her shock maul into the side of the enforcer's thigh. The man yelled in pain, and dropped to the ground, losing his shotgun and clutching his deadened leg. A second blow put him out of the fight.

Jenna followed up her attack by diving forwards as the first enforcer brought up his shotgun. She rolled beneath his shot, and slammed the butt of her shock maul into his groin. He grunted in pain, but stayed upright, which was more than she'd expected.

Jenna sprang to her feet, agile even in armour, and whipped her shock maul around and into the mirrored faceplate of the enforcer's helmet. The metal crumpled, but held, and the man dropped. Without power, the shock maul was simply a solid lump of plasteel, but there were worse things to have in your hand when trying to put someone down.

Jenna heard the sound of a shotgun being cocked, and looked up to see a lithe enforcer in a grey body-jack kneeling on a splintered stub of floor slab a few metres above her. Even with the reflective visor of the helmet down, Jenna knew the identity of this enforcer.

'Clever,' said Jenna.

She tightened her grip on the shock maul, her muscles tense and ready for action.

'You always run here,' said the enforcer. 'Why is that?'

Jenna didn't answer, twisting and hurling her shock maul at the enforcer as the barrel of the shotgun erupted in flames.

A shock maul wasn't designed with aerodynamics in mind, and her missile flew wide of the mark. Jenna tensed in expectation of pain, but she laughed as she realised that the enforcer had also missed. The solid shot had blasted into the creaking wooden floor.

The slide of the combat shotgun racked once more.

'You missed,' said Jenna, raising her hands in surrender. 'Going to have to work on your aim, Enforcer Apollonia.'

'I wasn't aiming at you,' said the enforcer, lowering the shotgun.

Jenna looked down, seeing where the impact of solid shot had destroyed the end of the joist supporting the portion of the floor she was standing on.

'Oh, hell,' said Jenna as the splintered timbers cracked and gave way beneath her.

She dropped through the floor, crashing down onto a pile of fallen stone and smashed plaster-work. Her armour took the brunt of the impact, but the breath was driven from her as she rolled over onto her side.

'Don't move,' said a breathless voice beside her, and Jenna looked up to see a tall, powerfully built enforcer standing over her, his shotgun pointed at her chest. Blinking away the lights in front of her eyes, she looked up through the billowing cloud of dust her fall had thrown up to see another weapon aimed at her through the hole in the floor.

'Nicely done, Enforcer Dion,' said Jenna, between heaving gulps of air. 'I had a feeling it would be you two that caught me.'

She pushed herself to her knees, one hand pressed to the old gunshot wound in her stomach.

'Are you all right, ma'am?' asked Dion, flicking up the silvered visor of his helmet.

'Yeah, I'm fine,' said Jenna, reaching up and unclipping the vox-mic attached to her armour's gorget, 'just a bit winded is all.'

The enforcer nodded and made his weapon safe.

'All units,' said Jenna Sharben, Commander of the Brandon Gate Enforcers, 'the exercise is over, I repeat, over. Everyone assemble in Liberation Square for debrief.'

Jenna led her trainees from the ruins of the Arbites precinct, following a winding route through mossy piles of fallen plasteel and granite facing stone towards Liberation Square. A high wall of re-inforced rockcrete, topped with razor wire and studded with gunports had once surrounded the precinct, a grim, foreboding edifice in the heart of Brandon Gate that served to remind the populace of their duty to the Imperium.

Clearly, it had not been a strong enough reminder, thought Jenna.

Those were bloody days, when the influence of the cartels that were the industrial backbone of Pavonis had reached a critical mass of power and ambition, and Virgil de Valtos had attempted to overthrow Imperial rule.

Jenna had only seen the opening shots of that revolution fired.

While attempting to evacuate Governor Mykola Shonai from the Imperial palace, an aide in the pocket of de Valtos, a worm named Almerz Chanda, had shot and almost killed Jenna. An Astartes healer had saved her, and, though she had fully recovered, the phantom pain of it still troubled her, now and again.

Jenna climbed over the fallen slabs of masonry that were all that remained of the wall. A shiver passed through her as she thought back to the sight of squadrons of tanks blasting their way through the wall, their guns mowing down the surviving Judges as they crawled from the wreckage of the bombed structure.

No one had ever figured out how the agents of de Valtos were able to smuggle an explosive device inside the Arbites precinct, but however it had been managed, the resulting blast devastated the entire building, effectively ending any meaningful resistance to the de Valtos coup from the ranks of the Adeptus Arbites.

Virgil Ortega, her former mentor, had died in the fighting; a Judge of rare courage and honour, and a man whom she felt could have taught her a great deal. She dearly wished he were here now, for the training of an entirely new cadre of enforcers was not something she had anticipated when she had been posted to Pavonis.

In the days before the rebellion, each of the cartels had raised and trained its own corps of enforcers, resulting in numerous private armies that were loyal only to the cartel that paid them. These enforcers were little more than corporate sponsored thugs, who enacted the will of the cartels with beatings, coercion and scant regard for the rule of Imperial Law.

One of the first acts of the Administratum, upon establishing its presence on Pavonis following the coup, had been to disband these private militias, putting thousands of men out of work. Mykola Shonai had protested at such drastic measures, but she had been serving out the last months of her term of office and her concerns were ignored.

As the last remnant of an Adeptus Arbites presence in Brandon Gate, the task of recruiting and training a new breed of enforcer had fallen to Jenna Sharben, a task she had quickly realised was more complex and demanding than anyone had imagined.

Anyone with strong cartel affiliations was suspect in the eyes of the Administratum, and Jenna had been forced to turn away many promising recruits for past associations with blacklisted cartels. Such restrictions were galling, and cared nothing for the fact that anyone who wanted employment before the rebellion *had* to have been attached to one of the cartels.

Despite such setbacks, Jenna had persevered. With help from Lortuen Perjed, the Administratum aide to the governor and former acolyte of the late Inquisitor Barzano, she had managed to recruit nearly two hundred enforcers, secure them weapons, uniforms and training, and had established a headquarters in a secure facility on the edge of the city.

Their base of operations was a rundown prison facility that had been burned out and looted in the wake of the rebellion, but which had been brought back to basic functionality in the last year. Its official name was the Brandon Gate Correctional Facility, but it was known locally as the Glasshouse.

It was a far from perfect base from which to police an entire city, but it was a beginning, and every endeavour had to start somewhere.

Jenna shook herself from her gloomy thoughts as she and her trainees gave a wide berth to the blue walls of the Ultramarines battle fortress. Under the watchful gaze of its guns, they approached a checkpoint manned by Guardsmen of the 44th Lavrentian Hussars. Each of the approach routes leading into Liberation Square had such a checkpoint, a staggered emplacement of piled sandbags and rockcrete beams that housed a squad of Guardsmen in polished silver breastplates and emerald green breeches.

Banners depicting a heroic golden soldier on a rearing horse hung limply above each checkpoint, and a Chimera AFV was parked threateningly behind it.

Jenna knew the Lavrentians were tough soldiers, hardened fighters who'd spent the better part of the last seven years fighting greenskin marauders on the Eastern Fringe. Being rotated to Pavonis, far from the front lines, was a cushy number for them, yet Jenna had seen no let up in their training regime or discipline.

She heard the cocking of heavy bolters as they approached the checkpoint. The turret-mounted multi-laser on the Chimera tracked her every move, despite them having passed the same checkpoint only four hours earlier en route to their hunt/capture exercise. A captain and protection detail emerged from the emplacement, and Jenna knew he would be as thorough in his ident-checks and counts as before.

The captain, whose name was Mederic, scanned her transit tags with a wave of a data wand, and repeated the procedure for each of the enforcers as they passed beneath the watchful gaze of the gunners manning the heavy bolters.

'Good exercise?' asked Mederic, as the last enforcer was cleared.

'Could have been better,' admitted Jenna. 'It took them three hours to run me down, but they got me in the end.'

'Three hours,' said Mederic with a roguish smile. 'If I set the Hounds of the 44th on you, I'd have you bound, gagged and at my mercy in three minutes.'

'You wish,' said Jenna, reading Mederic's lingering glance at her athletic figure, which her Arbites armour did little to conceal. 'I'd have your Hounds chasing their tails.'

'Yeah?'

'Yeah.'

'I'll have to put that boast to the test sometime, Judge Sharben,' said Mederic, waving her through. 'Our scouts are the best in the sector.'

'That's pride, Captain Mederic,' said Jenna defiantly. 'It doesn't suit you.'

She turned and made her way past the Chimera to catch up with her enforcers.

'I'll be in touch,' chuckled Mederic. 'Count on it.'

Mederic had irritated her, having done little to conceal his attraction to her. She told herself it was his obvious desire and disparaging of her skills that had annoyed her, but it was more than that. It was the fact that he didn't belong here. He was an outsider.

Never mind that she too was not native to Pavonis, this was her world because she had fought to defend it. Though the Lavrentians were here to safeguard her adopted home world, their presence was a visible symbol that the Imperium did not trust the people of Pavonis.

'Everything all right, ma'am?' asked Apollonia, glancing back down the street.

Apollonia was a petite woman, with cropped dark hair and wide, almond shaped eyes, who had proved to be one of Jenna's finest recruits. Many people, including Jenna, had underestimated her, but she had proven to be an object lesson in not judging people by their appearance. She was tougher than she looked, and had excelled in every area of training.

'Yes, it's fine,' replied Jenna. 'Just Guardsmen being Guardsmen.'

'The sooner they're gone the better,' said Dion, dropping back to walk alongside them.

'Secure that talk, Enforcer Dion,' warned Jenna. 'That's the kind of sentiment that will keep them here longer. Understood?'

'Understood, ma'am,' said Dion with a crisp salute.

'Apollonia?'

'Yes, ma'am. Understood.'

Jenna nodded, putting the incident from her mind as the approach road widened out and she stepped into the central plaza of Brandon Gate.

Liberation Square had once been a meeting place popular with the wealthy of Brandon Gate, a place to gather, perambulate and gossip, but since the uprising it had largely been forsaken.

Too many memories, Jenna supposed. Too many had died here.

Even now, she sometimes woke with the hate and fear-filled shouts of the Workers' Collective ringing in her ears, the sounds of booming shotguns, the screams of the wounded and dying, or the urgent sound of her pounding heartbeat.

Instead of a gathering place for the people of the city, Liberation Square was now a symbol of the planet's past failures. Some citizens still passed through it, but not many, although Jenna saw a few hundred people gathered at the centre of the square.

Looking closer, she saw why.

The crimson-painted Rhino of Prelate Culla was parked at the foot of the great statue of the Emperor from which the traitor Vendare Taloun had been hanged. Braziers burned from ebony skulls fitted to the glacis of the tank, and curling bronze organ pipes rose from behind an onyx pulpit, broadcasting hectoring words to the crowd gathered before him.

Standing tall atop his mobile shrine, Culla was a fearsome-looking preacher with an enormous fiery chainsword and bolt pistol raised to the heavens. Robed in the emerald chasuble of a predicant of the Lavrentian 44th, Culla trained for battle with the soldiers to whom he daily preached. He was a man whose appearance looked quarried from rock instead of crafted by birth, and his forked beard and tattooed, shaven head gave him a threatening appearance that was entirely deliberate.

Choral servitors in hooded smocks sang uplifting hymns, as golden-skinned cherubs, trailing prayer banners, hovered in the clouds of devotional incense that billowed from the Rhino's smoke dispensers.

In the wake of the rebellion, ships from the Ministorum and Administratum had brought hosts of new clerks, scribes and preachers to restore spiritual and bureaucratic stability to Pavonis, but none had been zealous enough for Culla, who had taken to the streets to preach his own fiery brand of the Imperial Creed.

From the sound of the crowd, Culla was already in full swing, and Jenna paused to listen.

'It behoves us all to cast out the unbeliever. Such creatures have no value whatsoever as human beings. In fact, you must not even consider them human, but as inhuman animals, since they are nothing but miserable liars, cowards and murderers!'

Culla's devotees, mainly indigent workers and itinerant labourers, were cheering at his words, and Jenna couldn't deny that the prelate's words were affecting.

The preacher swept his arms out, the fiery sword leaving bright afterimages on Jenna's retinas. 'Do not cry for the unbeliever who lives amongst you, though they may be your friend or a member of your family. No one should weep over the rotting corpse of a worthless unbeliever! What else is there to say? Nothing at all. There should be no last words, no rites and no remembrance. Nothing. Every time an unbeliever or alien dies, the Imperium is better off, and their Emperor-forsaken souls will burn forever in the depths of the warp!'

'Looks like we'll need to find another place for debrief,' noted Dion.

'Yeah, we'll head back to the Glasshouse, do it there,' said Jenna, the words of Prelate Culla and the cheers of his audience ringing in her ears.

THE TWO RHINOS travelled south as far as Olzetyn, the City of Bridges, before turning eastwards, and then following Highway 236 northwards along the river towards Brandon Gate. The highway was well-maintained, since it was the major arterial route connecting the planetary capital and the coastal port-city of Praxedes, and the Ultramarines made good time as they completed their patrol circuit. What traffic there was on the highway gave the Rhinos a wide berth, the cupola mounted storm bolters tracking any vehicle that came too near until the driver hurriedly pulled away.

The outer suburbs of Brandon Gate were heavily indus-trialised belts of manufacture, sprawling districts of production, assembly and distribution, a great deal of which was now sitting idle. Some of the manufactorum still churned with the sound of machines, but many more sat empty and abandoned, their workers deprived of employment thanks to their previous cartel affiliations.

Stopping only to transfer the tau prisoner to the cus-tody of the enforcers at the fire-blackened compound of the Glasshouse, the Ultramarines drove swiftly onwards. They passed the sheet steel walls of Camp Torum, the headquarters of the 44th Lavrentian regi-ment, before entering the city proper via the northern Commercia Gate.

The manufacturing hub of Pavonis had changed a great deal since Uriel had last seen it.

The city walls were reinforced with Lavrentian Hydra flak tanks, and armed patrols of green-jacketed Guardsmen in silver breastplates roamed the streets to keep the peace that Uriel and his warriors had won.

Their route took them through the financial heart of the city, where much of the trading that had made Pavonis one of the economic powerhouses of the sub-sector had been done. Uriel had time to admire the elaborate architecture of the Carnelian Exchange House, with its high towers and gilded arches, before it was lost to sight as they crossed Liberation Square.

Imperial Guardsmen controlled entry to the vast space, but the Ultramarines vehicles were not stopped, rumbling past awed soldiers making the sign of the aquila. They skirted around the giant statue in the centre of the square, where a preacher atop a crimson Rhino hectored a gathering of the faithful. Uriel's heart sank as he saw that this place, which had once been dedicated to the glory of the Emperor, was now home to the ugly practicality of roadblocks and checkpoints.

The Ultramarines had set up their base in Belahon Park, a once pristine area of greenery, lakes and rarefied beauty, but which was now an overgrown wasteland with a stagnant lake at its heart. On the park's southern edge, the spires of the iron-sheened Templum Fabricae dominated the skyline, overshadowing the more modestly constructed Library of Deshanel.

The Rhinos drove towards a modular defensive fortress of high blue walls, angled bastions and defensive turrets. Designated Fortress Idaeus, it had been constructed by the company's Techmarines and servitors next to the ruins of the former Arbites precinct. As the Rhinos approached, Codex-pattern recognition protocols passed between the vehicles and the gun towers before the gate rumbled open.

The two Rhinos swept inside the fortress, and no sooner had they ground to a halt beside a trio of massively armoured Land Raiders, the most powerful battle tank in the Space Marine arsenal, than the assault ramps dropped. The drivers revved out the last of the journey from the engines, and Uriel stepped from the vehicle, rotating his head on his shoulders to loosen his muscles.

Prefabricated structures were spaced at regular intervals within the compound, the basic necessities of a Space Marine battle company at war: command centre, armoury, apothecarion, refectory and barracks. Groups of Space Marines practised targeting rituals, while others trained in close-quarters combat in small groups under the supervision of their sergeants. Techmarine apprenta worked on the engine of a Land Raider, while tower-mounted Thunderfire cannons scanned the surrounding urban landscape for threats.

In the centre of Fortress Idaeus, held by an unmoving warrior wearing the full battle dress of the Ultramarines and a cloak of brilliant green, the 4th Company banner flapped in the wind. Depicting an iron gauntlet clutching the icon of the Ultramarines against a golden laurel, it was a symbol of courage and honour to all who fought beneath it, and Uriel felt great humility at the sight of so noble a standard.

An immaculately maintained Chimera, painted in the colours of the Lavrentian 44th, was parked beside the command centre, together with an altogether less impressive half-track, emblazoned with the white rose of the Pavonis PDF.

'Looks like we have guests,' said Learchus, coming over to join Uriel, his stride sure, and looking like he'd just stepped from the parade ground.

'Looks like,' agreed Uriel. 'Lord Winterbourne and Colonel Loic by the vehicles.'

'Do you wish me to join you?'

'Eventually,' said Uriel, 'but we must honour the banner first.'

Uriel and Learchus marched towards the centre of the company fortress, and stood before the warrior who bore the standard. His name was Peleus and his title was Ancient, a rank only ever given to those who were pure of heart and soul, and who had won the right to bear the company's banner through the fires of countless battlefields.

Peleus had carried the banner of the 4th for over thirty years.

The eagle on his breastplate shimmered, and the white wings of his helmet were dazzling. Scarlet cords secured the cloak around Peleus's shoulders, and a host of oath papers and purity seals were affixed to his shoulder guards. Sunlight caught the silver and gold threading on the banner, and the pride that filled Uriel as he took hold of the fabric was like a panacea.

'The banner is a credit to you, Ancient Peleus,' said Uriel. 'It has never looked so good.'

'Thank you, my lord,' replied Peleus. 'I am honoured to bear it.'

The Space Marines Uriel had led on this latest patrol mission formed up behind him without any orders needing to be given. Uriel dropped to one knee before the banner, and his warriors followed suit, heads bowed as they acknowledged the awesome weight of its legacy. Never in its history had the banner been allowed to fall, though enemies of every stripe had sought to bring it low.

'In the name of the Emperor and primarch, whom we serve, I offer you my life and the lives of these warriors,' said Uriel, his hands clasped across his chest in the sign of the aquila. 'I offer our devotion, our skill and our courage. To the service of this banner, our Chapter and the Emperor, I offer you our lives.'

The warriors behind him spoke their own oaths, each one personal to the man that gave it, and Uriel waited until the last had finished speaking before rising to his feet. As Uriel gave his oath to the company standard, he felt a warm sense of acknowledgement swell within him, as though everything it stood for welcomed him back into the ranks of 4th Company.

He turned to Learchus. 'Set the men on their post battle ministrations and join me in the command centre when you're done.'

'Yes, sir,' replied Learchus with a crisp bow.

Uriel turned on his heel, and made his way towards the oblong structure that served as the command centre for the company. Its sides were deep blue, and a surveyor dish rotated amid a bristling forest of vox aerials on its armoured topside. The symbol of the Ultramarines was stencilled on its side, and two Space Marines with their blades unsheathed stood at attention to either side of the entrance.

Both warriors hammered the hilts of their swords against their chests as Uriel punched in the access code and entered the command centre.

The interior was lit with a soft, green glow from the numerous data-slates fitted to the walls. Cogitators hummed with power, and, though spinning fan units on the ceiling dissipated the heat from so many machines, it was still uncomfortably warm. Binaric cant chattered in the background, a companion to the hiss of machine language burbling from the mouths of output servitors.

Techmarine Harkus sat upon a silver-steel throne at one end of the command centre, connected to the workings of the various logic-engines via hard-plugs in his arms, chest and cranium. Flickering light pulsed behind his eyes as he collated the myriad data streams being gathered by the surveyor gear on the roof and the *Vae Victus* in orbit.

A handful of Chapter serfs attended to incense burners, anointed the guardian of the company's technology with sacred oils and recited mantas pleasing to the spirits of the machines.

At the hub of the command centre, a hololithic projection table of dark stone was lit by the translucent holo-map that bathed the three figures gathered around it in a lambent glow.

The nearest figure to Uriel was Colonel Adren Loic, commander of the local defence forces. Since the rebellion, partial control of the armed men of Brandon Gate had fallen to an officer chosen by the Administratum, a man selected as much for his lack of cartel affiliations as for his competence as a soldier. That he was a political appointment was clear to Uriel, but what was less clear was whether he had any merit as a leader of fighting men.

The collar of Loic's cream uniform jacket was open, and his florid skin was beaded with perspiration. The man's bullet scalp was shaved bald, and he dabbed at his forehead with a wadded scarf before standing to attention at Uriel's arrival. He carried a pistol and duelling sabre at his side, though Uriel doubted he knew how to use the latter with any real skill.

Beside Loic stood two senior commanders of the 44th Lavrentians. Uriel had met them on a number of previous occasions, and both officers had impressed him. Their first meeting had been when the Ultramarines had made planetfall, the second when formalising the chain of command, and the latest when delineating sectors of responsibility.

The regiment's colonel, Lord Nathaniel Winterbourne, was a flamboyant nobleman with genteel manners and a respect for etiquette that at first made him appear effete. After their first meeting, however, Uriel quickly realised that there was a core of iron to him. Winterbourne was a commander who demanded and got the best from his Guardsmen, no matter that there was precious little glory or honour to be gained on this assignment.

Tall and rakishly thin, his emerald green frock coat seemed too large for his spare frame, yet there was an undeniable strength to the man that Uriel liked. His features bore all the hallmarks of good breeding, careful juvenat work and the eager hunger of a career soldier.

Two richly dressed aides stood discretely behind Winterbourne, one holding the colonel's emerald-plumed helmet, the other the long leashes of two wolf-like creatures: slender beasts with glossy black and gold fur, vicious looking jaws and predators' eyes. One of the creatures was missing its left foreleg, yet appeared no less aggressive for its loss.

Winterbourne was the fiery heart of the regiment, but his second in command, Major Alithea Ornella, was all business. Unsmiling and hard to warm to, Ornella was meticulous and precise, as dedicated as her colonel in ensuring that the regiment's soldiers upheld the fine tradition of the Imperial Guard. Like her superior officer, she was dressed in a long frock-coat, though she came without pets or an aide to carry her helmet.

'Lord Winterbourne, Major Ornella,' said Uriel, unconsciously addressing the soldiers in order of respect, if not proximity. 'Colonel Loic.'

'Ah, Uriel, my good man,' said Winterbourne. 'Damned sorry to drop in on you like this, but we got word that you'd had something of an encounter with alien trespassers.'

'That's correct, Lord Winterbourne,' said Uriel. 'Tau Pathfinders and their vehicle.'

'Call me Nathaniel,' said Winterbourne with a dismissive wave of the hand. 'Everybody does. Or at least I tell them to, but they never listen.'

The three-legged hound nuzzled the colonel of the 44th, and he stroked its ferocious-looking head, which was more than Uriel would have done had it come near him.

'Anyway, to business, to business,' continued Winterbourne, patting the beast. 'The damned tau infest the Eastern Fringe like burrow-ticks on old Fynlae here's hide. We've fought them before and they're slippery buggers, got to keep an eye on them or they'll be behind you in a flash. I remember once on Ulgolaa they–'

'Perhaps we should concentrate on the matter at hand?' suggested Major Ornella, smoothly forestalling her colonel's reminiscence.

'Of course, yes,' agreed Winterbourne, shaking his head. 'Talk the hind leg off a grox if Alithea didn't bring me to heel every now and then. So, these tau, where did you encounter the scoundrels, Uriel?'

Winterbourne appeared to take no offence at his underling's intervention, and Uriel stepped up to the hololith table that was projecting an image of the environs around the command centre to a radius of three hundred kilometres.

The major cities were shining blobs of light, the geographical features projected as stylised representations of mountains, rivers, forests and hills. Brandon Gate sat in the centre of the map, with Praxedes on the western coast and Olzetyn roughly at the midpoint between the two cities. Madorn lay just south of the Tembra Ridge

Mountains, a great saw-toothed barrier three hundred kilometres to the north.

Further east, Altemaxa nestled amid the sprawling Gresha Forest. The Abrogas cartel had once maintained sizeable estates in this area, but a malfunctioning magma bomb from the *Vae Victus* had fallen there during the rebellion, obliterating many of them, along with whole swathes of forest that burned in the subsequent fires.

To the south, the slum city of Jotusburg sat isolated from the other conurbations, shunned like a reeking plague victim. The city was a blackened sump that housed the tens of thousands of Adeptus Mechanicus labourers who toiled in the Diacrian Belt, a hellish region of smoking refineries and drilling rigs that blackened the eastern and southern reaches of the continent. Where other cities *had* ghettoes, Jotusburg *was* a ghetto.

Uriel detached a light-stylus from the table, and drew a holographic circle around the Owsen Hills, sixty kilometres west of Brandon Gate.

'Right here,' said Uriel.

'Damn, that's close,' said Colonel Loic. 'That puts them practically right on our doorstep.'

'You're not wrong, Adren,' agreed Winterbourne, ignoring or oblivious to Loic's discomfort at the more senior officer's familiarity. 'Damned aliens will be sitting at our dinner table soon. What do you make of it, Uriel?'

'I think Colonel Loic is correct,' he said. 'The tau are too close and too bold for my liking. Given what I observed, they appeared to be plotting a route for a larger force.'

'Preliminary groundwork for an invasion, eh?' said Winterbourne. 'Think they can just take a world of the Emperor from us, do they?'

'We've heard nothing from sector command about a renewed offensive,' said Alithea Ornella. 'After your Chapter's victories at Zeist and Lagan, Imperial Strategos are of the opinion that the tau have withdrawn to their previous holdings.'

'The Masters of the Ultramarines came to the same conclusion,' said Uriel, 'but the fact that tau forces are on Pavonis is undeniable and unacceptable. If they are scouting routes for an army, then it follows that they are planning to invade. Perhaps not soon, but eventually. It is our duty to deny them any intelligence that will aid them in any aggression towards this world, whether the threat is imminent or merely theoretical.'

'Of course,' agreed Ornella. 'So that's what you think this is, a scouting mission?'

Uriel considered the question. 'No, I think there's more to it than that.'

'Oh?' said Winterbourne. 'So tell me, Uriel, what do you think these xenos are up to?'

Uriel looked back at the hololithic projection and said, 'I think they are here in far greater strength than encountered numbers might otherwise suggest. It wouldn't surprise me if the tau have been on Pavonis for quite some time.'

'I assure you, Captain Ventris, my PDF long-range patrols have found nothing to support that suspicion,' said Colonel Loic.

'I'm sure they haven't, colonel,' said Uriel. 'I'd be surprised if they had.'

Loic's face reddened, but Uriel held up a placating hand. 'I mean no disrespect to your men, colonel. Even we were only able to locate the tau thanks to information gained at the cost of Astartes lives on Augura.'

'I'm all for soldier's intuition, Uriel,' said Winterbourne, 'but you'll have to do better than a suspicion.

Lay it out for me. Why do you think the tau are here when cleverer thinkers than us all say they've gone home to lick their wounds?'

'It's this world,' said Uriel.

'What about it?' asked Loic defensively.

'I think the nature of Pavonis makes it an attractive prospect for the tau,' said Uriel, circling the table as he gathered his thoughts. 'Before the de Valtos rebellion, it was the hub of the sub-sector trade networks. As much as the cartel system placed a dangerous amount of power in the hands of individuals unsuited to wield it, those individuals were formidable merchants as well as producers. Trade is in the blood of this world. Look at how it's ruled; the central hall of governance is called the Senate Chamber of Righteous Commerce and its chief official is the Moderator of Transactions.'

'So, how does that make it a prime target for the tau?' asked Loic.

'It fits how these aliens work,' said Uriel. 'In practically every instance where Imperial forces have fought the tau, it has been on worlds where xenos diplomats or traders have first made secret overtures to the planetary leadership through its mercantile concerns, offering co-operation and commerce. If the planet's leaders are foolish enough to accept this offer, trade links are quickly forged, and the tau influence grows as the planet's rulers become wealthy. Soon after, the tau establish a military presence, which transforms into a full-scale occupation within the space of a few months. By the time the populace realise what is happening, it is already too late, and an Imperial world has become part of the tau empire.'

'Despicable,' said Winterbourne, shaking his head in disbelief. 'To think that Imperial citizens would lower themselves to treat with xenos.'

'The tau aren't like other races you've fought, Lord Winterbourne,' said Uriel, choosing his words carefully. 'They are not like the greenskins or the hive fleets. They do not lay waste to worlds indiscriminately or seek destruction for destruction's sake. Their entire race works for the good of the species, and, in fact, there is much to admire about them.'

'But they are aliens,' protested Winterbourne, 'degenerate xenos with no regard for the sanctity of human life or our manifest destiny to rule the stars. Intolerable!'

'Indeed, and any world the tau set their sights on that does not welcome their advances will be attacked with all the fury their armies can muster. The tau offer a simple choice: either join their empire willingly, or you will be conquered and *made* part of the empire.'

'And you think that's what's happening here?' asked Winterbourne.

'Yes. The tau will believe that the commercial mindset of this planet's leaders makes them receptive to their advances when the time comes to begin the assimilation of Pavonis.'

'If it hasn't already begun,' pointed out Ornella.

'Exactly,' said Uriel.

℧
THREE

ALONE IN HIS arming chamber, Uriel allowed the simple act of caring for his battle gear to set his mind at ease. Honouring the memory of the warrior who had last borne these weapons and armour into battle came as naturally to Uriel as breathing, and helped him to better process his thoughts. He worked a finely textured brush across the breastplate, taking care to work the red dust of Pavonis from between the carved feathers of the golden aquila.

As captain of a Space Marine battle company, Uriel was permitted his own chamber in the modular barracks structure: a three metre square, steel-walled cell with a compact bunk and weapons shrine on one wall, and a reversible ablutions cubicle on the other. A gunmetal grey footlocker at the end of the bed contained Uriel's few personal belongings: his training garments, his hygiene kit, a sharpening block for his sword, the glossy black claw of the stalker creature he had captured on Tarsis Ultra and a ragged fragment of an enemy battle flag he had taken on the battlefields of Thracia.

A Space Marine had no great need for privacy in the normal run of things, and shared virtually every moment of his life with his battle-brothers. Such unbreakable bonds of brotherhood allowed the Adeptus Astartes to fight as one, and to make such war as was unthinkable to mere mortals.

The rest of Uriel's armour stood in the corner of the chamber, each plate having been removed from his enhanced body and placed reverently upon a sturdy frame by a company serf an hour before.

The Savage Morticians had brutally cut the bulk of Uriel's original armour from him on Medrengard, and he had been forced to discard the few remaining fragments on Salinas. Necessity had seen him don power armour belonging to the Sons of Guilliman Chapter for a short time, but now he had another suit of battle plate to call his own.

Before leaving Macragge, when the time had come to renew his Oaths of Confraternity, the Master of the Forge had escorted Uriel into the vast, torch-lit vaults of the Armorium to choose his new armour.

Scores of armoured suits stood in the sacred repository of the Chapter's wargear like warriors on parade, and Uriel had the powerful sense that these vacant suits were simply waiting for warriors of courage to bear them into battle once more. Firelight danced upon the polished plates as Uriel reverently made his way through their ranks, knowing that the spirits of fallen heroes were silently, invisibly, judging his worth as a warrior.

Each suit was a creation of forgotten science and art, any one of which it would be an honour to wear. The unique bond between armour and warrior went beyond anything that could be understood by those without the depths of faith of a warrior of the Adeptus Astartes.

No sooner had Uriel set eyes upon the gleaming plates he now polished than he had known it was the armour for him. He reached out and placed his open palm on the golden breastplate, and felt a connection to the armour on a level that he could never fully explain.

'The armour of Brother Amadon,' said the Master of the Forge approvingly, his voice little more than a hoarse croak, as though coming from a forgotten place deep within the towering warrior's chest. Only rarely did the warden of the Armorium deign to use his flesh-voice, and Uriel was savvy enough to know that the honour was not for him, but for the armour.

'Brother Amadon fell during the storming of the breach at Corinth, brought low by a barbarian green-skin warlord as he fought alongside our beloved Chapter Master.'

'Corinth,' said Uriel, unwilling to desecrate the echoing silence of the Armorium with anything above a whisper. 'The battle that took Ancient Galatan from us.'

'The same,' agreed the Master of the Forge, watching as Uriel circled the armour, feeling as though Brother Amadon's soul was speaking to him from across the gulf of centuries that separated them.

'It's magnificent,' breathed Uriel. 'I felt something similar on Salinas when I saw the armour belonging to the Sons of Guilliman, but this is so much more. It's as if... it *needs* me to wear it.'

'The heroic deeds of every warrior to wear a suit of armour adds to its legacy, Captain Ventris. Only when the souls of armour and bearer are in accord will each be able to achieve true greatness.'

Uriel smiled at the memory as he set the breastplate aside, satisfied that he had removed all evidence of the last few days in the field. He hung the breastplate back on the frame, and drew his sword from its battered and stained leather sheath. He supposed he could have requisitioned a new scabbard, but this was how his former captain had given the sword to him, and he was loath to change any aspect of the weapon that did not require it.

He lifted the sharpening block from his footlocker and worked it along the length of the blade, closing his eyes and feeling more alone than he could remember.

Sometimes, solitude was to be cherished, and many a warrior had found illumination within one of the Chapter Solitoriums to be found in the furthest reaches of Macragge.

This was not one of those times.

Even before his elevation to captaincy of the 4th Company, Uriel had fought shoulder to shoulder with Pasanius, one of the finest sergeants to be found within the ranks of the Ultramarines. Together, they had faced down an ancient star god, defeated a tendril of the Great Devourer, and brought down a fell champion of the Ruinous Powers.

Pasanius was his oldest and dearest friend, a brother who stood at his side through all the battles and tribulations they had faced since their earliest years.

Now, even that was gone from him.

THE COMPLETION OF their Death Oath was, as it turned out, simply the first step on the road to rejoining the ranks of their illustrious Chapter. Their courage and loyalty were not in question, and never had been, but they had broken faith with the Codex Astartes, and had travelled to worlds polluted beyond redemption by the foul and corrupting touch of Chaos. Uriel had fought enough of the servants of the Ruinous Powers to know that a man might earnestly believe himself free of taint, and yet carry a hidden canker in the dark corners of his soul.

No sooner had the gates of the Fortress of Hera closed behind them, than a fifty-strong escort of warriors from the 1st Company had marched them directly to the Apothecarion.

Uriel and Pasanius had been subjected to punishing procedures designed to test the purity of their flesh and detect any abnormalities in their gene-stock. Every aspect of their physical makeup was examined with greater thoroughness than that endured by potential recruits, whose bodies were examined down to the cellular level for any latent weaknesses.

Such tests were gruelling and painful, and lasted many weeks, but both warriors endured them willingly.

Eventually, the Chapter's Apothecaries declared Uriel free of corruption, his flesh as pure as it had been on his induction to the Ultramarines over a hundred years ago.

Pasanius was less fortunate.

The veteran sergeant had lost the lower half of his arm on Pavonis in combat with a diabolical alien creature known as the Bringer of Darkness, though he had fought on as Uriel faced the creature down and forced it to flee. Adepts from Pavonis had replaced his missing limb with a bionic arm, which had proved almost as effective as the one he had lost. Only later, when a greenskin warrior had smashed its monstrous blade into his forearm in the depths of a space hulk, had Pasanius realised the nature of the hideous change wrought upon him.

The silver-skinned Necrontyr warriors that served the Bringer of Darkness were fashioned from an alien form of metal that could spontaneously self-repair, undoing even the most catastrophic damage. By some dreadful transference, a measure of that power had passed into the augmetic arm grafted to Pasanius, enabling it to perform similarly impossible feats of metallic regeneration.

Ashamed, Pasanius had kept this secret from Uriel until his arm's miraculous power eventually came to light in the damned fortress of Khalan-Ghol, domain of the Warsmith Honsou. The surgeon creatures of Honsou had cut the arm from Pasanius for their dark master, taking the taint of the Necrontyr with it, but that did nothing to change the fact that Pasanius had lied to his captain – an infraction of the utmost seriousness.

Once declared free of physical taint, Uriel and Pasanius were transferred to the incense-wreathed Reclusiam, and the care of the Chapter's Chaplains. In the Temple of Correction they relived every moment of their ordeals since leaving Macragge before the magnificent, immobile form of Roboute Guilliman. Both warriors told of their adventures, time and time again, and every tiny detail was exhaustively picked apart and retold, until the guardians of the Chapter's sanctity were satisfied that they knew every detail of what had transpired during the fulfilment of the Death Oath.

Many aspects of Uriel's tale: the Faustian pact with the Omphalos Daemonium, the freeing of the Heart of Blood and the alliance with Ardaric Vaanes's renegades had raised damning eyebrows, and, though such devil's bargains were unwholesome, none doubted the noble intent of Uriel's motives in making them upon hearing the outcomes.

Uriel haltingly spoke to Chaplain Cassius of the Unfleshed, and of his failure to honour his oath to keep them safe and offer them a better life. Of all the tales Uriel told, the death of the Lord of the Unfleshed caused him the most pain. Though its eventual fate had been the only possible outcome to the creature's wretched, blighted life, the sadness of its ending had lodged in Uriel's heart and would never be forgotten.

Many aspects of their Death Oath were fantastical and beggared belief, but an Ultramarine's truth was his life, and not even Uriel's detractors, Cato Sicarius of the 2nd Company being the most vocal, doubted his word or honesty. Despite this, Uriel and Pasanius had consented to truth-seekers from the Chapter's Librarius Division verifying every aspect of their odyssey at every stage of their testing.

Satisfied that their hearts were still those of warriors of courage and honour, the Chaplains sent Uriel and Pasanius onwards for the last, most crucial, stage of their testing.

THE LIBRARY OF Ptolemy was one of the marvels of Ultramar, a repository of knowledge that stretched back tens of thousands of years to a time when fact and certainty blurred into myth and fable. Legend told that it had been named for the first and mightiest of the Chapter's Librarians, and the breadth of knowledge contained within its sprawling depths was greater than the Agrippan Conclaves, more diverse than the Arcanium of Teleos and, it was said, contained practically every word crafted in all human history.

An entire spur of the mountain range upon which the Fortress of Hera was constructed was given over to the library. Its many wings, archives, colonnades and processionals formed a manmade peak of gleaming marble and granite to rival the highest mountains of Macragge.

The tops of soaring columns were lost in the deep shadows of the distant roof, and the floor of veined green marble gleamed like ice. Towering bookcases of steel and glass rose to unimaginable heights to either side of a central nave, each stacked with an impossible number of chained books, scrolls, info-wafers, maps, slates, data crystals and a thousand other means of information storage.

Graceful marble arches spanned the chasms between the mighty bookcases, forming separate wings and kilometres of stacks that required detailed maps or guide-skulls to navigate. Only the Chapter Librarians fully understood the layout of the library, and much of its twisting depths and dusty passageways had remained untrodden for centuries or more.

Wordless servitors clad in long cerulean robes ghosted through the echoing silence of the library, some on wheels, and some on telescoping legs that allowed them to reach the higher shelves, while other, more specialised retrieval drones floated on individual grav-plates. Servo-skulls trailing long parchments and carrying quills in clicking bronze callipers floated through the air, the glowing red orbs of their eyes like drifting fireflies in the sepulchral gloom.

Uriel had spent a great deal of time within the Library of Ptolemy in his years of service to the Ultramarines. Here, he had learned the legacy of his Chapter and its heroes as well as the broader scope of Imperial history and politics. However, the majority of his time had been spent memorising the tenets of his primarch's greatest work, the Codex Astartes.

Such thoroughness was at the heart of Astartes training. Though bred and equipped for war, a Space Marine was not simply a thoughtless killing machine wrought from the bones of ancient science. His decades of training enabled him to become more than simply a warrior. Each Astartes embodied the finest qualities of humanity, courage, honour and a capacity to fight not simply because he was ordered to, but because he knew why.

Uriel's sandalled footsteps echoed on the floor, disturbing both the dust and the reverent silence that filled the library with a heavy quality all its own. Pasanius walked beside him, likewise stripped of his armour and dressed identically to Uriel in a chiton of deepest black that was secured around his waist by a belt of knotted rope.

These were the robes of the penitent, yet the knotted belt was that of an aspirant, signifying that their trials were almost at an end. The Apothecarion had decreed their bodies free from corruption, and the Chaplaincy had found their hearts to be pure.

The final decision as to whether their names would be entered once more into the honour rolls of the Ultramarines rested upon the shoulders of Marneus Calgar, and the Chapter Master's decision would be based on the word of his Chief Librarian.

The Arcanium was the heart of the library, its approaches guarded by silver-armoured warriors who bore long polearms with shimmering blades, and whose helmets were high hoods veined with psi-disruptive crystalline webs. None had challenged them as they approached, but Uriel was not surprised, for these guardians would already know of their purpose, and could divine any ill-intent.

The interior of the Arcanium was a twenty metre square cube with an arched doorway in each wall, softly lit by thick candles held aloft in iron sconces worked in the forms of eagles and lions rampant. Its walls were constructed from bare timbers, weathered and bleached, as though reclaimed from a distant shoreline, and the floor was made of dark slate. The character of the room was quite out of keeping with its surroundings, having the appearance of a far more ancient structure that had existed long before the arrival of the library.

A heavy table of dark wood filled the centre of the chamber. Upon this table were four enormous tomes, their spines a metre long and thick enough to enclose a book a third of a metre deep. Each book was secured to the table by a heavy chain of cold iron through the faded gold leaf edging of their leather bindings, and the pages were off-white vellum that had yellowed with the passage of millennia. Tightly wound script filled each page, each letter precisely formed and arranged in perfectly even lines of text.

Uriel took a deep breath at the sight of these books, letting the myriad aromas settle in the back of his throat and transport his mind back to the age of their creation. He tasted the tannic acid, ferrous sulphate and gum arabic of the ink, the warmth of the hide used in the vellum and the chalk used to prepare the surface to accept the ink. But most of all, his senses conjured the image of the singular individual that had penned these mighty tomes, a god amongst men, and a figure to whom uncounted billions owed their lives.

These works of genius had lived in Uriel's dreams for decades during his training, but until now, he had only been allowed within the presence of copies.

'Is that what I think it is?' began Pasanius.

'I think so,' said Uriel, stepping towards the books with an outstretched hand.

Both men stared at the enormous books, too lost in their reverence for the instructional words that had guided the Ultramarines for ten thousand years to notice that the door behind them had shut and another had opened.

'I wouldn't touch that if I were you,' said a resonant voice. 'It would be a shame if the Arcanium's defences killed you before I could pass my recommendation to the Chapter Master.'

Uriel snatched his hand away from the book, and looked up into the hooded eyes of the Chief Librarian of the Ultramarines, who stood on the other side of the table, though neither he nor Pasanius had been aware of his arrival.

Varro Tigurius was an imposing figure, though he stood no taller than would Uriel were he clad in his armour. Rather, it was the depth of knowledge and immense stature his rank and power conferred upon him that made Tigurius so vast and terrible.

Uriel felt a tremor of fear down his spine at the sight of the Librarian, his heavily ornamented armour bedecked with wax seals and carved script-work. Wards and sigils of unknown origin spiralled around his gauntlets and across every facet of his battle plate. A set of bronze keys hung on a thick chain around his neck, and his skull-topped staff of office seemed to glitter as though fashioned from corposant made solid.

Tigurius's eyes were infinitely deep pools, bright and glittering with wry humour, though only the Librarian ever knew the source of that amusement. His pale skin and sunken cheeks gave his features a sharp, angular edge uncommon amongst the ranks of the Astartes.

The Chief Librarian stepped towards them, and Uriel felt his skin crawl at the nearness of the mighty warrior. Though Tigurius had fought with courage and honour for the Ultramarines for hundreds of years, and had saved the warriors of the 4th Company on the desolate heaths of Boros, he was no brother as other Space Marines were brothers.

His powers and wealth of hidden knowledge ensured that he remained an outsider, even within a Chapter of warriors bound by oaths of brotherhood stronger than adamantium. To some, Tigurius was little better than a warlock, a wielder of powers more commonly ascribed to worshippers of unclean spirits or warp wyches, while to others, he was a warrior guided by the Emperor himself.

Tigurius's prescient warnings had saved the Ultra-marines from destruction at the claws of hive fleet Behemoth, had predicted the approaching war fleet of Warmaster Nidar, and had sent Uriel and Pasanius to Medrengard.

As much as Uriel honoured the might, power and rank of Tigurius, he had been through too much, due to this warrior's visions, to ever truly like him.

'Centuries of wisdom are contained within these hallowed pages,' said Tigurius, circling the table, and turning a page of the nearest tome without touching it. 'Our beloved primarch wrote much of its earliest passages here as a boy. Did you know that?'

'No,' said Uriel, surprised that he did not, for every warrior of the Ultramarines studied the history of the Chapter's gene-father, memorising his life, his battles and his teachings as part of his intensive training on the road to becoming a Space Marine.

'Few do,' said Tigurius. 'It is a small part of the primarch's story, and not one I am keen to promulgate, for I enjoy the solitude of this place and do not wish it to become a lodestone for pilgrims. Could you imagine this place with thousands traipsing through it like the Temple of Correction?'

Uriel shook his head, and glanced over at Pasanius. His friend was similarly close-mouthed, the sergeant's innate understanding of when to speak and when to shut up allowing Uriel to do the talking.

'I think it would be crowded,' said Uriel.

'Crowded, yes,' agreed Tigurius, as though the idea had only just occurred to him. 'As a youth, the primarch would come here with his books to read when he wished to escape the politicking of Macragge City. Hundreds of kilometres from the nearest settlement and higher than any man had climbed upon Hera's Peak, it was the perfect place to find peace. It still is, and I intend to keep it that way.'

'Then why summon us here?' asked Uriel, surprised at the tone of his question, which bordered on the disrespectful.

'Why do you think?' countered Tigurius.

'I don't know.'

'Then think harder,' snapped the Chief Librarian. 'You are a warrior with a modicum of intelligence, Captain Ventris. I expect more from you.'

'Because of these,' suggested Uriel, pointing towards the enormous books.

'Just so,' agreed Tigurius. 'The Codex Astartes. Tell me, what do they represent?'

Uriel looked down at the books, feeling humbled and awed once again that he was in the presence of artefacts touched by the hand of Roboute Guilliman.

'They are what makes us who we are?' ventured Uriel.

'Why?'

'Why what?' asked Uriel.

Tigurius sighed. 'Why does the Codex Astartes make us who we are? After all, it is just a book is it not? What makes it different to any other text penned over the millennia?'

In that sigh, Uriel understood with sudden clarity that his fate was hanging in the balance.

The instinctive, marrow-deep, detachment most warriors felt from Tigurius as a brother was blinding Uriel to that stark fact, and he forced down his impatience at the Librarian's obtuse nature. If he failed to convince Tigurius that he and Pasanius were worthy of reinstatement, then their lives were forfeit, with only the prospect of execution at Gallan's Rock awaiting them.

He stared down at the volumes of the Codex Astartes, letting the honour of standing in their presence flow through him. He had memorised entire tracts of his primarch's works, an amount of knowledge beyond even the most gifted of mortal savants, but even that was but the smallest fraction of knowledge contained within their pages, for no one without the magnificent cognitive faculties of one of the Emperor's lost sons could ever hope to memorise its entirety.

'It is more than just a book,' said Uriel. 'Its teachings were the building blocks that laid the foundations for the Imperium in the wake of the Great Heresy. Its words were the glue that held the forces loyal to the Emperor together when the rebels were defeated.'

'Good,' said Tigurius, nodding eagerly, 'and what does it teach us, the Ultramarines?'

'It sets out the tenets by which a Chapter should be organised,' said Uriel. 'Before the Heresy, the Legions were autonomous fighting formations, equipped with their own ships, manufacturing capabilities and command authority. The Codex broke that up and set out how the Space Marines should be organised so that no one man could ever hold such power again.'

'A Space Marine learns that on his first day within the walls of his Chapter House,' spat Tigurius. 'A novice could tell me that. That is what the Codex *is*, but I want you to tell me what it *means*, what it means to you, right here, right now.'

Uriel struggled to imagine what the venerable Librarian wanted to hear, thinking back to the times he had fought with the Codex as his guide, the times its teachings had saved his life and the terrible, aching absence torn in his heart when he had forsaken it.

'Think, Uriel,' hissed Tigurius, his eyes seeming to flicker with hidden fires. 'To be in the same room as these relics of a time long gone is to be standing in the presence of history itself. Through these works, a man can reach back to a time when gods of war walked amongst men, and the founder of our Chapter led the Ultramarines in battle.'

'It is the keystone of what makes the Space Marines so formidable,' said Uriel with sudden clarity. 'Without it, we are nothing but gene-bred killers.'

'Go on,' said Tigurius.

'Without the Codex Astartes, the Imperium wouldn't have survived the aftermath of the Great Heresy. It binds every one of the thousand Chapters of Space Marines together, and gives us a common cause, a connection to the past and to one another. Every Chapter, whether they acknowledge it or not, owes its very existence to the Codex Astartes.'

'Exactly,' said Tigurius. 'It is living history, a tangible link to everything we are.'

'And that's why you summoned us here,' said Pasanius. 'To know where we come from is to know who we are and where we are going.'

Tigurius laughed. 'You do not say much, Pasanius Lysane, but when you speak it is worthwhile to listen.'

'I'm a sergeant, my lord,' said Pasanius. 'It's what I do.'

Tigurius turned another page of the Codex without touching it, and said, 'This mighty work, this legendary connection to our past and our brothers, guides us in all things, yet on Tarsis Ultra you saw fit to disregard its teachings. You broke faith with what makes us Ultramarines, and left your warriors to fight without you while you took command of the Deathwatch and flew into the heart of a tyranid bio-ship. Was that arrogance or merely hubris?'

'It was neither, my lord,' said Uriel. 'It was necessary.'

'Necessary? Why?'

'The Deathwatch commander, Captain Bannon, was dead, and his squad needed a leader.'

'Any one of Bannon's warriors could have taken command. Why did it have to be you? What makes you so special?'

'I fought with the Deathwatch before,' said Uriel.

'Could the mission have succeeded without you?'

Uriel shrugged, looking over at Pasanius.

'I don't know,' he said. 'Maybe. I know I should have stayed with my company, but we succeeded. Does that count for nothing?'

'Of course it counts,' stated Tigurius with solemn finality. 'Yes, you saved Tarsis Ultra, but at what cost?'

'Cost?' asked Uriel. 'I don't understand.'

'Then tell me of Ardaric Vaanes.'

'Vaanes?' asked Uriel, surprised to hear Tigurius mention the renegade warrior of the Raven Guard. 'What of him? I am sure you have read the transcripts from the Reclusiam. You must have heard everything about him by now.'

'True,' said Tigurius, 'but I want to hear it again. What did you offer him on Medrengard?'

'A chance to regain his honour,' said Uriel, 'but he did not take it.'

'And what became of him?'

'I do not know,' said Uriel. 'I imagine he is dead.'

'Dead,' repeated Tigurius. 'And what did you learn from him?'

'Learn from him? Nothing,' said Uriel, tiring of Tigurius constantly meeting his answers with further questions.

'Are you sure?' asked Tigurius. 'If not from his words, then by his poor example.'

Uriel thought back to Medrengard, though the memories were painful and unpleasant. The renegade Space Marines he and Pasanius fought alongside had, for a brief, shining moment, embraced their cause and journeyed into the heart of the Iron Warriors' citadel. But Ardaric Vaanes had, in the end, forsaken them, and left them to their fate.

Suddenly, it was clear to Uriel.

'Vaanes's fate could have been my fate,' he said, with the growing confidence of epiphany. 'He let ego blind him to his duty and shared brotherhood. He believed he knew better than the teachings of his Chapter.'

'Ardaric Vaanes is a classic example of a fate that can overcome even the best of us if we are not vigilant,' said Tigurius, and Uriel heard the warning in the Librarian's tone. 'Every one of us constructs self-enhancing images of ourselves that make us feel special, never ordinary, and always of greater stature than we are. This is at the core of what makes a Space Marine such a fearsome opponent, the complete and utter belief in his ability to achieve victory no matter the odds against him. It boosts his courage, his self-esteem, and protects him from the psychological tribulations of being sur- rounded by death and forever immersed in battle. After all, every one of us thinks we are better than the average. Isn't that so?'

Uriel nodded, though the admission was uncomfort- able. 'Perhaps I once thought like that.'

'I know I did,' admitted Pasanius sourly. 'There wasn't a task I delegated that I didn't feel I'd have done better.'

'As much as they help us, these egocentric biases can be maladaptive,' said Tigurius, 'blinding us to our fail- ings and obscuring the awful truth that people exactly like us behave just as badly in certain evil situations. You assume that other people will fall to their vices, but not you, and do not armour your soul against tempta- tions, believing that nothing bad can affect you, even when you know how easily it can happen.'

Tigurius placed an open palm on the table, and bade Uriel and Pasanius approach.

'When you were an aspirant and you learned of the Great Heresy against the Emperor, I imagine you concluded that you would not do what the forces of the Warmaster had done. You shook your head and wondered how anyone could have travelled such a road. Am I right?'

Uriel nodded as Tigurius continued. 'Of course. I am sure you felt you simply *could not* have done what they did, but experience has shown that to be a lie, you *can* do such things. That belief is what makes us all vulnerable to such temptations, precisely because we think ourselves immune to them. Only when we recognise that every one of us is subject to forces beyond our control does humility take precedence over unfounded pride, and we can acknowledge our potential to tread the path of evil and engage in shameful acts. Tell me what that teaches you, Uriel.'

'That in the right circumstances, any one of us can fall.'

'Or the wrong circumstances,' added Pasanius.

'I fell once, because I believed I couldn't,' said Uriel, 'but on Medrengard I saw where that path ultimately leads: degradation and damnation.'

'Is that a fate you wish for?'

'No,' said Uriel with utter finality, 'absolutely not.'

'Then you have learned something of value,' said Tigurius.

♉ FOUR

IMPERIAL COMMANDER AND System Governor of Pavonis, Koudelkar Shonai was not, at first, an impressive sight, with his soggy physique, weak chin and receding hairline. A warrior he was not, though, as Lortuen Perjed had come to learn in the last year, his appearance was deceptive and there was a clever mind and hard heart concealed behind Koudelkar's unimposing appearance.

The second of two sons, it had been Koudelkar's brother, Dumak, who had been widely tipped to succeed Mykola Shonai as the next governor of Pavonis. However, Dumak had been slain by an assassin's bullet during one of the many worker riots in the days before Virgil de Valtos's attempted coup. In the wake of that rebellion, when Mykola Shonai's term of office was approaching its end, Lortuen had swiftly groomed Koudelkar to take his aunt's place.

It was a far from ideal situation, but as the senior adept of the Administratum on Pavonis, Lortuen had made the best of what was left to him. Most of the cartels were tainted with affiliations to traitors, and his masters had only accepted the scions of the Shonai as candidates for the role of Imperial Commander once they had agreed with his recommendation that no outsider be appointed to the position.

It was a recommendation that Lortuen had come to regret many times, but his former master had been fond of saying that regrets were like weights; they were only a burden if you held on to them. Ario Barzano, Inquisitor of the Ordo Xenos, had been full of such aphorisms, but he had died at the hands of a malevolent eldar warrior beneath the northern mountains, depriving Lortuen of a thoughtful master and trusted friend.

Since then, it had been a thankless task to restrain the policies of the young Shonai governor, whose idea of careful reconstruction was to aggressively pursue trade links with off-world conglomerates and merchant houses. With little infrastructure left in place, the planet's economy was fragile at best, but Koudelkar was not a man given to timidity, and the newly reconstructed palace was forever host to delegations from nearby systems, each seeking exclusive trading rights with Pavonis.

It made for a heady, cosmopolitan atmosphere and had certainly brought revenue to Pavonis. None of which would be a problem were Lortuen not tasked with keeping track of the young governor's comings and goings. Appointed permanent Administratum observer to Pavonis after the rebellion, Lortuen was finding this assignment almost as exhausting as travelling the stars in service to an Imperial Inquisitor.

Lortuen Perjed was not a young man anymore, his body aged well past the time when juvenat work would have done him any good. His mind was as sharp as ever, but his wrinkled flesh was liver-spotted, and even a brisk walk with his ivory-topped cane would tire him out. Had there been any justice, he would have been allowed to spend the rest of his days sequestered in some distant library with nothing but the study of dusty books and quiet contemplation to occupy his time.

Lortuen closed his eyes and smiled at the prospect, but the sound of angry voices brought him back to reality with a jolt. He opened his eyes and swept his gaze around the governor's expansive meeting chamber.

He sighed, realising that his dream of a quiet retirement was an ever more distant prospect.

The Senate Chamber of Righteous Commerce was the heart of Pavonis's traditional governorship, but with the dismantling of the cartels' power it had fallen into disuse. In lieu of a formal debating chamber, Koudelkar Shonai had constructed a long, glass-panelled atrium in the heart of the Imperial palace from which to conduct his gubernatorial duties.

Though open to the skies, thanks to rotating louvres in the curved roof, mast-borne voids secured the room from attack and wall-mounted vox-dampers prevented eavesdropping. Two gene-bulked skitarii in archaic-looking breastplates, hung with fetishes and carved with binaric oaths, provided more immediate protection for the governor.

The skitarii had been a gift from High Magos Roxza Vaal, the highest-ranking Mechanicus adept of the Diacrian Belt, for the swift restoration of machine imports to the refinery belt of the south-east.

Their swollen, bio-mechanical bodies and weapon implants were capable of immense violence, harking back to a barbarous age of gladiatorial combats, and truth be told, they scared Lortuen more than the Space Marines. You knew where you stood with the Adeptus Astartes, but these cybernetic monstrosities were a law

unto themselves. Both were heavily scarred and tattooed, looking more like deep-sump hive-world
gangers than guards appropriate for a Planetary Governor.

A long, reflective table of polished wood from the
fused remains of the Gresha Forest filled the centre of
the room, and brass cogitators softly chattered along the
entire length of one wall, with ticker-tape data-streams
of the sector markets fluctuations, raw material prices
and system currencies.

Liveried servants, for Koudelkar would not consider
something as prosaic as servitors when there were men
standing idle, stood holding silver ewers of wine with
their heads bowed at the mirrored doors, ready to
respond to their master's dictates.

The meeting, requested by Lord Winterbourne of the
44th Lavrentians, started poorly when Clericus Fabricae
Gaetan Baltazar pre-empted the order of business by
immediately demanding that Governor Koudelkar have
Prelate Culla arrested, or, at the very least, prevented
from spreading his fiery rhetoric through the streets of
Brandon Gate. As highest-ranking representative of the
Adeptus Ministorum on Pavonis, Baltazar objected to
the stirring up of the populace at a time when unity and
rebuilding were the order of the day.

Lord Winterbourne responded with a scathing remark
concerning the insipid nature of the preachers within
the walls of the Templum Fabricae, who seemed more
inclined to preach a doctrine of introspection and quiet
industry than the persecution of the Emperor's enemies.

Lortuen sat to the right of Governor Koudelkar, who
seemed content to let the two men vent their frustrations. Heated words passed back and forth between the
Lavrentian colonel and the Clericus Fabricae, but
Lortuen let the words wash over him as he accessed his

augmetic memory coils to consult the data he held on the various luminaries attending the governor.

The senior Imperial Guard commanders sat to the governor's left, formally clad in full dress uniforms, gleaming plumed helmets and scarlet capes. Lord Winterbourne had the lean, pinched look of a man used to campaigning, and Major Ornella faithfully transcribed the furious words passing between her colonel and the Ministorum priest.

Across the table from Winterbourne, and on Lortuen's right, sat Colonel Loic, commander of the Brandon Gate PDF, who in deference to his commander in chief had come unarmed. Loic observed the argument with grim stoicism, and Lortuen knew that behind the purely political appointment, Adren Loic was a dependable, if unimaginative, soldier. Which, he recalled, accounted for his selection to the post.

The ochre-robed Gaetan Baltazar sat beside Loic, resplendent in his chasuble and tall, gilded mitre. As he argued with Lord Winterbourne, Baltazar constantly worked prayer beads between his fingers.

Beside the Ministorum priest, Jenna Sharben of the Brandon Gate enforcers sat with her hands clasped tightly before her. Lortuen liked Sharben. She had been Ario's guide in the days when he had been investigating the cartels, and had proved to be a resourceful, determined woman. It had been Lortuen's directive that had seen her begin the establishment of a new cadre of enforcers, and, looking at the sunken hollows beneath her eyes, he saw the strain that role was placing on her.

As important and impressive as these individuals were, they were nothing compared to the dominating presence of the three Space Marines, who sat at the end of the table. Captain Uriel Ventris, a sergeant named Learchus, and a brutish warrior in gleaming black armour filled the room with their armoured bulk. The third warrior's helmet was worked in the form of a grinning skull, and his bellicose body language spoke volumes of his impatience and desire to be elsewhere.

Lortuen had met Uriel and Learchus before, though the other warrior was unknown to him. As pleased as he was to see Captain Ventris, Lortuen was surprised at the change he saw in him.

In Lortuen's time with Inquisitor Barzano, they had cause to fight alongside several Space Marines, many of whom had become staunch allies over the years. One facet that always amazed Lortuen was the apparent unchanging physicality of Space Marines. Though decades might pass between meetings, the genetic superiority of the Adeptus Astartes rendered them functionally ageless to the perceptions of most humans. Not so Uriel Ventris, who now carried hard-won wisdom in his eyes that spoke of horrors endured and lessons learned in blood.

Lortuen knew that look; he had seen it in his master's eyes in the months before his death.

Eventually, the argument between Winterbourne and Baltazar ended when Koudelkar slammed his palm down on the table.

'Enough!' snapped Koudelkar. 'Your prattle is hurting my ears. I have better things to do with my time than listen to you two argue.'

Gaetan Baltazar looked set to answer the governor's outburst with one of his own, but wisely kept his counsel, and simply nodded his head. Lord Winterbourne, clearly not used to anyone coming between him and a good argument, also bit his lip, and laced his hands together before him.

'Thank you,' said Koudelkar, his tone more even and placating. 'We are reasonable men, are we not? I am sure that between you, this issue can be resolved. After all, we each wish for a secure, stable world where trade can flourish and the teachings of the Imperial Creed are heard by all.'

'Of course,' said Baltazar, 'but all this predicant Culla preaches is hatred. He forgets the guidance and protection the Emperor represents. He fans the flames of fear, and that is not conducive to the stability you crave, my lord.'

'Culla is a scrapper, and a damn fine one too,' said Winterbourne. 'I've seen him go toe to toe with greenskins, come out on top, covered in blood, and then go back for more. We're out on the Eastern Fringe, Baltazar, and in case you hadn't noticed, we're a long way from Terra. The only protection we can rely on are our guns, tanks and swords.'

'Heresy!' spat Baltazar. 'The Emperor protects! A soldier like you should appreciate that.'

'Oh, be quiet, man,' said Winterbourne. 'The Emperor indeed protects, but I don't expect Him to do it all for me. What you need is a good–'

'Be silent!' barked the black-armoured Space Marine. His voice was deep and authoritative, a voice used to giving orders and having them obeyed without question. 'Did you not hear your commander? You should be ashamed of yourselves, arguing petty points of jurisdiction when you are gathered to discuss a deadly threat to your world. Captain Ventris?'

The gathering was suddenly cowed, the skull-faced warrior's outburst silencing them all in an instant. Uriel Ventris nodded his thanks to the warrior and rose to his full height, which towered over the gathered officials, and even the two skitarii.

Uriel folded his arms across his wide chest. 'Chaplain Clausel speaks bluntly, but he is right to do so.'

'A deadly threat?' demanded Koudelkar, leaning forwards and steepling his hands before him on the table. 'To what does your comrade refer?'

'There is a xenos presence on Pavonis, Governor Koudelkar,' said Uriel. 'Yet your senior officials argue and bicker while an enemy plans routes of invasion through your lands.'

Lortuen's eyes widened at Uriel's statement, shocked that such a threat had only now come to light.

'Are you sure?' he asked. 'We have seen nothing to suggest such a thing.'

'Adept Perjed,' said Uriel with a nod of respect, and Lortuen was a clever enough orator to recognise that Uriel was pausing to gather his thoughts in the face of uncertain facts. 'We ambushed a forward reconnaissance unit of tau Pathfinders in the Owsen Hills recently. It is my belief that these aliens were scouting routes towards Brandon Gate, possibly for a larger force to advance along.'

'Saints preserve us,' gasped Gaetan Baltazar, turning to the governor. 'We must mobilise all reserve units of the PDF, and deploy the 44th immediately!'

Koudelkar held up a hand and took a deep breath before answering the dismayed Clericus Fabricae. 'Calm yourself, Baltazar. A full deployment of our armed forces would achieve little save to cause panic.'

'If we are under attack, then–'

'Do we appear to be under attack?' snapped Koudelkar, rapping his fingertips on the smooth surface of the table. 'If what Captain Ventris says is true, and these are merely scouts, then we have some time to formulate an appropriate response.'

'An appropriate response would be to authorise a deployment of the 44th and to raise your alert level,' said Winterbourne. 'Then activate the Secondary and Tertiary Reserves.'

Koudelkar shook his head. 'These are delicate times for Pavonis, Lord Winterbourne. I do not expect a fighting man like yourself to understand the subtleties of planetary rule, but I am engaged in complex negotiations with several powerful subsector trading conglomerates to assure this planet's future prosperity. It would seriously jeopardise, if not utterly wreck, those negotiations were we to suddenly turn our world into an armed camp on the strength of one encounter with some easily bested aliens.'

Lord Winterbourne bristled at Koudelkar's words, his spare frame shaking with anger.

Uriel saw that anger and said, 'Governor Koudelkar, it would be a mistake to underestimate the tau. Their technology is highly advanced, and their warriors are skilful enemies.'

'So I have heard, but I notice that you choose words that suggest you are not certain of your conclusion, Captain Ventris,' said Koudelkar. 'Aside from the presence of this one unit of aliens, what proof do you have of your suspicions?'

'Nothing concrete,' said Uriel, 'but where Pathfinders are found, others are sure to follow.'

'But you have seen no sign of any others?'

'That is correct,' admitted Uriel.

'Lord Winterbourne? Colonel Loic?' asked Lortuen, 'Have either of your forces discovered any sign of these aliens?'

'We have not,' said Loic crisply. 'My long-range patrols have seen neither hide nor hair of any alien presence.'

'Nor have mine,' said Winterbourne, in control of his anger now, 'but, my lord governor, I am inclined to agree with Captain Ventris. His Chapter has experience in fighting the tau, and if he believes there are alien forces on Pavonis, then I concur that we should prepare for battle.'

'If the threat becomes credible, we will act upon it, I assure you,' said Koudelkar.

'What will it take for it to become credible?' demanded Chaplain Clausel, and even Koudelkar flinched from his razor tone. 'A tau honour blade opening your throat? An enemy battle flag planted atop the palace?

The governor composed himself in the face of the Chaplain's anger, and squared his shoulders. 'Would I be correct in assuming you killed all the tau you encountered?' he asked.

'No, there was one survivor,' said Uriel. 'We transferred her to the custody of Judge Sharben's enforcers at the Brandon Gate Correctional Facility.'

Koudelkar turned his attention to Jenna Sharben. 'And has this prisoner furnished us with any actionable intelligence or the location of any others of its kind?'

Sharben shook her head. 'No, my lord. The xenolexicon servitor has enabled us to communicate with the alien, but it has so far refused to give us anything beyond its name, rank and designation.'

'Then you must be more forceful in your questioning, Judge Sharben,' said Koudelkar, staring hard at Sharben. 'Find out what it knows, and do it quickly. Do I make myself clear?'

'Yes, my lord,' said Sharben with a curt nod.

'Are you going to mobilise our armed forces?' pressed Adren Loic. 'Given the Administratum restrictions we are under, any order to take up arms must come from the Imperial Commander and be ratified by the Administratum.'

This last, barbed, comment was directed squarely at Lortuen, and he smiled benignly.

'You sound entirely too eager for war, Colonel Loic,' said Lortuen. 'I assume you remember that those restrictions were put in place to ensure there is no repetition of the de Valtos incident.'

'De Valtos was a madman,' barked Loic. 'This is completely different.'

'Maybe so,' said Lortuen, 'but I will only ratify any deployment order if further indications of xenos presence come to light, or if Judge Sharben informs us that the tau prisoner has furnished useful information. Governor Koudelkar is entirely correct not to risk this planet's recovery and future prosperity on a suspicion unsupported by evidence.'

Uriel leaned over the table, his brow thunderous at what he would no doubt be seeing as a betrayal by a former ally. 'My warriors are not subject to the authority of the Administratum, Adept Perjed. Therefore I respectfully inform you, Governor Koudelkar, that the Ultramarines shall be assuming a war footing. I urge the armed forces of Pavonis to do likewise before it is too late.'

'Duly noted,' said Koudelkar, rising to his feet and ending the audience. 'We will reconvene in a week to discuss any further developments, but until then there will be no overt military operations beyond current deployments.'

Flanked by his towering skitarii, Koudelkar made his way from the audience chamber. As the chamber's door slid open, he turned to address the room.

'Now, if you will excuse me, gentlemen, I am late for an appointment with my aunt, and those of you acquainted with her will know that Mykola Shonai is not a woman who likes to be kept waiting.'

URIEL SAT ON a marble bench in the gardens of the Imperial palace. Its surface was worn and pitted, and he remembered the last time he had sat here. Nothing much had changed, which, having met Koudelkar Shonai, surprised him, since the new governor seemed like a man not given to sentiment. The grass was freshly cut and the flowers of the garden well cared for, the scent of their blossoms providing pleasant counterpoint to the ubiquitous, burnt metal aroma of Brandon Gate's industry.

A high wall enclosed the garden, one of the few areas of the palace to have escaped extensive damage during the rebellion, and Uriel felt more at peace than he had in a long time. This was where his last expedition to Pavonis had ended, sitting before the grave of Ario Barzano, a brave man who had died to save it from a madman's nightmarish plot.

The simple headstone in front of Uriel was a plain oblong of pale stone quarried from Tembra ridge, the words carved by Uriel's own hand:

> *Each man is a spark in the darkness*
> *Would that we all burn as bright.*

Barzano had been a garrulous, charismatic individual, but also a dangerous one. His word and Inquisitorial authority might have seen this world destroyed, but he had been willing to take a chance to save it, and for that reason alone deserved Uriel's respect.

'I never thought I would return,' said Uriel, leaning forward and resting his elbows on his knees, 'but it seems appropriate that we talk here, don't you think?'

'Indeed it does, Captain Ventris,' said Lortuen Perjed, appearing from an arbour behind Uriel. 'How long have you known I was there?'

'Since you entered the garden. Your cane and stoop give you a distinctive sound when you walk, adept.'

Lortuen awkwardly lowered himself to sit beside Uriel.

'I suspected I might find you here.'

Uriel shrugged. 'It seemed like the right thing to do.'

'It was.'

'You keep the garden well-tended.'

'It seemed the right thing to do,' replied Lortuen with a smile. 'After all, this world owes its survival to Ario, and to you.'

Uriel said nothing and studied Lortuen Perjed more closely, shocked by how different he appeared from the last time he had come to Pavonis. Adept Perjed had been old then, but now he seemed little more than a breath away from his grave. His skin was mottled and leathery, his hair ghostly wisps of silver clinging to his skull, and Uriel could clearly see the dull gleam of his savant augmetics behind his ear.

'You look much older than when last we were here,' said Uriel.

'These have been trying times since you left, Captain Ventris,' said Lortuen. 'The rebuilding of a planet so recently in rebellion is… exhausting work. While we're on the subject, I could say the same for you. I didn't think Space Marines aged, but time has caught up to you. I mean no offence.'

'None taken,' said Uriel. 'We age, but at a much slower rate than mortals.'

'So what happened to change you so much?'

'Things I would prefer not to talk about.'

'Ah, fair enough. I apologise for prying,' said Lortuen, resting his hands on the ivory pommel of his cane. They sat in companionable silence for a few moments before Lortuen said, 'So what do you make of Governor Koudelkar?'

Uriel looked away, clasping his hands and staring hard at Barzano's grave before answering.

'I think he is being naive, and governorship of a world on the Eastern Fringe is no place for naivety,' said Uriel. 'The tau are on Pavonis right now, and we must act expeditiously to stop them, or more lives will be lost when Koudelkar finally wakes up to the fact that the tau empire does not scout worlds without purpose.'

'You may be right, Uriel, but we are trying to rebuild this world. We are on the verge of securing a number of lucrative contracts with nearby systems. To jeopardise that would condemn Pavonis to ruin and its people to poverty for centuries to come.'

'To do nothing will condemn them to slavery,' pointed out Uriel.

'If you are right,' countered Lortuen. 'You must admit that you have not given us more than a vague suspicion that the tau plan anything immediate. Koudelkar is a businessman, and he is thinking of the future of his world.'

'Wrong,' said Uriel, rounding on Lortuen. 'He is an Imperial governor of a world of the Emperor, and he should be thinking of the danger facing his world *right now.*'

Uriel pointed at the gravestone and said, 'Do you think Ario would have hesitated to act? Imagine he were here right now. What would he do?'

'Ario was always one for spur of the moment decisions,' said Lortuen. 'I, on the other hand, am more considered in my deliberations. I believe we must proceed with caution, but I will meet you halfway, Uriel. I will issue readiness orders for the Secondary Reserve of the PDF.'

'And the 44th?'

'For now, their orders remain the same,' said Lortuen, pushing himself to his feet with the help of his cane. 'Foot patrols only and garrison duty. No active deployments. I do not wish to cause panic in the streets of our cities.'

'I'm sure the sight of a tau hunter cadre will do that for you,' said Uriel.

A HUNDRED KILOMETRES north of Brandon Gate, high upon Tembra Ridge and far above the cloud layer where the air was thin, the Kaliz Array spread itself over the tallest peaks on Pavonis, like a vast forest of pollarded trees constructed of latticework steel. The array was a jagged spine of ten thousand vox-masts, none less than five hundred metres high, secured by wire-wound guys anchored deep into the rock of the mountain.

It allowed long-range vox-units to function, gathering, relaying and transmitting communications traffic across the surface of the planet. Such was its power that even interplanetary communication was facilitated, albeit with a significant time lag.

The Kaliz Array had been constructed by the Vergen cartel nearly eight centuries ago, and its structures were sheened with verdigris and required constant maintenance. The hundred adepts, techs, maintenance workers and servitors tasked with keeping the array functional were housed at Mechanicus Station Epsilon in a collection of boxy structures huddled together in the lee of a sheer cliff far below the swaying masts.

Topped with leisurely rotating dish antennas and sheltered from the worst of the biting winds, the structures were nevertheless draughty, damp and cold. Even in such uncertain times, where money and employment were scarce, rumours of brain malignancies caused by vox radiation and the inhospitable conditions ensured that only the very desperate volunteered for duty at the Kaliz Array.

Workers stationed here did their best to stay indoors at all times, but as a particularly fierce squall blew in from the north, a trio of dejected figures made their way towards a malfunctioning series of masts in a region known simply as Deep Canyon Six.

Third Technician Diman Shorr pulled his glossy slicker tightly around himself and cursed the names of everyone he knew back at Epsilon who'd managed to dodge this duty. He'd reached thirty names when Gerran tugged at his sleeve to let him know they'd finally arrived at the end of the Deep Canyon Six chain.

The mountain paths were lined with steel posts connected by jangling chains, which were notched with angular markings that allowed a tech to find his way around without the aid of a map or the need to remove his helmet. Such chain paths allowed maintenance workers to navigate the myriad routes that twisted and curved through the array without getting hopelessly lost.

Hissing rain, solid enough to almost be considered hail, battered him, and crazed the visor of his helmet in streaming patterns of dirty water as he looked into the stepped gully that wound down into the canyon. Rainwater poured down its length in a tumbling waterfall, and they were going to have to be careful not to slip and break a leg. Getting med-evac out here would be next to impossible.

His hood billowed, and the icy wind bit into his body like a scavenger worrying a bone, threatening to toss him back down the slopes they'd spent most of the day climbing. His foul-weather slicker was old and thin, and he was tired, cold and wet through. He couldn't afford to replace the slicker, and the adepts of the Machine-God seemed disinclined to care overmuch for their techs by issuing heavy-duty ones.

For the better part of ten hours, he and Gerran had slogged along the chain paths through the wind and rain from the Mechanicus Station towards Deep Canyon Six in the company of a silent pack servitor with an elongated spine, gene-bulked shoulders and a simian posture that enabled it to carry huge loads across rugged, mountainous terrain unsuitable for vehicles. The servitor carried all their food and water, as well as basic medicae kit, ropes, an all-weather vox and a pair of battered lascarbines.

'My bones are getting too old for this,' he muttered, stepping into the torrent of icy water pouring down the gully. The breath hissed from his mouth at the jolt of freezing cold.

'Did you say something?' asked Gerran, and Diman knew he'd forgotten to switch off the inter-helmet vox.

'Nothing,' he said. 'It doesn't matter. Come on, let's see what the hell's wrong with these damned masts. See if it's something that needs an adept to repair. Sooner we're back inside the better. I don't want to die of exposure out here.'

'How come we had to do this anyway?' grumbled Gerran. 'I just finished an inspection shift over on Topper's Ridge.'

'Because we're just lucky, I guess,' replied Diman, carefully picking his route downwards.

'Lucky?' asked Gerran, missing Diman's sarcasm. 'Don't feel lucky to me. I tell you, Adept Ithurn has it in for me. She knew I'd just come off a shift and she still sends me out. It ain't fair, it just ain't.'

'Well you can always quit,' said Diman, weary of the younger man's carping. Things were miserable enough without him making it worse. 'Plenty of others be willing to step into your boots. Y'ought to be thankful you was part of the Shonai before the fighting. Only reason you were able to keep working for the Mechanicus.'

'Yeah, well, I might just do that,' said Gerran.

Diman was about to tell Gerran not to be so foolish, but he looked through the driving rain and saw a faint glow coming from the bottom of the gully.

'Damn it all,' he hissed. 'Looks like Ithurn's already sent a crew out to fix the masts. Bloody woman doesn't know one end of a work order from the next.'

Diman let Gerran squeeze past him, and waved the pack-servitor over, the lumbering beast oblivious to the heavy rain and freezing temperatures. He rummaged in one of the panniers for the battered vox, and extended its aerial, though it was doubtful the reception would be up to much in the narrow gully. A hissing burp of static issued from the speakers, and Diman turned the volume way up to try and pick out anything resembling a Mechanicus signal.

'Typical,' he said, when all he was rewarded with was white noise. 'A thousand vox-masts and I can't get nothing. Bloody thing needs junking, not a blessing.'

'Diman?' said Gerran, and he turned to see the younger man standing at the mouth of the gully, illuminated by the faint glow he'd seen earlier. 'You're gonna want to come see this.'

'What is it?' he asked. 'Another work crew?'

Gerran shook his head, and Diman sighed, turning the vox off and stowing it back in the servitor's panniers, before descending the last steps to the end of the gully and the entrance to Deep Canyon Six.

The planed rock floor stretched out for hundreds of metres in all directions, rising to steep cliffs on either side of a dark valley filled with humming generators and silver steel vox-masts. A hundred or so filled the canyon, but it wasn't the masts that caught Diman's attention.

It was the group of alien soldiers.

'I don't think that's another work crew,' said Gerran.

℧
FIVE

THERE WERE ABOUT forty of them, a mix of armoured soldiers in olive-coloured plates of armour with long, rectangular-barrelled weapons, and others dressed in the heavy-duty coveralls of engineers or labourers. A pack of fierce-looking creatures with wiry physiques and glossy pink skin stood apart from the soldiers. Flexing crests of spines sprouted from the backs of their beaked skulls, and they carried long rifles that looked almost primitive.

The glow Diman had seen from the gully shone from a handful of flattened discs hovering above the aliens, but he was more concerned by the boxy devices the alien engineers were carefully wiring between the generator relays.

A trio of vehicles with curving sides and enormous engine nacelles hovered behind the group, blurring the air, and turning the rainwater to hissing spray with antigrav fields. The soldiers were helmeted, but the flat, grey and utterly alien faces of the engineers were clearly visible. They worked with swift precision, and Diman saw that whatever they were doing, they were almost finished.

None of the aliens had noticed them. The warriors were too intent on the progress of the engineers and the heavy rain helped to obscure the two Mechanicus techs, but such luck couldn't hold forever. Diman immediately recognised the significance of what this act of sabotage could mean to Pavonis, and began backing slowly towards the pack servitor and the all-weather vox.

'Come on,' hissed Diman, 'we need to get out of here.'

Gerran stood, open-mouthed, at the entrance to Deep Canyon Six, transfixed by the sight of the aliens.

'What are they,' he asked, 'and what are they doing?'

'I don't know, but it's sabotage of some kind,' replied Diman urgently. 'You want to stick around and find out? Come on, let's go.'

'Sabotage?' said Gerran, horrified. 'Why?'

'Why the hell do you think?' snapped Diman, trying to keep his voice low, even though their words were spoken over their helmet-mics. That, combined with the noise of the wind and rain, would mean it was next to impossible for the aliens to hear them. 'If they take out the DC6 generators and masts, overload traffic will clog the rest of the network in a few hours.'

Diman reached the pack servitor, and hurried to slip the lascarbine from its waterproof holster with fumbling fingers. He slung the weapon over his shoulder and unbuckled the snap fixings of the pannier, hauling on the aerial of the vox-set.

Gerran joined him and lifted the second lascarbine from its holster before setting off up the foaming, water-slick steps out of the gully. He'd climbed six metres before realising that Diman wasn't following him.

'What the hell are you doing?' asked Gerran. 'You said we had to go!'

'We do, but we need to call this in.'

'Do it when we're away, for crying out loud.'

'Shut up, Gerran.'

Diman flicked the toggle to transmit, and an angry burst of feedback squealed from the handset, deafeningly loud in the confines of the gully.

'Shit!' he cried. 'The volume!'

He mashed the power switch to the off position, but the damage had been done.

'You bloody idiot!' shouted Diman. 'Run!'

Almost immediately, the diffuse glow from the end of the canyon surged in brightness, and spots of light blazed down into the gully. Diman looked up through the rain to see a pair of the floating discs bobbing in the air above him. Lights flickered around their circumferences, and Diman knew their luck had run out.

'Sweet Capilene, mother of mercy!' cried Diman, turning and sprinting as fast as he could up the steps after Gerran, leaving the hulking pack servitor behind.

The lights followed them up the gully, and Diman felt his heart hammer like a rapid drumbeat in his chest as he fought his way through the foaming waterfall pouring down the gully. His work boots felt as though they had weights attached to them, and he fell to his knees as a blistering pulse of light flashed above him and impacted on the wall of the gully.

A blizzard of light and noise washed over him, momentarily blurring his vision, and sending a spasm of nausea through him. Diman stumbled as glowing splinters of rock showered him like grenade fragments. The wind snatched his hood away, and cold darts of air stabbed the skin of his face through the cracked plastic of his visor.

Diman threw a panicked glance over his shoulder in time to see the pack servitor brought down by a pulsing volley of blue-hot beams of light. Smoking holes were blasted clean through its meaty bulk, and Diman didn't want to think about the kinds of weapons that could inflict such damage on a pack servitor or what they would do to *his* body. Scrambling forms darted into the gully, but the rain and mist of blood obscured them from clear sight.

Whatever they were, they were fast.

Diman scrambled to his feet, and snapped off a couple of shots down into the gully before pushing onwards. He didn't think he'd hit anything, but perhaps his fire might keep their heads down for a while.

The flying discs still floated above the gully, and Diman fired wildly into the air, hoping to bring one down, but the damned things seemed to anticipate his aim, and flew erratic, zigzagging patterns in the air.

'Move yourself!' shouted Gerran from the entrance to the gully, and Diman almost laughed with relief. He slipped and scrambled upwards as he heard a strange sound, a clicking, scratching noise like flint on stone.

He was no more than three metres from Gerran when a blurred creature of pale pink flesh, like a giant flightless bird stretched out into the semblance of a humanoid form, rose up behind the other man. Its limbs were lean and sinewy, and its monstrous head was crested with a mass of rigid spines. The creature's arms whipped up, almost too fast to follow, and Diman saw a jagged blade erupt from Gerran's stomach.

A screeching, squawking war cry ululated from the creature's beaked maw, and it wrenched the blade from Gerran's body with a brutal twist of its wrists. Gerran collapsed, his spine severed by the blow, and the water pouring down the gully was turned red with his blood.

Twin bandoliers crossed the creature's chest, and its patterned loincloth put Diman in mind of the pictures he'd seen of feral world predators. It carried a long barrelled rifle with a cruelly curved blade fitted to either end.

Long ago training from his days in the Tertiary Reserve kicked in, and Diman dropped to one knee with his lascarbine pulled in tight to his shoulder. The creature let loose another screeching cry, and spun its rifle to a firing position.

Diman fired first, and Gerran's killer was punched from its feet, a ragged, smoking hole blasted in its chest. The ancient lascarbine hissed in the rain as it fired, and Diman hurriedly cycled the firing mechanism as he heard the strange clicking, scratching sound once more.

Beams of light swept over him from above, but he ignored them and carried on, the breath heaving in his lungs at this rapid exertion. A stuttering volley of solid rounds blasted into the rock beside him, and he ran crouched over, emerging from the gully as a shot creased his shoulder and sent him sprawling.

Diman lost his grip on the lascarbine as he was spun around by the impact. He hit the ground hard and rolled, feeling the sharp rocks tear up his overalls. His helmet was smashed from his head, and the impact left him dazed as the cold hit him like a blow.

Bright lights danced before his eyes, and Diman lifted his head, feeling blood pouring from a gash on his forehead. He tried to push himself from the ground, but his limbs were leaden and uncooperative. Screaming pain in his thigh told him he'd broken his femur.

A pack of the skinned-looking creatures emerged from the gully, and gathered around the creature Diman had shot, their movements inhumanly quick and birdlike. Their quills stood on end, with colours rippling down their lengths. One of the creatures was of greater stature than the others, with powerful muscles and a crest of bright red quills. It carried a weapon of obvious sophistication, with a short-barrelled, under-slung launcher of some kind.

At its side was a hideous trio of quadrupeds that must surely have escaped from a realm of nightmares. They resembled nothing so much as skinned wolves. Their pink flesh glistened in the rain, and manes of spines stood erect on their powerfully muscled shoulders. Diman whimpered in fear as he saw that they shared evolutionary roots with their masters, having the same spine of rigid quills and jagged, beak-like jaws.

The red-quilled leader emitted a series of high-pitched squawks and whistles.

In response, two of its pack knelt by the body of the dead beast, and began attacking it with long-bladed knives, carving off strips of flesh and gulping them down. Within moments, they had efficiently butchered the body, and passed out dripping chunks of their former comrade's flesh to each member of the pack.

Diman felt his gorge rise at the sight, the blood of the slain beast drooling from their beaked jaws as they threw back their heads and screeched to the sky. He sobbed as the alien hounds joined the macabre chorus.

Redquill barked something in his vile alien language, and the three hounds sprinted over the rocks towards Diman.

He tried to pull away, but knew it was hopeless as his leg flared in unbelievable agony. The monstrous hounds screeched at him as they bounded over the rocks, their jaws frothing with thick saliva.

Diman expected the searing pain of their bites, but, instead, they circled him with their heads low and their jaws wide, hissing and spitting. Their breath was hot, and reeked of dead flesh and rancid milk. He closed his eyes and curled himself into a tiny ball, prayers he'd learned as child spilling from his lips.

'Emperor, who art with me in all things, protect your humble servant...'

A powerful hand flipped him over onto his back and seized him by his neck. The reek of alien flesh caught in the back of Diman's throat, and he gagged at the pungent, oily sweat of the creature.

He opened his eyes and found himself staring into a pair of milky white eyes without pupils, set deep in an alien skull topped with spines that had deepened from red to crimson. Fear like nothing he had known seized him.

'Redquill,' he said.

The creature cocked its head to one side, a thin membrane nictitating across its eye. Its jaw worked, and a grating, clicking sound emerged from its beak. It repeated the sound several more times until Diman realised that it was trying to repeat what he had said.

He nodded and smiled through the pain, hoping and praying that this moment of connection might save his life. At last, the monster seemed to have mastered the vowel sounds, and it croaked, 'Radkwaal...'

'Yes,' nodded Diman. 'You. Redquill.'

'Radkwaal,' said the creature again.

It turned its head towards its fellows, and squawked the name Diman had given it, followed by a further series of clicks and whistles.

Any hope that Diman's fleeting communication might have saved his life was snatched away as the creatures drew their butcher knives.

BRANDON GATE CORRECTIONAL Facility covered a square kilometre and had a total of twenty guard towers encircling its perimeter. Within its boundaries, it was a small city, partitioned into five walled enclosures, each designed to hold a particular kind of prisoner, but which presently served as vehicle pools and firing ranges.

Only a thousand prisoners were held here, although the facility had once held close to twenty thousand unfortunates within its hellish interior. Though much had changed since the rebellion, the prison was no less horrendous a place to be sent, either as a guard or as a prisoner.

A circular tower stood in the centre of its open yard, ringed with mosaics and bas-reliefs of uplifting scripture and religious imagery intended to inspire the rehabilitation of its inmates, but which only served to give them a focal point for their hatred. Atop this tower was a polarised glass dome, from which the enforcers could command a panoramic view of the city, and which gave the facility its more usual name of the Glasshouse.

Stuck on the edge of Brandon Gate beyond the Commercia Gate like an afterthought, the facility had an unsavoury reputation, even before the de Valtos rebellion, as a place of torture and execution. It had been a favourite dumping ground for undesirables rounded up by the cartel's enforcers for any activity deemed a crime by their paymasters.

Those unwise enough to demand rights for workers injured in the line of duty, or to voice any opinions on the cartels deemed subversive, would soon find their doors smashed down in the middle of the night. Squads of enforcers would drag them from their beds and toss them into the hellish confines of the Correctional Facility.

In the wake of the rebellion, many of its former inmates had escaped when vengeful relatives and friends attacked the prison complex, and looted it of anything of value. The prison had been brought back to operational use by Jenna Sharben's newly established enforcers in lieu of any other facility capable of handling criminals. Conditions within its mouldering cells and debris-strewn enclosures made it resemble something from an active warzone instead of a functioning centre of law enforcement.

The corridor Jenna Sharben walked along was dim and thick with dust, the sputtering lumen strips set into glass blocks in the wall barely providing enough illumination to avoid the tangled piles of inert cabling and debris. Water pooled on the floor, and the stench of mould and a thousand filthy cells hung like a miasma upon the air.

Enforcer Dion walked alongside her. Jenna suspected that, in time, he would make an enforcer of which Brandon Gate could be proud. He was cut from a rugged cloth, his manner powerful yet fair and even-handed. Like her, he carried his helmet in the crook of his arm and had his shock maul strapped across his back. Dion and Apollonia were the best she had trained, and, by their example, the tarnished reputation of the enforcers would be restored to one of honesty, integrity and justice.

'So, what's the word from on high?' asked Dion as they drew near the cell where the alien captive was being held. The Ultramarines had deposited the prisoner a couple of days ago, and a xenolexicon servitor the day after, though it hadn't helped with getting any actionable intelligence from the prisoner.

'The word is that it's time to get tough,' said Jenna.

'What does that mean, exactly?' asked Dion.

That was the big question, thought Jenna.

'It means that Governor Koudelkar wants information from the prisoner,' she said, leaving out the part where she felt that the governor wasn't too interested in how that information was obtained. That didn't seem like a message that ought to be literally carried down the chain of command.

'So what sort of information are we after?' asked Dion.

'Anything we can get,' said Jenna. 'If the Ultramarines are right, and the tau are on the verge of invasion, then we need to bring the governor some hard evidence of that.'

'And you know how we do that?' asked Dion. 'I suppose you had training in interrogation techniques in the Adeptus Arbites.'

'I did,' agreed Jenna, 'but those techniques require time and the eventual co-operation of a prisoner. One we don't have, and the other, we're not likely to get any time soon.'

'Then what's our game plan?'

'We go in hard and see what we get,' said Jenna, turning a corner and halting before a steel door fitted with a mag-lock that was obviously new. Two enforcers stood outside, and both snapped to attention when they saw Jenna.

She pulled on her helm and said, 'Put your helmet on, and slide the mirror visor down.'

'What for?'

'Just do it,' said Jenna. 'It makes it easier.'

'For the prisoner?'

'No,' said Jenna, 'for us. And once we're inside, no names.'

She turned to the guards at the door.

'Open it up,' she said.

The door was opened, and Jenna and Dion stepped through into a windowless room that reeked of stale sweat and a pungent, alien smell that was deeply unpleasant for its very unfamiliarity. The cell was bare rockcrete, the walls scratched and defaced by the hundreds of lost souls held there over the years. Incense burners sat in each of the cell's four corners, emitting aromatic smoke inimical to xenos creatures, though they did little to counter the noxious odour of the room's occupant.

Enforcer Apollonia stood at the back of the cell with her hands behind her, the mirrored visor of her helmet pulled down. The tau sat on a stool with her strange, four-fingered hands laced before her in her lap.

Sitting opposite, its hands laced in front of it in imitation of the prisoner's posture, was the xenolexicon servitor the Ultramarines had provided. Robed in a pale blue chiton with gleaming implants and a well-maintained flesh tone, the bio-mechanical hybrid was a fine example of the Mechanicus's skill.

Its ears had been replaced by broad-spectrum receptors, and the lower half of its face was a nightmarish melange of moving parts formed from brass and silver. Designed to mimic the mouth shapes of a dozen different alien races, its jaw was a bulbous mass of constantly rotating, shifting metal with artificial mandibles, teeth and a multitude of artificial tongues that could adapt its structure to match that of the subject.

Jenna stood beside the xenolexicon servitor and addressed the prisoner. 'I am going to ask you some questions. It would be better for you if you were to answer them truthfully. Do you understand me?'

The servitor's mouth clicked and whirred as it formed the internal anatomy of a tau mouth and repeated the words she had said in the alien's language, a language that was strange, and bore little resemblance to any human tongue. Briefly, Jenna wondered how the builders of the servitor had known what structure to construct in order to form the word groups and syllables of the tau language.

Study and dissection of tau skulls, she supposed, untroubled by the thought.

Although the flat features and lack of a nose made it difficult to read the tau female's facial expression, Jenna thought she detected a faint revulsion on her face. Was the servitor's rendition of its language so bad?

The prisoner said the phrase she had been saying since they'd put her in the cell, the words rendered tonelessly by the servitor.

'My name equals La'tyen Ossenia. Shas'la of Vior'la Fire Warrior team Kais.'

Jenna circled the prisoner, drawing her shock maul from the sheath on her back. 'I see. You think you're being a good soldier, but all you're doing is making this harder for yourself. You're going to tell us what we want to know, and, the sooner you do, the easier this is going to be for you.'

Once again, the servitor relayed her words, and once again it repeated the phrase the prisoner had said countless times before.

'My name equals La'tyen Ossenia. Shas'la of Vior'la Fire Warrior team Kais.'

Jenna slammed her shock maul against the prisoner's lower back, and she fell to the floor with a wordless cry of pain. Another couple of swift strikes to the shoulder and hip had the tau prisoner curled up in a tight ball of pain.

Jenna rolled the tau female onto her back with her boot, and planted the tip of her shock maul against her throat. She took no pleasure from such violence, but such was the role in which she had been cast, and she would play it to the best of her ability.

'That's a taste of how bad things are going to get for you if you don't co-operate.'

She heard the servitor translating her words, and pressed down harder on the captive's chest. 'That was without the shock field activated. Imagine how much pain you'll be in when I turn it on.'

Three times more, Jenna asked the tau questions, and each time received the same answer.

'My name equals La'tyen Ossenia. Shas'la of Vior'la Fire Warrior team Kais.'

Each obstinate refusal to answer only infuriated Jenna more. Didn't the creature realise that she was trying to spare it pain? She delivered stinging blows to the captive's knees, stomach and ribs, each carefully weighted to cause extreme pain but no long term damage.

After half an hour of beatings, Jenna hauled the prisoner to her knees, and thumbed the activation stud on her shock maul. She held the humming weapon in front of the prisoner's face, and was gratified to see a trace of fear enter her amber eyes.

'Still won't talk, eh?' said Jenna, nodding to Dion and Apollonia. 'Then it's time for the gloves to come off.'

The screams of the tau prisoner echoed throughout the Glasshouse long into the night.

THE TWO AIRCRAFT banked around a jutting headland of rock, hugging the mountainside, and flying high across the craggy landscape in a roar of engine noise. Nap of the earth flight was impossible so close to the Kaliz Array, for vox-masts appeared over the horizon without warning, and could easily tear a wing from an unwary aircraft.

One of the flyers was a bulky gunship, its wings bristling with missiles, and a multitude of guns studding its frontal sections and upper deck. This was a

Thunderhawk, the workhorse of the Adeptus Astartes, and an aerial chariot without equal. Its armoured skin was a vivid blue, the glacis beneath the pilot's compartment emblazoned with a brilliant white inverse omega symbol of the Ultramarines with a golden eagle set upon it.

The second aircraft was a smaller Aquila-class lander, its swept forwards, eagle-wing design giving rise to its honourable name. Its wings and side panels bore the golden horse heraldry of the 44th Lavrentian Hussars, and its pilot was careful to keep close to the larger Astartes gunship.

Both bled speed as they drew near a wide canyon cut in the rock, and set down in a wash of flaring retros and rock dust. The landings were difficult, the aircraft buffeted by high winds blowing over the mountains from the north, but these pilots were the best, and within moments, both gunship and lander were safely down.

The assault ramp on the front of the gunship dropped, and a host of Space Marines emerged, dispersing swiftly from the troop compartment, and assuming defensive positions around the aircraft. Nearly thirty warriors of the Ultramarines fanned out from the gunship, forming up in a Codex deployment pattern.

Uriel jogged down the ramp of the Thunderhawk, his bolter held loosely at his side, and his sword a reassuring presence at his hip. A light rain pattered his armour, but he didn't feel the cold or wet.

'Looks quiet,' said Learchus at his side.

'It does indeed,' replied Uriel, scanning the ground before him and forming a mental map in his head, 'but I'd expect that.'

Learchus nodded, and set off to join the scout squad forming up on the western edge of their deployment zone without another word. Uriel stepped from the ramp of the Thunderhawk onto the Tembra Ridge Mountains, his enhanced faculties for spatial awareness identifying the best positions to occupy: from where an effective assault could be launched or defence mounted.

Without orders needing to be issued, each squad of Ultramarines was already positioning itself correctly, and Uriel felt proud to be part of such an awesomely effective fighting machine.

Chaplain Clausel took up position with his assault squad, warriors who went into battle with bulky jump packs fitted to their armour. These allowed them to take the fight to the enemy and descend upon them from the skies on wings of fire. They were Astartes of the highest calibre, warriors who excelled in the brutal whirlwind of close-quarters fighting. As ferocious as they were, assault troops were not mindless killers, but carefully chosen fighters with an innate understanding of the ebb and flow of battle.

An Assault Marine knew when to smash the enemy with force, and when to withdraw.

Clausel had said little to Uriel since his return from his Death Oath, and every now and then he would catch the Chaplain's stern, uncompromising glare upon him. Which, he supposed, was entirely fair. After all, this mission was as much to test Uriel's ability to command his warriors as it was to ensure that the hard-won peace was holding.

Techmarine Harkus, detached from the command centre and incongruous in his red armour and hissing servo harness, ministered to the Thunderhawk, ensuring that the rough landing had not offended the aircraft's spirit. The black and white of the Icon Mechanicus stood out on Harkus's right shoulder guard, while the blue of the Ultramarines remained on his left. The sight of an Ultramarines warrior in armour that bore another's heraldry sat ill with Uriel, but the union of the Adeptus Astartes and the Mechanicus of Mars was an ancient one.

Uriel set off towards the canyon ahead of him, as the Aquila lander lowered its internal compartment to the ground and Lord Winterbourne emerged, resplendent in his green frock coat, high boots, golden helmet and ebony walking cane. Growling and pulling urgently on their leashes were the two hound creatures that accompanied the colonel everywhere he went. Uriel had learned that they were called vorehounds, and their noses darted from side to side as they sniffed the wet rocks.

Four Lavrentian storm-troopers, in gleaming golden breastplates and carrying bulky hellguns, shadowed their colonel, followed by a robed scribe with clicking quill-armatures and a glassy-eyed vox-servitor.

'Uriel,' said Winterbourne, 'good of you to help out. My lads were itching for some action, but it would take us quite some time to get up here, what? You and your fancy gunship are a real boon.'

'Happy to help, Lord Winterbourne.'

'Nathaniel,' said Winterbourne automatically. 'Damned unusual business this.'

'Yes,' agreed Uriel, enhancing the thermal imaging display of his visor to better penetrate the shadows of the mountain. 'Unusual and conspicuous.'

'Seems to support your suspicions, does it not?'

Uriel nodded. 'If you're going to attack someone, first knock out their communications.'

Reports had come to the Ultramarines command centre of a system-wide failure in a great many of the planetary vox-networks. Such glitches in the system were common enough not to raise immediate suspicion, but the timing of such a failure immediately raised a red flag in Uriel's mind.

The Kaliz Array was hundreds of years old, and the Adeptus Mechanicus and local technicians had their hands full maintaining its venerable generators and relays. It would take days for PDF units or Guard forces to reach Deep Canyon Six, the location the Adeptus Mechanicus had identified as the source of the initial system failures. Uriel had immediately offered the services of the Ultramarines.

'So, how do you want to do this?' asked Winterbourne.

'We go in expecting a fight,' said Uriel. 'We will take one approach down, you and your men will take the other. If there are any enemy units there, we destroy them and see what damage they have done.'

'Simple. I like it,' said Winterbourne, fighting to hold the vorehounds at his side. 'Damn it! Germaine! Fynlae! Heel!'

The beasts paid their master no heed, and continued to tug at their leashes, foam gathering at the corners of their mouths and their desperate barking echoing from the mountainside.

'What is the matter with them?' asked Uriel.

'Damned if I know,' cursed Winterbourne. 'Heel! Heel, I say!'

With a final surge, the vorehounds broke free of Winterbourne's grip, and bounded across the rocks towards the nearest gully leading down into Deep Canyon Six. Uriel and Winterbourne set off after them, with the storm-troopers hot on their heels.

It didn't take long to catch up to the hounds, one of which sniffed the ground and growled at the entrance to the gully. The three-legged beast circled a patch of rocks downhill, eagerly barking with feral hunger.

Winterbourne caught up to his pets, and struck at their flanks with his walking cane.

'Damned unruly beasts!' he shouted, gathering up their leashes and hauling their choke chains tight. 'No discipline, that's your problem. I ought to have you shot.'

Uriel knelt by the ground the vorehounds had been sniffing, and ran his fingers over the slick rocks. His enhanced vision and auto-senses could already detect the lingering residue and aroma of an all too familiar substance.

'Blood,' he said.

'Human?' asked Winterbourne, and Uriel nodded.

'Yes, and no more than a day or so old.'

'How do you know that?'

'The smell's too fresh. Any longer and the rain would have washed away all traces of it. Your hounds aren't the only ones with sharp senses, Lord Winterbourne.'

'That bodes ill,' said Winterbourne, handing the reins of his vorehounds to the vox-servitor, and drawing his sword, a magnificently fashioned sabre with a curved blade and a network of crystalline filaments worked along its length that crackled with fire.

Uriel passed the word of what the hounds had discovered to his warriors, and there was a noticeable shift in the posture of the Ultramarines, each warrior now expecting battle instead of merely anticipating it.

'I suggest you join your soldiers, Lord Winterbourne,' said Uriel. 'It is time to move out.'

'Just so,' said Winterbourne, unsnapping the catch on the holster at his hip. The colonel of the Lavrentians drew his sidearm, a simple laspistol with a matt black finish. The weapon was standard issue and old, very old, but clearly well cared for. Uriel was surprised at the lack of ornamentation on the weapon, having seen many a colonel seek to impress with the ostentation of their battle gear.

Winterbourne saw his look and smiled.

'It was my father's pistol,' he explained. 'Got me through a few damned tight scrapes, let me tell you. I look after it, and it looks after me.'

Uriel nodded to Winterbourne's storm-troopers and left the colonel to their care. He jogged over to his squad, and quickly ran through the pre-battle ritual of preparedness. Each warrior inspected the battle gear of one of his brothers, checking armour and weapons that had been checked thrice already, but which were checked again because that was the Ultramarines way.

When the icons for each of his squad members flashed green on his visor, Uriel broadened his scope of view, seeing icons flashing to life for every warrior under his command. All were ready.

Chaplain Clausel approached, and Uriel offered his hand.

'Courage and honour, Chaplain Clausel,' he said.

'Courage and honour, Captain Ventris,' replied Clausel, leaving Uriel's hand unshaken.

'My warriors will go in through the gully,' said Uriel, masking his irritation at Clausel's manner. 'Your assault troops will await my signal to manoeuvre.'

'Remember the teachings of the Codex,' said Clausel. 'It will guide you in all things.'

'I will, Chaplain,' promised Uriel. 'You do not need to worry about me. Librarian Tigurius reminded me of my duty to the teachings of our primarch.'

'Aye,' agreed Clausel. 'I'm sure he did, but Tigurius cannot see everything.'

'What does that mean?'

'It means he wanted you back within the ranks of the Ultramarines,' said Clausel, 'for his own reasons as much as for the good of the Chapter.'

'You doubt me, Chaplain?' asked Uriel. 'My honour is intact, my loyalty undoubted. The senior masters of the Chapter agreed on it.'

'Not all of them,' said Clausel, turning away. 'Just know that I remain to be convinced that your return is a good thing. Fight well and you may yet persuade me that one who fights within the Great Eye can come back unchanged.'

'I am not unchanged, Chaplain,' whispered Uriel as Clausel rejoined his warriors.

Uriel put the grim Chaplain's words from his mind, and issued his orders. The Scouts would remain with the Thunderhawk while Uriel would lead one squad through the southern gully towards the base of the canyon. Lord Winterbourne and his storm-troopers would take the northern approach. Chaplain Clausel and his assault troops would climb to the top of the cliffs that overlooked the base of the canyon and await Uriel's order to deploy.

Uriel drew his warriors close, Learchus at his side, and stared into the darkness of the gully that led down through a narrow cleft in the rocks to shadow. He remembered the last time he had travelled into these mountains with war in his heart.

He and his warriors had dropped thousands of metres into a deep core mine, and had faced the Bringer of Darkness in a forgotten tomb built when the galaxy was young. Ario Barzano had died there, and Pasanius had lost his arm, a grievous wound that had brought him nothing but pain and punishment.

A punishment that had seen Uriel go to war without his dearest friend.

Ʊ
SIX

A COLD WIND blew down from the east, the bite of a harsh Macragge winter easing up now that spring was breaking and the snows on the lower slopes were melting. The landing platforms sat near the foot of the mountains upon which Ptolemy's Library and the Sword Hall were built, the eastern winds an omen of changing times and good fortune.

Uriel did not feel fortunate as he marched from the upper cloisters to a flight of marble steps that led down to where the 4th Company stood in ordered ranks before five Thunderhawk gunships. Steam rose from the edge of the platforms, the aircraft growling as the Techmarines feathered their engines. The banner held proudly aloft by Ancient Peleus flapped noisily in the wind.

Over a hundred warriors in the dazzling blue of the Ultramarines stood as still as statues on the platform, their arms locked by their sides and their heads held high as they awaited the order to embark on this latest mission. The Chaplain, Techmarines, Apothecaries, artificers, drivers and pilots, and ancillary company staff had gathered for the official Company Commencement. Not since the 4th Company had deployed to Tarsis Ultra had its duly-appointed captain led it into action, and such a moment demanded recognition.

Uriel had dreamed of this ever since he and Pasanius had been banished from Macragge, and now that it was here, he found that redemption tasted bitter. For this new beginning marked the first time he had been forced to leave a battle-brother behind.

ESCORTED BY FOUR armed Vanguards, Pasanius had come to bid Uriel farewell in the company chapel the previous evening as he prepared to don the armour of Brother Amadon for the first time. Uriel was clad in a form-fitting under-suit, and was surrounded by four red-robed artisan-apprenta from the Armorium.

Uriel had prepared his flesh with fasting, oils and physical exertion.

His soul was steeled with reflection and speaking the catechisms of battle.

He was ready to be clad in the armour of a Space Marine, and the apprenta recited binaric cants pleasing to the Machine-God as they applied sacred oils to the hard plugs that allowed the armour to interface with his body.

The chapel was a long, vaulted space of silver stone, brightly lit with a dozen flaming brands and the glow from a rose window set high on the western wall. Firelight reflected from the walls, and from the burnished battle-plate that hung on a sturdy frame before a great statue that stood in the curved chancel. Rendered in polished bronze by the hand of Mellicae, the greatest warrior artificer of the Ultramarines, the towering form of Roboute Guilliman stared down at Uriel with eyes fashioned from sapphires the size of a Space Marine's fist.

The Vanguards led Pasanius into the chapel with their weapons bared, and it broke Uriel's heart to see his friend so ignobly treated. The apprenta backed away from Uriel with their heads bowed as Pasanius halted before him, still dressed in the black chiton of the penitent. Like Uriel, he had been found free of corruption in flesh and soul, but, for the crime of failing to disclose the truth of his infected arm, he had been judged guilty of breaking the Chapter's Codes of Rectitude.

'You can go,' Uriel told the warriors escorting Pasanius.

'We are ordered to remain with the prisoner at all times,' said one of the Vanguards, a black-bladed sword held across his shoulder. 'He begins his sentence at sunset.'

Each of the Vanguards was clad in armour forged by masters of their craft, decorated with gold and silver trims, and polished to a reflective finish. No two were alike, yet each warrior had earned the right to wear such armour on uncounted battlefields, through acts of valour that would be unbelievable were any save a warrior of the Ultramarines to relate them.

'This man is a hero of courage and honour,' said Uriel. 'You will not address him as "prisoner" in my presence again. Is that understood?'

'Yes, my lord,' said the Vanguard. 'Our orders come from Chaplain Cassius himself.'

'I am sure Pasanius is not going to try and escape,' said Uriel dryly. 'Are you?'

'No,' said Pasanius. 'I'm in enough trouble as it is without adding attempting to escape to my list of crimes.'

For breaking the Codes of Rectitude, Pasanius had been sentenced to a hundred days in the Chapter cells and to endure exclusion from the ranks of the 4th Company for the time it took Macragge to orbit its sun. In addition, he had been reduced in rank from sergeant to battle-brother. To be kept apart from his brothers for even a day longer than necessary was a punishment as severe as any that could be meted out to a warrior of the Ultramarines.

'We will wait for you outside, brother,' the Vanguard told Pasanius as they withdrew from the chapel.

'I'm obliged to you, and I'll be with you directly,' Pasanius assured them as the heavy wooden doors of the company chapel closed behind the veteran warriors.

'You'll want help with that,' said Pasanius, nodding towards the armour.

'I have the apprenta from the Armorium,' said Uriel, indicating the robed acolytes who waited at the foot of the statute.

'Apprenta?' scoffed Pasanius. 'What do artisans know about the wearing of battle plate? No, you need a brother warrior to fit you into that armour. It's only right and proper. After all, this is the nearest I'll get to power armour until you get back.'

Uriel turned towards the apprenta and said, 'Leave us.'

The robed acolytes bowed and made their way from the chapel of the 4th Company.

'A hundred days,' said Uriel when they were alone. 'It's not right.'

'Don't be soft,' chuckled Pasanius. 'I'll do a hundred days no problem; it's no more than I deserve. I lied to my brothers, and more importantly, I lied to you. It's a just punishment. You and I both know it, and I'm not going to complain about it.'

'You're right, I know,' said Uriel. 'You'll be missed within the ranks.'

'I know,' said Pasanius without arrogance, 'but you've good men there as sergeants. Venasus, Patrean... Learchus.'

'I've heard good things about Learchus from the men,' said Uriel. 'You read the honour rolls after the 4th's deployment to Espandor?'

'I did,' confirmed Pasanius, kneeling to remove the first section of the armour from the rack. 'A gargant and a greenskin horde. Not bad.'

Uriel laughed at the understatement in his friend's tone. 'It was a grand achievement, Pasanius, as you well know.'

'Yes, but it galls me we weren't there for it,' said Pasanius. 'It feels wrong, knowing our warriors went into battle without us. It feels like we let them down.'

'We did, but the past is done with, and I have a company to lead. When this expedition to Pavonis is over, you'll be reinstated to the ranks, and we'll fight side by side once more.'

'I know that, Uriel,' said Pasanius. 'Just...'

'Just what?' asked Uriel when Pasanius didn't continue.

Pasanius looked uncomfortable, and glanced towards the sealed doors of the chapel.

'Come on,' pressed Uriel. 'Out with it.'

'It's Learchus.'

'What about him?'

'Watch him.'

'Watch him?' said Uriel. 'Why? Because his accusations saw us condemned? You know he was entirely correct to speak up.'

'Yes, and I hold no grudge against Learchus for that,' said Pasanius. 'It took courage for him to do the right thing, I see that now.'

'Then what?'

Pasanius sighed. 'Learchus promised he would look after the company until our return, and by the looks of things he's done a grand job: fine recruits, hard training and warriors we can be proud of. Not only that, he led them all into battle on Espandor against a horde of greenskins that would have tested the mettle of a veteran battle company.'

'Then what troubles you?'

'No one expected us to come back alive, Uriel,' said Pasanius. 'Learchus was one of the few who did, but even he had begun to believe us dead. On Espandor, he got a taste of proper command and he liked it. I'm thinking that with us long gone, he figured he'd be the logical choice to take command of the 4th.'

'And then we returned,' finished Uriel.

'Exactly,' said Pasanius. 'Now don't get me wrong, Learchus is a great warrior and I trust him with my life, but he'd be less than human if there wasn't some part of him that didn't resent your reinstatement.'

'I think you are wrong, my friend,' said Uriel.

Pasanius shrugged. 'I hope so, but enough talk, let's get this armour on, eh?'

Uriel nodded, and, piece by piece, Pasanius clad him in the armour of Brother Amadon. He began with the boots, and worked up to the greaves on Uriel's shins and the cuisse plates protecting his thighs. The locking belt snapped together around Uriel's hips, and, once the power coils were attached, Pasanius reverently lifted the eagle and skull-stamped breastplate and fitted it over his chest.

As each segment of armour was fitted to Uriel's body, Pasanius recited the actions the armour had been part of, speaking the names of heroes long dead and battles long since fought. Every honour won and every plaudit earned was spoken, and, soon, both warriors were giving voice to the armour's illustrious heritage.

The plates protecting Uriel's upper arms came next, together with the pauldrons, vambraces and gauntlets. With his arms sheathed in plate, Pasanius lifted the heavy, auto-reactive shoulder guards, and allowed the armour's fibre-bundle musculature to mesh with the internal gyros and motors within.

Lastly, Pasanius hefted the heavy backpack that provided power to the armour, and the heat exchangers that allowed it to function. Uriel felt its immense weight, and tensed his muscles, but no sooner was the backpack mounted than the armour hummed with life, and energy flowed through Uriel.

He felt the bio-monitoring dendrites link with the hard plugs implanted in his flesh, and his muscles swelled with power. His awareness of his body's subtle rhythms heightened, and he became one with the armour. It was an extension of his flesh that enabled him to fight and move as though clad in the lightest chiton, yet would protect him from the slings and arrows of a hostile galaxy.

Uriel remembered a similar sensation when being clad in the armour of the Sons of Guilliman on Salinas by the artificers of the Grey Knights, but that was a pale shadow of this experience. The battle plate that had protected him during the fighting within the House of Providence was merely borrowed and no bond had formed between him and the armour.

This was different. This was a level of connection that Uriel had not felt since he had first been honoured with his own armour many decades ago. That sense of unity was like a forgotten golden memory coming to the surface, made all the sweeter for its sudden reappearance.

As the armour came to life around him, Uriel felt light-headed as the legacy of heroic endeavours, of which it had been part, filled him. The expectation of honourable service and duty applied to them both, and Pasanius took hold of his shoulder to steady him.

'How does that feel?' asked Pasanius.

'Like I've come home,' said Uriel.

Pasanius nodded, and looked up past the mighty figure of Roboute Guilliman to the fading red glow shining through the rose window. Uriel watched his friend's face harden as the sun set over the distant mountains.

'It's time?'

'It is,' said Pasanius.

Uriel extended his hand, and Pasanius shook it, wrist to wrist, in the grip that symbolised the bond between warriors who had fought and bled in defence of the human race. Pasanius pulled Uriel into an embrace, his enormous frame almost a match for Uriel in his armour.

They had been friends even before their ascension to the Ultramarines, and the bonds of loyalty between them were as enduring as any of the legends told of the long lost primarchs.

They were closer than friends, closer than brothers.

They were Astartes.

'I'd better go,' said Pasanius, nodding towards the chapel doors. 'They'll be waiting.'

'I'll bring the 4th Company back soon,' said Uriel, his voice choked with emotion. 'We'll hardly be gone. It's only a short tour to Pavonis to make sure the peace is holding.'

'I know,' laughed Pasanius, 'and I'll be waiting.'

'Courage and honour, my friend.'

'Courage and honour, Uriel.'

* * *

URIEL STEPPED ONTO the landing platform, and marched to stand before the warriors of the 4th Company. His warriors were armoured in their battle plate, their faces hidden by their helmets, yet each was known to him.

Space Marines might look faceless and identical to mortal eyes, but nothing could be further from the truth. Each warrior was a hero in his own right, one who had his own legends and a roll of honour that was as magnificent as anything that could be invented by all the poets and taletellers of the Imperium.

It was an honour to stand before them as their captain, and Uriel recognised that this moment was one he would never forget. To have travelled to the places he had seen, and to have survived the horrors he had endured was an achievement few could match, and the pride he felt was for himself, too.

Uriel stood erect as another figure descended the steps that he had just come down, a giant of a man clad in armour of brilliant blue from which a golden cloak billowed like a great wing in the wind.

Marneus Calgar, Lord Macragge, marched towards Uriel with his normally stoic and craggy features open and filled with joy. The Chapter Master of the Ultramarines halted before Uriel, and looked him up and down with a critical eye.

Calgar's legendary deeds were known across all human space, heroic battles that painted him as a mighty warrior who crushed entire armies before him and toppled the mightiest of foes with but a glance. Truth be told, Marneus Calgar was no taller than Uriel, though his shoulders were broader and his waist thicker.

The Chapter Master was a brawler to Uriel's swordsman.

Marneus Calgar was a giant, but it was the sheer power and dynamism within him that made him so.

Vitality and strength seemed to ooze from his pores, and just being near Marneus Calgar energised those around him with surety of purpose and determination.

Daemons of the eldar and the Ruinous Powers had fallen before Calgar, and some, jealous of his stature and tally, called him proud, but Uriel knew that was not so. The pride that drove Calgar was that which drove all warriors of noble virtue to war, the defence of those who could not defend themselves.

'Brother Amadon's armour,' said Calgar, his voice rich with approval.

'Yes, my lord,' said Uriel, standing tall and with his shoulders back.

'It looks good on you,' nodded Calgar, reaching out to touch the brilliant white 'U' on Uriel's shoulder guard. 'The last time I saw you armoured thus it was without heraldry, and you were leaving to an unknown destiny.'

'That was another life,' said Uriel. 'I see now why we have our code.'

'I know you do. Varro told me of your words within the Arcanium, and he is a good judge of the hearts of men. He says you have learned what you needed to learn.'

'I have,' agreed Uriel. 'Some lessons are learned the hard way.'

'Some men need to learn their lessons that way or they're not lessons at all.'

'And what lesson will this mission teach?' asked Uriel.

Calgar smiled and leaned in close so that only he could hear his words. 'It will teach those who watch from above that you are a true warrior of Ultramar.'

Uriel nodded, and looked over Calgar's shoulder towards the gallery where the Masters of the Chapter currently on Macragge had gathered to watch the 4th

Company's departure. Here were the warriors who had once sat in judgement of him, but who now gathered to see him become one of them again.

Agemman of the veterans stood at the forefront of the masters, his noble features brimming with pride, and Uriel gave an almost imperceptible nod of respect to the Regent of Ultramar. This great warrior had spoken to Uriel the night before judgement was pronounced upon him. It had been Agemman who had convinced Uriel to accept his punishment for the good of the Chapter, and for that he would forever be in the First Captain's debt.

Beside Agemman were three of the battle captains of Macragge, Masters of the Ultramarines and guardians of the Eastern Fringe. Their names were legend, their deeds mighty and their honour boundless: Sicarius of the 2nd, Galenus of the 5th and Epathus of the 6th.

Of all the warriors here gathered, only Sicarius's eyes were as cold as a winter sky, his unflinching gaze never leaving Uriel as the 4th Company snapped to attention in unison, the sound like a hundred hammers slamming down.

'Lead with courage and honour, and you will win over your doubters,' said Calgar, following Uriel's gaze.

Uriel hammered his fist against the eagle upon his breastplate.

'Permission to depart Macragge, my lord,' he said.

'Permission granted, Captain Ventris,' replied Lord Macragge.

The roar of the Thunderhawks' engines surged in volume, and Uriel gratefully took the hand his Chapter Master offered him.

'It is fitting that this mission should be to Pavonis,' said Marneus Calgar.

'I remember,' said Uriel, 'my first mission as captain of the 4th Company.'

'Let us hope that this tour is not as eventful.'

'As the Emperor wills it,' said Uriel.

THE BASE OF the canyon was planed smooth, and Uriel recognised the application of Mechanicus scale meltas in the rippling, liquid texture of the rock. Lingering rain pooled in the darkness of Deep Canyon Six, and shadows from the high cliffs kept the temperature low. Patches of thick scrub, and wiry clumps of overgrown mountain gorse clung to the edges of the canyon. Tendrils of clammy fog drifted through the upper reaches of the forest of vox-masts that filled the canyon.

Uriel kept still and scanned the canyon. Nothing moved save streams of water pouring from cracks in the rock and the wind-blown undergrowth, yet Uriel had the acute feeling he was being watched.

Every one of his senses told him that this canyon was deserted, yet ones he could not name told him just as clearly that he and his warriors were not alone. He eased from the stepped gully that had brought them from the Thunderhawk's landing site, and the rest of his squad moved out with him. Two hundred metres to the north, he could see Lord Winterbourne's green frock-coat emerge from a narrow gap in the rocks, his storm-troopers forming a protective cordon around him. Uriel shook his head as he saw one of the storm-troopers holding the leads of the vorehounds. Taking unruly pets like that into a potential firefight was madness.

Uriel held his bolter out before him, scanning left and right, and allowing his auto-senses to gather information on his surroundings. The air had an electrical tang to it, which wasn't surprising, but it also had a strange, meaty aroma that the softly falling rain couldn't entirely mask.

'Combat formation,' ordered Uriel over the internal vox-network. 'Primus envelop right, Secundus left. Nice and slow. Harkus, you're with me.'

Proximity to the huge mast array was degrading communications, and his words were overlaid with squalls of biting static. To ensure there were no misunderstandings, Uriel placed his right fist in the centre of his chest and moved it in a slow outwards arc. He transferred his bolter and repeated the gesture with his left fist, slowly advancing towards the vox-masts.

The Space Marines spread out, Uriel and five warriors curving their route to the left as Learchus led the others along the contours of the canyon walls. Uriel advanced with Harkus at his side. The Techmarine had a bolt pistol drawn, and carried a cog-toothed axe, reminding Uriel that, despite his loyalty to Mars, Harkus was a warrior of the Ultramarines first and foremost. The armature limbs of his servo-harness were drawn in tight, soft spurts of gas venting from exhaust ports on his back.

'What can you make out?' asked Uriel, knowing Harkus would see the terrain in a very different way to the rest of the formation.

'The arrays are non-functional,' said Harkus, his voice flat and devoid of tone. A whirring lens apparatus clicked into place over the Techmarine's right eye. 'The residual flux readings tell me the generators are still functional, and...'

'And what?' said Uriel, holding up an open palm and pulling it down to his shoulder.

Instantly, his warriors halted and dropped to their knees with weapons trained outwards.

'I can see a number of attached devices that do not belong on this equipment,' said Harkus, scanning his head from side to side.

'What kind of devices?'

'Unknown, but they are not of Imperial manufacture.'

'Tau?'

'The energy patterns match previously encountered xenotech,' confirmed Harkus.

Uriel passed the word to Clausel and Winterbourne. 'Looks like the tau have definitely been here.'

'We have the northern approach covered,' said Winterbourne.

'In position on the ridge above,' reported Clausel.

Uriel looked over to Learchus and nodded.

Both combat squads moved out, advancing carefully towards the array of vox-masts. The air snapped and fizzed with discharge, and Uriel's auto-senses were fluctuating wildly with the distortion and interference generated by the masts. An army of greenskins could be hidden within a hundred metres of him and he wouldn't know it. With a thought, he disengaged all but the most basic of his auto-senses, knowing that his instincts for danger would serve him better.

Step by step, they drew closer to the array. Uriel could see the devices that Harkus was talking about attached to the base of around fifty of the vox-masts and a few of the generators. Rectangular in shape, they were about the same size as a Space Marine backpack and formed from a hard, plastic-looking material. Etched into the surface was a circle that encompassed a smaller circle drawn from the larger circle's apex.

Uriel recognised it as a tau icon that represented one of their settled worlds, but he had no idea which one.

'What are they?' asked Uriel.

'I cannot answer that with certainty, Captain Ventris,' replied Harkus, the arms of his servo-harness unfolding and flexing like a collection of scorpion tails. 'Not without disassembly and study.'

'Then give me your best guess.'

Harkus didn't move, but the arms of his servo-harness seemed to shrug, as though the very idea of an acolyte of the Machine-God guessing at something was abhorrent. The light behind the lenses of Harkus's helmet flickered as the Techmarine accessed the vast wealth of knowledge implanted in his augmetics.

'Assessment: the interference in the vox networks suggests they are jamming devices, which would explain the build up in unknown spectra of wavefronts I am detecting.'

'Can you disable them?'

'Potentially,' replied Harkus, 'if I can ascertain the power source of the devices.'

'Do it,' said Uriel.

Harkus crouched before the nearest of the devices, the servo-arms of his harness extending a number of strange devices and tools. Uriel left the Techmarine to his work, and moved to where Learchus held his combat squad in readiness for action.

'Re-form the squad,' ordered Uriel. 'Set up a perimeter and hold at a hundred metres.'

Learchus nodded and asked, 'What are those things?'

'Harkus thinks they're jamming devices.'

'Tau?'

'Yes. I recognise the markings on them.'

'This should be all we need to make Governor Shonai mobilise his armed forces,' said Learchus. 'Not even he can ignore this.'

'I hope so,' said Uriel. 'I just pray we're not too late.'

No sooner were the words out of Uriel's mouth than the devices attached to the vox-masts exploded.

Fire and light surged out and upwards in a series of percussive detonations. Uriel was hurled from his feet by the blast wave, and slammed into Learchus. The two of them were smashed to the ground, and Uriel felt the breath driven from him. He lost his grip on his bolter and tasted blood.

A handful of red icons flashed to life as his armour registered breaches. His visor was opaque, an automatic reaction to the blinding light, but it was already returning to normal.

He was lying on his back, looking up at the high cliffs of the canyon and the flaring remnants of a blooming cloud of debris. Shards of broken metal and rock were raining down, and he could hear a terrible groan of tortured metal.

Uriel quickly checked the status icons of his squad, and was relieved to see that everyone was alive. Shaking off the disorientation, Uriel rolled to his feet and saw his bolter a few metres away. He retrieved it quickly, and checked for the rest of his warriors.

Pulverised rock dust billowed around Uriel, and he heard a sharp snapping sound, like the crack of a whip, which was quickly followed by a succession of identical sounds.

At first, he thought they were gunshots, but a second later he realised what he was hearing.

'Move!' he shouted. 'Get to the canyon walls!'

The smoke twitched in front of him, and he threw himself flat as a whipping guy wire slashed through the air above him like a scythe blade. Another sliced past, and then another. Uriel pushed himself to his feet, and ran towards the edge of the canyon as metal buckled and the towering vox-masts began to fall.

The huge towers twisted as the high winds and gravity did their work, tonnes of metal crashing down in a graceful, almost leisurely fashion. Height and proportion rendered the vox-masts slender and delicate, but they were incredibly solid pieces of engineering, and slammed down with the force of artillery strikes.

One after another, the masts thundered to the ground amid the noise of snapping wires and screaming metal. The canyon shook with the power of the impacts, and Uriel staggered like a drunk as he fought through the chaos of destruction. Something struck his shoulder-guard, and he stumbled, dropping to one knee under the weight of the blow.

A snapped spar of metal hammered into the rock beside him, like a spear hurled by a vengeful god, followed by chunks of spalled metal and shattered rock. Uriel swore and pushed onwards, weaving a Codex evasion pattern before realising that it would be ineffective against randomly falling debris.

He felt the presence of others around him, but could only identify them through the icons on his visor, such was the thickness of the dust thrown up.

At last, Uriel reached the edge of the canyon and pressed his body against the rock wall. Looking around, he could see other members of his squad. They were battered and scarred by the explosion, but appeared otherwise unhurt.

'Rally on me!' ordered Uriel as the destruction of the vox-masts continued unabated.

His warriors formed up around him, and Uriel whispered a quick thank you to his armour as Chaplain Clausel's voice came urgently over the helmet vox.

'Uriel! Uriel, are you reading me? What happened down there?'

'Devices attached to the vox-masts,' said Uriel. 'Turns out they were explosives as well as jammers.'

'Casualties?'

'No one is hurt,' said Uriel. 'Though I cannot see Tech-marine Harkus yet.'

'We shall drop into the canyon with you.'

'No. Remain where you are, Chaplain,' ordered Uriel. 'I don't want to bring anyone else in until we're sure there are no secondary charges.'

'Very wise,' conceded Clausel. 'Very well, I shall await your orders.'

Uriel shut off the link as Learchus edged towards him along the canyon wall. The sergeant looked as though he'd been through a boarding action, the frontal plates of his armour dented and scarred from multiple impacts. Blood leaked from a gash in his armour somewhere below his right shoulder.

'You're hurt,' said Uriel.

'It's nothing,' said Learchus. 'What in the name of Guilliman just happened?'

'I'm not sure. Harkus was examining the devices and, well, you saw what happened after that.'

'They must have had anti-tamper traps worked into them,' said Learchus.

'No. Harkus would have found them,' said Uriel, as a new and unwelcome thought arose in his mind. 'They were detonated manually.'

'That means the enemy is close.'

Uriel nodded. 'Take your section and see if Harkus is still alive.'

'What are you going to do?'

'I'm going to link with Winterbourne.'

Learchus passed the word, and, as his combat squad formed up, yet more sharp cracks echoed from the sides of the canyon.

This time, Uriel was sure it was gunfire.

♉
SEVEN

KOUDELKAR SHONAI LIKED to think of himself as a direct man, a man who could take action when it was needed and who could be trusted not to vacillate needlessly. It was a character trait he expected in others, and his temper frayed when those around him did not meet such expectations.

His temper was fraying now. It had been two days since he had arrived at Galtrigil, the sprawling ancestral home of the Shonai family, and his aunt's promised business venture had yet to materialise.

The Shonai estates nestled in a basin of undulant hills at the western end of Tembra Ridge on the shores of Lake Masura, comprising over five thousand hectares of ornamental gardens, forests and hidden follies. The magnificent house, all turrets, towers and arches, had been built nearly a thousand years ago by the founder of the Shonai Cartel, Galt Shonai, and was an opulent palace of marble, steel and glass. It had been a wonder of its day, a monument to wealth and status, but it now felt like a prison.

His mother and aunt dwelt here, and the friction their relationship generated made a house that had once been bright and full of laughter feel like a mortuary. Koudelkar had spent the better part of the last two days promenading the lakeside gardens and terraces in order to escape. The fresh air was invigorating, the scenery spectacular, and, best of all, it kept him from the frosty atmosphere within the house.

Though he was patently in no danger at Galtrigil, protocol, and that damned old fool Lortuen Perjed, demanded that he be accompanied at all times by his brutish skitarii and a squad of heavily armed Lavrentian soldiers. His mother hated having armed men in the house, and even his normally unflappable Aunt Mykola seemed nervous around the skitarii. Given the internecine strife that had torn at Pavonis some years ago, he supposed that was understandable.

Koudelkar stopped beside a carved wooden bench that looked out over the lake, a glittering expanse of frigid water fed by glacial melt-water that poured down the flanks of Tembra Ridge. The sun was midway through its descent into the west, and the surface of the water foamed with whitecaps. A stiff wind sprang up as he took a seat, carrying the bite of cold from mountains that reared like jagged fortress walls to the north.

He remembered golden summer days, running through the gardens and swimming in the lake with his brother, but that was a long time ago, and Koudelkar forced the memory from his mind. Dumak was dead, killed by an assassin's bullet intended for his aunt, and the pain of his murder was still strong. His mother had never really recovered from the loss, and a seed of resentment had built in her heart towards her sister.

More than the solitude and respite from his relatives' carping, the spectacular vista afforded Koudelkar the opportunity to process the multifarious transactions and business deals he was negotiating.

Many of the deals were with off-world clients, powerful guild entities in nearby systems, and even one in a neighbouring sub-sector. He had come to Galtrigil at the behest of his Aunt Mykola, who had promised him a meeting with a representative of powerful business interests with a great desire to work with the Shonai and assure Pavonis a prosperous future.

Koudelkar had been sceptical, and had the proposition come from anyone other than the former Planetary Governor of Pavonis, he would never have agreed to meet with this man. The meeting had been scheduled two days ago, but the representative had failed to arrive at the appointed time, much to Koudelkar's chagrin.

He had been on the verge of returning to Brandon Gate, but Aunt Mykola had persuaded him to stay, reminding him that no one could predict exactly when a ship might arrive from a distant world.

Reluctantly, he had agreed to stay, and had spent the last two days taking the air and restoring his soul in the sculpted wilderness of his family's estates. Truth be told, he was glad to be away from Brandon Gate. The city had become more of a barracks than the thriving metropolis he fondly remembered from before the troubles. The Administratum's policy of branding those with suspect cartel affiliations had put a great many people out of work, and resentment towards the planet's new masters was simmering beneath the surface.

Naivety and false expectations had squandered many of the opportunities that had arisen in the wake of the de Valtos coup, and it would not take much to reignite the flames of rebellion. It astounded Koudelkar that supposedly intelligent people couldn't see that. The populace were hungry and frightened, which made for a potent mix of discontent. People without coin in their pockets and food in their bellies were capable of almost anything.

As much as he had berated Gaetan Baltazar and Lord Winterbourne concerning the fiery rhetoric of Prelate Culla, he knew that he would need to order the colonel of the 44th to restrain the man. He was stirring up a hornet's nest of unrest, and that could only end badly.

The business deals he was attempting to put together would bring much needed employment to Pavonis, and the personal esteem that came from earning a living would ease much of the building pressure amongst the populace.

Aunt Mykola promised that this deal could ease the suffering of the people and bring undreamed of prosperity to Pavonis. It sounded like grand hyperbole, but his aunt had always had a silver tongue when it came to swaying people to her cause.

His ruminations were interrupted when he heard the familiar shuffle, click, shuffle of Lortuen Perjed. The old man was wrapped in the thick brown habit of an adept of the Administratum, yet still seemed troubled by the mildness of the early evening, and the hand that grasped the top of his cane was white.

'What do you want?' asked Koudelkar, not bothering to hide his irritation at this interruption. 'Can't you see I'm busy?'

'Your aunt sends for you,' said Perjed.

Koudelkar sighed. 'What does she want now?'

'She says that the representative you are here to meet is on his way.'

* * *

URIEL JOGGED THROUGH the smoke and dust of the vox-masts' destruction, his bolter held loosely across his chest. He could pick out little through the haze, but the snapping exchange of gunfire was getting louder, as was a high-pitched, skirling screeching sound. Amid the after-echoes of the detonations, Uriel could pick out the heavy bark of hellguns, as well as the sharper crack of a weapon type he didn't recognise.

He saw shadows moving in the clouds of dust ahead, and caught a flash of light reflecting from a gold breast-plate. He angled his course towards it. The strange screeching sound came again, louder this time, and Uriel swung his bolter up, moving forwards and the weapon's barrel scanning in tandem with his gaze. A man screamed in agony, a horrible shriek that was abruptly cut off.

The warriors accompanying Uriel spread out, their weapons raised. Four were equipped with bolters similar to his, while the fifth carried a bulky flamer, its wide nozzle hissing with a cone of heat.

A shot ricocheted from Uriel's armour, a solid round, but he continued without a break in his stride. He didn't think the shot had been aimed at him.

Emerging from the dust of the explosions and into the smoke of battle, Uriel saw that Winterbourne's scribe and vox-servitor were dead, killed by the explosion or mangled in the cascade of falling debris. Uriel was relieved to hear the clipped tones of Lord Winterbourne directing the fire of his soldiers. His storm-troopers were still fighting, trading shots with a swarming pack of pink-skinned aliens, whipping spines trailing from their bizarre avian skulls.

'Kroot,' snarled Uriel, recognising the aliens as a mercenary race in thrall to the tau.

They moved as though their muscles were rapidly uncoiling springs, bounding and leaping with a hideously unnatural gait. The horrid screeching sound was coming from them, and they wielded long rifles shaped like black-powder weapons used by feral world barbarians.

Nathaniel Winterbourne fired his battered laspistol from behind the cover of a tangle of fallen metal. His frock coat was in tatters, and his helmet had been torn from his head. Blood coated the right side of his face and streamed from a long cut on his arm, but the wiry colonel still raged at the foes before him. His hounds stood beside him, barking furiously at the kroot.

One of the kroot vaulted the debris sheltering Winterbourne, the jagged blades fixed to the ends of its rifles slashing for his head. Winterbourne shot the creature square in the face, the blast tearing away most of its skull. The momentum of the kroot's leap carried it onwards, and its corpse bore the colonel to the ground.

The vorehounds savaged the body, and Uriel moved on as he saw Winterbourne pick himself up, his jacket stained with the alien's blood. The distinctive hard bangs of bolter-fire joined the cacophony of battle, and a handful of kroot were instantly cut down, blown in half or simply exploding under the impact of the shells. Dozens more survived the fusillade, their squawking war cries rising in urgency and ferocity.

A storm-trooper dropped as a solid shot took him low in the gut, and another fell as a kroot fighter slammed a serrated blade into his chest. Uriel drew a bead on the killer, a heavily-muscled beast with a flaring crest of red quill-spines, but it bounded clear of its victim with a throaty screech, and Uriel lost sight of it in the billowing dust.

The intensity of gunfire was building, and Uriel felt a trio of impacts on his armour, but none were serious enough to trouble him. Kroot were swarming over the storm-troopers, and yet another was brought down, hacked down by four kroot with bloody beaks and stabbing knives. A shadow moved beside Uriel, and he swung around as a hissing kroot warrior hurled itself at him.

Uriel caught it in midair, his iron grip closing around its throat as its blade scored down his breastplate. One swift twist and its neck snapped. It died without another sound. A second beast came at him from his right. Uriel dropped the dead kroot, spinning and drawing his sword in the same motion. The blade sang out in a golden arc and neatly beheaded his attacker.

Uriel quickly scanned the combat, his enhanced battle-sense reading the ebb and flow of the fight in a moment. Liquid fire bloomed from the flamer, and a host of alien warriors shrieked in pain as they were immolated. Bolter-fire beat a merciless, relentless tattoo, and only occasionally did the sharper crack of the alien weapons pierce its symphony of destruction.

'Forward!' shouted Uriel. 'Take the fight to them! Chaplain Clausel, we need your warriors! To me! Now!'

His Space Marines were shooting and killing with methodical precision, moving and firing with the practiced ease of the galaxy's finest warriors. The surviving storm-troopers were fighting hard, but the kroot were too many for them to contain.

The commander of the Lavrentians was fighting a pair of kroot warriors blade to blade, and though the wiry colonel was holding his own, Uriel saw that he wouldn't last much longer. Uriel ran through the fighting to join Winterbourne, cutting down the first of the colonel's opponents with his sword, and putting a bolt-round through the other's chest.

Winterbourne swept his sword around and gave Uriel an elaborate bow, his face breaking open in an expression of relief.

'My thanks, Uriel,' gasped Winterbourne. 'I'm obliged to you. I don't think I could have held them much longer.'

'We're not out of this yet,' said Uriel as a handful of kroot came at them. Uriel scooped up the corpse of one of the aliens and hurled it at the charging beasts. One was tripped by the body, but the others easily sprang over it. Uriel surged to meet them.

A blade snapped against his armour, and he smashed his shoulder-guard into the kroot's chest, pulverising its ribcage and hurling it back. He felt a rifle blade hook around his leg, and stepped into the attack, stamping down on the weapon. It snapped, and he thrust his sword into the kroot's belly, tearing it upwards and out through its collarbone.

It fell with a horrendous screech of pain as the kroot Uriel had tripped with the corpse sprang to its feet. Winterbourne's sword lanced out and tore through its chest, but no sooner had he delivered the deathblow than he was punched from his feet by a powerful beast with foaming jaws and slashing claws.

At first, Uriel thought one of the colonel's hounds had turned on its master, but then he saw that the creature was lithe and wrought from the same stock as the kroot. Its jaws snapped shut on Winterbourne's arm, and the man's scream of pain was hideous.

Uriel had no time to aid the colonel as the remaining two kroot attacked. One fired its rifle at point-blank range, the round impacting on Uriel's breastplate and leaving a perfectly round dent in the centre of the eagle. Uriel's sword swept up and hacked the alien's weapon in two as the second monster, the heavily-muscled creature with the crest of red quills, slammed the butt of its weapon against Uriel's helmet.

* * *

THE ALIEN HOUND'S eyes were like cloudy pearls, and they locked with Nathaniel Winterbourne's as it bit through the heavy fabric of his uniform jacket. Blood streamed down his sleeve, and he felt its fangs close on the bones of his forearm. He kicked out at the vile beast through the haze of agony as he fumbled for his pistol.

The weapon had fallen from his grip when the creature bore him to the ground and might as well have been a hundred kilometres away. His sword was buried in the chest of another alien and just as far out of reach. He kicked and punched, but the beast was oblivious to his attacks. Winterbourne cried out as he saw another two alien hunting beasts barrelling through the smoke and dust of battle towards him, their jaws wide and ready to tear him apart.

They never reached him.

Two black and gold bullet-like forms intercepted them in a flurry of snapping fangs and tearing claws. Winterbourne's heart swelled as his faithful vore-hounds, creatures he'd acquired during a deployment to Vastian's World, leapt to his defence. Germaine rolled in the dust with one of the hounds, while Fynlae, scrapper Fynlae who'd lost his leg in the storm of an artillery strike on Boranis, faced off against the other.

Fresh agony coursed down Winterbourne's arm, and he reached up with his free hand to jab his fingers into the eyes of the attacking beast. It yelped in pain, and relaxed its grip a fraction. He tore his limb from its jaws in a welter of blood, and scrabbled over the rock towards his fallen laspistol. His hand closed on its grip as an immense weight landed on him, pinning him to the ground.

He smelled the hot, rank breath of the creature on his back. Saliva sprayed from its jaws and spattered the back of his head. He tried to roll the beast off, but it was too heavy. Before it fastened its jaws on his neck, the weight was suddenly gone, and he felt a growling, howling scrum of fur and flesh thrashing behind him. Winterbourne propped himself up on his good arm, seeing Fynlae locked in a battle of fang and claw with the alien beast.

His vorehound's missing leg had not dimmed its ferocity, and it fought in a frenzy to protect him. Bared teeth flashed, and blood sprayed into the air. The alien hound gave a screeching yelp of pain, and Winterbourne let out a wordless shout of pride as Fynlae ripped its throat out.

Winterbourne glanced over his shoulder, and his heart sank.

Germaine was dead, her belly torn open and her eyes staring glassily at the sky, but so too was her killer, the vorehound's jaws locked around its throat. The beast that Fynlae had faced earlier was dead, its face a mask of blood where the old, war-scarred hound had crushed its skull in his jaws.

Behind the dead animals, Captain Ventris was on his knees, struggling with a pair of kroot fighters. One circled the combat, darting in to stab at Uriel's armour with a long-bladed knife, while a brute of a monster with a crest of flaming red spines attempted to drive its rifle-blade into Uriel's neck.

Uriel's bulk was so much greater than the kroot's, that it should have been a mockery of a competition, but the alien's powerful physique was proving to be a match for that of the Space Marine.

Winterbourne raised his pistol, fighting to hold it steady as the creature forced its long blade towards Uriel's throat.

* * *

MYKOLA SHONAI HAD aged in the years since Pavonis had been saved from the insurrection of Kasimir de Valtos. Her grey hair had turned white, and, though the sharpness of her green eyes was undimmed, a genetic defect in her retinal structure meant that she was an unsuitable candidate for ophthalmic surgery, and was now forced to wear eyeglasses to see much beyond her immediate surroundings.

In her long cream robes, she looked like a matronly famulus, but Koudelkar knew her well enough not to let her appearance fool him into underestimating her intelligence. She had once ruled a planet of the Emperor and such an achievement was not to be taken lightly.

His aunt was pacing along a marble flagged path in the south arboretum when he found her. She claimed she did her best thinking when she paced, and when she turned to face him, the excitement that radiated from her was palpable. The air in the arboretum was hot and humid, and Koudelkar could see his bodyguards sweating in their heavy armour, though the skitarii seemed unaffected. He wondered if they could alter their metabolism to better cope with changing environments.

Evening sunlight shone through the treated glass walls and ceiling, creating a sweltering environment better suited to raise the plants cultivated from the few stems recovered from the wasteland of the Gresha Forest.

She rushed over to him and looked him up and down. 'You'll be changing into your dress uniform, won't you?'

The words were phrased as a question, but Koudelkar knew his aunt's mannerisms well enough to know that it was actually a statement. Mykola brushed at his shoulders and shook her head.

'Yes, I think so. You'll want to make a good impression,' she said.

'A good impression on whom?' asked Koudelkar, stepping away from her fussing.

'The representative, who else?' she said, as if he were being obtuse, and began straightening his hair with a moistened palm.

Koudelkar threw Lortuen Perjed a confused glance. 'Adept Perjed told me he was just about to arrive.'

'Hmm... oh, yes, of course,' said Mykola, straightening his jacket. 'Oh well, this will serve, I suppose.'

'You want me to make a good impression on a man I don't even know,' said Koudelkar, prising away her hands. Aunt Mykola always fussed over him, more than his mother ever did, but this was extreme, even for her. 'Does he even have a name?'

'Of course he does.'

'Then what is it?'

Mykola hesitated, looking away for the briefest moment, but Koudelkar read the unease in her body language.

'He's called Aun.'

'Aun?' asked Perjed, with a sharp intake of breath. 'What manner of name is that?'

Mykola shrugged, as though the nature of the representative's name was a matter of supreme indifference to her. 'It's an off-world name, Adept Perjed. It's strange, I know, but no stranger than ours are to him, I expect.'

Koudelkar decided he'd had enough of his aunt's evasive answers and looked her straight in the eye.

'Well, does he have a last name? And who or what does he represent? You know, you've told me next to nothing about this person or how you know him. You've spun me a grand tale of how he can offer

Pavonis great things, but unless you tell me who he is and what organisation he represents, then I am leaving right now.'

Mykola folded her arms and turned away from him. 'You're just like your grandfather, do you know that?'

'If you mean I'm not about to put up with vague answers to specific questions, then I suppose I am. Don't change the subject or try and make me feel guilty. If I am going to do business with this person then I need to know more about him. I cannot negotiate from a position of ignorance.'

Mykola turned to face him, and he almost backed away from the steely resolve he saw in her eyes.

'Very well, you want to know the truth?'

'I do.'

'You'll see it's for the best,' said Mykola, glancing over at his bodyguards and Lortuen Perjed, 'but you're not going to like it at first.'

'I assure you, Aunt, I like lies even less.'

She nodded and said, 'I've never lied to you, Koudelkar, but I've deliberately shielded you from some knowledge until the time was right.'

'That sounds like more evasion,' said Koudelkar. 'The right time is now, so get to the point.'

'I'm getting there if you'd let me,' snapped Mykola, walking towards him. 'Aun represents a collective from the Dal'yth sept.'

'Dal'yth?' hissed Adept Perjed. 'Emperor's tears, what have you done, woman?'

'Be quiet, you insolent little man,' snapped Mykola.

'Never heard of them,' said Koudelkar, alarmed by Perjed's exclamation.

'That shouldn't surprise you,' said a voice behind him, and Koudelkar recognised his mother's caustic tones.

'Keep out of this, Pawluk,' said his aunt.

Koudelkar sighed in exasperation. His mother and aunt sharing the same room was like putting two hungry tigers in a cage. Why they insisted on living in the same house, even one large enough for them to avoid each other, was a constant puzzle to Koudelkar.

Pawluk Shonai's face was as pinched and hostile as ever, her lifeless grey hair pulled back in a tight bun. He felt the tension ratchet up a notch. Despite the warmth of the arboretum, a distinct chill entered with his mother.

For an amused moment, Koudelkar wondered if the plants would suffer from the chill.

'Hello, Mother,' he said. 'Won't you join us?'

His mother linked her arm with his and glared at his aunt.

'Well?' she asked.

'Well what?' asked Mykola.

'Aren't you going to tell him? About this Aun?'

'Tell me what?' asked Koudelkar.

His aunt pursed her lips, and Koudelkar could see her anger threatening to boil over. 'I was just about to tell him, Pawluk.'

'Governor,' said Lortuen Perjed urgently, 'we must get you out of here.'

'Why, what's going on?'

Before Perjed could answer, Koudelkar heard the approaching thrum of engines from outside the house. He looked up and saw three aircraft swoop over the glass roof of the arboretum. Waving fronds, leaves and climbing flowers obscured the details of them, but it was clear that they were of a design he had never seen before.

'What manner of craft are these?' he asked. 'I don't recognise the pattern.'

'Governor,' repeated Perjed. 'We have to go. Now.'

The aircraft were a drab olive colour and striped with camouflage patterns, but Koudelkar could make out little else of their shapes. Two appeared to be smaller, wedge-shaped fighters and the third was a four-engine transport craft of some sort. Each was gracefully proportioned and flew with a grace and an agility that was quite out of keeping with any Imperial aircraft in which Koudelkar had flown.

As the smaller fighters circled overhead, the transport craft rotated on its axis and descended through the growing dusk towards the stone terrace beyond the arboretum on a rippling column of distorted air. Mykola threw open the large doors leading to the terrace and beckoned him to follow her.

His aunt's evasive answers, and Adept Perjed's insistence that he leave, gnawed at his resolve. He looked down at his mother, alarmed at the panic he saw there.

'I didn't know until today, I swear,' she said. 'She made me promise not to tell you.'

Deciding that it was time he find out what was going on, Koudelkar walked out onto the terrace, warm gusts from the aircraft's descent billowing his coat and hair. Perjed, the Lavrentians and skitarii followed him, and he spotted that they carried their weapons to the fore with the safeties off. He shielded his eyes from flying grit as a wide ramp lowered from the transport craft's rear and an armoured machine stepped from its brightly lit interior.

It was humanoid, standing at least twice the height of a man and was a thing of beauty. Fashioned from plates of what looked like olive green ceramics, it was constructed with a fine sense of craftsmanship as well as aesthetics. Its rectangular head mount turned towards him, and, though it resembled nothing so much as a remote picter, Koudelkar felt sure there was intelligence lurking behind the blinking red light of its lens.

Was this a machine at all, or was it crewed by a living creature? It was certainly large enough for someone to pilot. At first glance, the machine looked like an automated loader servitor, but the lethal-looking weapons mounted on each arm told Koudelkar that this creation was not designed for labour, but for battle.

His appreciation of the machine's construction evaporated, and his mother's grip on his arm tightened. Koudelkar felt some of her fear transfer to him as he saw that the Lavrentians had their hellguns aimed squarely at the machine's chest, and that the implanted rotary cannons of the skitarii were spooling up.

Koudelkar realised that the situation could turn ugly very quickly, and struggled to project an air of calm authority. Two identical machines followed the first, each moving with a smooth grace and autonomy not normally found in mechanised creations, finally convincing Koudelkar that the fighting machines were crewed by living pilots.

His mouth was dry with tension, but he turned to his bodyguards and said, 'Hold your fire, but be ready.'

The three machines stepped to the right of the aircraft and another three emerged from its interior, taking up position to the left. Koudelkar knew nothing of their capabilities, but felt sure that, in a firefight, he and his men would come off worst.

'Mykola,' he hissed, 'what have you done?'

'What needed to be done to save our world from being taken from us by outsiders,' said his aunt, sending a withering glance towards Adept Perjed as she strode towards the aircraft. Its rear engine nacelles rotated into a lateral position in line with the running lines of the hull, and his aunt halted at the bottom of the ramp as a slender figure appeared at the top.

The figure was clad in long robes of white and gold with a shimmering crimson weave, and its head was framed by a high collar of enamelled silver and crimson. It carried a short, caramel-coloured baton topped with a glinting gem in each hand, holding them crossed over its chest. Its face was grey, the colour of a winter sky at dusk, and its flat, alien features were devoid of expression.

His aunt bowed to the figure, and then turned towards him.

'Koudelkar, allow me to introduce Aun'rai of the Dal'yth sept and envoy of the Tau Empire,' she said.

PART 2

UNTAINTED BY DOUBT AND UNSULLIED BY SELF-AGGRANDISEMENT

℧
EIGHT

THE KROOT WAS a monster, its strength phenomenal. Uriel's helmet had saved him from the worst of its blow, and he fought to hold its heavy blade at bay as another beast stabbed at him with a long knife. His armour was holding, but it wouldn't take much for the alien to get lucky and find a weaker spot. Though the blows weren't penetrating his armour, he could feel the pain of each impact.

The creature's muscles bunched and swelled in unnatural ways, somehow able to meet the genhanced strength crafted into Uriel's body and that of his power armour. It squawked and spat in his face, its breath reeking of meat and blood. Uriel heard the snapping discharge of a laspistol, and a flaring bolt of light slashed across the kroot's shoulder. It screeched in pain, and Uriel rammed his helmet into its face. In the moment of respite, he hurled himself backwards, pulling the creature up and over him.

Its blade stabbed into the ground and snapped as it sailed over his head with a surprised squawk. Uriel rolled onto his side and swept up his sword. The knife-armed kroot came at him, its blade slashing for his face. Uriel swayed aside and hammered his blade into its belly, almost cutting it in two.

Lord Winterbourne staggered over to him, cradling his bloody arm tucked into his uniform jacket and holding onto his laspistol with the other. The three-legged vorehound padded alongside him, its flanks heaving and furrowed with bloody gouges.

Winterbourne nodded, but Uriel had no time to thank him for his aid as yet more kroot came at them, a pack of screeching fighters with rifles held like quarter-staffs, their blades glittering in the weak light. He risked a glance behind him to check what had become of the red-quilled monster, but it was nowhere to be seen.

'Come on then, you whoresons!' shouted Winter-bourne, emptying the last of his laspistol's powercell into the charging aliens. One kroot fell with a chunk blasted from its stomach, and another came on, despite a dreadful wound to its shoulder.

Then the heavens blazed with light, and a host of screaming angels of death dropped into the fight on wings of fire. They bore roaring swords of silver, and were led by a black-armoured avenger in a bone-white death mask. This mighty apparition carried a winged golden staff, and slew his enemies with brutal sweeps of its crackling, fiery edge.

Chaplain Clausel and his Assault Marines slammed into the battle with a searing flare of howling jump packs and the hammering of boots on rock. The kroot scattered like pins as the furious slaughter began, and their screeching filled the air.

Uriel pulled Winterbourne clear of the swirling melee as pistols boomed and chainswords bellowed. In moments, the kroot were butchered, the ferocity and suddenness of the assault leaving only torn carcasses in its wake.

Clausel hacked down the last of the kroot, standing tall amid the carnage, and never had the Chaplain looked so mighty and terrible, his weapon coated in blood and his skull-faced helmet red with the stuff.

The noise of battle changed in an instant. No longer did the sound of kroot weapons punctuate the roar of bolter-fire. Even the actinic crack of hellgun-fire had ceased. The dust thrown up by the collapse of the towers and the fighting settled, and a curious calm descended upon Deep Canyon Six.

'All forces, rally on me,' ordered Uriel, retrieving his bolter and replacing the spent magazine with a fresh one. He sheathed his sword as Clausel strode towards him.

'We should pursue,' said the Chaplain. 'Kill them all.'

'No,' said Uriel. 'These were nothing. A token force to kill any who survived the blasts.'

'Nevertheless, we should finish them,' urged Clausel.

Uriel shook his head. 'I won't go charging blindly into the unknown against an enemy skilled in evasion, who has a greater knowledge of the local terrain.'

Clausel bowed. 'That is, of course, the correct course of action, captain.'

'We will secure the battlefield and return to the gunship,' said Uriel warily. 'Governor Shonai needs to know what happened here.'

'As you wish,' said Clausel, turning away as Uriel let out a deep breath. His racing metabolism had begun to slow as Lord Winterbourne and his vorehound approached. Uriel removed his helmet, and ran a hand over his scalp and chin.

'Thank you for saving my life,' said Winterbourne, holding out his hand.

'I should say the same, colonel,' said Uriel, taking the proffered hand and nodding towards the vorehound, which snarled and bared its teeth at the kroot corpses.

'That is a fierce beast, colonel,' he said. 'Proud and loyal.'

'Indeed he is,' agreed Winterbourne through a mask of blood. 'Once a vorehound has adapted to its new master, it will protect him unto death. That alien monstrosity almost had me back there, I don't mind telling you. Bugger would have done for me if it weren't for old Fynlae here. Earned himself a commendation for valour, and no mistake. Didn't you, lad?'

'I think they both did,' said Uriel, spying the body of the other vorehound.

'Yes,' sighed Winterbourne, patting the head of his hound. 'Poor Germaine. It's a shame, but then I suppose they're fighting beasts. It's what they do. One mustn't get too attached to them, you know, but it's hard. Still, I suppose we've got more important things to worry about now.'

'It certainly looks that way,' agreed Uriel.

THE SPACE MARINES and surviving storm-troopers began securing the battlefield with practiced efficiency, treating wounds and gathering the bodies of the honoured dead. The wounded were carried from the gully to the Aquila lander and med-evaced back to Brandon Gate, while the dead aliens were unceremoniously dumped on a pyre and set alight by a sustained burst of promethium from an Astartes flamer.

None of Uriel's warriors had fallen in the fight with the kroot, and Learchus and his combat squad found Harkus alive, buried amongst a huge pile of wreckage at the base of a fallen vox-mast. His servo-harness had taken the full force of the blast, but both his legs were crushed beyond repair, and much of his torso had been burned away. Only the superlative endurance of a Space Marine had kept him alive, and Uriel immediately despatched four warriors to carry Harkus back to the Thunderhawk for emergency medicae treatment.

His armour's systems would keep Harkus alive for now, but his body would require the ministrations of Apothecary Selenus back at Fortress Idaeus if he were to survive. He and Harkus were not close, but Uriel felt a profound sadness as he watched his battle-brothers carefully lift the wounded Techmarine and bear him away. Harkus would probably live, but his time as a warrior was over. His body had suffered too much damage, and, even with replacement limbs, he would never be fit for frontline duty again. Uriel wondered if Harkus would mind that much of his body would now be artificial, or would he view that as becoming closer to the Machine-God?

With the battlefield secured, Uriel was the last to leave the canyon, climbing back the way they had come, and leaving the devastation of the array behind. He reached the top of the cut stairs and emerged onto the plateau above.

The engines of the Thunderhawk rumbled and strained, as though eager to be away from this place, and Uriel didn't blame it. The mountains were dismal and forsaken, and he wondered if some part of that was due to the monstrous creature that had been buried beneath them for uncounted eons. Even with it gone, perhaps the echoes of its imprisonment were strong enough to taint the world with the memory of its bleak and horrifying presence.

Uriel put such morose thoughts from his mind as Learchus emerged from the Thunderhawk, his manner brisk and his face grim.

'What's wrong?' asked Uriel, already sensing something awry.

'A communication from Admiral Tiberius,' said Learchus. 'He tried to reach your armour's vox, but the distortion of the array prevented direct communication.'

'What's the message?'

'He reports numerous contacts matching previously encountered energy signatures appearing across the surface of the prime continental mass,' said Learchus.

'Tau?'

Learchus nodded. 'It would appear so.'

'Then the destruction of the array has acted as an attack signal,' said Uriel, running for the Thunderhawk. 'Where is Governor Shonai? Has he been secured?'

'Lord Winterbourne has contacted Major Ornella at Brandon Gate,' said Learchus. 'She says that Koudelkar Shonai is still at his family estates on the shores of Lake Masura.'

Uriel climbed the ramp to the Thunderhawk's interior as the last of his warriors embarked and took position in the bucket seats along the fuselage of the aircraft.

'What protection does he have?'

'A squad of Lavrentian storm-troopers and a pair of skitarii,' said Learchus, consulting a wall-mounted dataslate. 'Plus, whatever personal bodyguards and security measures are in place at his aunt's estates.'

'That won't be much,' said Uriel.

'No. A basic surveyor/alert system and few armed retainers at most.'

'How far is Lake Masura?' asked Uriel urgently. 'Can we reach it?'

Learchus bent to consult a glowing map on a nearby screen. 'It is a hundred and fifty kilometres west, in the foothills of these mountains. We are carrying enough fuel to get there, and back to Brandon Gate, but that's about it.'

'I'll bet that was one of the first places to register a signal.'

'It was,' said Learchus. 'How did you know?'

'Because that's what I'd do,' said Uriel. 'First you cut off communications, and then you cut off the head of the command structure.'

An alien was standing before him. Of course, Koudelkar had *heard* of the tau, who on the Eastern Fringe did not know of this expansionist xenos species? But being introduced to one while standing at his family's estates on a chilly evening was unexpected to say the least. He had always hoped he might one day see a xenos creature, but had imagined it would be down the barrel of a gun or as he gazed at its preserved corpse in a museum.

The robed figure descended the ramp from his ship, and Koudelkar was struck by his grace and poise. Aun'rai moved as though he floated just above the ground. Keeping the batons crossed over his chest, Aun'rai bowed to him and then to his aunt.

'Greetings, Guilder Koudelkar,' said Aun'rai, his voice soothing and flowing like honey.

'Don't speak with it,' hissed Lortuen Perjed. 'Xenos filth!'

Koudelkar said nothing, more because he did not know what to say than through any desire to follow Perjed's advice. The alien took no notice of Perjed's hostility.

He glanced over his shoulder at the Lavrentian soldiers and his skitarii. His confusion mounted. The tau were their enemies. Shouldn't these men be shooting at them? Even as the thought formed, he arrived at the

conclusion his soldiers and the skitarii defence protocols had reached long before him.

If shots were fired, they would all die. The giant fighting machines standing to either side of the humming
aircraft would kill them in a matter of moments, and,
looking beyond Aun'rai, Koudelkar could see at least a
score of armed xenos soldiers inside the aircraft.

As much as he knew he *should* order his men to open
fire, Koudelkar was not so far removed from his mandatory service in the PDF that he didn't appreciate the
difference between courage and suicide.

'Welcome to our home, Aun'rai,' said his aunt, when
Koudelkar did not speak. 'You are most welcome, and
may I say what a pleasure it is to finally meet you in person.'

'The honour is mine, I assure you,' replied Aun'rai
smoothly, uncrossing his arms and sliding his batons
into ceramic sheaths at his side. 'To meet one of such
wisdom and foresight is a rarity in these troubled
times. It is my fervent hope that we can begin a new
phase in our relations that will allow peaceful trade
and co-operation to flourish. Such relations will prove
to be for the greater good of both our peoples, I am
quite certain.'

'You are too kind,' said Mykola. 'Please, will you join
us for some refreshments?'

'Thank you, no,' said Aun'rai. 'We have taken suste-
nance already.'

'Of course,' said Mykola. 'Koudelkar? Would you
escort Aun'rai within?'

'I will not,' he said at last. 'It's a xenos. Here. At our
house.'

'Koudelkar,' said his aunt, and he recognised the icy
threat thinly concealed by her tone. 'Aun'rai is our
guest.'

Anger rose within him at her presumption of superiority, and he turned to his aunt. 'I think you're forgetting who's governor, Mykola. Contact with aliens is a crime, have you forgotten that? Sharben will toss you in the Glasshouse for this, and that will be the end of you. Even I can't overlook this, for heaven's sake!'

'I thought you of all people would be more open-minded, Koudelkar,' said his aunt with what he knew to be contrived disappointment. 'After all, aren't you always the one complaining about how the Administratum is keeping your hands tied?'

This last comment was directed at Lortuen Perjed, who looked fit to burst a blood vessel, such was the hue of his skin.

'Have you lost your mind, Mykola?' spat Perjed. 'You'll be shot for this, you know that, don't you?'

'This is a chance to rebuild Pavonis,' she continued, ignoring Perjed's threat. 'You just have to be willing to take a small step beyond your comfort zone.'

'Comfort zone? This goes way beyond a "small step". This is treason,' said Koudelkar.

'Don't be dramatic,' scolded his aunt. 'This is just a business negotiation. The tau can offer us technology that makes the Mechanicus gear look like tinker toys. They're willing to locate a great many of their most dynamic industries on Pavonis, Koudelkar. Think of what that could mean for us and our people: employment, currency, trade, and a position of leadership in the sector markets. Isn't that what you've been striving for these last few years?'

Before Koudelkar could reply, the tau envoy reached out and placed a hand on his shoulder. His first instinct was to shrug it off as repugnant, but he did not, and he felt a curious feeling stirring within him, not acceptance, per se, but interest. If there was even a grain of truth to what his aunt was saying, perhaps it was worth hearing what this alien had to say.

After all, Koudelkar had broken no laws. If there were any price to be paid, it would be borne by his aunt. She had set up this meeting. She had brought the aliens here. Koudelkar was blameless, and if he listened to what the creature had to say, well, what was the harm?

'I will hear him out, but I make no promises,' said Koudelkar, amazed that he was actually saying the words, but feeling wholly natural in doing so.

'Koudelkar!' cried Lortuen. 'Don't be a fool. This is wrong and you know it.'

His aunt glared at the adept of the Administratum, and Koudelkar felt his irritation grow at the wizened old man who had held him back from fully realising his potential as governor of Pavonis. Perjed had worked with him to pull his world back from the abyss of rebellion into which it had almost plummeted, but now all Koudelkar felt towards him was antipathy. The feeling was strange, and he wondered how he had not realised the true scale of his dislike for the man until now.

'Be silent, adept,' said Koudelkar. 'Know your place. I am governor, and I will decide who I talk to and who I do business with. I will listen to Aun'rai, and if, at the end of our discussions, I do not wish to deal with him, he will be free to leave and things will continue as they have always done.'

'If you believe that, you are a fool,' said Perjed. 'This can only end in blood.'

MAJOR ALITHEA ORNELLA rode across the brightly lit parade ground of Camp Torum on a chestnut gelding named Moran, accompanied by her command squad. Riding was Ornella's passion, and, though her rank normally precluded her from charging into battle on the back of such a fine beast, she took the opportunity to saddle Moran whenever the chance arose.

She slowed the horse with a gentle pull on the reins and a light pressure of her thighs, watching the purposeful activity around her with a satisfied eye. Blazing arc lights on the edges of the camp dispelled the gloom of gathering night and illuminated the preparations of a regiment of the Emperor's Imperial Guard as it made itself ready for battle.

Armoured vehicles lined three sides of the parade ground: Leman Russ Conquerors, Hellhounds, Basilisk artillery pieces and row upon row of Chimeras. Each mighty vehicle swarmed with mechanics and enginseers as their crews went through pre-deployment checks and blessings. Ornella felt a curious mix of excitement and tension at the thought of going into battle once more; excitement because she would have the chance to serve the Emperor, and tension because who relished the thought of going into harm's way?

It had been good to rest the regiment on Pavonis after sustained front-line operations, for the strain had begun to tell in the number of disciplinary infractions and combat fatigue citations sent up the chain from platoon commanders.

Pavonis had been a relatively easy deployment, a chance to ease down from the stress and exhaustion of combat operations, and an opportunity to refresh the soldiers in urban pacification duties. Such work was inglorious, but necessary, and Ornella ensured that any duty given to the 44th Lavrentian Hussars was completed to the highest standards.

Camp Torum was home to Sword Command of the 44th Lavrentian Hussars, the largest and most heavily armed of the four commands deployed to Pavonis. Of the other commands, Lance were based on the coast at

Praxedes, Shield at the bridge city of Olzetyn, and Banner on the outskirts of the Jotusburg slum, each comprising three thousand mechanised infantry, light armour units and mobile artillery.

Named for the first colonel to take command of the regiment at its founding on the great steppe plateau of Lavrentia, Camp Torum spread out on the northern fringe of Brandon Gate, close to the arterial route of Highway 236. It was a sprawling complex of utilitarian structures, uniformly constructed with only functionality in mind, which was just how Ornella liked it.

Portal-framed hangars clad in ochre sheets of corrugated iron were scattered throughout the camp, medicae stations and barracks separated by sand-filled barriers that could take a hit from a missile launcher and remain unbreached. Some eight thousand soldiers were based at Torum, nearly half of the regiment's strength on Pavonis.

Their few super-heavies sat in hardened shelters originally designed for aircraft, but with the heavy fighting further out on the fringe, most of the planet's air power had been stripped by Battlefleet Ultima. Sentinels patrolled the edge of the camp, a high berm of bulldozed earth, reinforced with segmented plates on both sides. Hardened watchtowers were set at regular intervals around the circumference of the wall, and six Hydra flak tanks scanned the heavens for aerial threats.

Over the clatter of tanks, shouted orders and marching Guardsmen, Ornella heard a sound like a sheet of cloth flapping in the wind, but dismissed it as she and her horsemen rode across the parade ground. Ornella was pleased at the sense of urgency that invested the Guardsmen. As demanding as urban operations were, an inevitable sense of complacency soon set in. Patrols became routine, boredom crept up and patterns became predictable. Though no professional soldier relished the thought of being shot at, they soon began to chafe at the forced idleness of garrison duty and actually longed to get back to an active warzone.

The communication from Lord Winterbourne had come as a welcome shock, and Ornella was pleased to have the opportunity to test her new rapid reaction procedures. So far, they appeared to be working like clockwork, Guardsmen forming up outside their barracks before moving out to their transports, and tank crews prepping their machines for a pre-battle blessing from the regiment's preachers.

Prelate Culla's Rhino rumbled up and down the parade ground, his strident tones blaring from the augmitters on the upper deck of his vehicle. Culla stood atop his pulpit, his fiery sword cleaving the air to punctuate his words. Ornella smiled as she saw him, pleased that the 44th had such an inspirational figure to put fire in the bellies of the regiment's soldiers.

She rode down the line of tanks, her mounted command squad following behind her as she turned towards the centre of the parade ground. One of her squad eased his horse alongside hers.

'All looking good, major,' said Captain Mederic.

'Yes,' she agreed, trying not to sound too pleased. Mederic was a good officer. He was intelligent, seasoned and a hell of a fighter, although he clearly disliked being on horseback. Mederic commanded the Hounds, the 44th's Scout Platoon, and was a man used to operating on his own initiative. Despite that, he was also a man who could be trusted to follow orders.

'So what's the word, ma'am? This a real deployment or an exercise?'

'It's real, captain,' she said. 'Lord Winterbourne and the Ultramarines have engaged the enemy in the mountains to the north.'

'Is it tau? That's what the scuttlebutt's saying.'

She nodded. 'Yes. It looks like they've taken out a significant amount of the vox-network, and we're going on alert to secure the major cities once confirmation comes in from the Administratum.'

'We still have to wait for that? Even now?'

'I'm afraid so,' said Ornella. 'It's frustrating, but given what happened here, I understand the need for such controls.'

'Not me,' said Mederic. 'This planet's about to be hit by xenos raiders and we need to wait for some form-stampers to give us the go ahead to defend it? Begging your pardon, ma'am, but that's just grade A bull.'

'Maybe so, captain, but those are our rules of engagement, and we must abide by them.'

'Any idea when we're gonna get that confirmation?'

'Not yet, no.'

Mederic grunted in disgust, but Ornella left him to his misgivings. Privately, she shared them, but if Alithea Ornella had learned anything in her ten years of active service it was that only by following explicitly worded orders could a regiment function. She and Lord Winterbourne had inculcated the 44th to function as a well-oiled machine whereby orders were issued with alacrity and obeyed without delay.

With clear orders, the regiment functioned. Without them, it did not.

She glanced upwards as she heard the sound of flapping cloth again, but the lights blazing on the edge of the camp compromised her night vision and she could see nothing in the darkness. She turned in the saddle. The rest of her command squad sat in a loose semicircle around her: two Guardsmen with lasguns slung over their shoulders, a vox-operator and the regimental banner-bearer.

She was about to write the noise off as the banner flapping in the wind, before realising that there was no wind. Puzzled, she looked up once again.

'Everything all right ma'am?' asked Mederic.

'Hmmm? Oh, yes, captain,' she said. 'Just thought I heard something.'

THE TEMPLUM FABRICAE was busy, even though there was no public service until the morning. Hard times had a way of bringing out the devotion in people, and Gaetan Baltazar struggled not to feel contempt as he made his way through the devotees kneeling in the pews and praying to the anthracite statue of the Emperor at the end of the nave.

To see so many people crowding his temple should have brought him joy, but such conditional devotion was abhorrent to Gaetan. In times of plenty, people would attend the bare minimum of mandatory prayers, but in times of woe and destitution, everyone came to prayers morning, noon and night to ask the Emperor for a boon. Gaetan knew he should be thankful for so many eager worshippers, but it was difficult when he knew they came for personal salvation, not the glorification of the Emperor.

Clad in his ochre vestments and carrying his broad-bladed eviscerator before him, he made his way to the altar to recite the Prayer of Day's Ending before retiring for the night. Though skilled in the use of the monstrous, chainblade sword and the heavy inferno pistol buckled at his waist, he did not like to carry them at worship. Their presence made a mockery of his belief in the Emperor's power of forgiveness and mercy, but they were as much part of his robes of office as the aquila, and could not be discarded.

The acolytes in steel-dust robes that followed him bore similarly enormous blades, and even the chittering prayer cherubs that floated above him carried small daggers and implanted laser weaponry. The scent of their anointed skins was a sickly sweet fragrance that caught in the back of Gaetan's throat, and, not for the first time, he wished that the vaunted tech-priests of Pavonis would fix the ventilation systems of the templum.

A tall building of exposed structure and machined parts, the Templum Fabricae was a monument to the Emperor in his dual aspect of Master of Mankind and Omnissiah, though the priests of Mars would have a hard time rationalising the constant machine failures that were its bane. Given the planet's troubled history, perhaps they wouldn't, he reflected sourly.

The walls were adorned with sheet iron sculptures and welded plates with etched scripture. Private side chapels had once been dedicated to the Emperor by the cartels, each paying a substantial tribute to the templum's coffers to secure a burial place for their departed leaders. Gaetan had thought the practice repugnant, but Bishop Irlam, the templum's former master, had been little more than a mouthpiece for the cartels, and his pockets had been lined with their silver.

In the wake of the rebellion, Irlam had been disgraced, and the Administratum had decreed that the chapels be re-consecrated to the glory of the Emperor without favour to any one organisation. Gaetan had taken great pleasure in instructing the templum servitors to remove any indication that the chapels had once been devoted to private citizens.

That had been the only time the directives of the Administratum had proven to be helpful, and Gaetan railed against such interference whenever he could. It was difficult when bureaucrats controlled every aspect of the planet's workings, men with no understanding of faith and the importance of devotion. For the sake of unity, Gaetan reluctantly obeyed their directives, and continued to preach his doctrine of quiet industry and devotion to the Emperor.

He knew it was not a doctrine that found much favour on the Eastern Fringe, but it was one that had served him well over the years, and he was too set in his ways to change. Out here, preachers who bellowed for war and filled the hearts of men with hatred were the norm.

The confrontation with Lord Winterbourne over the zealot Culla had only served to reinforce that view, and, while he could appreciate the value of such doctrine on this frontier of mankind's dominion of the galaxy, it was not a creed he would willingly preach. Hatred and violence only bred more of the same, and to oppose such things with the light of the Emperor's wisdom was the lonely path trodden by Gaetan Baltazar alone.

He remembered the day he had taken his final vows at the Temple of the Blessed Martyr on Golanthis nearly two decades ago. Abbot Malene, his spiritual mentor and friend, had spoken to him the night before he took ship to the Eastern Fringe.

'I fear you will have a hard time convincing people of your beliefs where you are going,' the venerable abbot had said, sipping a honeyed tisane. 'The Eastern Fringe is a place of war.'

'Then it is exactly the right place for me,' he had countered.

'How so?'

'How better to end war than by preaching peace?'

'The Emperor's creed *is* war,' Malene reminded him. 'His doctrine was spread from Terra through the barrels of guns and on the blades of swords. It has survived because we defend that faith. That's not just a flowery term, Gaetan. It has meaning. You think the Ecclesiarchy schools you in the arts of war for no reason?'

'No. I know why we are trained to fight, but I do not believe that violence is the key to the Emperor's wisdom. There is much to His teachings that are beautiful, and have nothing to do with war and death. Those are the parts of His word I wish to take to the people of the Imperium.'

'Aye, there is beauty,' agreed Malene, 'but even a rose needs thorns to defend it. How will your doctrine of hard work turn aside an enemy intent on slaying you? How will it give those to whom you minister the faith to stand against the many threats that lurk in the darkness? There are vile foes in the galaxy that care nothing for our teachings, races that will meet your pretty words with murder. I fear you have set yourself an insurmountable task, my friend.'

'I know, but even an avalanche begins with a single pebble,' said Gaetan.

Those words seemed now foolish to him, yet he held to them as a dying man would cling to his last breath of life. Gaetan reached the altar and set his enormous sword upon it before lifting his robes to kneel before the polished anthracite. He worked his prayer beads between his fingers, and lifted his head towards the reflectively black statue of the Emperor.

Beyond the statue, the chancel was a long, tapered vault with exposed ironwork, and supports from which hung gilded lanterns, incense burners and silken devotional banners. Shadows flickered and danced in the swaying lantern light, and Gaetan blinked as he saw a ripple of movement in the upper reaches of the chancel.

The opening words of his prayer faltered as he saw the blurred distortion of incense on a wide, horizontal girder. For a moment, it had looked as though a human shape had been standing there looking down at him. He peered into the upper reaches of the chancel, shielding his eyes to better penetrate the shifting and uncertain light.

There *was* something there, but he couldn't make out the details. It was as if the light was somehow distorting around something unseen, which did not wish to come into view.

Gaetan had heard tales of priests who claimed that angels of the Emperor watched over them from on high, but he hadn't taken such stories literally.

He turned to his acolytes and pointed to the chancel roof.

'Do you see that?' he asked.

໐
NINE

URIEL STALKED THE length of the Thunderhawk, his metabolism moving into readiness for combat once more. His
armour monitored his heart rate, blood flow and oxygen
levels, ensuring his entire body was optimally primed for
the business of killing. Learchus moved along the fuselage,
checking that every warrior was equipped with a full load
of ammunition and had observed the correct pre-battle rituals. His warriors had fought well against the kroot, but if
Uriel's suspicions were correct, they would soon be in
battle with more technologically advanced foes.

Chaplain Clausel stood by the assault ramp, feet
planted firmly on the deck and his crozius arcanum
held lightly at his side. The towering warrior-priest
recited the catechisms of battle, his booming voice cutting cleanly through the roaring of the Thunderhawk's
engines. Dried blood coated his skull-faced helmet,
and, though rough thermals from the mountains
caused the gunship to buck alarmingly, he neither held
to the ready line nor the walls to keep steady.

They were ten minutes out from Lake Masura, flying low and keeping hard to the mountain's flanks. Flying like this cost precious fuel, but it was the only way to avoid detection by enemy countermeasures. As yet, there was no response from the governor or Lortuen Perjed, despite repeated attempts to reach them. Presumably, the jamming technology the tau employed at Deep Canyon Six was being used to keep the governor in the dark as to the presence of aliens on his world.

Uriel hoped he would not find out the hard way.

Lord Winterbourne's Aquila lander was already en route back to Brandon Gate, despite the colonel's bluster that he was fit enough to fly into battle with the Ultramarines. After a brief, but one-sided, discussion, Uriel had convinced him of the need to evacuate his wounded, and to return to his regiment and oversee its mobilisation. Harkus had been placed within the Aquila, and Winterbourne promised that the bloodied Techmarine would be taken to Fortress Idaeus as soon as they landed.

Uriel cleaned the congealed blood of the kroot he had slain from his sword, knowing that soon it would probably be coated in the vital fluids of another living being. Learchus marched down the length of the gunship, and took his seat opposite Uriel. The sergeant's face was serious and drawn, dried blood caking one side. He drew his weapon, a sword similar in design to Uriel's, and began reciting a prayer to honour its war-spirit.

Uriel let him finish before speaking. 'This will be a tough fight, sergeant.'

'I expect so,' agreed Learchus. 'Any word on support from Brandon Gate?'

'Ancient Peleus was all set to prep the other Thunderhawks, but he will need his warriors in place to defend the city if this is the first stage of an attack. In any case, they would not reach us in time.'

'So we are on our own for this one?'

'We are,' said Uriel, 'but we're not going in on a full engage and destroy mission.'

'We are not?' asked Learchus.

'No, we're going in to retrieve the governor and get out.'

Learchus rubbed a gauntlet over his chin. 'We are only a few squads and a gunship, potentially going up against an enemy of unknown strength and deployment that may be dug in at a fortified location. I hope you have a plan?'

'I do. We make a single pass in the Thunderhawk to ascertain what we can of any enemy presence in and around the Shonai dwelling. Then we execute a hot landing at the weakest point of their perimeter. If they have taken refuge within the building, we do a standard room by room clearance, killing any tau we find.'

'It is a sound plan, but if there are hostages, they may be caught in the crossfire.'

'Our priority is to retrieve the governor,' said Uriel, 'nothing more.'

'Understood,' said Learchus, checking their time to arrival. 'Five minutes out,' he said.

'Are the men ready?' asked Uriel.

'Yes,' said Learchus, sheathing his sword and laying his bolter across his lap. 'They were ready the moment they boarded the gunship.'

'Good. They are a credit to you, Learchus. The entire company is a credit to you.'

'Thank you, captain,' said Learchus, a familiar shadow passing over his features. 'I promised I would look after the men of the company while you were... away.'

'And you have done a grand job,' said Uriel. 'I could not have wished for finer recruits to be raised to the 4th. Captain Idaeus would have been proud.'

Learchus nodded stiffly, and Uriel leaned forward. 'We have a few minutes until Lake Masura, and we need to clear the air between us before we go into battle.'

'What do you mean?' asked Learchus, his blue eyes wary.

'The fact that I am here troubles you, that much is obvious,' said Uriel, 'as does the fact that I am captain again. Part of you wishes I had not returned.'

'That is ridiculous,' snapped Learchus. 'You completed your Death Oath and returned to Macragge with your honour restored. There is nothing else to say.'

'I think there is,' pressed Uriel. 'You feel no bitterness at my return?'

'None.'

'Are you sure?'

'I am sure.'

Uriel leaned back in the shaped metal chair and paused before saying, 'I wish Pasanius were here.'

Surprised at Uriel's change of tack, Learchus nodded slowly. 'His strength would be of great value in the coming fight.'

'It would, but that is not what I mean,' said Uriel.

'Then what do you mean?' asked Learchus, clearly exasperated.

'I mean that I *wish* he were here, but I understand that it is right he is not.'

'He broke the Codes of Rectitude and is being punished for that.'

'He broke those codes by lying, Learchus,' said Uriel, 'as you are lying to me now.'

Learchus's face flushed. Uriel saw his jaw tighten as anger rose within him, only to be swiftly quelled.

'What am I lying about, captain?' demanded Learchus.

'About your ambitions.'

'What ambitions?'

Uriel leaned forwards, resting his forearms on his knees. 'I know you led the 4th Company to Espandor in my absence. I know of the battles you fought there, the victory of Corinth Bridge and the defence of Herapolis. You destroyed a gargant, a war machine with the power to level cities, and you saved that world from the orks. You led our company to Espandor a sergeant, but in your heart you returned as a captain. Tell me I'm wrong.'

'You are not wrong,' snarled Learchus. 'Am I to be dishonoured now for having ambition?'

'Of course not. A warrior must always test himself, seeking new foes and new challenges against which to fight. Without ambition, we would never achieve anything of greatness. A Space Marine *needs* ambition, it is what drives him to be the very best he can be. You have been a loyal sergeant and a proud warrior of the 4th, but this company is mine to lead.'

Learchus looked down at the deck, and to Uriel, he seemed to shrink a little in his armour.

'You were gone so long,' said Learchus eventually. 'Everyone believed you were dead. Even I had begun to lose hope that you would ever return to the Chapter.'

'But I did,' said Uriel. 'I am captain once more, and you must accept that.'

'I rebuilt the 4th, I trained it and I fought as its commander,' said Learchus. 'I grieved for the dead and carved their names on the wall of the Temple of Correction. I earned the right to lead it.'

'And in time you *will* receive a captaincy, of that I am certain.'

'But not now, and not the 4th?'

'No,' said Uriel with a wry smile, holding his hand out to Learchus. 'But who knows, I might die in this coming war. If that is to be my fate, then I could imagine no finer warrior to take my place. I need you with me, Learchus. The 4th Company needs you. Are you with me?'

Learchus stared at Uriel's hand for a long moment, but, at last, he nodded and took it.

'I am with you,' he said.

THOUGH KOUDELKAR FELT much calmer now that his aunt had explained her motives in inviting the tau delegation to Galtrigil, a nagging sense of unease gnawed at his veneer of calm. Try as he might, he couldn't quite identify its source, even though he felt it should have been obvious to a man of his insight and perspicacity.

'I think we might be able to do business,' he said, smiling at the grey-skinned tau.

Aun'rai took his hand from Koudelkar's shoulder and bowed.

'That is a wise decision, Governor Shonai,' said the tau. 'You will not regret it.'

'Damn you,' hissed Lortuen Perjed, pushing between Koudelkar and Aun'rai.

The old man had his stick raised, and was poised to strike the alien when one of the giant fighting machines took a step forwards. Standing apart from the others, Koudelkar now saw that it was etched with different markings. Its head unit was pale blue with a striped pattern on its left side, and there was a flaming sphere painted in the centre of its chest panel and upon one shoulder guard.

The machine raised its weapons, one a huge cannon with multiple barrels, the other a thick tubular gun with a hemispherical muzzle. Naked fear rose in Koudelkar as the lenses on the battle machine's head whirred and a thin beam of targeting light reflected from Lortuen Perjed's glistening pate.

Lortuen slashed his walking cane at Aun'rai, but the alien's batons flashed into its hands, and the cane was knocked from the adept's hand.

Koudelkar was impressed. The tau envoy was faster and more skilled than he looked.

The battle machine leaned down.

'Step back or die, Gue'la,' it told Perjed.

The voice was mechanically rendered, though it still carried the resonance of the speaker's voice superbly. Even though he was deathly afraid of the machine, Koudelkar wondered why the Adeptus Mechanicus could not develop something similar. Surely, if these aliens could invent such technology, the priests of the Machine-God could as well.

Koudelkar took hold of Lortuen's arm and held the adept tightly.

Aun'rai waved the battle machine back, and Koudelkar thought he saw a trace of anger in the envoy's features.

'My apologies, Governor Shonai,' said Aun'rai. 'The noble El'esaven is very protective of me and sometimes forgets himself.' The alien then turned its amber eyes on Lortuen Perjed and said. 'And you should know that the silent alarm signal in your cane is being jammed.'

'Filthy creature!' shouted Lortuen, shrugging off Koudelkar's grip. Aun'rai stepped back to avoid his outburst. 'How dare you?'

'There's someone inside that?' asked Koudelkar, indicating the tall machine, though Aun'rai had as good as confirmed his earlier suspicion that each one was crewed by a living pilot. The notion that the tau were jamming an alert signal registered as strange, but the thought vanished as Aun'rai spoke again.

'There is indeed a pilot within,' said Aun'rai. 'El'esaven is a commander of great repute and skill.'

'And that machine is his... armour?'

'In a way, yes, but it is so much more than merely armour. In your language, the best translation of its name would be "battlesuit".'

'Stop talking to it!' demanded Perjed. 'Don't you see what's happening here?'

'Adept Perjed, control yourself!' shouted his aunt. 'Your behaviour is unconscionable.'

Perjed spun on his heel, rage lending his aged limbs strength. '*My* behaviour? You have made pacts with xenos creatures, you stupid, stupid woman! They are not here to negotiate; they are here to take over! Open your eyes, damn you!'

Koudelkar felt Lortuen's words tugging at his mind, and he turned back to Aun'rai. 'My military advisors tell me you have other soldiers on Pavonis, is this true?'

The tau smiled, or at least that was what Koudelkar assumed the movement of its features signified. 'We do have some... lightly armed reconnaissance troops on Pavonis, yes. Purely as a precaution, you understand? Given your society's intolerance of other species, I felt it was prudent to ensure that Pavonis was ready for my arrival.'

'I am not sure I am comfortable with your armed forces on my world,' said Koudelkar as a powerful feeling of revulsion and anger began taking shape within him.

Aun'rai stepped towards him once more, but his mother put herself in his way.

'Don't you touch my son,' she said. 'Don't you lay a finger on him, I'm warning you.'

'Mother!' hissed Koudelkar, but the implications of what Aun'rai had said were worming their way through the haze surrounding his thoughts with ever greater force. The nagging sensation of something being horribly wrong was growing in strength, and he looked up at the threatening bulk of the battlesuit warrior that threatened Adept Perjed.

This was an alien soldier, one of high rank if he was a noble, and businessmen did not bring armed men to a negotiation. His anger rose in a tide, and Koudelkar felt the desire to talk with these aliens fade like a half-remembered dream. He shook his head. What had he been thinking? Dealing with xenos creatures? The very idea was ludicrous.

With that thought, the last of whatever subtle manipulation had been worked upon him vanished and he saw the truth of Lortuen's words.

'In fact,' he continued, 'I find the notion of your troops on Pavonis a gross insult. This is an Imperial world of the Emperor, and your presence here consti tutes an act of war.'

'Koudelkar!' cried his aunt. 'No! Think of what you're saying. Think of Pavonis!'

'Oh, I am, Mykola,' he said. 'I'm saying what you should have said long ago and what I would have said had this bastard not influenced me with some form of xenos mind control!'

Koudelkar drew himself up to his full height and pushed out his thin chest. 'Aun'rai, you are an enemy of the human race, and you are in violation of the Emperor's will, by whose glory and beneficence is the galaxy ruled. You must leave this planet and never return, or else face the full might of the Imperium's wrath.'

Aun'rai sighed. 'This is most regrettable. I was led to believe you would be willing to enter into a partnership with us for the greater good of all.'

'Then I am happy to disappoint you,' said Koudelkar, shooting a poisonous glance towards his aunt.

'I have come to expect such narrowness of vision from your species, but I hoped this time would be different,' said the alien envoy. 'But make no mistake; Pavonis *will* be part of the Tau Empire. It would have been better if you had embraced the idea and become part of this planet's future, but I see now that you are just as blinkered and hate-filled as the rest of your selfish race.'

'You see, Mykola?' hissed Lortuen Perjed. 'See now the true face of these xenos! They come not with co-operation in mind, but conquest.'

'You are wrong about us, Adept Perjed,' said Aun'rai, with a faint trace of regret, 'but it is too late for a peaceful resolution.'

As if to confirm that statement, one of the circling tau aircraft exploded, tumbling from the sky in a flaming cartwheel until it slammed into the lake with an almighty splash.

The sudden violence of the explosion acted like a flamer to a drum of promethium.

Koudelkar looked up to see a thundering blue craft, boxy and ungainly, scream overhead. Its guns blazed with light and noise, and he knew he'd never seen a more welcome sight.

THE BLOODSHED SIMMERING just beneath the surface of this encounter erupted in a crescendo of violence. Koudelkar's skitarii, who had been itching to wreak harm on the tau, finally gave in to their warlike urges, and a number of things seemed to happen at once.

The battlesuits cycled their weapons up to fire, and the bronze-armoured skitarii with an implanted cannon and grenade launcher opened fire. One of the Lavrentian soldiers barrelled Koudelkar and his mother to the ground, and a hurricane of gunfire erupted all around him.

Koudelkar jammed his palms over his ears at the deafening, terrifying volume of it. One of the battlesuits collapsed, its upper half a smoking ruin where a series of grenades had blown it apart. Both skitarii were firing, howling and exultant, their guns roaring as they unleashed the full fury of their maker's lethal skills.

Koudelkar rolled as barking hellguns opened up and squalling bolts of las-fire flashed overhead. His mother screamed in fear, and Koudelkar saw Mykola throw herself to the ground and crawl in panic towards the house. Lortuen Perjed was curled into a tight ball, covering his ears and keeping as low to the ground as possible.

Then the battlesuits opened fire.

Three of the Lavrentians were immediately slain, shredded in a blitzing storm of fire. Their bodies literally ceased to exist as limbs were torn from bodies and torsos were vaporised in the relentless hail of shells. The survivors scattered, but, to their credit, they were still fighting, snapping off shots at their attackers as they ran for cover. Another battlesuit was brought down by their fire, its chest punctured and cratered with las-burns.

'Come on!' screamed the soldier that had borne him to the ground. 'Move it!'

'What?' cried Koudelkar. 'I can't hear you!'

The man dragged the collar of his frock-coat and pointed. 'Get to the house! Go!'

'Get Lortuen,' shouted Koudelkar over the din of firing. The soldier looked set to disobey him, but nodded and crawled over to the venerable adept.

Koudelkar put an arm across his mother's back, and together they began crawling towards the house. The walls of the arboretum blew out and fell to the ground in crashing panes of glass as the trees within splintered under the storm of fire. Shards of glass sliced Koudelkar's palms as he crawled, and he gritted his teeth against the pain.

One skitarii dropped to its knees with a smoking, fist-sized hole blasted in its chest. Even as it died, it sent a string of grenades sailing into the troop compartment of Aun'rai's drop-ship. Flames and smoke erupted from within the aircraft, and Koudelkar heard horrifying screams of pain from the tau soldiers within. Flaming bodies tumbled from the craft, which sagged on its skids as secondary explosions blew out its sides and an engine.

Screams and smoke filled the air, and Koudelkar felt sure the shot that was going to kill him would come at any second. He heard another explosion, but couldn't tell where it had come from. All was chaos: las-bolts, alien weapons' fire and cries of pain. It was impossible to tell what was happening. Koudelkar's terror rose to new heights at the thought of dying like this.

'They'll think I'm a traitor,' he said. 'If I die here, they'll think I'm a traitor.'

'What?' cried his mother, her face streaked with tears.

He shook his head. They were almost there. Ignoring the pain of his gashed hands, Koudelkar reached the door to the arboretum and almost wept with relief. Fresh shots echoed from the walls of the house, some high-pitched and whining, others booming like distant artillery fire.

A huge shadow enveloped him, and Koudelkar looked up to see the battlesuit with the flaming sphere device worked onto its chest.

It towered over him, and he cried out as it reached for him with mechanised gauntlets.

URIEL DROPPED FROM the assault ramp of the Thunderhawk. The howling gale of its engines as it hovered behind the tau craft was like a fiery hurricane blast, the grass flattened and burning beneath the gunship. Smoke boiled from the stricken tau vehicle, some kind of drop-ship by the look of it, and enemies poured from its interior. Some were ablaze and dying, others were burned, but fighting.

Learchus and a squad of Ultramarines dropped to the ground and began shooting. Behind them came Chaplain Clausel's assault troops as the scouts fanned out behind the battle squads, positioning themselves to deliver covering fire.

'Are we too late?' shouted Learchus.

'I think we arrived at exactly the right moment,' answered Uriel. 'Let's go!'

As the Thunderhawk had passed overhead, Uriel scanned the dynamics of the firefight, mapping out the shape of the battle in a second. A furious exchange of fire was underway on a stone-flagged terrace. Tau infantrymen, flying discs with under-slung weapons, and tall battle machines like elongated Dreadnoughts traded shots with a few Guardsmen and what looked like one of Governor Shonai's skitarii.

Gunfire fizzed past Uriel, streaking darts of light that hissed and spat as they struck the armoured hull of the Thunderhawk. Tau warriors, around a dozen of them, were forming up in the shadow of the wrecked drop-ship. An enemy soldier in a pale red helmet was directing their fire, and two of the battlesuits turned from the firefight on the terrace to add their support.

'Chaplain, the terrace!' bellowed Uriel. 'Learchus, your squad with me. We take those tau at the drop-ship, and then hit them in the flank!'

Clausel and his warriors powered away on columns of fire, the roar of their jump packs cutting through the stuttering cacophony of gunfire. Uriel set off towards the downed drop-ship, his Space Marines following behind him through the torrents of fire, their bolters locked before them.

Searing beams of pulsing weapons fire slashed the air as Uriel and his warriors charged towards the slumped drop-ship. He heard impacts of hard energy against ceramite plates as several shots struck home. One pulse hit the curve of his shoulder-guard and ricocheted past his helmet, another struck his greave. Neither was powerful enough to stop him.

His bolter bucked in his hand as he fired. One of the tau pitched backwards, his chest and shoulder blown out by the mass-reactive bolt. Another volley flashed, and Uriel felt one tear through the weaker joint at his waist. Even as the pain registered, balms dulled it, and medicae systems began treating the wound.

A volcanic blizzard of fire streaked above Uriel, and the tau drop-ship bucked and heaved as the frontal guns of the Thunderhawk tore it apart. Uriel emptied the last of his magazine before slinging his bolter as the gunship's suppressing fire was shut off.

He reached the blazing drop-ship's perforated remains, and slammed his back against it.

'Frags!' he shouted, unsnapping a pair of textured discs from his belt harness.

Uriel lobbed the grenades over the drop-ship and counted three seconds as he drew his sword. Other grenades followed his, and a series of dull bangs rocked the drop-ship. Uriel heard the ringing impacts of razored fragments pinging from its hull.

Uriel swung around the drop-ship with his blade raised at his right shoulder. Behind the drop-ship, a dozen or so tau warriors picked themselves up from the horror of the grenades' detonations. Their fatigues were torn and bloodied, but, more importantly, the blasts had broken their readiness to fight.

Uriel's golden blade leapt with azure fire, and he drove it through the chest of the nearest tau warrior. His victim fell without a sound as Uriel stepped over his body and took the fight to his foes. The aliens were bloodied and disorientated, but Uriel gave them no chance to recover their wits, cleaving his blade through another warrior's armour, and tearing it free in a wash of blood.

The tau rose to meet his charge, and, though full-enclosing helmets obscured their faces, Uriel saw the panic in them. They had come here expecting an easy mission, but were now in a fight for their lives. A few snap shots flashed past him. Uriel's squad followed him into the fight, but this moment was his and his alone.

He hammered his boot into the chest of the next tau, and smashed his sword through the armour of the warrior behind him. More tau turned their weapons on him, but he was already among them, and it was too late for guns. This was a close-quarters fight that required the brutal skills of a killer, and there were no finer killers than the Space Marines. Uriel fought with total economy of motion as he struck the tau like a thunderbolt. No blow was wasted, and, each time his sword or fist connected, an enemy fell.

The tau were helpless against him, for he was a warrior of the Adeptus Astartes and he was fighting for more than just victory, he was fighting for the glory of his Chapter. For too long, Uriel had fought for redemption or simply for survival.

This fight was for the honour of the Ultramarines.

Learchus stood next to him, his sword cleaving a bloody path through the tau. Side by side, they fought like the mighty gods of battle they were. Uriel was always on the move, slaying his foes without mercy or fear. He swayed aside from knives and rifle butts, smashing skulls and slicing open armour with every blow. Decades of training and a century of war had moulded him into a warrior without peer. He was a killing machine that had never tasted defeat, and he fought with all the skill encoded into his flesh by the most fearsome training regime imaginable.

Shots banged around him, blades tore flesh, and blood flowed in rivers. Within moments the tau were dead. Nearly a score of enemy warriors lay scattered on the ground, scorched black by fire, cut to pieces by blades or blown apart by explosive bolts. Uriel registered the deaths without emotion, and drew close to the drop-ship.

'Precious little glory in this,' sneered Learchus. 'They have no stomach for a real fight.'

Uriel nodded, kicking one of the tau rifles. 'They rely too much on their weapons and not enough on blade-work.'

'How does our Chaplain fare?'

Uriel looked over towards the terrace where Clausel's assault warriors fought. Smoke and flames obscured much of the battle, but the sound of shooting and the clash of blades told him that there was still a fight to be won.

'Let's go and find out,' he said, hefting his bloodied sword once more.

♉
TEN

Blood swilled around his feet, and the stink of seared flesh filled the cramped transport compartment of the Aquila lander. Nathaniel Winterbourne took shallow breaths as he tried to focus on the streams of data flowing over the slates fitted around the circumference of the observation canopy's circular cupola. Alithea had outdone herself, and operational readiness icons were flashing to life for virtually all units of Sword Command.

He drew in a sharp breath as the pain of his wounded arm flared again. The kroot hunting beast had bitten deep and, now that the adrenaline of combat was draining from his system, his arm felt like it was on fire. He'd accepted a shot of morphia to dull the pain and had swabbed the wound with half a bottle of counterseptic. Hopefully, that would be enough to counteract any xenos toxins that the beast's bite might have carried.

Beneath him, in the passenger compartment, injured men groaned in pain, their wounds far more severe

than his. Three of his soldiers were dead as well as his
vox-servitor and scribe. Germaine too had been killed,
and he grieved for her loss keenly. She would receive a
commendation along with the soldiers who had fought
so valiantly beside him. He stroked Fynlae with his
uninjured hand, careful to avoid the gouges torn in the
vorehound's flanks during his fight with the alien beast.

The wounded Ultramarines warrior lay unmoving.
For all the life he displayed, he could have been dead.
The man's wounds were horrific, and it was a source of
amazement to Winterbourne that anyone, even a Space
Marine, could suffer such hideous trauma and live.
Truly, the Adeptus Astartes were a race apart, and Win-
terbourne gave a short prayer of thanks that they fought
for the divine Emperor of Man.

The commander's seat of an Aquila was mounted
above and behind the pilot's cockpit, and Winterbourne
had a panoramic view of the moonlit landscape below
him. Behind him, the dark wall of Tembra Ridge serrated the horizon, and the diffuse glow just ahead was
the city of Brandon Gate. A ribbon of light stretched
away from the city, curving in a concave arc as it made
its way south-west towards Olzetyn before reaching
Praxedes on the coast. Beyond Brandon Gate, the horizon was a glowing line of fire, the skies stained with
light and fumes from the unceasing labours of the
Adeptus Mechanicus within the Diacrian Belt.

The lander dipped its wings and began its descent to
Camp Torum on the northern edge of the city. Winterbourne looked down into the passenger compartment
once more, relieved beyond words that his men were
soon to receive proper medical treatment. It had been
foolish to travel to Tembra Ridge without a full medicae
team, but he'd been so damned insistent about going
with the Ultramarines that he hadn't prepared properly.

Without warning, the aircraft banked sharply to the right, and his wounded arm slammed against the sharp metal rim of the cupola. Hot pain lanced up his arm, and he roared in anger.

'Emperor's wounds, man!' he shouted at the pilot. 'Watch what you're doing or I'll have your damn wings!'

The man didn't answer, and Winterbourne was about to rebuke him when he saw the streams of fire blazing into the sky from below. Ribbons of light spat upwards, almost lazily, and painted the heavens with blooms of light. Nearby, explosions cracked and spat, the sound of them rolling over the aircraft seconds after the flash. The sky above Torum was thick with waving streams of tracer fire. Winterbourne recognised it as flak from Hydra tanks. His tanks.

And they had been on the verge of flying into it.

The pilot's quick reactions had undoubtedly saved their lives, and Winterbourne made a mental note to apologise for his stern rebuke once they were safely on the ground.

'What in the name of Torum's balls is going on down there?' he yelled.

'I don't know, my lord,' said the pilot, pulling the Aquila in a wide, anticlockwise circle around the southern reaches of the city. Winterbourne attempted to raise someone on the ground, but every channel either hissed static or binaric interrogation cants.

Winterbourne recognised them as Hydra targeting logisters checking to see if they were a friendly or a hostile contact. Glancing at the slate to his left, he was relieved to see that the transponder was broadcasting his personal ident-code. He reached out to touch the black and white cog symbol etched into the metal rim of the cupola, and whispered a quick prayer of thanks to the spirit of the Aquila.

Satisfied that he wasn't about to be blown out of the sky by his own flak tanks, Winterbourne peered through the darkness to try and make some sense of what was happening below. His practiced eye quartered the city, scanning back and forth to spot anything out of the ordinary.

He didn't have to look for long.

Something was burning in the southern wedge of the city, a large structure with tall, metallic spires and iron flanks. The rippling glow of the flames illuminated the structure, and Winterbourne's eyes widened as he realised that the Templum Fabricae was ablaze.

'Merciful heavens,' he hissed. 'Are we too late already?'

He quickly scanned the rest of the city, but could see nothing else amiss.

'Get us on the ground,' he said. 'Now.'

'Where, my lord?' asked the pilot.

'Camp Torum, where do you think?' snapped Winterbourne. 'And make it fast. Men will die if you don't get us down quickly.'

'Yes, my lord,' replied the pilot. 'The sky's too hot for a normal descent, so we're going to have to come in from the city side. We'll be low and fast, so hold onto something.'

The pilot immediately pulled the Aquila into a sharp downward arc, angling the nose to the north-west and losing altitude rapidly as he flew over Brandon Gate. The aircraft shot over the ruins of the Arbites precinct, and across the open expanse of Liberation Square, before pulling into a screamingly tight turn over the Commercia Gate. The wings of the aircraft spread, and the nose came up alarmingly, as the pilot threw the aircraft into its landing mode and rapidly bled off the last of its forward momentum.

Winterbourne was hurled forwards; only his restraining harness and a firm grip prevented him from smashing his skull against the toughened glass of the observation dome. Even so, the rapid deceleration was blindingly painful on his torn up arm. Fynlae yelped as he was thrown around, and cries of alarm came from the passenger compartment.

The Aquila levelled out, and Winterbourne saw that it wasn't just the Hydras that were firing into the sky. Tank commanders were shooting their turret-mounted guns upwards, and even Guardsmen on the ground were aiming their lasguns towards the heavens. A few even turned their guns on the Aquila as it roared into view, but held their fire as they saw their regiment's heraldry on its wings and fuselage.

The lights of Camp Torum were blazingly bright, and Winterbourne saw no evidence of damage or signs of attack as the lander skimmed over its vast hangars and barrack buildings. Just what the hell had happened here, and why was the sky above the camp awash with exploding flak?

'Set us down over there,' ordered Winterbourne, spotting a knot of Guardsmen in the centre of the parade ground, clustered around a horseman holding the emerald and gold banner of the 44th aloft.

The pilot brought the Aquila in low, and set it down hard in a billowing cloud of engine smoke. Even before the forward skid was down, Winterbourne slammed his palm against his harness release, and pulled the lever to lower his command chair from the observation dome. Fynlae jumped down, and Winterbourne slid from his seat as the passenger compartment descended.

Guardsmen with raised rifles awaited him as he stepped onto the parade ground, and their expressions told him that something serious was afoot. Medicae staff ran towards him, but he waved them away.

'There are men in there need help more than me,' he said. 'See to them first.'

Winterbourne pushed through the scrum of soldiers surrounding him, and stalked towards the horseman with the banner. Any senior officer would be there. Heated voices were raised and he sensed panic.

'Can someone please inform me why I was almost shot out of the sky above my own damn base?' he shouted, the years of authority in his voice cutting through the babble.

Heads turned to face him.

'Make a hole!' he bellowed, and the soldiers parted before him to reveal a scene of carnage. Dead men and dying horses lay in spreading pools of blood as medicae in red-spattered uniforms fought to save the wounded.

'Oh no,' he said, and his heart sank as he saw Captain Mederic cradling the body of Major Alithea Ornella. Her uniform coat was sticky with blood, and black where it had been burned by weapons fire. He dropped to his knees beside her, and reached out to touch her cheek. It was still warm.

'Mederic? What happened?' he asked.

'We were attacked,' said his captain of scouts, 'by those.'

Winterbourne looked over to where Mederic was pointing, and saw a host of dead creatures with leathery skin of mottled blue chitin and wide wings of what looked like textured silk. They were repulsive beasts, hybrid by-blows of reptiles and insects, and they leaked a viscous yellow sap-like blood from scores of las-wounds. Strange-looking weapons with oddly-angled grips lay beside them, and dead, multi-faceted eyes stared glassily out over the parade ground.

Winterbourne's lip curled in distaste.

'Stingwings,' he hissed.

'They came out of nowhere,' said Mederic. 'One minute we were supervising the mobilisation, the next we were under fire. Two dozen of them dropped out of the sky and tore into us. We got them all, but not before…'

His words trailed off as he indicated the dead body of the 44th's second in command.

'Alithea will be avenged, captain,' said Winterbourne. 'Make no mistake about that.'

'I believe you, my lord,' said Mederic.

Winterbourne stood and drew himself up to his full height and addressed the Guardsmen around him with the full weight of his authority.

'Right, let's get this army ready to fight,' said Winterbourne. 'I want us ready to roll out of here and fit to fight within the hour. Is that understood? Now go!'

Mederic saluted as the Guardsmen of the Lavrentians rushed to obey Winterbourne's orders.

'What about the Administratum?' Mederic asked. 'We're still awaiting their authorisation.'

'To hell with that, son,' said Winterbourne. 'We're at war, and I'm not waiting for some damn pencil pusher to tell me I can march out with my soldiers. Now make it happen!'

THE FIGHT, AS it turned out, was brief. Chaplain Clausel's warriors had been thorough in their destruction, and only a handful of the flying discs and a single battlesuit had still been functional by the time Uriel and Learchus led their squad into the battle. With the last of the tau machines brought down, a curious silence fell over the battlefield.

Glass and bullet casings crunched underfoot, and the moans of wounded tau were the only other sounds to disturb the quiet. As Uriel's scouts secured the few alien prisoners, the assault troops gathered up their fallen brothers. Three Space Marines were dead, and Uriel stood aside to allow Clausel's warriors past as they were borne towards the Thunderhawk.

Uriel approached Clausel. The Chaplain's face was a mask of blood, red droplets falling from the eye sockets of his death mask like ruby tears.

'Well met, Chaplain,' said Uriel, gripping Clausel's wrist. 'Who did you lose?'

'Brother Phaetus, Brother Ixios and Brother Ephor,' said Clausel. 'They will be remembered.'

'That they shall,' Uriel assured him. 'I will carve their names myself.'

Clausel moved away, and Uriel turned his attention to the aftermath of the fighting, angered at the deaths of the three warriors. Stepping carefully through the detritus of battle, he saw half a dozen of the automated flying drones the tau employed lying scattered like dented silver mirrors. The drones lay amid the bloodied remains of a handful of Lavrentian Guardsmen, and, such was the destruction wreaked upon their corpses that Uriel found it next to impossible to tell exactly how many had died.

His anger built at the sight of their bodies. It was obscene that the lives of warriors should be ended by an enemy without feelings, emotions or a spirit. Machines that killed were anathema to the Imperium, and even the death-dealing technology fabricated by the priests of Mars was imbued with a fragment of the machine-spirit or crewed by a living, breathing human being.

Two skitarii, the ones Uriel had seen during the audience with Koudelkar Shonai, were also dead, their heavily augmented bodies burned and cratered by multiple gunshot wounds. Brutal and animalistic killers they might be, but they had died in defence of their master.

Uriel counted four destroyed battlesuits, their armoured casings broken open and leaking hydraulic fluids onto the bloodied stone of the terrace. Through the cracked plating, Uriel could see torn grey flesh, and he could smell the strange, musky odour of alien blood. He walked through the scene of slaughter, coming at last to the splintered doors and smashed glazing of a botanical hothouse.

'Looks like it was quite a fight before we got here,' said Learchus, appearing at his side.

'Aye, that it does,' said Uriel, 'but I do not see the body of the governor anywhere.'

'Maybe he got inside,' suggested Learchus. 'I think these doors were open before they were shot out.'

'Possibly,' said Uriel, his eyes narrowing as he spotted something out of place beneath one of the battlesuits. He stepped over a pool of congealing blood, and knelt beside the blackened shell of one of the tau armoured fighting suits.

'Over here,' he said. 'Help me with this.'

Learchus joined him, and together they heaved the wrecked battlesuit onto its side. The machine was startlingly heavy, a solid, immobile hunk of metal now that whatever power source drove it was inactive.

'Guilliman's oath,' hissed Learchus at the sight of what was revealed.

Beneath the battlesuit lay the body of another tau, but one that was clearly not a warrior. Its robes were stained with blood, though none appeared to be its own. Its robes were white and gold, embroidered with a shimmering multi-coloured thread. A high collar of polished gems and enamelled chips was crushed beneath its head and its eyes flickered with life.

'Looks like someone important,' said Learchus.

'Yes,' agreed Uriel, 'one of their leader caste. A diplomat or some kind of noble perhaps.'

The fallen alien groaned, and his chest rose and fell with breath now that the pinning weight of the battle-suit had been removed. Learchus took hold of the alien, his massive gauntlet easily able to encircle its neck. 'Do you think he's the one in charge of them?'

'Given that he's here at the governor's residence, that seems possible.'

'Then his death will greatly hinder them,' said Learchus, tightening his grip. The tau reached up with thin arms and weakly pulled at the sergeant's wrists.

'No, do not kill him,' ordered Uriel. 'Secure him and get him onto the gunship. If he is a senior commander, we could learn a lot from him.'

Learchus nodded and hauled the tau to his feet. 'I will personally keep this one secure. What do you want to do now?'

'Search the grounds and the house,' ordered Uriel. 'Find any survivors.'

IN THE END, the search of the house revealed fifteen servants, who had gone to ground when the fighting had started, but Governor Shonai was not amongst them. Of the survivors, none were of especial note save for Mykola Shonai, the governor's aunt, whom Uriel had previously seen on his last expedition to Pavonis at Ario Barzano's grave. The scouts had found her hiding in the shredded ruin of the arboretum, curled under a stone bench with her eyes closed and her hands pressed firmly against her ears.

Uriel was pleased Mykola was alive, but this pleasure soured as he saw the guilty fear in her eyes as she was brought before him. If Uriel had been shocked by the change in Pavonis, it was nothing compared to the change he saw in Mykola Shonai.

Gone was the confident, strong-willed Planetary Governor, who had faced down an Imperial inquisitor over the fate of her world, and in her place was a weeping, mud-stained woman with thinning grey hair and a deeply lined face. Tears and snot mingled on her face, and Uriel felt a stab of sadness that she could have fallen to such a level.

'Uriel…? Oh, Emperor protect me,' she whispered. 'Oh, no… I'm sorry. No, no, no.'

Mykola looked away, and dropped to her knees as she saw the bodies strewn across the bloodstained terrace. Uriel shot Learchus a confused look as she covered her eyes and wept.

'I'm sorry, I'm sorry… I never meant for this to happen,' she cried. 'I didn't know they'd take them, I swear.'

Uriel dropped to one knee before her. Gently, he raised her head. 'What happened here, Mykola? Where is Koudelkar?'

Mykola shook her head. 'No, I can't. It's too much.'

'You have to tell me everything,' pressed Uriel, 'and you have to do it now.'

'They said they came to negotiate,' cried Mykola, 'to do business. They said they could help bring prosperity back to Pavonis, and that's what I wanted. That's all I've ever wanted.'

The implications of her words were clear, and Uriel's heart sank. 'You invited the tau here, didn't you? They approached you with offers of trade and you listened to them. That's what happened, isn't it?'

Mykola nodded. 'You don't understand, Uriel. We'd won our world back from the brink of damnation. We were saved, but it was being taken away from us piece by piece by bureaucrats who had never even heard of Pavonis, let alone knew how bad things had gotten. The tau offered us a way out.'

'That is not what the tau offer, Mykola,' said Uriel. 'They offer you slavery and call it freedom, a prison you do not know you are in until it is too late. They offer a choice that is no choice at all.'

Something Mykola had said earlier now registered, and Uriel gripped her shoulder tightly. 'Koudelkar, they took him. The tau have your nephew, don't they? Is that what you meant when you said, "I didn't know they'd take them"?'

Mykola didn't answer at first, but she nodded between sobs. 'Yes. One of the battle machines took him and my sister. Another took Lortuen... I mean Adept Perjed.'

Uriel looked over his shoulder at the smouldering wreckage of the tau drop-ship, matching its shape and features with the knowledge he'd assimilated from the myriad briefing files and after-action reports collated by the Ultramarines in the wake of their battles against the tau.

Such drop-ships were designated Orcas by Imperial Lexicographers, and Uriel quickly ran its troop capacity against the number of tau corpses he'd seen. The numbers didn't add up.

'Learchus, count the number of enemy dead,' he ordered. 'All of them: warriors, battlesuits and drones.'

'What for?'

'Just do it,' snapped Uriel, although he feared he already knew the answer. Learchus turned to the task with alacrity, and within the space of a minute, he had returned.

'Well?' asked Uriel.

'Four destroyed battlesuits, twenty-four dead soldiers and eight drones accounted for. Looks like three crew on the drop-ship that were killed when the Thunderhawk opened up.'

Uriel swore. 'An Orca can carry six battlesuits. Are you sure there are only four here?'

'Absolutely,' said Learchus. 'I'd stake my honour on it.'

'Damn it, Mykola, where have they taken him?' asked Uriel.

'I don't know, I swear on my life! Once the shooting started, I didn't see much of anything. I saw one of the battlesuits, the one Aun'rai called El'esaven, lift Koudelkar and Pawluk. Then another one picked up Lortuen, but then I got inside the arboretum, and I didn't see anything after that!'

'Aun'rai and El'esaven?' said Uriel. 'Who are they?'

'Aun'rai was the envoy,' said Mykola, wiping her face with the hem of her robe, 'the lying bastard who set this all up.'

'A tau in robes, not armour?' asked Uriel.

'Yes, uh… creamy white robes and no armour,' agreed Mykola.

'And El'esaven?' said Learchus. 'Is he a warrior?'

'I think so,' said Mykola between heaving gulps of air. 'He was wearing a battlesuit. I never heard of him before today, but I got the feeling he wasn't happy about what was happening, like he wanted to just open up on us instead of talk.'

'Did you see where they took the governor?' demanded Learchus. 'It is imperative that we retrieve your nephew. The fighting forces of Pavonis need a figurehead.'

Mykola shook her head.

'I didn't see,' she said with complete and utter self-loathing. 'I was too busy keeping my head down.'

Uriel sighed, saddened to see a once-noble servant of the Emperor brought low by her own flawed character. Though Mykola Shonai was now a traitor in the eyes of the Imperium, Uriel could well understand how she had come to this place, having walked a similar path not so long ago. Any censure heaped upon her would be nothing compared to the crushing anguish she would be lavishing on herself, though that fact would carry no weight with those who decided her punishment.

Uriel wanted to hate Mykola Shonai for what she had done, but found he could not. All he felt towards her was pity. He nodded to the scouts. 'Take her onto the Thunderhawk and secure her with the rest of the prisoners for transfer to the Glasshouse.'

The two scouts lifted the distraught Mykola and dragged her away.

'We're not taking her to Fortress Idaeus?' asked Learchus. 'She needs to be interrogated.'

'Fortress Idaeus is now our base of operations for war,' said Uriel, 'and that is no place for prisoners. Judge Sharben's enforcers will undertake the interrogation.'

Learchus nodded. 'Very well. And the governor? What do we do about Koudelkar?'

'You are going to get him back,' said Uriel.

'Me?' said Learchus. 'Surely we should follow their trail in the Thunderhawk.'

'No. With the prisoners and survivors of this attack aboard, we don't have enough fuel to mount an aerial pursuit and get back to Brandon Gate. I need you to take the scouts and find the trail of this El'esaven. Machines that big should be simple enough to track. Follow them, find them and kill them. Then bring the governor back.'

'Very well,' said Learchus, slamming a fresh magazine into his bolter. 'What are you going to do?'

'I'm going back to Brandon Gate,' said Uriel. 'The fighting is only going to escalate, and the warriors of the 4th Company need their captain to lead them.'

Learchus smiled and said, 'Perhaps you did learn something on your Death Oath after all.'

'So it would seem,' agreed Uriel, gripping his sergeant's wrist.

'Courage and honour, captain.'

Uriel nodded.

'I want the governor back,' he said. 'Find him for me.'

'We will find him,' vowed Learchus. 'On my honour, we will find him.'

♈

ELEVEN

THE FIRST ATTACK came at Praxedes in a blaze of light, and the first warning the port city's defenders had was the booming metallic cough of shells detonating above them. Sentries turned their gazes upwards, Hydra flak tanks swivelled their quad-mounted cannons to the heavens, and, a moment later, the warm glow of the sun was eclipsed by a sky-wide explosion of incandescent fire. Targeting auspex fused and shorted out, retinas were irreparably damaged, and delicate surveyor gear was instantly obliterated.

Where some enemies of the Imperium attacked under the cover of darkness, the tau came in the searing glare of a thousand stars.

A host of wedge-shaped craft flew in from the western ocean in the wake of the blinding detonation. Launched from floating platforms, brought to the surface in secret and concealed with alien technologies, they had awaited the execute order from El'esaven for many months. Caught unawares and blinded by the blazing skies, the air defences of the coastal city had no time to engage the attacking aircraft. The first wave began their attack runs as alert sirens roused the majority of Lance Command's Guardsmen from their bunks.

Twenty-five Barracuda air-superiority fighters of the Burning Star Hunter Coalition screamed over the airfields of Praxedes with their chin-mounted cannons blazing. It was the largest port facility on Pavonis, and the majority of its structures were built on the slopes of an ancient crater that was now open on its western edge to the vast expanse of the cold black ocean. Its sprawling landing fields and jib-platforms jutted out to sea like branches of a silver tree stripped of its leaves.

Some of these jibs were laden with freighter craft and bulk-lifters used to ferry cargo to orbiting mass conveyors, but many more were empty. Precious few of the city's flyers were combat aircraft, and those few that were able to get airborne were blown out of the sky within minutes of the first warning.

Explosions mushroomed skywards as fuel bays were hit, and stuttering pulses of light stitched across the vast hangars and container lines of the port. Panic gripped the city. Lance Command was based in a fortified enclosure on the side of the docks, and interceptor guns began opening fire as the Barracuda came in for another pass. Blazing tracer fire lit the sky, and a few tau aircraft tumbled downwards, torn in two, or their engines blown off by the barrage from below. No sooner had the tanks opened fire than invisible beams of laser light from teams of spotters concealed on the bluffs overlooking the city were painting their flanks.

Shoals of missiles detached from the wings of the surviving aircraft, and, like hunting hounds with the scent of blood, they roared towards the Imperial guns. Within moments, Lance Command was a scene of carnage as no fewer than four missiles slammed into the topside of each of its six anti-aircraft batteries.

Percussive detonations rolled over the base as each flak tank was silenced, and blazing plumes of thick, tarry smoke boiled skyward from the wrecks. Flames and explosions lit the night with a hellish orange glow as the Barracuda circled overhead like carrion birds.

With the city's air-cover stripped, four enormous aircraft with wide wings, like those of a great undersea monster that had forsaken the depths for the air, flew in low from the ocean. Flaring bow waves of frothing dark water travelled before them, rocking the platform jibs and throwing out great breaths of hot, magnetised air.

These giant aircraft were known and feared by Imperial forces as Mantas, monstrously powerful carrier aircraft that bristled with weaponry, and which could transport the equivalent of a battle company. Streaking bursts of explosive shells swept across the landing platforms, clearing them of any last defenders.

Each of the alien craft swooped in low over an empty platform and rotated on its axis before smoothly setting down amid sprays of ionised water and debris. A lower deck opened up, and each carrier disgorged four graceful skimmer tanks that moved on rippling cushions of anti-grav energy. The tanks were a mix of lightly armoured Devilfish, more heavily armed Hammerheads and missile-laden Sky Rays. No sooner were the armoured vehicles disgorged than ranks of battlesuits marched behind them. Each hulking war machine was heavily armed and followed the tanks as they swiftly pushed into the landing facility.

With their heavy payloads deployed, telescoping ramps slid down from upper decks, and squad after squad of armoured warriors hustled from the enormous bays. A handful of drones flew above the soldiers, hardened fighters from the world of Sa'cea, who called themselves Fire Warriors. The sensor spines of the drones tracked left and right, relaying their findings to each squad leader.

The entire deployment had taken less than a minute, and, as the first Manta pulled away, another four flew in to set down yet more troops. Within ten minutes, over thirty armoured vehicles, sixty battlesuits and four hundred infantry were pushing out through the buildings and command structures of the port.

Support tanks showered the interior of Lance Command's fortifications with barrage after barrage of lethally accurate missiles, each one guided to its target by the unseen observers on the cliffs. Barracks buildings were reduced to rubble, defence emplacements flattened and vehicle hangars set ablaze as underground fuel bunkers were breached by perfectly coordinated strikes.

Hundreds of Lavrentian Guardsmen died in the opening moments of the attack, shredded by shrapnel from the exploding missiles or crushed to death as their base collapsed around them. Hundreds more were killed as a wave of olive-coloured battlesuits dropped from the sky on streaking plumes of jet fire. Cycling cannons strafed the esplanades and eye-wateringly bright bolts of blue fire exploded among knots of panicked soldiers.

Shouting captains tried to organise a coherent defence, but engaging the battlesuits at close quarters was like trying to grip smoke. Heavy weapon teams set up and opened fire, but their targets were like flitting insects, darting through the air on precisely controlled bursts of jets. Weapons fire blazed through the interior of the Lavrentians' compound, criss-crossing in webs of light. A number of battlesuits were brought down, but casualties amongst the Guardsmen were far more numerous, and panic began to turn to terror.

Of the armoured strength of Lance Command, barely a handful of Leman Russ Conquerors rolled out from the hellish firestorm of the camp. They emerged from the roiling clouds of acrid smoke to take the fight to the enemy, with Chimera transports following in their wake. Such defiance was noble and courageous, but the Imperial forces were pitifully few compared to the full strength that had been deployed to Pavonis months before.

In the battle that followed, the hopelessly outnumbered and outgunned Imperial tanks were blown to pieces by hyper-velocity slugs that ripped their guts out and reduced them to smouldering piles of twisted metal.

Within the hour, the tau had secured their hold on Praxedes, and the coastal spaceport was now a bridgehead for invasion. In addition, over a thousand Lavrentian Guardsmen were taken prisoner, making the city's fall the worst defeat the regiment had suffered in its long and illustrious history.

The fall of Praxedes, however, was just the beginning of a night of bloodshed.

WITH THEIR BRIDGEHEAD secure, the forward elements of the tau army moved out from the coast in a swift advance. Yet more armed forces were ferried to the docking jibs of Praxedes by the giant Mantas, and every hour brought hundreds of Fire Warriors, battlesuits and armoured vehicles to the surface of Pavonis.

Under a thin curtain of Barracuda fighters, tau recon forces pushed along Highway 236, the arterial expressway that followed the line of the river towards Olzetyn. Second only to Brandon Gate, Olzetyn was a magnificent city, built upon a host of mighty bridges spanning great chasms carved in the earth by the confluence of three mighty rivers that merged into one mighty watercourse that flowed west to Praxedes. Its structures were clustered like miniature hives upon the bridges, the largest and most ornate of which was the gold and marble majesty of the Imperator Bridge.

Colonel Loic commanded the PDF forces stationed at the mighty city of bridges, bolstered by nearly three thousand Guardsmen of Shield Command. Alerted to the danger facing them, Colonel Loic and Captain Gerber of the 44th rallied their soldiers to face the tau with commendable speed, and the first attacks were beaten back with only minor losses.

The rest of the night was spent in hard-fought skirmishes as tau scout teams probed the outer defences of the city, but the assault on Olzetyn was only one of the tau offensives.

THE SLUM-CITY OF Jotusburg eternally sweltered beneath a hot roof of rank smog. The teeming slums and wretched hives were home to the millions of Mechanicus labourers that toiled in the forges and weapon shops of the Diacrian Belt. Hundreds of miles of silos, ore barns, milling hangars, generator stations and smelteries covered the foothills of the Sudinal Mountains, a vertiginous barrier that kept the cities safe from the howling, polluted winds of the southern wastes.

The south-eastern haunches of the continent were sprawling anthills of iron-sheathed forges and stone chimneys that produced much of the energy and raw materials for the manufactorum of Pavonis.

But those anthills had been roused to swift action.

As alert bells chimed through the squalid alleys and rat-runs of the reeking city, flickering ether-lamps were lit, and grimy units of dirt-stained PDF hurried to their muster stations. Units of tech-guard and skitarii efficiently mobilised and took up their posts, yet they were a small fraction of the defences. Guardsmen of Banner Command went to high alert as word came from Lord Winterbourne that they were to stand ready for combat operations.

The first warning that the enemy were inbound came, once again, from the Hydra flak tanks. The combat-logisters of each vehicle swiftly registered multiple solid returns from high-altitude flyers moving in from the west. With a weapons free order from their commander in chief, the flak tanks opened fire, and bright streams of shells and explosions burst within the smog above Jotusburg in diffuse yellow flares of igniting gases.

The defenders of Jotusburg watched the strobing skies as ominous shapes twitched the fog above them, waiting with fear-taut nerves for the high-pitched shriek of descending bombs or screaming drop-ships on attack runs. The tension was unbearable, but as minute after minute passed, it seemed the tau craft might simply be flying on a reconnaissance mission.

That hope was cruelly dashed when the smog was split by hundreds of glittering discs falling from the sky like a rain of silver coins dropped from a giant's hand. The sky was thick with the falling shapes as nearly a thousand gun drones dropped en-masse from converted Tiger Shark bombers.

The drones slashed downwards, weapon pods slung beneath the upper disc sections firing indiscriminately at whatever targets presented themselves. The drones split into roaming hunter-killer squads, zipping through the warren of twisting streets, arched processionals and darkened hubs with their weapons blazing.

They moved without pause, strafing assembling tech-guard, ambushing running PDF units before vanishing into the fume-laced shadows. Power relays, vox-masts and transit hubs were attacked, as well as anything else that could be destroyed to hamper Imperial response.

The streets of Jotusburg echoed with screams and bellows of confusion as the drones infested the city like a virus, never stopping, always hunting, and the mobilisation that had begun with such speed ground to a virtual halt as the city's defenders turned inwards to purge the enemy from their midst.

ALL HE HAD known since waking was pain, excruciating, maddening pain that threatened to send his mind screaming into a dark corner of madness to escape it. Even with the morphia, his body was one seething mass of agony. No corner of his flesh was exempt, and he wept bitter tears from lidless eyes.

Gaetan Baltazar stared unflinchingly at the ruin of his body. His chest, torso and limbs were wrapped in swathes of burn dressing, his hands little more than fused claws of bone enclosed in sterile gel packs. Any semblance of humanity had been burned away in the fires that had destroyed the Templum Fabricae.

Though he couldn't see his reflection, he knew his head too was a scarred mess of blackened tissue, one eye a dribbling, glutinous mess. Through the fog of pain and medication, he knew he was lying supine on a soft bed within a vaulted chamber of pale stone.

Devotional banners depicting armoured warrior-women protecting a shining candle hung above him. The air reeked of incense, counterseptic and death.

The Hospice of the Eternal Candle…

How had he come to this place?

His memory was like a fractured pane of glass, each shard reflecting a different aspect of the horror that saw him confined to a bed within the hospice and tended by white-robed Sisters Hospitaller with expressions that alternated between horror and pity.

Gaetan remembered the flames and the screams. He remembered the shimmering invisible forms of the daemons that ran riot through the Templum Fabricae.

Most of all, he remembered the fire of the terrible weapons mounted on their arms.

No sooner had he seen them gathering, than they dropped from the iron girders of the chancel. Slivers of refracted light gave them a semblance of form: broad, hunched and heavy enough to smash the marble slabs of the nave as they landed. Gaetan had blinked furiously until their shapes finally resolved, and he saw the armoured daemons as they opened fire.

Blazing tongues of fire ripped through the templum, and screams of panic and pain soon followed them. The unrelenting echoes of gunfire formed a brutal hymnal of death as the hundreds gathered in the Templum Fabricae sought to escape the deadly salvoes, running for the wide doors at the end of the nave or hurling themselves beneath the splintering pews.

Escape was impossible as the invisible daemons moved through the templum with methodical remorselessness, walking streams of explosive shells through the panicked mass of fleeing worshippers. Braziers, lamps and candles were overturned in his congregation's desperation to escape, and flames licked at the walls. The statue of the Emperor rocked under a series of impacts, and shards of burning anthracite fell from His splintering form.

Furious rage built within Gaetan, and he swept his eviscerator from the altar. He could not tell how many daemons there were, but he had to fight them, and he hurled himself at the nearest blurred outline.

'In the Emperor's name, I smite thee hip and thigh!' he screamed, bringing the monstrous eviscerator down on the daemon's head. Adamantine teeth ripped into the daemon in a flaring shower of sparks, hydraulic fluids and spraying blood. It fell to the ground, and, as it did so, the veil of illusion that kept its repulsive form concealed was dispelled.

Its cloven body was armoured in olive-green plates, its bulbous, elongated head like the carapace of some hideous insect. This was no daemon; this was some form of tau warrior, a trespasser and defiler of this holy place. Captain Ventris had been right after all, the warriors of the tau were on Pavonis, and they sought to tear the heart of its faith from its people.

Blood poured from the beast, and Gaetan looked up to see sheets of flames ripping through the templum, consuming worshippers, pews and the silken banners with equal hunger. Gaetan dragged his eviscerator from the corpse of the tau warrior, and set off towards the nearest blurred outline of his enemies as hot chips of stone fell around him in a black rain.

The aliens saw him coming and turned their guns upon him, but Gaetan had no thought for his survival. All that mattered was that the vile xenos be made to pay for what they had done. Time compressed, and Gaetan knew he would never reach the alien warriors before they cut him down.

Then, the head of the Emperor's statue fell from its shoulders and exploded into shards of hard, hot coals as it struck the altar. The alien warriors were swept away in the explosion of razor-sharp fragments. The impact hurled Gaetan from his feet, and he landed on the soft and yielding flesh of dead bodies. He rolled from them in horror as flames bloomed around him, the heat of them scorching his skin and burning the hair from his scalp. He surged to his feet, the fabric of his robes ablaze and the pain unimaginable.

In moments, he was a living torch, a burning fury of insensate agony. He ran, his limbs obeying the instinctual urge for self-preservation as they carried him along the nave towards the golden doors that led to the cold night beyond. Gaetan felt the skin slough from his shins, the fabric of his robes searing to his flesh and the skin of his face peeling back under the awful, intolerable heat of the merciless flames. His temple burned behind him, but he had no thought but survival now, and even that seemed certain to be denied.

He knew not how long he had run for, but he remembered screams of fear and horror, blessed cool air on what remained of his skin, and the twin joy and pain of fire suppressants bathing his body. Then he knew darkness, agonising pain beyond imagining and almost beyond sanity. He knew shouts, lights and stinging needles, faces peering at him, and voices calling his name.

Hymns. He remembered hymns.

He woke to pain, and wept as it bathed his entire body, knowing that, beneath the counterseptic-soaked bandages that wrapped him he was barely alive, that his life hung by the thinnest of threads. Pain balms allowed his mind to wrench itself free of physical sensation, retreating into the furthest corners of his mind, but, as the agony overcame each dose, he would be dragged back to his misery.

Rows of beds stretched out either side of him, their wretched, miserable occupants filling the echoing chamber with their cries. The Sisters of the Eternal Candle that tended to his ruined flesh mouthed banal platitudes, but he had long since stopped listening to them, repulsed by the pity in their eyes. All they saw was a ruined preacher, a man destined to spend the last breaths of his life in terrible, unendurable agony. They sought to ease him into his death, thinking they did him a mercy.

Only one visitor to his bedside had come without pity in his heart.

'Truly you endure the price of peace and forgiveness,' said Prelate Culla, standing above Gaetan with a copy of the Imperial Creed held close to his chest. The predicant of the Lavrentian regiment was a towering presence, an emerald-robed warrior priest with a red chainsword sheathed over his shoulder.

Culla's shaven head reflected the weak light of the hospice chamber, and his beard had been braided into two forks, one silver and one black. Golden flecks in his eyes glittered with faith, and Gaetan winced as he pictured the fire that had crippled him.

His blistered tongue licked the lipless gash in his face that was all that remained of his mouth, and he heard the hiss of the atomiser as it puffed a mist of sterile moisture over his eyes.

'Culla,' he said, his voice cracked and little more than a rasping hiss, 'if you have come to gloat, leave me be. I am dying.'

'Aye,' agreed Culla, 'you are, and I come to you as a fellow keeper of the flame.'

Gaetan searched Culla's face for mockery, but finding none said, 'What do you want?'

'You are a defender of the faith, Gaetan Baltazar,' said Culla. 'Though ye walk through the fires of the iniquitous, ye shall rise again to smite the blasphemer, the heretic. Aye, and the alien too. Truly, I envy you, Clericus Fabricae.'

'Then you are a fool. I am dying,' hissed Gaetan. 'Why would you envy me?'

Culla reached down and placed his hand on Gaetan's chest. He winced at the pain as Culla said, 'Suffering brings us closer to the Emperor. We are clothed in His image, yet we walk freely beneath the sun while He suffers in our name upon the Golden Throne. In pain, we draw closer to Him and know a measure of his sacrifice. All men of faith should rejoice in such a fate. You will live to fight again, my friend.'

'We are not friends, Culla,' gasped Gaetan. 'All you preach is death and hatred.'

'That is all there is, Gaetan,' pressed Culla. 'Can you not see that? Hatred is what keeps us strong, what gives us the strength to defeat our enemies. Surely you now see the deception of tolerance? The evil of acceptance? There must be no peace amongst the stars, Gaetan, not while unclean xenos species and unbelievers are allowed to exist. Rejoice, for an eternity of carnage and battle awaits us. Embrace your hatred, for it is necessary. Hatred is good. You cannot tell me that you do not hate the tau for what they have done to you.'

Culla's words were like whips of fire on his soul, for he felt the pain of them even beyond that of his burned flesh. He *did* hate the tau. He hated them for the agony he suffered with every last shred of his life. He tried to hold onto his belief in redemption, forgiveness and brotherhood amongst the stars, but a tidal wave of bile and venom washed it away.

Gaetan wept at the ease with which his convictions crumbled before this hatred, and Culla smiled as it took shape in his heart. The Lavrentian preacher bent and lifted something heavy from beside the bed, placing it next to his hand.

'You understand at last, my friend,' said Culla.

'Yes,' said Gaetan, curling his clawed, burned hand around the blackened grip of his eviscerator, 'I do, and it breaks my heart.'

'Olzetyn is sure to be next,' said Lord Winterbourne, cradling his wounded arm in a sling as he stared at the gloomy projection on the hololithic table. The Lavrentian colonel had changed out of his bloodied shirt and uniform jacket, but was otherwise as Uriel had last seen him in the mountains. 'Jotusburg is infested with those damn drones, and Praxedes is… well, it's just gone. Damned if I thought I'd see the day a Command of the Lavrentians would be taken so easily.'

Uriel sympathised with Winterbourne, having learned of the death of Major Ornella and the night of fighting on the west of the continent. The morning had brought little respite for the Imperial forces. The 4th Company were ready to go to war, and the remaining Commands of Lavrentians had assumed a defensive posture in response to the tau invasion, but there was no doubting they were still reeling from the speed of the attack.

Winterbourne, Uriel and Clausel gathered in the command centre of Fortress Idaeus, watching as hazy icons flickered on the surface of the projection table. The wounded vorehound sat at its master's feet, gnawing on a bone that didn't look as though it came from any livestock Uriel knew.

The data-slates embedded in the command centre's walls streamed with what information the surveyor gear on the roof could gather, and Chapter serfs passed it to the Techmarine hard-plugged into the throne at the end of the command centre. Harkus was fighting for his life in the Apothecarion, and Techmarine Achamen had taken his place. Binary code whispered from his lips as he sifted through the data being fed to him, and relayed it to the hololithic table.

'None of us expected it. That was our first mistake. Let us make sure it is our last,' said Uriel. 'But Praxedes *did* fall, and we need to get our forces moving to meet the tau advance. The xenos fight a rapid war, and, unless we act now, we will be too late to stop them.'

Clausel said, 'Then we must take the fight to them, immediately.'

'And we will, but not without first planning that fight,' said Uriel, indicating the table. 'These are the last plots we received from the *Vae Victus,* before Admiral Tiberius had to pull back to the Caernus asteroid belt.'

'Pull back?' said Winterbourne. 'Damn, but I was counting on your vessel to pull our backsides from the fire, Uriel. Why the devil has she pulled back?'

'The tau have a number of ships in orbit more powerful than the *Vae Victus,* at least two carriers, a warship and a number of escorts.'

'A small fleet for a planetary invasion,' noted Clausel. 'Even a system patrol fleet could defeat that. Would that we had one!'

'Agreed,' said Uriel. 'Admiral Tiberius postulates that this is an explorator expedition, not a full invasion fleet, perhaps a probe to test the defences of this arc of the Eastern Fringe in preparation for a renewed assault.'

'Then it is even more imperative we defeat it,' said Clausel.

'How recent are these images?' asked Winterbourne, looking down at the host of red and blue icons on and around the representations of the cities.

'They are around three hours old,' said Uriel.

'Then they are as good as useless,' snapped Winterbourne. 'The tau move at speed, and this will bear no resemblance to the situation on the ground.'

The vorehound's head snapped up at Winterbourne's angry tone, a low growl building in its throat.

'True enough,' said Uriel, 'but it is all we have, and, if nothing else, it may give us an indication of our own dispositions and plans.'

'Plans? How can we plan to fight without knowing the disposition of the enemy?' shouted Winterbourne. 'We should be hammering that tau you captured at Koudelkar's estate for intelligence. He'll know what their game is. Him and that traitor, Mykola Shonai, they'll have information we can use, I'll warrant.'

'I have faith that Jenna Sharben will get them to talk,' said Uriel.

'Pah! Sharben is an amateur,' said Winterbourne. 'I've sent Culla to get the truth. He'll break them, and then we'll learn something of value.'

'Perhaps,' said Uriel, but Winterbourne wasn't finished yet.

'The tau have us on the back foot, Uriel. The initiative lies with them, how do you propose we get it back?'

'We fight,' said Uriel, leaning over the plotting table. 'We meet the invaders head-on, and we wrest the initiative from them at the end of bolter and the edge of a chainsword. The loss of Major Ornella was a blow, but you need to control your grief, Nathaniel.'

Winterbourne looked set to retort angrily, before realising that Uriel had called him by his first name. He took a deep breath and pinched the bridge of his nose between his thumb and forefinger.

'Yes, of course, of course, you're right, Uriel,' sighed Winterbourne. 'I'm sorry, I'm just a bit shaken up, you understand. Alithea dying, Praxedes falling… it's a lot to take in.'

'That is no excuse,' said Clausel, towering over the colonel. 'You command a regiment of the Emperor's soldiers. You do not have the luxury of grief while there is a war yet to fight. Mourn the dead after the songs of victory are sung.'

Uriel locked his gaze with Winterbourne's. 'Now that we understand one another, let us look at what we have available to fight.'

For the next hour, Uriel, Winterbourne and Clausel discussed the strategic situation as best they could. Communication was the key to any response, and with the Kaliz Array down Lavrentian techs had rigged a linked series of encrypted master vox-units to allow coordination of the various commands.

Convoys of armoured vehicles were, even now, en route to Olzetyn, Jotusburg, Madorn and Altemaxa to deliver the cryptographic codes to allow coordination of forces. A few had already reached their destinations, and information was slowly beginning to flow between Imperial forces on the status of the defences.

Praxedes was clearly in enemy hands and was no doubt acting as a bridgehead from which the tau carriers could freely drop fresh troops and supplies to the planet's surface. If the invasion were to be defeated, Praxedes would need to be taken, but before any such assault could be launched, the tau had to be contained. Initial attacks against the redoubts at Olzetyn had been beaten back, but it was unlikely the tau could be held there for long without support.

'What about your forces at Jotusburg?' asked Uriel.

Winterbourne flipped through a plastek binder. 'There's still fighting in the streets, but it's a warren down there. It's pretty confused, but I'm getting reports of sporadic ambushes and power disruptions. Banner Command is under Captain Luzaine, and he has three thousand men and six hundred armoured vehicles. Factor in some six thousand PDF and maybe a skitarii legion and you're looking at close to ten thousand soldiers at full alert. Aside from the kill teams hunting drone infiltrators, Luzaine hasn't yet reported any significant contact with the enemy.'

'And what of the Mechanicus facilities?' asked Clausel.

'They've suffered damage,' said Winterbourne, 'but Magos Vaal assures me that supplies of ammunition and weapons will be unaffected once the Hundred Rituals of Reparation are complete.'

'The war could be won or lost by then,' protested Clausel.

'I thought you of all people would understand the importance of ritual, Chaplain.'

Clausel did not reply, but Uriel sensed his grudging acceptance of Winterbourne's words.

'Then we will plan our fight accordingly,' said Uriel. 'What is the strength of Shield Command, Nathaniel?'

'Captain Gerber has two and a half thousand soldiers and four hundred tanks,' replied Winterbourne. 'Colonel Loic is there too, with perhaps five thousand PDF. They're good lads, but I can't vouch for them in a fight. Only a few of them saw action during the rebellion, the rest are boys and old men who've never fired a rifle in anger.'

'Then we need to reinforce Olzetyn,' stated Uriel. 'It is the main route to Brandon Gate, and the tau appreciate the symbolism of capturing a planetary capital as well as any foe. I think you are right, colonel, they will seek to smash through Olzetyn and seize it as soon as possible, hoping that its capture will break the will of Pavonis to win.'

'They might be right,' said Clausel. 'The fighting spirit of this world is lacking. Its people are more concerned with making money than doing battle, but why would the tau bother to fight their way through Olzetyn? Surely with their skimmer tanks they don't need to capture the bridge city? They can cross the rivers anywhere.'

'To attack on such a wide front will take time and numbers,' said Winterbourne. 'It means spreading their forces, and, if your Admiral Tiberius is correct, and this *is* an explorator fleet, they probably don't have the numbers to mount such an offensive.'

Uriel nodded. 'And if they can break through quickly they will split our forces in two.'

'We can't allow that to happen,' said Winterbourne. 'If it does we are lost.'

'I will lead the bulk of the 4th to Olzetyn,' said Uriel. 'It is imperative the city holds. The tau need to win quickly, and we need to hold them for long enough for reinforcements to arrive.'

'And how long will that be?'

'I am not sure,' admitted Uriel. 'Admiral Tiberius will have sent word to Macragge and sector command. Help will be on the way. We just have to hold on long enough for it to get here.'

'What do you require of me, Uriel?' asked Winterbourne, standing to attention.

'Guard our flanks. I believe the tau will seek to make a decisive thrust through Olzetyn, but it is also likely they will try to encircle us and trap us in a pocket. If they succeed, this war is over.'

Winterbourne saluted with his good arm. 'You can count on the 44th.'

'I know I can, Nathaniel,' said Uriel.

At that moment, Techmarine Achamen emitted a blurt of binary code that cut across their words. The augmitters fitted within the hololithic table crackled to life as they translated the binary into Imperial Gothic. The artificially rendered voice was devoid of any sense of urgency, but the words galvanised everyone who heard them.

'Incoming enemy aircraft,' said the voice. 'Multiple target tracks inbound on this location. Assessment: altitude, bearing and formation consistent with airborne assault patterns.'

TWELVE

THOUGH KOUDELKAR HAD no frame of reference by which to judge its merits, the prison camp on the shores of Praxedes was certainly more comfortable than he had been led to believe such institutions were typically appointed. He and his mother had been given a private chamber within a smooth-walled structure containing another fifty prisoners, though the soldiers shared one long dormitory room and a single ablutions block.

Built on one of the vacant landing platforms that jutted out to sea, the structure was clean and comfortable, blandly furnished, softly lit and apparently impervious to graffiti or carving. Along with another twenty such structures, Koudelkar's new home sat within an enclosure bounded by thin posts topped with domed discs and patrolled by armoured squads of what he learned were called Fire Warriors.

Some Guardsmen had tried to escape on their first day of imprisonment, but painful jolts of invisible energy coursing between the posts had hurled them back. Koudelkar sat on the steps of his structure, looking out to sea and enjoying the warm sunlight as it tanned his skin. His mother was inside, lying on her back and staring at the featureless ceiling, almost catatonic in her resignation.

'How can you just sit there?' asked Lortuen Perjed, limping unsteadily now that the tau had taken his walking cane. 'We should be planning our escape.'

'Escape? To where?'

'It doesn't matter where, Koudelkar,' said Lortuen, sitting beside him. 'And it doesn't even matter if we succeed. All that matters is that we try. I've been speaking to some of the senior sergeants and they agree that it is our duty as Imperial citizens to inconvenience these xenos scum any way we can.'

Koudelkar looked over at the rippling force barrier that surrounded their enclosure. Beyond the unseen energy field, a number of heavily armed battlesuits moved through the subjugated port city as yet more of the wide-winged craft descended from orbit with fresh supplies and soldiers.

'I don't think we'd inconvenience them that much, Lortuen.'

'So we just sit here, meek and compliant?'

He sensed Adept Perjed's steely glare and shrugged. 'What would you have me do, Lortuen? Organise a revolution? We are surrounded by an enemy army, and I don't think we'd last too long if it came down to a fight.'

'It doesn't matter,' pressed Lortuen. 'You are the Planetary Governor and these men look to you for leadership.'

'These men?' hissed Koudelkar. 'These men are Lavrentians, they think of me as little more than a puppet ruler that they're here to watch as much as to serve.

They don't need me for leadership, but if you want to foment rebellion, then go ahead and die for it.'

'A man should have the courage to die for what he believes is right, and fighting these aliens is what's right.' Perjed waved a liver-spotted hand at the tau warriors. 'We don't know what's going on beyond Praxedes. By sitting here and doing nothing, more and more of these abominable Fire Warriors might be freed to fight on the front lines. If we cause trouble, then they have to stay here and guard us. That could make all the difference in the war.'

'You don't know that.'

'No, I don't,' agreed Lortuen, 'but I could not live with myself if fighting men died because I did nothing. How will you look yourself in the mirror every day with those deaths on your conscience? Think of your honour!'

'We are prisoners of war,' said Koudelkar. 'What honour do we have?'

'Only what we bring with us,' said Lortuen wearily, lapsing into silence.

Lortuen's words struck a chord within Koudelkar, and he knew he should be filled with righteous anger and hatred for the aliens. But instead of anger, all he felt was fear and a growing sense of abandonment. He looked away from Lortuen, gazing out to sea once more.

The awful carnage at Galtrigil was still fresh in his mind: the spraying blood, the torn up bodies blown apart from the inside by superheated plasma, or cut in half by sawing blasts of bullets. He could still smell the stench of blood and emptied bladders. He could hear the frantic screams of the dying men before more bullets had silenced them.

Though battle still raged, the battlesuit with the flaming sphere insignia had carried him and his mother from the fighting, before heading south in a series of running bounds, while its companion carried Lortuen. His mother had screamed nearly the entire journey south to Praxedes, and while Koudelkar had been frightened, he had not been unduly worried. If this El'esaven planned to kill them, he could have simply gunned them down when the bullets started flying.

Clearly, the tau recognised some worth in having him as a captive, and now, a few days after their arrival at the Praxedes camp, Koudelkar had begun to form an idea of what his value might be.

'I wonder if my aunt is still alive,' he said apropos of nothing. 'Perhaps she is in some other prison camp. Or maybe the Ultramarines rescued her.'

Lortuen grunted. 'I know which fate will be worse for her.'

'You must hate her,' said Koudelkar.

'Don't you? She consorted with xenos, and, thanks to her, we are in their prison camp.'

'I am angry with her, yes, but try as I might I can't hate her. It must have been galling to see everything she and others had worked for over the years taken from them like toys from an unruly child.'

'Pavonis had rebelled,' Lortuen said, as if Koudelkar needed reminding. 'It was only my recommendation that allowed Mykola to retain her role as governor. Look where *that* got us!'

'Yes, but for the remainder of her term of office as Planetary Governor, Pavonis was, for all intents and purposes, under martial law, with the governor relegated to a figurehead role.'

'You tried to change that, I know,' said Lortuen. 'Perhaps I should have let you.'

Koudelkar sighed. 'I believe I was making some progress too, but all that good work has been undone by my aunt's meddling. This will never be our planet again, will it? Not now.'

'No, it won't,' agreed Lortuen, shaking his head. 'Even if the tau are defeated, Pavonis will be turned into a garrison world. One incident might be forgiven in time, but two?'

Koudelkar had known that would be Lortuen's answer, and he fought against the bitterness that was taking root within him at the unfeeling, heartless bureaucracy of far distant Terra, a world he had never seen and probably never would.

'Tell me,' said Koudelkar, wishing to change the subject, 'have you seen any sign of Aun'rai since we were brought here?'

'No.'

'Nor have I. Strange, don't you think? I have come to the conclusion that he was more than simply an envoy. In fact, looking at our guards, it seems as though they are beside themselves at his absence. I believe that Aun'rai is a personage of some importance, perhaps even of a similar rank to me.'

'It's possible,' said Lortuen. 'El'esaven deferred to him, so I imagine he is important.'

'Perhaps the Ultramarines captured Aun'rai and they will use him as a bargaining chip to secure our release.'

Lortuen laughed, though Koudelkar heard precious little humour in the sound.

'What?' he asked. 'Did I say something funny?'

The old man shook his head sadly. 'No, quite the opposite in fact.'

'Explain.'

'If Captain Ventris did indeed capture Aun'rai, then exchanging him for us will be the last thing on his mind, I assure you. In any case, we have been taken prisoner by xenos and our lives are forfeit.'

'What are you talking about?'

'Don't you see?' explained Lortuen. 'We are tainted by contact with these aliens, and even if we are rescued we will probably face an executioner's bullet.'

'You're joking, surely?'

'No. Remember, I served an inquisitor of the Ordo Xenos. I know how these things work.'

'But I am a Planetary Governor!' protested Koudelkar.

'And you think you are not expendable?' asked Lortuen sadly. 'Trust me, Koudelkar, the Imperium will shed no tears for us if we die here.'

URIEL WATCHED FROM the commander's hatch of his Rhino as flocks of wide-bodied tau aircraft swooped in over Brandon Gate. Five Rhinos had surged from Fortress Idaeus, racing to plug the biggest gap in the city's defences. A pair of Predator battle tanks completed Uriel's armoured convoy, one on each flank with their turret-mounted autocannons traversing as the gunners searched for targets.

Imperial Guard Hydras filled the air with explosive flak, and a number of tau craft vanished in clouds of fiery debris. They tumbled from the sky, but many more came in their wake. This was no bombing raid or show of force. This was an assault, and only the timely warning from Techmarine Achamen had given the Ultramarines time to deploy.

The tactical feed from the command centre was projected on Uriel's visor, and he followed the spinning dance of hostile icons as they circled the city, before separating in a graceful ballet that would have been admirable had it been an Imperial display of prowess. The larger of the tau craft were flying in low along Highway 236 on a course for the southern Commercia Gate. Winterbourne's tanks and Guardsmen were ready to meet any force that deployed against the city's main approach, and Uriel had faith in their ability to stand.

'Echelon formation,' he ordered, and the trailing Rhinos fanned out smoothly behind his. Fire and noise filled the air, and, though his attention was fixed firmly ahead of him, Uriel saw more tau aircraft spinning downwards and trailing thick plumes of smoke.

A thudding series of booming explosions sounded behind him, and Uriel risked a glance over his shoulder in time to see a monstrously large pillar of smoke and fire rising from the south wall. Streaking arcs of missile fire pounded the gate, and strange, insect-like creatures dropped from the sky on wide, flaring wings, but Uriel could afford to spare the devastation no more attention.

His vehicle halted on the reverse slope of a ridge of crushed stone. Uriel hauled himself from the command hatch and dropped to the ground, running, crouched over, to the crest of the ridge to stare down into the latest battleground of the war. The south-eastern wedge of the city looked much as it had during the latter stages of the rebellion, a desolate hinterland of collapsed structures, rubble and heaped debris. The walls by the Justice Gate had been blown down in the de Valtos rebellion, leaving a readymade access point into the heart of Brandon Gate.

If an enemy were to hold this region, they would be able to infiltrate the entire city.

Uriel scanned the ground, forming a three-dimensional map of the area in his head. Jenna Sharben had told him it was a favourite training ground for her new cadre of enforcers, and he could see why.

Plenty of places to hide and lots of cover.

Minefields, razor wire and Thunderfire cannons had blocked entry through this breach, but smoke billowed from deep craters where compact grid formations of missile impacts had cleared a path. Huge gaps had been torn in the lines of razor wire, flattened areas of molten ground showed where mines had been detonated, and the shattered remains of a number of the automated weapon systems littered the wasteland.

The tactician in Uriel was forced to admire the methodical precision of the tau forces' preparatory bombardment, even as he knew it would make this battle more difficult. Supporting forces were already en-route from Fortress Idaeus to refortify the area, but Uriel's warriors would have to deny it to the enemy first. A number of tau skimmer tanks were already riding over the twisted remains of the shattered wall, while dismounted Fire Warriors darted through the rubble.

The sheer amount of debris would make it impossible to hold this area simply with guns; the tau would need to be pushed out with blades and brute strength.

'Disembark!' yelled Uriel. 'Assault pattern Konor!'

GAETAN WAS WOKEN by the brutal thump of explosions and the crack of small-arms fire. At first, he thought he was reliving the horror of the attack on the Templum Fabricae, but dismissed that thought as he realised the city was under attack.

Rising from a drug-induced slumber, his gaze was drawn towards the gentle light of the stained glass windows that ran the length of the ward, each brightly coloured and depicting the Emperor in his role as a healer and saviour, ministering to the sick, dispensing alms to the needy and welcoming the dispossessed to his mercy.

Foolishness, he now knew. Mercy and forgiveness had no place in the Imperial Creed, such things were for those cosseted in far-off shrine worlds, where the threat of the xenos, the heretic and the mutant were shadowy bogeymen to cow the weak-minded.

Bright light flashed behind the windows, and they blew out in a storm of whirling fragments. Hot winds of explosions billowed into the Hospice, and Gaetan screamed as flying shards of glass sliced his face. Fragments lodged in his skull, but the pain only served to fuel his anger and strength. Hate swelled in his breast as fighting sounded from somewhere within the walls of the Hospice. The screams of wounded men and women echoed through the ward, but Gaetan paid them no mind. Another explosion sounded nearby, and the great doors to the ward were smashed asunder.

Flames billowed from the chamber beyond, and he finally understood what was happening.

The daemon creatures had come to finish him off.

Part of him recognised how unlikely that was, but the pain and trauma of his wounds had driven the rational part of Gaetan's mind to the furthest corners of his skull. In his mind, the tau were coming to finish him off, but he swore that the hateful xenos creatures would not find him meekly awaiting his fate. He was Gaetan Baltazar, Clericus Fabricae of Pavonis, and a warrior of the Emperor.

If the tau wanted him dead, they would find him on his feet with a weapon in hand.

He gritted his teeth as he pushed himself into a sitting position. Fire screamed along every nerve-ending in his body, but he fought against it as the sound of screams and gunfire sounded even louder than before.

Gaetan ripped away the wires and tubes attached to his body with his free hand, and the machines next to his bed warbled with alerts. He roared in pain as he swung his legs to the floor and saw a neat pile of dark clothing sitting on a stool next to his eviscerator.

Gaetan's lipless mouth pulled back over his teeth as he saw that they were fresh vestments. He guessed that Culla had brought them for him, and swiftly dressed, the pain of the rough fabric on his burned skin a blessed reminder of his duty to the Emperor.

The robes were those of a Mortifex, and Gaetan tied them at his waist with a jagged belt of iron hooks that pierced the black robes and pricked his flesh. Until now, he had always looked upon the cult of the Mortifex with distaste, thinking of them as deranged lunatics who sought only to die in the service of the Emperor. Culla had chosen well.

His fused fingers reached for the handle of his eviscerator.

Gaetan looked at the flaring eagle wings that formed the hand-guard of his weapon, and his mouth opened wide in a skeletal grin. Just holding the weapon gave him strength, and he pushed himself to his feet, the pain vanishing in the time it took to notice its absence. He took a deep breath, feeling hot air rasp in his tortured lungs. The burnt iron taste of war came from beyond the windows, and Gaetan rejoiced in the bark of gunfire echoing through the city's canyons of stone and steel.

War and death were calling to him, and he could no more resist their siren song than he could stop the beat of his heart. This was the reality of faith on the Eastern Fringe, and, though he grieved at the realisation, he knew it was by such faith that his race endured amongst the stars.

He set off towards the ruined doors, and passed through them in time to see a host of armoured warriors pushing into the Hospice. Their armour and weapons were unmistakably alien, and he squeezed the activation trigger of his eviscerator. The weapon roared to life with a throaty growl, its adamantium teeth a deadly cutting edge that could shatter steel and tear through the thickest armour.

The aliens saw him, and he relished their cries of terror. Weapons turned on him, but he was already amongst the tau, hacking left and right with his terrible blade. Blood sprayed the walls of the chamber as he cut through them, the roar of his eviscerator drowning out their death screams.

The battle was over in seconds, the blood of his victims soaking his robes and gleaming wetly in the firelight from outside. Gaetan lifted his eviscerator to the heavens.

'The Emperor set a fire in their hearts that they might burn the iniquitous and the impure from his sight!' he screamed. 'And the light of that flame shall be a beacon to the faithful, a light that shines in the darkest places!'

The words he had rejected as a novice were now the sweetest clarion call in his soul, and he recognised the truth of them even as he despaired. Beyond the walls of the Hospice, Gaetan could hear the sound of battle, the hungry scream of war: the voracious predator ever eager for flesh and bone to grind to dust, and eternally hungry for souls to send to their ending.

This was the reality of life.

This was the essence of death.

Gaetan Baltazar hefted his eviscerator, and went out into the maelstrom of battle with a song of doom on his lips.

A GROUP OF Fire Warriors huddled in the cover of a wide crater that had once been a minefield, firing over the crater's lip of compressed rubble and dirt. Behind them, a blackened Devilfish lay on its side, black smoke spewing from its shattered engines. Burning lines of tau rifle-fire hammered the knotted mass of rusted girders that Uriel and his squad sheltered behind, and he ducked back as white sparks flared from the impacts.

Uriel slammed a fresh magazine into his bolter and racked the slide. He rose to a crouch, ducking his head quickly around his cover to appraise the course of the battle as the tau attempt to force a path through the breach continued.

Gunfire pulsed and roared across the wasteland in withering streams, the killing ground between the walls and the city ablaze with wrecked vehicles and tau corpses. The Fire Warriors wore substantial armour, but it was no match for disciplined volleys of bolter-fire.

Behind Uriel, the Predators poured fire into the battlefield, their lascannons hurling unimaginably powerful spears of energy to obliterate enemy tanks, while their autocannons chewed up Fire Warriors in roaring salvoes of high-velocity shells. Both had taken hits, their armoured hulls dented and burned, but both were still shooting. Between them, they had already claimed nearly a dozen skimmer tanks, each of their kills spewing smoke and flames as the warriors they carried burned to death inside.

Spread across the crest of the ridge, Devastator Squad Aktis fired deadly accurate missiles into the enemy: whickering, explosive storms of frags keeping the enemy pinned down as Uriel's squad advanced directly towards the breach in the walls. Tactical Squads Theron and Nestor pushed out on Uriel's flanks, relentless volleys of bolter-fire raking the rubble-strewn ground before them. Sporadic fire lanced out to meet them, and, though a few warriors had fallen, Uriel saw that none had been killed.

The warriors Uriel led were normally designated Squad Learchus, but while their sergeant hunted for

Governor Koudelkar, they had temporarily been renamed squad Ventris. Learchus had insisted on the change, and Uriel recognised the honour for what it was. These were Learchus's men, and it was Uriel's duty to watch over them until such time as the sergeant returned.

As Learchus had done for the 4th Company, so Uriel would do for his squad.

The Fire Warriors had been held so far, each alien APC blown apart before it could reach a position of cover. Two of the heavier tau tanks sheltered behind the wrecks, darting out to shoot under the cover of salvoes of missiles launched from support tanks beyond the walls. Explosions shook the ground, and piles of debris rained down from the sagging structures around the edges of the battlefield, but the strikes were undirected, thanks to the pinpoint accuracy of Uriel's Devastators in taking out the enemy artillery spotters.

Uriel's visor darkened as a blazing rod of molten light stabbed overhead and struck one of the Predators on its armoured front glacis. The hyper-velocity slug tore through the tank's hull as though it were as insubstantial as mist. Uriel watched as a plasma trail of kinetic energy ignited the weapon charges inside the Predator, and its turret blew off with a thunderclap of electrical discharge and fire. The top half of the tank spun ten metres into the air before slamming down to earth with a dreadfully final clang. Uriel knew that no one inside could have survived such terrible violence.

As the smoke from the explosion cleared and Uriel fought his shock at the destruction of the battle tank, he looked up to see a pair of bobbing silver-skinned drones hovering a few metres behind his position. He swung his bolter around, before seeing that neither drone appeared to be armed. Each flying disc sported a bulbous device slung on a rotating gimbal mount that looked more like a picter than a weapon. Were the tau recording the battle for study?

Then, he saw a faint cluster of concentric circles of light projected onto the girder next to him and realised the threat these devices represented.

'Valkyrie's Mark!' he shouted, vaulting the iron girders towards the Fire Warriors in the crater. 'With me!'

His warriors obeyed instantly, surging to their feet, and following him over the top as a screaming roar of guided missiles streaked from beyond the walls and slashed downward. Barely a second later, a pounding series of impacts slammed into the ground. Uriel was hurled from his feet as the shock wave of the detonation obliterated the girders and blasted a six-metre crater in the earth.

Uriel felt the heat of the blast wash over him, keeping his bolter pulled in tight to his chest. Smoke obscured his vision, and the ringing echoes of the detonation pounded within his helmet. He rolled to his feet, instantly regaining his sense of spatial awareness as his auto-senses picked up the crunch of earth underfoot, and shouted, 'Incoming. On my mark.'

Figures moved in the billowing cloud of dust and falling debris, and he pulled the trigger, firing off a rapid volley into the emerging shapes. He heard screams and three of them dropped instantly. A blazing beam of light punched into his chest, and he staggered as his breastplate hissed and spat bright gobbets of molten ceramite.

He fired another burst, and ducked beneath a spray of gunfire as the Fire Warriors advanced under the shadow of the bombardment. Uriel slung his bolter and drew his sword, the rest of Squad Ventris following his example. The tau expected to find them battered and disorientated, and Uriel relished the chance to make them pay for that error.

He lifted his sword to his shoulder and shouted, 'Into them!'

Uriel saw a Fire Warrior ahead of him, and swung his sword in a two-handed blow that split him from collar-bone to pelvis. The alien soldier fell without a sound, and Uriel dropped to his knees as another white-hot bolt slashed the air above him. Space Marines fanned out around him, shooting as they charged, and each round blasted through olive green armour plates with a resounding crack.

A shadow loomed over Uriel, and he dived to one side as a pair of heavy, mechanical feet slammed down with a terrific crash of alien armour on stone. A battle-suit with a tubular cannon on one arm and a crackling khopesh blade mounted on the other towered over him, a rippling heat haze shimmering above its rear-mounted jets.

The khopesh slashed down, and Uriel blocked the blow with his sword. The impact was tremendous, and sent the sword spinning from his grip. Uriel was driven to his knees by the force of the blow as his warriors turned to face this new threat in their midst. More explosions rocked the earth, the deafening crescendo punctuated by barks of heavy gunfire and the sound of shells on armour.

An alien blade flashed, and two Space Marines went down, their armour cloven by the energy field sheathing the blade. Another warrior was clubbed down by the battlesuit's heavy fist, his helmet a crumpled mass of shattered plate and bone.

Another battlesuit hammered down, and then a third. Uriel scrambled back as the battlesuit turned to face him, and a blinding stream of light erupted from the tubular weapon. He rolled again, trying to put one of the other battlesuits between him and the plasma weapon as a second white-hot blast turned the ground molten. The third battlesuit stepped in towards Uriel, and he kicked out, hammering his boot against its knee joint.

The machine staggered, but it didn't fall. Uriel's instinctive reaction had bought him a few seconds, but it was all he needed to retrieve his sword. As it came at him again, he swung the blade at its thigh, the energised blade hacking the lower half of the battlesuit's leg from its body.

The alien battle machine collapsed, and Uriel sprang to his feet as the second stepped in. Space Marines swarmed the battlesuits, firing their bolters at point-blank range. Another Space Marine was pummelled to the ground as yet more Fire Warriors charged into the fight. Uriel swayed aside from a roaring blast of heavy calibre shells, and spun inside the battlesuit's guard to ram his sword up into its torso.

He buried the blade up to its eagle hilt, and wrenched it out through the machine's hip. A wash of sparks, hissing black hydraulics and blood flowed from the crackling wound, and the battlesuit fell to its knees, the light in its helmet lenses dying along with its pilot.

Uriel turned from the destroyed machine in time to see the lead battlesuit's khopesh slash towards him. Desperately, he tried to block, but the blade slammed into his shoulder-guard, and tore through the exterior plates before sliding up over his helmet and slicing through the upper layers of protection.

Red light flooded Uriel's vision, and he threw up his sword to block the reverse cut he instinctively knew would be coming to finish him. He angled the blade to direct the impact away, but was driven to the ground by the force of the impact. The battlesuit lashed out with its heavy foot, and Uriel was hurled back, the plates of his armour buckling in protest.

Uriel rolled onto his back as the battlesuit loomed over him, its khopesh poised to deliver the deathblow.

A deafening roar, like tearing steel, sounded, and a blazing plume of sparks obscured the top half of the battlesuit. A flaring line drew across the machine's midriff, as if a monstrous buzz-saw was slicing through it. Uriel saw the angular form of an armoured giant standing behind the battlesuit as its top half was smashed from its lower half. The machine's legs crumpled, and Uriel saw the welcome sight of Brother Zethus standing before him.

The Dreadnought stood with the barrels of its assault cannon still spinning and fragments of the battlesuit's armour falling from its enormous power fist. Behind the Old One, Uriel saw a pair of Whirlwind support tanks appear alongside the massively powerful form of a Land Raider. A rippling salvo of multiple rocket launches streamed from the Whirlwind's missile rack as the Land Raider began systematically destroying the tau vehicles still fighting.

'Supporting forces on station as ordered, Captain Ventris,' said Brother Zethus.

ʊ
THIRTEEN

PRIDE. CERTAINTY. EXCITEMENT. These emotions were uppermost in Nathaniel Winterbourne's mind as he watched his forces ride to battle. Leman Russ Conquerors and Vanquishers rumbled through the wide, fume-choked streets of Brandon Gate's outer fabriks.

Within the star-shaped city, the buildings were fine edifices of stone, steel and marble, but beyond the rarefied atmosphere of the walls, the blackened reality of the industry that lay at the heart of Pavonis reasserted itself.

Tangled warrens of giant, portal-framed hangars, towering ore silos, hammering weapon shops and thousands of kilometres of hissing pipe-work spread out from the oasis at the centre of the industrial hinterlands.

It was, thought Winterbourne, a lousy place to fight a battle.

Tanks were never safe in such an urbanised landscape, where a single infantryman armed with a rocket launcher could disable or kill an armoured vehicle. This landscape was the domain of the foot soldier, but Winterbourne wasn't about to let that fact of war dissuade him from meeting the tau offensive head-on.

The 44th's tanks within Brandon Gate – fifteen Leman Russ Conquerors and half a dozen Chimeras – had rendezvoused in Liberation Square before rolling south-west along the gilded streets of the Via Commercia towards the city's southern gateway. PDF vehicles were assembling at road junctions, as heavy earth movers formed berms of rubble and Lavrentian combat engineers unspooled barriers of razor wire.

Winterbourne had little faith that these PDF units would hold against a concerted push by the tau, but if the enemy reached this far into the city, the fight was already lost. A few outraged civilians argued with PDF officers about the destruction of the roadway, but the majority of the city's populace were barricading themselves in their homes, desperate to protect what few possessions remained to them.

He felt a moment of contempt for these people. Any Imperial citizen able to hold a gun ought to be on the streets and manning a barricade. The Eastern Fringe was no place for shirkers, and to sit idly by while others fought an alien foe at their very gates spoke of the lowest cowardice.

Winterbourne's armoured convoy passed through the Commercia Gate, a solid portal of bronze-sheathed adamantium engraved with the transactions of the founding members of the cartels. An enormous circular tower of polished grey granite flanked the gate. Its curving walls depicted scenes of trade and commerce, and was intended as a monument to their guiding principles of integrity, philanthropy and resolution.

Too bad their descendants didn't match up to those ideals, thought Winterbourne.

Beyond the city, tank squadrons surging from Camp Torum assembled and deployed in the concrete ribbon that partitioned the inner city from the industrial heartland that surrounded it. Much of the region was in ruins, decimated in the fighting during the de Valtos rebellion.

Carried from Fortress Idaeus in a Chimera AFV, Winterbourne had disembarked with his new protection detail and marched towards *Father Time*.

The scale of it was enormous, and it never failed to amaze Winterbourne that such a colossal mass of iron could even move, let alone fight.

Father Time was an immense Baneblade that had served as Winterbourne's command vehicle since his promotion to colonel. It was one of the mightiest tanks ever to roll off the Martian production lines, a vehicle so powerful that nothing short of an engine of the Titan Legions would dare to stand before it. Winterbourne's tank was one of a handful of these incredible war machines that could trace its pedigree back to the assembly yards of the Tharsis Montes, its honour roll and legacy of battle inscribed on the inner faces of its turret ring.

A pitiful few of the Mechanicus forge worlds could still manufacture these behemoths to such an exacting standard, their inferior copies regarded by the priests of Mars as second generation war machines at best.

Now, sealed within the belly of his magnificent vehicle, he stared in frustration at the auspex display as it bounced and squalled with interference.

'Can't you clean this damned image up, Jenko?' he demanded. 'Can't see a bloody thing.'

'Trying to, sir,' said Jenko. 'It's all the damned metal structures around us. The composition and conductivity is messing with the returns. There's so much bloody interference, the auspex signal's bouncing around like a sand-raptor on a griddle.'

Despite the tension, Winterbourne smiled at the boy's unconscious mimicking of his speech patterns and colourful metaphor. *Father Time's* target acquisition officer was barely out of his teens, but the lad could send an armour piercing shell up the arse of an enemy tank before veteran gunners with decades of experience even noticed it. The lad had an affinity with the venerable tank, and that made him an integral part of the crew.

'Hurry it up, lad,' said Winterbourne. 'We can't fight an enemy we can't see.'

'I've almost got it,' said Jenko. 'It's just a matter of syncing our auspex to filter out certain frequencies.'

'I don't care how you do it,' said Winterbourne, 'just get me a clear view.'

Winterbourne's command chair sat high in the main turret, behind the crew of his vehicle: nine highly trained soldiers, hand-picked to serve him on board. The interior of a Baneblade, like any Imperial tank was a cramped, oily, noisy and dangerous place, which had apparently been designed at a time when only midgets and famine victims were picked to be crews.

Winterbourne looked back down at his auspex reader as Jenko said, 'Got it, sir! Signals coming in, sir. Approaching vehicles. Signature matches say enemy.'

Rippling contours of static hazed the auspex panel, but they faded into the background as a host of hostile contacts lit up the threat board.

'Hell and damnation,' swore Winterbourne. 'They're almost on top of us!'

He flipped his toggle over to the squadron vox-net. 'All vehicles, be alert for imminent contact,' ordered Winterbourne. 'Lavrentia expects every man to do his duty. Fight like your fathers are watching!'

Winterbourne switched back to his internal channel and said, 'Raise the flag!'

'Aye, sir,' confirmed Lars, the Baneblade's vox-operator.

Though he couldn't see it, a telescoping antenna had just risen from the tank's hull bearing the green and gold banner of the 44th Lavrentian Hussars. Winterbourne knew it was foolhardy to mark himself out, but he would never dream of going into battle without the regiment's colours flying above *Father Time*.

He leaned forward to stare through the vision blocks above the main gun, seeing a slice of the outside world through the scuffed and crazed armaglass. Darting armoured shapes were moving through the tangled mass of structures ahead. A graceful tau tank slid from behind a blackened refinery structure, and in its wake came a host of skimming vehicles with heavy guns or racks of missiles mounted on their turrets.

'Enemy in sight.' shouted Winterbourne. 'All tanks engage!'

Something slammed down onto the hull of his Baneblade with a resounding clang of metal on metal, and Winterbourne jumped back from the vision blocks in surprise. Incredibly, he saw what looked like a pair of armoured legs, as of some bipedal war machine, and recognised them as belonging to a battlesuit. A flare of blinding light filled the turret as a weapon discharged, and a host of alarm bells began chiming.

'Contact!' he yelled, gripping the commander's turret controls and wrenching them to the side. The metal of the turret squealed, and the motors roared at such harsh treatment. Winterbourne's view spun as the turret slewed around. He felt the impact of the main gun striking something, and when he looked back through the vision block, the battlesuit was gone.

'Get me a target, Jenko!' he shouted.

'Hammerhead, ten o' clock. Six hundred metres!'

'I see it!' said Winterbourne, swinging the turret to bear. 'Acquiring target. Loader, anti-tank!'

'Anti-tank, aye!'

Ancient mechanisms no longer understood by any save the priests of Mars whirred and hissed as they aligned the Baneblade's main gun with the target. It swam into view on Winterbourne's threat board, a brass panel with two enamelled pistol grips to either side.

Winterbourne gripped the handles as a green bulb lit up on the threat board.

'Up!' called the loader. 'Fire!'

'On the way!' yelled Winterbourne squeezing the triggers.

Such was the power of the main gun that even the incredible weight of the Baneblade rocked back under the force of the recoil. Despite layer upon layer of armour and acoustic damping material, the booming crack of the shot was deafening, and acrid fumes seeped into the crew compartments from the huge gun's breech as the spent shell-casing was ejected.

'Got you!' shouted Winterbourne, seeing the tau tank reduced to pulverised metal by the force of the impact.

'Multiple Devilfish,' snapped Jenko, 'on our eleven, twelve and one!'

'Loader! High explosive rounds! Sponson gunners engage!'

THE MISSILE ARCED up, then down, slamming into the thinner topside armour of the Devilfish. The vehicle exploded with a booming crack. Flames and smoke billowed, and the floating tank ground its nose into the dirt as its engines blew out.

'That's for Alithea,' hissed Captain Mederic, slithering back down a slope of twisted metal and crumbled stonework, and handing the smoking missile launcher off to his loader, a new inductee to the Hounds by the name of Kaynon.

Mederic wiped sweat from his eyes as Duken, his secondary shooter, dropped from the edge of the berm to join him.

'Hit?' he asked.

'Yeah,' nodded Duken, 'Sky Ray. It's dead.'

'Outstanding,' said Mederic, slapping a hand on Duken's shoulder, where the insignia of the Hounds, the 44th's scout company, was emblazoned. 'Now let's get out of here.'

'No arguments from me,' agreed Duken.

'Displace!' yelled Mederic, chopping his hand along the length of the berm of rubble. He scrambled along the debris crouched over, knowing that, even now, a tau tank would be drawing a bead on the origin point of their shots. His six-man squad of Hounds needed no instruction to relocate after shooting, but Major Ornella had drilled them in the proper procedures, and the soldiers of the 44th were nothing if not well-drilled.

A blast of ionised air rolled over them as the area behind them erupted with violet fire and a hot, electrical discharge of alien weapons' fire.

'Too slow,' he chuckled as he dropped to his knees, and peered through a gap in the piles of shattered rockcrete and steel.

The battlefield before the walls of Brandon Gate was a hellish vision of shattered buildings, blazing plumes of fire and roiling banks of stinging smoke. Imperial tanks duelled with those of the tau in the warrens of the industrial belt that encircled the city – a raging hellstorm of shellfire and actinic energy beams.

Mederic and his Hounds were right in the thick of it, helping to even the odds by getting around behind the tau. Five other squads were pushing through the ruins to wreak havoc within the enemy lines. Being in the middle of a tank battle on foot was not generally where Mederic liked to deploy, but it was sure as hell keeping his survival instincts honed.

Tanks burned, their crew dead, and dismounted Guardsmen fought Fire Warriors from the charred wreckage of their former transports. This wasn't a glorious tank charge as told in the regimental records, but a down and dirty brawl of armoured units, hunting each other through obscuring banks of black smoke.

The circular tower that had once flanked the gate now lay in pieces before the shattered remains of the great bronze gate and a sizeable portion of the walls. A coordinated missile strike had smashed much of this section of the city's perimeter to ruins, and the tau were pushing hard for the breach.

The 44th were holding firm, with Lord Winterbourne's *Father Time* in the thick of the fighting, destroying all that came near it with relentless precision and ferocity. The Baneblade was the anchor of the Imperial defence, with the Leman Russ and Hellhounds that fought alongside it like armoured bodyguards.

Tanks fought through the ruins at close range, kills made with snap shots and point-blank volleys that tore through armour and exploded with fractions of seconds between launch and impact. Basilisk and Medusa artillery pieces within Brandon Gate pounded the rear elements of the tau advance, but the gunners dared not fire too close to the walls for fear of shelling their own men.

Mederic saw a scarred and pitted Leman Russ – he thought it was *Thunder Runner* – sweep past in a blur, quickly followed by the dark forms of *Terra Volta* and *Star of Lavrentia*. He had no idea where they were going, but wished them good hunting.

Blinding streaks of impossibly bright light speared from the roof of a nearby ore barn, and *Star of Lavrentia* exploded. The tank rocked up onto its right track with the force of the impact before toppling over. Bright streaks of ignited air drifted along the flight path of its killers' weapons' fire, and Mederic looked up to see a trio of thick-shouldered battlesuits silhouetted against the smoke and flames of battle.

Each bore a pair of enormous weapons like flattened battle cannons mounted on huge rigs fitted to their backs. They cycled through a sophisticated motion that could only mean they were readying themselves to fire again. Another volley like that and they'd reduce the other two Imperial tanks to scrap metal.

'Targets!' Mederic shouted. 'On our high six! Take 'em out!'

His loader handed him the launcher tube, and he pressed the targeter to his eye, seeing the three enemy units in stark monochrome. He pressed the range-finding stud on the back of the firing grip and was rewarded with a warbling tone in his ear.

'Lock on!' he cried.

The battlesuit in the centre of the group immediately turned its head towards him. The battlesuits' arms snapped up, and Mederic saw racks of warheads cycling in launchers.

'Crap!' shouted Kaynon. 'They made us! Shoot!'

'Clear!'

The missile leapt from the tube, ejected to a safe distance before the rocket motor ignited and hurled the projectile upwards. Two others joined it and slashed through the air on a path towards the tau battlesuits.

'Move!' shouted Mederic.

He didn't bother handing off his launch tube to Kaynon, but simply sprinted towards the nearest cover he could see. His men followed him, arms pumping as they sought to escape the tau retaliation. The ground behind them heaved as a flurry of anti-personnel rockets slammed into the ground with a roaring string of thudding detonations.

Mederic was hurled to the ground, a drizzle of rock dust and earth falling around him in a rain of debris. He coughed smoke and dirt, and shook his head clear of the ringing echoes of the nearby detonations, rolling onto his back to throw off rock fragments. Behind him, he saw that a pair of his soldiers were dead, lying in mushy piles that were all that remained of their lower extremities.

He looked up to see that one of the battlesuits was gone, but two were still standing. One had lost a gun from its shoulder-mount, but the other appeared to have escaped the worst of the missile impacts. The battlesuits trained their enormous shoulder-weapons on them, which meant that he and his men were as good as dead.

Then, like a long-dormant volcano suddenly returned to life, the top of the ore barn vanished in a searing fireball as a pair of high explosive shells slammed into it, and the unmistakable echo of cannon-fire rolled over Mederic.

He propped himself up on one elbow in time to see *Thunder Runner* and *Terra Volta* rumble away, the barrels of their mighty guns returning to their centre positions now that the threat had been neutralised.

'If we get out of this alive, remind me to buy those guys a drink,' said Duken, crawling towards him.

'I don't think they even knew we were here,' replied Mederic, taking the buckled and bloody dog tags from the dead soldiers. Each tag was shaped like the head of a snarling hound, and they were worn proudly by all the 44th's scouts.

'Maybe not, but I'll take whatever help I can get.'

'I hear that.'

'Where to next?' asked Kaynon, shouldering his satchel of rockets.

'We move out,' said Mederic lifting the dusty missile launch tube from the ground. 'They ain't paying us to bring missiles back with us.'

BLOOD RAN DOWN Winterbourne's cheek from where his head had struck the inner face of the turret after a particularly fearsome barrage of fire from a formation of Hammerheads. A trio of hyper-velocity slugs had slammed into the side armour of *Father Time*, tearing off the side gunner's compartment and throwing the rest of the crew around the interior.

Winterbourne had blacked out for a moment, and when he'd come to, all three tau tanks were dead. *Terra Volta* had killed the first, *Pride of Torum* another, and a series of missiles from one of Mederic's Hound squads had taken out the last one.

Spalled fragments from the impacts had shredded his vox-operator and one of the loaders. The interior of the vehicle stank of blood and oil and sweat, and Jenko was now doubling as his link to the rest of his fighting vehicles as well as his target acquisition officer.

'Any word from Uriel?' asked Winterbourne.

'None, sir,' replied Jenko, pressing the sticky vox-set to the side of his head.

Winterbourne swore softly to himself, returning his attention to the threat board.

The battle was a confused mess of wreckage, gunfire, moving armour and explosions. Imperial casualties were mounting fast. It was impossible to tell exactly how many tanks had been destroyed in the fighting, but each loss was a grievous blow. Winterbourne did not relish examining the butcher's bill at the end of this engagement.

Crater Maker rolled past his flank, its battle cannon roaring, and a segment of a milling shop disintegrated ahead of it. At first, Winterbourne thought the tank had missed its target, but then the upper storeys of the building came crashing down on a Sky Ray tank sheltering behind a ramp of collapsed slabs of rockcrete. *Gematria* and *Thunder Runner* displaced as their turrets rotated and fired into a mass of oncoming tau tanks, two Hammerheads and a Devilfish.

'Targets right!' he shouted, slewing the turret of the Baneblade around. 'Gunner, high explosive and keep them coming!'

'High explosive, aye.'

'Range two hundred metres!'

'Up! Fire!'

'On the way!' shouted Winterbourne as *Father Time* shuddered with the recoil from the main gun. The clanging of the breech opening and closing was lost in the deafening roar coming through the breach in the hull where the side gun had been torn off, and Winterbourne knew it would be days before the ringing echoes faded from his hearing.

One of the Hammerheads was dead, ripped apart by the heavy battle cannon shell, its turret torn from its hull and nowhere to be seen. The other was fighting a losing duel with *Gematria* and *Thunder Runner*, its engines burning and its hull broken open by armour piercing rounds. The Devilfish had sensibly taken cover and debussed its troops before fleeing from the vengeful guns of the Imperial tanks.

Hundreds of Fire Warriors darted through the ruins, and Winterbourne was forced to admire their courage. Advancing into the teeth of an armoured engagement required no small amount of bravery, and their guns, while no threat to the tanks, were reaping a fearsome tally amongst his dismounted Guardsmen.

Zipping drones sped through the battle, marking out targets for tau support tanks, and the air was filled with sparking las-bolts and solid rounds as Imperial soldiers sought to bring them down and give them some respite from the constant rain of missiles.

Loping Sentinels stalked the rubble and ruin of battle, duelling with agile battlesuits through the fallen remains of the industrial suburbs of Brandon Gate. Though outnumbered, the Sentinels fought hard, their autocannons raking the ground and chewing up enemies with every salvo. It was an unequal struggle, and, together with missiles guided in by the drones, the battlesuits eventually brought them down.

'We can't go on like this,' he whispered to himself, turning his attention to the threat board. The readings were confused, but it seemed as though the two sides were evenly matched. The tau seemed not to have the will to enforce their advance through the gap in the walls, while Winterbourne's force was holding its position without being able to push them back.

It was a deadlock that would only end when both forces had ground each other to dust.

'Sir?' said Jenko.

'This is wrong,' said Winterbourne, 'They're not pushing hard enough, and we're just letting them keep us engaged.'

Fierce yellow light shone through the vision block, and Winterbourne looked out to see the Hellhound *Emperor's Light* bathing a choked ruin of a processing plant in searing flames. A host of kroot were flushed from their hiding place, and Winterbourne relished their obvious pain. Only a single kroot warrior, one with a flaring crest of red quills, avoided the lethal spray of promethium to vanish into the rubble.

'That's the thing,' he said. 'Take the fight to them. We're just reacting to them.'

'Sir?'

'Damn me, Jenko, but they've got me dancing a jig to their tune,' cursed Winterbourne. 'Whatever game they're playing, they've got us to play along with it. Well, Nathaniel Winterbourne dances to no man's tune but his own. Send word to all our tanks! Full advance! Break their centre and push these bastards back down the highway!'

A nearby explosion rocked *Father Time*, but Winterbourne felt nothing, having come to that place in a warrior's mind where all fear is subsumed in the utter belief in his chosen course of action.

'All vehicles acknowledge your orders, sir!' shouted Jenko.

Father Time's engines roared, and coughed a filthy cloud of exhaust smoke before lurching forwards in a spray of rock dust. The armoured behemoth crushed iron and stone, churning the ground beneath it to powder on its unstoppable advance. Its main guns spoke with booming reports, each monstrously powerful shell obliterating whatever it was aimed at.

Its array of anti-personnel guns cleared the ground before it in scything bursts of heavy calibre gunfire, driving Fire Warriors before it in a bow wave of terror. Those not quick enough or sensible enough to retreat went under the Baneblade's tracks, pulped by its unimaginable bulk. Nothing could harm so mighty a war machine. The bright streaks of light from the guns of the Fire Warriors were doing little more than peeling the paint from its impenetrable armour plates.

In the wake of the huge tank came the charging armour of the 44th Lavrentian regiment: Conquerors, Vanquishers, Executioners, Hellhounds and Chimeras. Each tank commander followed the example of their leader, driving hard for the enemy lines, their guns roaring in a relentless barrage of shells.

A wedge of Hammerheads sought to intercept *Father Time*, but Winterbourne's driver saw them coming, and revved the engine as he turned his armoured charger towards them. Hyper-velocity slugs slammed into the frontal glacis of the Baneblade, tearing great gouges in the armour, but failing to halt its advance. One alien tank spun on its axis and fled, but the others stood their ground.

Father Time slammed into the first, its hull coming up as it mounted the tau vehicle. The armour of the alien tanks was strong and light, but it was no match for the three hundred tonnes of a Baneblade. Like a tin can crushed beneath the foot of a soldier, the tau vehicle was flattened in a blinding explosion of flaring electrical discharge.

The second vehicle fired one last shot before attempting to escape, but its crew's bravery had cost them their lives, and *Father Time* slammed into it side-on. The Hammerhead flipped onto its side, and was driven before the Baneblade for ten metres before finally going under the leviathan.

It was a glorious charge, but not one without cost. *Steppe Hunter*, the ambush predator that had broken the enemy line at Charos, vanished in a searing fireball as a close range burst from a battlesuit blew out its fuel tanks and ignited its magazine. *Crater Maker* took a direct hit that tore open its armour and killed its engine. No sooner had the crew bailed out than they were set upon by a host of kroot warriors, led by the red-quilled leader that Winterbourne had seen earlier.

The kroot ripped the crew of *Crater Maker* apart, but as they completed their slaughter, a lone figure in the black robes of a Mortifex emerged from the fire of battle with an enormous eviscerator held out before him. The howling priest hacked into the kroot, but was soon lost to sight amid the smoke and confusion of the armoured charge.

Winterbourne's charge was driving the tau back, but the aliens were making them pay a fearsome toll in blood for every metre reclaimed. A second line of tau tanks rallied at the south-eastern reaches of the burning ruins, and, as the Imperial tanks drove towards them, it was clear that it would be a bloody business to push them from these ad hoc redoubts.

Then the first of the tau tanks exploded, a searing lance of bright laser energy sawing through its vulnerable rear armour and detonating its energy core. Explosions mushroomed from the ranks of Fire Warriors, and stuttering bursts of perfectly coordinated gunfire brought down those few battlesuits still standing.

Emerging from the flaming wreckage of the tank assembly yards, the Space Marines came with fire and thunder. Whirlwind support tanks rained volleys of rockets down on the tau, while a trio of Land Raiders smashed into the rear of the tau formation, their side-mounted lascannon arrays tearing through the armour of the enemy tanks, and blitzing storms of bolter-fire adding their horrendous accompaniment to the battle.

Behind them came the Space Marines, warriors in ultramarine whose weapons were hymnals to war and whose gold and blue flag was a beacon of righteousness among the slaughter. Mighty Dreadnoughts stomped through the wreckage, weapons blazing and power fists crushing the life from anything that could not escape their inexorable advance.

Caught between two such implacable foes, the tau broke and fled for the safety of the highway south, but it was an illusory safety.

Shredded in the deadly crossfire, only two-dozen enemy vehicles survived to reach the highway, but within minutes they had been bracketed by artillery fire and reduced to blackened hulks littering the roadway. Their crews burned to death or scrambled from their blazing vehicles, only to be hunted down and killed by the pursuing Space Marines.

The engagement ceased to be a battle and became a massacre.

Lavrentian and Space Marine forces linked up in the glare of a burning weapons shop, the flames lighting up the sky with a hellish orange glow. *Father Time*, battered, gouged and war-scarred rumbled to a halt with a sigh of its engines, and Lord Winterbourne climbed down from his commander's hatch.

The colonel of the Lavrentians was smeared with oil and blood, but his eyes were bright and his stride sure as he marched over to meet the leader of the Space Marines. Like Winterbourne, Uriel was streaked with blood, though little of it was his own.

The two leaders met and shook hands, each man pleased to see the other alive.

'You're a damn welcome sight, my friend,' said Winterbourne, rubbing his hands on his uniform jacket in a vain attempt to clean them.

'As are you, Nathaniel,' said Uriel.

'A decisive blow, wouldn't you say?'

'The victory was decisive, yes,' agreed Uriel, 'but I do not believe this assault was ever expected to take and hold Brandon Gate.'

Winterbourne ran a hand through his hair and nodded. 'I know what you mean, Uriel. As fierce a fight as this was, there was no heart to it. They came with plenty of armour, but there weren't enough forces to hold an entire city.'

'Exactly. It fits with what we saw at the Shonai estates. This has all been part of the tau's attempt to decapitate the leadership of Pavonis. Communications have been disrupted, the governor has been captured, and they have tried to kill senior figures of the planetary leadership.'

'So this attack was what, a diversion?'

'I think so,' agreed Uriel. 'A blow to weaken us and divert our attention from where the real hammer blow will fall.'

'Olzetyn,' said Winterbourne.

'Olzetyn,' agreed Uriel.

ʊ
FOURTEEN

LEARCHUS PRESSED HIS body into the dry soil of the undergrowth, pulling the camo-cape over his bulky shoulders. The urge to look up was almost overwhelming, but he knew that to expose any part of his armour to the tau drones would only invite discovery.

He and his scouts sheltered in an undulant dip filled with the umber gorse that hugged the coastline southwards from Lake Masura towards Crater Bay. The ground between here and the Shonai estates was rugged and spectacular, easily the equal of many of the worlds of Ultramar. Where those worlds had a wildness to their geography, this landscape was clearly managed, the trees growing in regimented lines that appealed to Learchus's sense of precision, but seemed at odds with the natural order of things.

They had made good time in their pursuit of Koudelkar Shonai, easily able to follow the trail left by the two battlesuits as they moved south to the coast with their captives. Moving with the jet packs on their armour, the tau warriors had followed the coastline, making little effort to conceal their route. That spoke of arrogance, and Learchus was pleased to know that their foes had at least one weakness that might be exploited.

Learchus had set a punishing pace, marching his scouts hard through the sweeping terrain of the western coastline, through sprawling forests, over high ridges of granite and along sheer cliffs that plunged thousands of metres towards the dark waters of the ocean.

In the first few days of their pursuit, they had met no sign of the tau, but in the hours following the mighty burst of light that had exploded over the southern horizon the day before, that had begun to change. Learchus's scout sergeant, Issam, sent the team to ground when he spotted a number of small vehicles, like bulkier versions of the skimmer-bikes used by the eldar, darting across the landscape in pairs.

'Reconnaissance vehicles,' said Learchus, watching the light craft flit over the landscape in over watching bounds, 'working in pairs.'

'Do we ambush them?' asked Issam as the vehicles drew closer.

Learchus hesitated before answering. His every instinct and every tenet of the Codex Astartes was to order his warriors to attack the aliens, but to do so would effectively end their pursuit of Koudelkar. As much as he knew he *should* engage the enemy, the mission came first. It was the first and most important lesson learned by any initiate of the Ultramarines.

'No,' said Learchus, and the tau skimmers turned east and vanished over the horizon.

As he watched them go, Learchus felt a knot in the pit of his stomach, and he had a glimmering of how Uriel had come to choose the path that led to his expulsion.

For the next two days, they had evaded detection by yet more of the tau light skimmers, seeing that there appeared to be two versions. The first occupied a similar role to the Astartes Land Speeder as a light attack vehicle with a minimal weapon load, while the second appeared to be a purely scout vehicle.

None of the tau vehicles detected the presence of the warriors in their midst, for Ultramarines scouts were second to none in their abilities. The punishing landscape and unimaginably harsh training regime of Macragge schooled them in the lore of virtually any terrain, and Issam had a preternatural sense for danger that gave them plenty of time to take cover and deploy their camo-capes.

But now, sheltering in the dip of landscape with nothing but patches of wiry, rust-coloured gorse and their camo-capes to conceal them, Learchus felt acutely vulnerable as a flight of silver-skinned drones flew lazy spirals in the air above them. The drones had appeared out of nowhere, and only Issam's last minute warning had given them time to conceal themselves.

Learchus could feel the ripple in the grass nearby from the drone's anti-grav generators, and, though he told himself it was ridiculous, he swore he could feel the crawling sensation of their augurs hunting him. If the drones found them, they would have no choice but to fight. Such a fight would be short and easy, but it would undoubtedly alert the tau to their presence.

As much as it irked Learchus to allow the alien devices to remain unmolested, he knew it was the right thing to do. Not for the first time since they had left the Shonai estates, Learchus wished that his fellow battle-brothers were alongside him, for he felt adrift without them. Such were the bonds of brotherhood between the warriors of the Adeptus Astartes, that to be deprived of them felt like a piece of his soul was missing. Uriel and Pasanius had travelled to far distant worlds and fought the enemies of mankind with such a void within them, and Learchus knew then that to have done so made them true heroes of the Chapter.

He held still as he felt one the drones fly over him, the gentle pressure of its propulsion mechanism flattening the camo-cape across his wide back. His finger tensed on the trigger of his boltgun, but he fought the urge to roll over and send a shell into the drone's underside.

Learchus waited, the seconds stretching out before him, until he heard the buzz of the drones moving away. He let out a breath and eased his head up, watching as the pack of drones skimmed over the ground and vanished into the forested landscape further east.

Satisfied that they were in no danger of discovery, Learchus stood and shook the leaves from his camo-cape. The scouts gathered around him, and he could feel their frustration. Infiltration and destruction wreaked behind the lines was part of the scouts' purpose, and to have come this far and inflicted no damage upon the tau was anathema to these warriors.

'My lord,' said Issam, 'how much longer must we hold our force in check?'

'As long as it takes,' said Learchus.

'We could have taken those drones out in seconds,' pressed Daxian, one of Issam's youngest scouts. 'There would have been no warning sent back.'

'And when they are noted as being missing?' demanded Learchus. 'What then? This region would be flooded with tau scouts looking for what killed them. You are all fine scouts, and I have no doubt you would have the tau chasing their tails, but this is not a normal scouting mission.'

The scouts nodded, though Learchus could see the disappointment in their eyes as they gathered around him. Was this how Uriel felt when Learchus had called him to account for his actions?

'The Codex Astartes tells us that wherever possible we must discomfit the enemy,' said a scout by the name of Parmian.

'Our mission is to rescue Koudelkar Shonai,' said Learchus. 'Nothing must distract us from that purpose. Is that understood?'

'Yes, my lord,' said Parmian, 'but while we hide from the enemy, our brothers earn glory on the field of honour.'

'There is glory in all things, Parmian,' said Learchus, 'and not all of it is earned facing the enemy guns. Each of us must play our part in this drama, be it standing in the battle lines with bolter and chainsword in hand or behind the lines serving the greater good of the war.'

Learchus turned on his heel and began marching south once more.

'Fear not, my young brothers,' he said, 'you'll have your chance for glory soon enough.'

SCREAMS OF PAIN echoed from the filthy walls of the corridors, and Jenna Sharben felt each one as a knife to the chest as she made her way towards the Intelligence Room. The screams were alien and should have been music to her ears, but the sheer misery and horror in the sound tore at the essence of her soul that sought justice and craved nobility of spirit.

Every step was an effort, for there had been precious little sleep in the days since the tau attack on Brandon Gate. Flocks of the tau's winged auxiliary troops infested the city, and sniping attacks from above were a daily occurrence at the Glasshouse. Nerves were stretched taut and resentment towards the invaders was high. Added to that, resupply was late, and the enforcers stationed at the prison were deemed of lower importance than the soldiers fighting across Pavonis.

Jenna couldn't fault the logic, but it made it no easier to explain to her enforcers why they were going to have to continue on ration packs and recycled water. Forced to exist in the squalid barracks of the Glasshouse on a diet of freeze-dried food and brackish water that had passed through who knew how many digestive tracts wasn't a situation likely to ease tempers any time soon.

Tensions were high, but the enforcers had the perfect targets in their grasp to vent many of those frustrations. Since the prisoners had been deposited in the Glasshouse by the Ultramarines, the enforcers had found new and ever more inventive ways to harass, torture and discomfit them.

Each tau prisoner had their topknot cut, and any other identifying apparel or pieces of jewellery removed, before being hosed down with high-pressure water blessed by Prelate Culla. Dressed in identical smocks, they were herded like beasts into their overcrowded cells, forced to wear fetters that chafed their legs raw, and deprived of food and sleep for days on end.

And the net gain of actionable intelligence from this? Nothing.

Pretty much all any of the prisoners had said since they had been brought here was their name and what was presumed to be a serial number, not that Jenna had expected much. A prisoner subjected to physical torture would say anything to have his ordeal end, and any intelligence gained from such torture would have to be treated as suspect.

Jenna had come to this realisation after her first, fruitless interrogation of La'tyen, feeling strangely shamed by the level of violence she'd employed. After all, she had confined her interrogations to strictly verbal encounters.

She, however, was the only enforcer to do so...

She rubbed a hand across her face, feeling the dryness of her skin and the hollows of her cheeks from a diet of dried food sachets. Her blonde hair was dirty and unkempt, and she knew she looked nothing like the clean-cut Arbites Judge who had come to Pavonis full of idealism and fiery thoughts of justice.

Where was justice in this hellhole?

She passed cells where mirror-masked enforcers beat tau prisoners with their shock mauls, held them in stress positions for hours at a time or forced them into degrading positions with their cellmates. Worse even than the screams were the sounds of laughter that came from her enforcers. Despite the tension and food shortages, and the threat from the alien invaders, the enforcers she had tried to train as a cadre of honourable upholders of Imperial Law were actually enjoying their work.

The notion of it sickened her, but since the arrival of Prelate Culla there was little she could do to stop it.

The man had rolled through the prison gates in a glorious fanfare of hymnals, booming from the augmitters on his ridiculously ostentatious Rhino. Choking clouds of incense churned in the vehicle's wake, and half a dozen golden-skinned cherubs floated overhead, perusing the interior of the Glasshouse with doll-eyed expressions of distaste.

'I am here to interrogate the traitor!' Culla had declared upon climbing down from his fire-wreathed pulpit, a red-bladed sword of enormous proportions sheathed across his shoulders. The man towered above Jenna, his powerful physique muscular and intimidating. Culla's beard was waxed into two forks, one jet black, the other silver.

'Interrogating prisoners is our job,' Jenna had replied. 'You have no authority here.'

Culla drew the vast chainblade from across his shoulders and planted it in the hard ground before him. Resting both hands upon the skull pommel, he leaned forwards.

'I have the authority of the Emperor, girl,' boomed Culla. 'No traitor dares stand before me, and only traitors seek to bar me from my holy work. To know that one who has betrayed the Emperor still breathes within these walls is a sin, Judge Sharben, a sin that will not go unpunished.'

A sizeable crowd of enforcers had gathered, and, as distasteful as it was to allow the zealot within her walls, she did not relish a scene between her and the 44th's predicant. Reluctantly, she stood aside and allowed Culla into the prison, and for days he had been a fiery presence within its walls. When not washing the blood of prisoners from his muscular frame, Culla preached his credo of persecution to the enforcers, filling their hearts with fresh hatred for the tau and traitors.

Jenna absented herself from his sermons, trying in vain to catch up on her sleep or attempting to re-establish her command of the Glasshouse. Ever since Culla's arrival, the enforcers of Brandon Gate had turned to him for guidance, and her authority had eroded like sand before the sea.

She turned into the corridor that led towards the Intelligence Room, hearing Culla's shouts from beyond the iron door at the far end. Enforcers Dion and Apollonia stood to either side of the door, the mirrored visors of their helmets pulled down to cover their faces. Jenna didn't need to see their faces to know it was them, months of training had rendered their physiques and postures as familiar as her own.

'Open up,' she said when she reached the door.

'Prelate Culla doesn't like to be disturbed when he's questioning the traitor,' said Dion.

Jenna looked into his visor, seeing her own haggard reflection looking back.

'I don't give a crap what Culla wants,' she said. 'Open the door. This is still my prison, and you're still my damned enforcer, Dion. Now do as you're damn well told!'

Dion looked over at Apollonia, and Jenna said, 'Don't look at her. I'm your commanding officer, not her. Now open the door.'

'Yes, ma'am,' said Dion, standing aside to let Jenna past. She pushed open the door and entered a small room of bare concrete. A plain table sat in the centre, and a large window of one way glass looked into an interrogation cell entered through a featureless steel door in the wall next to it. A bronze eagle was set high on the far wall, a symbol of the Imperium for the condemned to gaze upon as they contemplated their fate.

Jenna saw Culla through the glass, standing in the centre of the room, stripped to the waist with his fists balled before him. He was shouting, but this was the one area of the prison with sound-proofing, and she could not hear his words. Jenna punched the code into the door keypad and entered the room. The reek of blood, human waste and terror hit her like a blow.

Culla turned to face Jenna, and his face was a mask of righteous fury. Given what she had seen of him, it was impossible to tell whether it was at her interruption or simply his normal state of being. Blood dripped from his knuckles, his body gleamed with sweat, and his chest heaved with exertion.

As she entered the room, Jenna saw the object of Culla's violent attention secured to a chair bolted securely to the floor.

Jenna was no stranger to the harm that could be wrought upon a human body, but even she blanched to see the violence done to this pitiful wreck of a person. Matted wisps of hair clung to a partially shaven scalp, and blood caked the side of a face blackened with bruises and ruptured with impacts.

One of the wretch's eyes was filled with blood, the other virtually closed over with swollen flesh. Both locked with Jenna, and despite everything she knew of this prisoner, Jenna felt nothing but pity.

Mykola Shonai whispered, 'Help me.'

CULLA SLAMMED THE door shut behind him as he joined Jenna in the anteroom, giving the broken and bleeding Mykola Shonai a moment's respite. He lifted a long cloth from his belt and wiped his forehead of sweat.

'Why do you interrupt me?' he demanded. 'I have work to do.'

'What kind of work demands that kind of abuse?' demanded Jenna, pointing through the one-way glass.

'The Emperor's work,' said Culla. 'You have sympathy with a traitor, Judge Sharben? It would be unfortunate if I had to bolt a second chair to the floor.'

'Of course I don't have sympathy with traitors.'

'Then why do you object to my right and proper treatment of this filthy collaborator?'

'She was once governor of this world,' said Jenna.

'And she betrayed her people the moment she consorted with xenos creatures,' pointed out Culla. 'What kind of craven wretch would do such a thing? Only a degenerate creature unworthy of inclusion in the human race. Only a disgusting, filthy xenos-loving animal.'

Jenna pointed towards the glass. 'Just what are you hoping to gain from this? If she knew anything of value don't you think she would have told you?'

'The ways of the xenos-lover are cunning,' said Culla, massaging his knuckles. 'Only through the purification of pain will they give up all their secrets.'

'Not if you kill her first.'

'Then I will have learned everything I wish to know,' said Culla, 'and the galaxy will be better for her death.'

'You are treating her worse than any of the tau prisoners.'

'The tau are xenos and do not know any better,' said Culla dismissively. 'They are simply ignorant beasts, responding to base desires and needs. They are vermin who should be hated and feared as imperfect creations. It is humanity's right and duty to cleanse such creatures from existence with fire and sword. Shonai should have known better.'

'I agree the tau need to be fought,' said Jenna, 'but like this? If we behave like this we'll lose our humanity, our honour.'

'That *thing* in there doesn't deserve to be called human.'

'Is that how you do it?' asked Jenna, leaning forwards over the table.

'Do what?'

'You don't even think of Mykola Shonai as human, do you? That's how you're able to do these things to her, isn't it?'

'Choose your words carefully, Sharben,' warned Culla. 'My army of the righteous does not tolerate dissenters in their midst. They know that the work they do is necessary.'

'*Your* army?' hissed Jenna. 'Last I checked I was still in command here. *I* am in charge of the Brandon Gate Enforcers, not you.'

'Cross me and you will find out if that is still true,' said Culla with a smile.

FROM HIS POSITION in the command hatch of his personal half-track, Colonel Loic watched the people of Olzetyn moving steadily eastwards across the Imperator Bridge as his driver slowly eased the rumbling vehicle through the crowds towards the western end of the bridge. Night was several hours old, but the span was still thronged with frightened people making their way from 'Stratum to Tradetown.

They travelled in ancient trucks, in wagons or on foot, carrying what possessions could be borne with them to safety. Or, at least, what they hoped was safety. The western reaches of Olzetyn on the far side of the gorges were considered too dangerous for civilians, which was a fair assessment, thought Colonel Loic.

Though a great host of people were on the move, the main thoroughfare over Imperator Bridge was by no means clogged. As colonel of the Pavonis PDF, Loic had imposed strict controls to guide and direct the flood of civilians crossing the river gorges. Some were diverted onto the Aquila Bridge to Barrack Town and then funnelled over the Owsen Bridge to Tradetown. Others were diverted across the Diacrian Bridge further south into the Midden and onwards east. Once across the bridges, some optimistic souls were remaining in Tradetown, but most continued onwards along Highway 236 to Brandon Gate.

There was fear, but little panic. The tau invaders were reported to have captured Praxedes, but had so far confined themselves to skirmishes and probes against the defenders of Olzetyn. Such caution was only natural, given the fearsome strength of the great bastions that protected the western approaches to the bridge city.

Imperator Bridge itself was the creation of engineering genius, a wondrously ornate suspension bridge spanning the gorges that marked the confluence of the main rivers of Pavonis. Marvellously tall towers of marble, adamantium and gold pierced the clouds at either end of the bridge, and cables wrought from some ingenious material supported the five kilometre span of the bridge in an elegant latticework arrangement that was immensely strong, yet also graceful and airy.

For centuries, it had been the wonder of the world, a single elegant structure that stood in splendid isolation upon the gorges, but over the last thousand years, the four main conurbations that made up Olzetyn, 'Stratum, Midden, Tradetown and Barrack Town had grown to the point where other, more prosaically designed bridges were required.

The Aquila and Omon Bridges connected east and west via Barrack Town on the northern spur, while the Diacrian Bridge crossed the southern gorge into the sprawling slums of the Midden. The aptly named Spur Bridge jutted from the tip of the Midden to link with the Imperator Bridge in the middle of its span, and what was once a graceful demonstration of ingenuity was soon little more than a monument to necessity.

But the final degradation of the Imperator was yet to come. As the city grew in importance, the once elegant structure of the bridge became home to the city's ever-expanding population. Sprawling habs, little better than garrulous shantytowns, began springing up along its length like fungal growths, faster than they could be removed, and tens of thousands now called the bridge home.

Despite such colonisation, it was still possible to see the towering bastions constructed on the western side of the bridge through the tangle of suspension walkways and drifting banks of smog.

Constructed from titanic blocks of glassy black stone hewn from the Sudinal Mountains by the great mining machines of the Mechanicus, each bastion was a magnificent structure, fully six hundred metres high and twice again as wide. To the left of the bridge stood the Aquila Bastion, its upper ramparts fashioned to resemble a pair of mighty pinions, while on the right was the might of the Imperator Bastion.

The wind whipped over the bridge, but with his cream uniform jacket pulled around him and a heavily padded fur chapka pulled down tightly over his head, he didn't feel the cold. Instead, he felt exhilarated at this chance to prove his mettle as a fighting soldier, for though he had trained as hard as any Guardsman, Adren Loic had never fired a shot in anger.

Few of the soldiers of the PDF had fought in actual combat since the de Valtos rebellion, and any of the men who had experience, kept quiet about it. No one who wanted a quiet life boasted of their actions during that shameful part of the planet's history.

He knew his appointment to the post of senior PDF officer was a political decision. Adren Loic was a man few could object to, since few had heard of him. All his life he had been undistinguished in his military endeavours, yet he had a sharp mind that made him uniquely appealing to the Administratum adepts who approved his appointment, for he was one of them.

In the years before his service in the PDF, Colonel Loic had served as a senior adept on the PDF Logistical Corps, and his understanding of the administration of a military force was faultless. He had never been tested as a warrior, but he knew how to organise and run a planet-wide force of armed soldiers better than anyone on Pavonis.

While Pavonis had been at peace, that had been enough.

Now he would be tested in war, and the thought of proving his worth galvanised him like nothing else in his career ever had.

The half-track emerged from the busy thoroughfares of the bridge into the wide, statue-lined esplanade between the two western bastions. Just being in the shadow of such colossal structures gave Loic a sense of calm, for who could imagine that two such powerful redoubts could ever be cast down?

Ahead, he saw Captain Gerber of the 44th Lavrentians, poring over a map unfolded on the front glacis of a green and gold Chimera. A number of junior officers and a commissar in a long black greatcoat clustered around him, and they bantered back and forth with the ease of professional soldiers who had fought together for many years.

Gerber was a rough type, brusque and to the point with his assessments and decisions. Had they met in the draughty chambers of 'Stratum's Tower of Adepts, Loic had no doubt they would have been at loggerheads, but as fellow warriors, they had unexpectedly (to both of them, he suspected) found a mutual respect for one another.

Loic dropped from his vehicle and marched over to Gerber's Chimera.

'Gentlemen,' he said as he reached the ring of officers. He received nods of acknowledgement from them all, but the earlier familiarity he'd seen amongst them vanished in an instant. The commissar, a quiet man named Vogel, shook his hand. Loic wondered, as he did every time he met Vogel, how many Guardsmen he had shot for cowardice. Having served with the Lavrentians for some time, Loic suspected that the number was very low.

'Busy night?' he asked.

Gerber looked up as Loic joined him. He shook his head. 'No, just the usual harassing attacks on the forward outposts, nothing my lads couldn't handle.'

'Where?' asked Loic, pointing at the map. 'Show me.'

Scribe logisters with telescoping arms held the ancient plans of the city, drawn by hand on wax paper, steady as quill-callipers sketched out what Gerber was saying.

'They're probing the defences at these points south of the river,' said Gerber as the logisters indicated a number of points on the map. 'Fire Warrior squads in Devilfish mainly, with skirmish screens of recon skimmers. Some of those bloody kroot are trying to get behind us, and there's always a flock of Stingwings overhead somewhere.'

'No heavy armour?'

'Not yet, but it's only a matter of time,' said Poldara, Gerber's lieutenant. The sandy-haired young man seemed absurdly youthful to be a soldier, let alone an officer. Upon first meeting Poldara, Loic had suspected nepotism or a bought commission, but he had quickly learned that the young man's rank was a reflection of his ability as a soldier. 'The attack at Brandon Gate shows they can move armour quickly, and it's Lord Winterbourne's belief that the tau are going to come against us in force, sooner rather than later.'

Loic nodded. 'That makes sense. Well, my lads are itching to get their hands bloody.'

He saw the doubt in their faces, recognising it as the Guardsman's instinctive mistrust of soldiers who never left their home world and who were tarred with the brush of treachery from the de Valtos rebellion. Indignation stirred in his heart, and he steeled his spine.

'Need I remind you that my men are fighting to defend their home world?' asked Loic. 'I know you think of us as less capable soldiers, but I assure you we won't let you down, gentlemen.'

Gerber searched his face for bravado and said, 'You'd better not, Adren. Your men are green and they've never been at the sharp end of a fight before. At least, not enough of them have. My men can't do this on their own, your PDF units are going to have to do their part too.'

'I assure you, we have been training harder than ever,' said Loic.

'That's all well and good, but it's no substitute for the real thing. I've fought the tau before and when they come at us it'll be with everything they've got. I still don't rate our chances better than one in four that we can hold them without reinforcements.'

'One in four!' asked Vogel. 'That sounds like defeatism, Captain Gerber.'

'It's not. It's realism,' said Gerber. 'Oh, we'll fight like the tough sons of bitches we are, but the numbers aren't on our side.'

'Surely these tau are no match for us?' said Loic. 'I've heard they're quite weak in fact.'

'Then you haven't fought the tau or seen how they make war,' replied Gerber. 'The most successful armies are the ones that coordinate their forces the best, the ones that know what force to apply where and for how long. Some might say it's also the force that makes the least mistakes. The tau don't make mistakes. Every soldier in their army is utterly dedicated to their goal and fights for his commander because he knows, *knows*, with utter certainty that he's fighting towards something greater than himself.'

'They sound almost like us,' joked Loic, then wished he hadn't when no one laughed.

'Without reinforcements, we don't have a prayer of holding for any significant length of time,' said Gerber. 'It's that simple.'

'Then I think those prayers have just been answered,' said Poldara, pointing back down the length of the bridge.

Loic turned and saw a convoy of blue armoured vehicles rumbling along the bridge: APCs, battle tanks and a host of Space Marines, who marched beneath an azure banner of a mailed fist. A pair of towering Dreadnoughts flanked the armoured giants, and darting blue speeders flashed overhead. A warrior in a billowing green cloak, secured with a pin in the shape of a white rose, marched over to them, one hand gripping the handle of a sheathed sword.

The Space Marine captain reached up and removed his helmet.

Uriel Ventris said, 'The 4th Company stands ready to defend Olzetyn.'

PART 3
BRIGHT STARS IN THE FIRMAMENT
OF BATTLE

♉ FIFTEEN

THE ATTACK ON Olzetyn began in earnest as dawn painted the sky with the first smudges of light in the east. Forward augers detected the presence of numerous aerial targets, yet none of the gunners in the Imperial interceptor guns switched their targeters to acquisition mode. Alert klaxons blared, and tired soldiers pulled themselves from their bedrolls, but none turned their gaze upwards.

Forewarned by those few units that had escaped the fall of Praxedes, the defenders of Olzetyn kept their heads down as a blaze of pyrotechnics scorched the sky with blinding, searing light.

As the heavens burned with deadly radiance, a host of tau armoured vehicles surged forwards. Scores of Devilfish and Hammerheads pushed towards the bridges, while packs of Stingwings swooped and dived overhead. If the tau hoped to catch the defenders of the bridge city with the same ploy as had worked at Praxedes, they were to be sorely disappointed.

The terrible illumination faded from the sky, and the order to open fire was given.

Flak tanks and static interceptor guns filled the skies above Olzetyn with explosive ordnance, and brought down dozens of tau aircraft. Shattered Barracuda and enormous Tiger Sharks were blown out of the air, their sleek and graceful hulls torn apart by the churning maelstrom of whickering shrapnel and fire.

Nor was the carnage restricted to the tau aerial forces. Expecting the Imperial defenders to be blinded and disoriented, the tau vehicles were advancing without caution. A withering salvo of heavy weapons fire and precisely directed artillery hammered the advancing foe without mercy. Tau transports were shattered, the warriors they carried immolated without firing a shot, and tanks were destroyed without their guns ever having found a target.

Within moments, the thrust of the tau attack had been blunted, the shock value of the Imperial response like a sucker punch to the guts of an overconfident boxer. Scores of armoured vehicles were destroyed, and hundreds of Fire Warriors slain before the battle had even begun, and what was hoped to be a decisive blow turned out to be anything but.

Without panic, the tau commander reacted to the changing circumstances of battle with frightening speed. Tanks peeled away in formation, using the contours of the ground and local cover to advance in bounding leaps, one group shooting while another darted forwards.

The Stingwings dropped from the sky en-masse to hamper the efforts of the defenders, and a glittering host of drones zipped around their flanks. Within moments, salvos of missiles were raining down, exploding with pinpoint accuracy and killing dozens of Guardsmen and PDF troopers with every blast.

With battle well and truly joined, the shape of the tau attack became clear, and while every portion of the Imperial lines came under attack, it was the trenches, redoubts and pillboxes protecting the approach to the Diacrian Bridge that bore the brunt of the assault.

THE BOOMING REPORTS of massed Thunderfire cannons were deafening, echoing from the far sides of the gorge. Some shells arced downwards and detonated among the tau, while others burrowed through the earth to explode beneath the delicate grav plates that kept the tau skimmer tanks in the air.

Armour cracked open and bodies were burned, but still the xenos force advanced. This close to the bridges, there was precious little cover to be had, and the enemy were forced to come at them head-on. Missiles streaked overhead and slammed into the raised bulwark protecting the Imperial troops, but without guidance, they were simply blasting earth.

Pushing into the teeth of guns manned by a prepared and determined enemy was the least desirable tactical situation for a commander to find himself in, and Uriel hoped to make the tau pay for their overconfidence. The majority of the 4th Company's squads protected the southern bridge of Olzetyn, for it was clearly the weakest part of the defence. Knowing the tau would come at it in force, Uriel had deployed his warriors here to bolster the ranks of the 44th and potentially drive the tau onto the western bastions, where Chaplain Clausel and his assault squads awaited them.

Uriel climbed onto the firing step of the raised earthen berm behind which he and the defenders sheltered. He raised his bolter high for all to see, and shouted, 'Stand to! For Pavonis with courage and honour!'

The hundreds of soldiers within earshot echoed his cry as they rushed from their dugouts to join him. That Space Marines from such an illustrious Chapter stood with these men was a potent symbol of their determination to resist the enemy at all costs, and Uriel knew that his very presence would be inspirational to them. Not a man among the 44th or the PDF wanted to be seen as weak before the Emperor's finest warriors, and they would fight to their last breath to prove their courage.

Uriel swung his bolter over the lip of the earthwork, his practiced eye taking in the details of the tau assault in the time it took to rack the slide. His Space Marines took up positions next to him as the hundreds of Guardsmen stationed to defend the Diacrian Bridge deployed with a clatter of boots on duck-boards. Banners waved, and the shouts of sergeants and officers cut through the crash of explosions and the crack of tau weapons' fire.

'We're slaughtering them!' cried Colonel Loic, clambering to the firing step beside Uriel.

'For now,' agreed Uriel, 'but they'll adapt soon enough and try something different.'

'They'll try to pin us in place with expendable troops while they advance.'

Uriel was surprised at Loic's insight and nodded. 'Any moment now I suspect.'

'I think you might be right,' said Loic, looking up.

Uriel followed the colonel's gaze as he heard a flapping, tearing noise, like a swarm of bats erupting from a cave mouth. High above, the sky was filled with a host of chitinous blue creatures with narrow wings and hideous insect-like features. They dropped hard and fast, lightly armoured assault troops set to disrupt the Imperial defences long enough for their tau masters to reach the lines.

'Stingwings!' shouted Uriel. 'Reserve squads, drop them!'

Fire support groups stationed further back from the front lines opened fire, their weapons aimed at the sky for just such an eventuality. Las-bolts streaked upwards, and the cries of the wounded xenos creatures could be heard over the volleys, until the interceptor guns and the heavy stubbers mounted on the cupolas of PDF Chimeras joined in.

'That won't stop them all,' said Loic.

'Probably not, but it should stop enough of them.'

Uriel was pleased to see a lack of fear on Loic's face. Political appointment he might be, but the man had courage. He returned his attention to his front as the Imperial guns continued to wreak havoc amongst the tau vehicles. Realising their transports were death traps, most of the tau squad commanders debussed their troops to advance on foot. Uriel saw darting tau warriors moving forwards in the cover of craters and wrecked tanks. Rolling banks of propellant smoke drifted across the battlefield, twitched by solid rounds and burned away by tau gunfire.

Behind the Fire Warriors, the bulkier forms of battle-suits moved through the smoke, the blue glow of their jet packs flaring and marking their passage. It was impossible to count them, but Uriel saw a worrying amount drawing close.

'Battlesuits coming in behind them,' he said, passing the word to the Ultramarines over the vox. 'Take out the heavier units where possible.'

Acknowledgements came through from his warriors, and the hard noise of bolters erupted as contact was made further down the lines. As the gap between the two forces shrank, withering storms of gunfire and explosions erupted along the Imperial defences. Tau shots fused the earth of the berm and punched Imperial soldiers backwards with the impacts, their armour offering no protection against the powerful energies.

Screams punctuated the din of battle, the dreadful pain of human beings and the welcome agony of their alien foes. Both Ultramarine Dreadnoughts, Brother Zethus and Brother Speritas, stalked the length of the redoubts, lending their incredible firepower to sections where the tau pressed hardest. The noise of their weapons' fire was like the thunder of the gods, their lascannons like bolts of lightning from the heavens.

Corpses littered the ground before the defences, and flames ripped through the battlefield from ignited fuel lines and cooking ammunition. Uriel fired streams of explosive shells into the ranks of the tau, each volley dropping a handful of enemy warriors, though many more forged on towards the defences.

This was what he was crafted for, this righteous slaughter of the foes of mankind, and Uriel felt a savage pride in his ability to deal death. He spared a glance to either side, seeing Space Marines firing with grim, remorseless accuracy into the tau. They fought like heroes, each one a warrior worthy of being immortalised in song and verse. Yet none looked for glory for its own sake, only for the Emperor and for the Chapter.

Amongst them, the soldiers of the 44th Lavrentians and the Pavonis PDF were fighting with equal fervour. As Colonel Loic had predicted, the fire of the reserve squads and interceptor guns had not been enough to prevent the Stingwing assault from hitting home, and a brutal, short-range firefight spilled out from the rear of the Imperial defences.

Even as he saw the spreading battle, so too did Colonel Loic. The PDF commander fired his pistol into the blue-winged xenos species, and led a savage countercharge into the midst of the aliens. Contrary to Uriel's earlier assessment, Loic was indeed proficient with his power sabre, and the energised blade clove a bloody path through his enemies. Loic caught sight of Uriel and raised his sword in salute to him before pressing onwards into the bloody melee.

What Space Marines brought to any fight was not just their awesome skill at arms; it was the *idea* of what they represented in the minds of those that fought with them and against them that made them so formidable. The Adeptus Astartes were symbolic of Imperial might, symbolism with the means to enforce the will of the Imperium wherever the Emperor demanded it.

That was what made the Space Marines a force beyond anything their numbers might represent. A man could be defeated, but a Space Marine was invincible, indomitable and unstoppable. The tau had learned this in the Zeist campaign, and they were about to learn it once again on Pavonis.

Uriel bent to swap out his bolter's magazine, the process completed with a practiced economy of motion. A bright bolt of superheated plasma exploded further along the line, showering him with glassy fragments of fused earth. Two Space Marines fell from the firing step, hurled back by the powerful blast, and a war-scarred battlesuit forced its way through the ruined parapet, its weapons trailing a glowing fuzz of smoke as they recharged.

A wedge of battlesuits followed behind it, blazing cannons clearing whole swathes of the berm of defenders as they began to spread out. Fire Warriors gathered around them, and Uriel saw the danger immediately. He slung his bolter, looking around to see what aid he could call upon. Drawing his sword, he charged along the firing step towards the battlesuits.

'Squad Ventris, with me!' he yelled. 'Brother Speritas, I need you at my location!'

LEARCHUS HUGGED THE ground as the convoy of tau tanks passed so close to his position that he could have run forwards and planted a melta charge on the nearest vehicle before its pilot would have a chance to react. The wake of the skimmers' anti-grav engines sent a warm ripple of air over his camo-cape as well as an unpleasantly alien reek of burnt metal. The proximity of the aliens threatened to get the better of him, but he viciously quelled his rising anger and disgust.

He knew they had a mission, but the further he and his scouts pressed south, the slimmer it seemed their chances of completing it became. They could travel barely a kilometre without a warning burst on the vox from Sergeant Issam sending them to ground. It had been many years since Learchus had been a scout, and with every enemy unit they concealed themselves from, he remembered why he had been so glad to be elevated to full Astartes status.

The tanks passed out of sight, and Learchus once again threw off his cape and pushed himself to his feet. His armour was filthy, and he brushed leaves and mud from the burnished plates with a grimace of distaste. Was this Uriel's way of punishing him for his ambitions?

Learchus immediately discarded that thought as unworthy, and took a deep, calming breath, silently reciting the catechisms of devotion to soothe his ragged temper as Issam ghosted through the long ferns towards the assembling scouts.

Learchus looked up at the sky. Clouds were drawing in from the ocean. A stiff breeze was building, and Learchus could taste the promise of lightning on the air.

'Stay down,' hissed Issam, running, crouched over.

Learchus dropped to his belly and pulled the cloak back over his armoured body. Issam dropped to the wet earth next to him, squinting out to sea and tugging Learchus's cloak to fully cover his body.

'Don't worry,' said Learchus, 'they're gone.'

'Storm coming in,' said Issam, ignoring Learchus's words. 'A big one by the looks of it.'

'I think so,' agreed Learchus sourly. 'Yet more joyful news.'

'It will help us move forward undetected.'

'There is that I suppose,' said Learchus. 'Then let us continue.'

Issam pressed his hand over Learchus's forearm and shook his head. 'No, we wait here in this hollow for a few minutes before pressing on.'

Learchus rounded on Issam angrily. 'We have a mission, Issam, and we cannot afford to spend time resting. We need to complete our mission and return to our battle brothers.'

'We're not resting,' said Issam. 'We're waiting in case there's a rearguard.'

Learchus cursed softly, but said nothing, waiting in silence as a soft rain began to fall. At length, another Hammerhead tank, escorted by a pair of the nimble scout vehicles, slipped past their hiding place on the same route as the heavier convoy.

Once Issam was satisfied there were no more tau forces, he issued orders to his scouts with a series of chopping hand motions. Learchus rose and squatted on his haunches, wringing his hands as he looked towards the south.

Learchus looked up at Issam, angry with himself for not thinking of a rearguard and angry at his exclusion from the fighting.

'How far to Praxedes do you think?' he asked without apology.

Issam drew a folded map from a pouch at his waist. The map was laminated and printed with contours, colours and symbols that Learchus knew he should recognise, but the meaning of which eluded him. Issam pointed to Praxedes and traced his finger northwards.

'Based on how far I believe we've come, I'd say another two days, but maybe longer if we have to keep taking refuge from the tau.'

'Three days,' said Learchus. 'The war might be lost by then!'

'Nevertheless, that's how long it will take.'

'That is too long,' said Learchus. 'We must be there quicker.'

The scout sergeant squared his shoulders. 'How long has it been since your elevation to full Astartes?'

'Ninety years, give or take,' answered Learchus. 'Why?'

'Some warriors relish the game of stealth, matching their wits against a foe in shadow games behind the lines, but not you. Scouting doesn't suit you, not any more.'

'No, it does not,' stated Learchus. 'I am a far more straightforward warrior. I desire only to meet my foes face-to-face and blade-to-blade where courage can be tested and honour satisfied. This mission flies in the face of everything that makes me who I am.

'You are forgetting your earlier lesson about the mission,' said Issam. 'You long to take the fight to the tau.'

'I do, with every fibre of my being,' said Learchus. 'The desire to attack those tanks was almost overpowering, but if Uriel's exile and return has taught me anything, it is the folly of abandoning the teachings of the Codex Astartes.'

'It *reminded* you of that, Learchus,' said Issam, 'but you never forget that lesson as an Astartes Scout. Abandoning the Codex when you're cut off from your brothers is a sure fire way to end up dead. Had you attacked those tanks or moved out we would all be corpses by now.'

'I know that,' snapped Learchus. 'I am not an initiate, fresh from the recruitment auxilia.'

'A fact of which I am acutely aware,' said Issam. 'If you were, you would listen to me and show me a bit of damn respect. I think you forget that I too am a sergeant.'

Learchus felt his already frayed temper threaten to get the better of him, but once again his iron control clamped down on it. He was being ridiculous. Issam was right.

'I am sorry, brother,' said Learchus. 'You are, of course, right. I apologise.'

'Accepted,' said Issam graciously, 'but I think our getting to Praxedes to rescue to the good governor is the least of our worries.'

'Those tanks that passed,' said Learchus.

'Indeed.'

'How many did you make it this time?'

'Including the rearguard, thirteen vehicles,' replied Issam, 'four Hammerheads, three Sky Rays and six Devilfish. The formations are getting larger each time.'

'Aye,' agreed Learchus, 'and heavier. What do you make of it?'

'Too many for a scouting or harrying force,' said Issam. 'This is a full flanking thrust.'

'That is what I was afraid of. We have to send word to Uriel.'

'The Codex states that to remain undetected Scouts should maintain vox-silence when behind enemy lines,' Issam reminded him.

'I know that too, but if we do nothing our brothers will be outflanked and surrounded. They will be destroyed, and this war will be over whether we get the governor back or not.'

Issam nodded. 'The tau will almost certainly pick up such a signal.'

'That is a chance we have to take,' said Learchus, feeling the certainties that underpinned his life melting away one by one.

THE LEAD BATTLESUIT stepped down from the firing step, and a Chimera exploded as a plasma bolt punched through its hull just beneath the turret ring. Colonel Loic and men of the 44th were reacting to the threat, but they would not be able to plug the gap. Only the Space Marines could do that. Uriel and his warriors fought their way through the fury of battle towards the breach as Fire Warriors clambered up the earthen bulwark.

The battlesuits had seen them and were turning to face them. All it would take would be for them to hold the Space Marines for a moment and it would be too late to seal the breach.

A voice laden with ancient wisdom and clinical detachment came over the vox. 'I am with you, Captain Ventris. Commencing hostile engagement.'

A searing blast of light came from behind Uriel, and the upper section of the first battlesuit exploded as though struck by a bolt of horizontal lightning. Its smoking shell remained upright for a few seconds before toppling over the parapet. Another flashing shot blew the head and shoulder mount from a second battlesuit, and yet another punched a ragged hole through the chest of a third.

Uriel's sword tore through the chest carapace of the nearest battlesuit, and he ducked below the slashing fist of its neighbour. A heavy calibre round nicked his hip and spun him around. He dropped to one knee as his attacker was slammed back against the berm by a ferocious impact that caved in its chest.

'Careful, Captain Ventris,' said Brother Speritas, his voice booming from his sarcophagus-mounted augmitters. 'You have not the armour to match mine.'

Brother Speritas, whose mortal flesh was all but destroyed on the daemon-haunted world of Thrax, towered over Uriel, the Dreadnought's armoured frame like a great slab of iron given shape and form to make war.

Tau weapons fire spattered from Speritas's hull without effect, and his monstrous, crackling fist smote another battlesuit to destruction as he waded into the tau armoured suits. Too close for weapons fire, the tau were no match for the up-close and personal fury of an Astartes Dreadnought.

Uriel ducked and wove his way through the combat, using the massive form of Speritas to weave a deadly path through the wedge of battlesuits. His warriors fanned out around him, shooting into the breach, and driving back the Fire Warriors using the battlesuits' assault to force their way in. Close-range bolter-fire turned the breach into a blitzing hurricane of explosions and ricochets through which nothing could live. Tau screams and the wet smacks of solid rounds on flesh punctuated the staccato barks of gunfire.

All Uriel could hear were explosions and the furious clang of metal on metal. He hacked the legs from another battlesuit, and spun his sword around before stabbing it down through its chest. Experience had taught him that the head section of these suits did not actually contain the wearer's cranium, and as he twisted his sword clear, its blade was stained red with tau blood.

At last there were no more foes, and Uriel swiftly scanned the battlefield. Colonel Loic and his men had taken up position on the firing step and poured volley after volley into the tau. A green and gold banner flew proudly above the fighting, and Uriel nodded to the PDF colonel as Brother Speritas crushed the life from the last of the battlesuits.

Space Marines secured the breach as earth-moving dozers moved to seal it once more.

Uriel switched back to his bolter, and checked the load as he climbed back to the firing step. Loic greeted him with a wide grin, his bald head streaked with sweat and blood. The man's chest heaved with excitement, and he slapped a gloved hand on Uriel's arm.

'By the Emperor, we did it!' he cried. 'I didn't think we could do it, but damn me if we didn't just give them a bloody nose they won't soon forget.'

Looking out over the battlefield, Uriel had to agree. Dawn's light was spreading across the wreck and corpse-choked wasteland, though drifting clouds of smoke obscured the full scale of the fighting. The first battle for the Diacrian Bridge had been won, but the cost had been high. Hundreds of the defenders were dead, but the tau had suffered the worst of the fight. Uriel estimated nearly fifty tanks were burning and that at least a thousand or more tau had been killed.

Colonel Loic wiped the blade of his sword clean on the tunic of a fallen tau soldier before sheathing the blade. He followed Uriel's gaze over the battlefield.

'They'll come at us again soon, won't they?'

'Yes,' said Uriel.

'Then we need to be ready for the next attack,' said Loic, waving over a vox-operator. 'I'll get extra ammunition distributed and have food and water brought.'

'That will take too long,' said Uriel. 'We need to make do with what we have.'

'No, I had supply stations set up just behind our lines,' explained Loic, between issuing orders over the vox. 'They're manned by PDF non-combatants, and they can have supplies to us inside of five minutes.'

'That was perceptive of you,' said Uriel, impressed at Loic's thoroughness.

'Simple logistics, really,' said Loic modestly. 'Even the bravest soldier can't fight if he's got no ammo or he's dehydrated, now can he?'

Uriel nodded. 'I underestimated you, Colonel Loic, and for that I apologise.'

Loic waved away his words, though Uriel saw that he was inordinately pleased with them.

'So how do you think they'll come at us this time, Captain Ventris?'

'Cautiously,' said Uriel. 'They were over-confident before, and they won't make that mistake again.'

'Captain Gerber said the tau don't make mistakes,' said Loic.

'They do,' said Uriel, 'but they don't make the same one twice.'

JENNA WATCHED AS Mykola Shonai was dragged from the cells, her bare and broken feet leaving glistening trails of blood on the wet floor. The woman's body was no more than a whipped and beaten mass of dead meat, and whatever secrets remained within her skull were going with her to the grave.

Two enforcers with their mirrored visors drawn down over their faces took her away, and Jenna felt a leaden weight settle in her stomach at the sight of the former governor's corpse, knowing that she bore a share of responsibility for Mykola Shonai's death.

She saw Culla through the door of the cell, naked to the waist and dousing his sweating torso with water from a battered copper ewer. Anger overtook her, and she stormed into the cell, her hands itching to reach for the predicant's throat.

Culla smiled as she entered the cell, his face serene and beatific in its sense of accomplishment. His beard was matted with dried blood and his fists were smeared with the stuff.

'You killed her,' said Jenna. 'You beat her to death.'

'I did,' said Culla, 'and the warp will devour her filthy soul forever. Rejoice, Judge Sharben, for one less heretic besets the Imperium. By such deeds are we made safe.'

'Safe are we?' hissed Jenna. 'Did you learn anything from her? Anything that will help us fight the tau armies?'

'Nothing she did not confess upon her arrest,' admitted the preacher, towelling himself dry with a linen cloth, 'but such wickedness ensured her a long and painful ending. Would that it had been longer and more agonising. Do you not agree?'

Jenna saw Culla's face transform from serenity to something loathsome and reptilian. His eyes glittered with a predatory hunger, aching for Jenna to say something foolish that would see her taking Mykola Shonai's place upon the chair bolted to the floor.

'She deserved death, that much we agree on,' said Jenna, choosing her words carefully, 'but a death decreed by Imperial justice. She should have been declared guilty by a conclave of Judges and executed by the proper authorities.'

'I already told you, Sharben, I have the authority of the Emperor,' said Culla, pushing past her and leaving the cell. 'What higher authority is there?'

Jenna let him go and sank to her haunches, letting her finger trace spirals in the blood on the floor. It was sticky and still warm. A human being had died here, a woman she had respected and admired. Mykola Shonai's actions had damned her, and there was no doubt in Jenna's mind that her crime not only warranted, but demanded, a death sentence.

Had she deserved to die like this, beaten to the bone by a madman who claimed a highly dubious direct connection to the Emperor? Imperial law was mercilessly harsh, but with good reason. Without such control, humanity would soon fall prey to the myriad creatures and dangers that pressed in from every side. Such harshness was necessary and vital, but Jenna had always believed that the law could also be just.

The blood on her fingertips gave the lie to that notion, and she felt her anger at Culla scale new heights. The preacher had violated the core of her beliefs and notions of the world, but that wasn't the worst part.

The worst part was that she had let him

She hated Culla, but she hated her complicity in his actions more. He had dragged her into his barbarity, and she had stood by and done nothing, even when she had known it was wrong.

Jenna took her fingers from the floor, rubbing the sticky blood between her fingertips. She lifted her head and looked up at the bronze eagle set high in the far wall of the cell. The symbol was supposed to remind the condemned what they had forsaken and who stood in judgement of them.

It served to remind Jenna who and what *she* served.

Culla claimed he worked with a higher authority, well, so too did Jenna.

She stood and turned in one motion, marching from the cell with a hard, jagged anger crystallising within her. Jenna slid her shock maul from its sheath on her shoulder, and strode through the dank corridors of the Glasshouse towards the sound of Culla's booming voice. He was in the section occupied by the tau prisoners, and Jenna felt a curious calm descend as the sound of his voice grew louder.

At last, Jenna emerged into the wide chamber that served as the holding pen for the tau, where a group of eleven of the dejected aliens were kept locked in cells two metres by three that were illuminated every hour of every day. The prisoners' effects, such as they were, were kept in the guardroom opposite the cells, as were the guards' myriad devices of torment.

Standing before the cells, Culla was being robed in his emerald chasuble by Enforcer Dion, while Enforcer Apollonia brought a number of items of excruciation from the guardroom. Knives, saws, pliers, devices of scarification and implements of burning were laid out on a long metal tray attached to a surgical table fixed to the floor. Culla's eviscerator sword was propped against the table like a favourite walking stick, and Jenna was struck by the random nature of her observation.

A third enforcer, rendered anonymous by his mirrored visor, held one of the prisoners. The remains of a shorn white topknot told Jenna that it was the tau female named La'tyen, the first captive brought to the Glasshouse. The tau's hands were bound before her, and Jenna saw that her defiance and hatred were undimmed. In the corner of the chamber, the xenolexicon servitor the Ultramarines had provided stood as an unmoving witness to events.

Culla sighed as he saw Jenna enter. 'Unless you have come to aid me in delivering the Emperor's wrath upon these degenerate animals, you have no place here. Be gone, woman.'

'I'm here to stop you, Culla,' said Jenna, her voice calm and controlled.

'Stop me?' laughed Culla. 'Why in the world would you want to do that? These are a filthy xenos species. You can't tell me you believe the likes of them deserve mercy.'

'You're right, I don't, but you violated Imperial Law with what you did to Mykola Shonai, and I am here to see justice done.'

'Justice?' sneered Culla. 'A meaningless concept in the face of the enemies our species faces. What does the xenos or the heretic know of justice? Save your petty notions of justice for children and simpletons, Sharben. I deal in harsh realities, and I have work to do.'

'Not any more,' said Jenna, moving to stand between the preacher and the cells. 'Dion, Apollonia, step away from Prelate Culla.'

Both enforcers hesitated, torn between loyalty to their commander and their recently engendered fear and awe of Culla. Jenna felt the moment stretch, her thumb hovering over the activation stud of her shock maul. Part of her recoiled at facing down an Imperial preacher with a weapon in her hand, but the core of what had driven her to become a Judge in the Adeptus Arbites knew that this was the right and just course of action.

Neither Dion nor Apollonia moved, and Culla's lip twisted in a sneer.

'The enforcers are mine now,' he said. 'I warned you not to cross me.'

'And I told you *I* was the commander here.'

Jenna's thumb pressed down, and she slammed the crackling shock maul into Culla's face.

♘
SIXTEEN

THE LAVRENTIAN PREACHER dropped, reeling from the unexpected blow, and Jenna stepped in to deliver a second. She could not afford to give Culla an opening for retaliation, and her weapon arced around to render the man insensible.

The blow never connected.

Enforcer Dion slammed into her, knocking her from her feet and driving the breath from her. She rolled with him as he took hold of her wrist and tried to smash the shock maul from her hand. Jenna squirmed from his grip and drove her knee up into Dion's groin. He hissed in a breath, but kept hold of her, using his weight to keep her pinned to the ground.

'What the hell are you doing?' Jenna yelled at him. 'I'm your commanding officer!'

Dion didn't answer, which was smart, saving his breath for the struggle. He smashed his forehead into her nose and she felt it break. Blood filled her mouth and bright lights burst before her eyes. Dion tried the

same move again, but she twisted out the way and his
head cracked against the floor.

He yelped in pain, and Jenna freed her left arm. She
hammered her fist into Dion's throat. He grunted in
pain, and his grip loosened on her other wrist. She
heard a shout of alarm and sounds of a struggle behind
her, but couldn't spare a second's focus to see what was
happening around her.

Though she hated to do it, she swung the shock
maul and slammed it against the side of Dion's skull,
finally dislodging him. Breathless, Jenna struggled
from beneath his suddenly prone form as she heard
the angry bellow of an eviscerator roaring to life. She
froze for a moment, the innate fear of such a painfully
lethal weapon like a bucket of freezing water to the
senses.

How had Culla recovered so quickly? The man must
be possessed of superhuman resilience to even be conscious after a shock maul to the face. A dreadful scream
filled the chamber, louder and more agonised than it
was possible to imagine. It was the sound of a human
being in the most insufferable pain, the sound of raw,
naked terror. A sound that was abruptly cut off and
replaced by an even more hideous noise.

Jenna rolled to her knees. Dizziness swamped her and
she fought to keep from vomiting. She saw Culla was
still on the ground, the skin of his temple burned by the
energy field of her weapon. Who had activated the eviscerator?

Blood sprayed the air in an arcing fountain, and Jenna
felt it spatter her face. She blinked it away, and saw the
source of the horrific screaming through a blur of tears
and red liquid. The enforcer that had been holding the
tau prisoner was on his knees, and he had been virtually
split in two.

The roaring chainsaw blade of Culla's eviscerator was buried in the middle of his stomach, having ripped downwards through collarbone, ribs and sternum. Jenna screamed as the weapon was torn free, removing the upper quadrant of the man's torso.

She caught motion from the corner of her eye. Apollonia was bringing her shotgun to bear. The eviscerator swung around and hacked through the weapon before she could fire. The blade bit into Apollonia's shoulder, and the jagged teeth of the sword chewed through plasteel, mesh, meat and bone to saw her arm from her body in a vile spray of mangled flesh.

Apollonia fell, blood squirting from her shoulder like a ruptured hydraulic line.

The enforcer was dead before she hit the ground. Jenna pulled herself unsteadily to her feet and yanked the alarm pin on her belt. Blaring klaxons erupted throughout the Glasshouse.

La'tyen advanced towards her. Jenna circled around the surgical table, keeping it between them, and trying to buy some time. The gigantic weapon looked absurd in the tau warrior's hands, almost too heavy for her to lift, but Jenna didn't doubt that hatred would give her the strength to wield it.

Her eyes flicked towards Culla and Dion, but both men were out of the fight for now. Jenna was on her own until more enforcers responded to her alarm.

She and the tau continued circling the surgical table, the room filled with the deafening roar of the enormous chainblade. Jenna tried not to think of how painful it would be to die being carved up by such a horrific weapon.

'It's over,' said Jenna. 'Put the weapon down.'

From the corner of the room, the xenolexicon servitor repeated her words.

Instead of attacking, La'tyen backed towards the cells and brought the giant sword down on the locking mechanism of the nearest door. It exploded in a shower of sparks as the adamantine teeth tore through the metal as though it were pulped wood.

The cell door swung open and one of the captive tau emerged. The eviscerator swung down again and another door was carved open. Jenna's eyes snapped towards the chamber's main entrance but there was no sign of other enforcers.

Once more the eviscerator tore through a door lock, though the tau that stepped from this cell was clearly no warrior. Taller than the others, he was possessed of a serene poise that the others lacked. This tau spoke a few words to the others, and Jenna saw the effect his words had on them. The warlike cast of their features softened, and their eyes grew a little wider, as though hearing the words of a revered saint or a god made flesh. The servitor repeated the words in Imperial Gothic, but the roar of the eviscerator drowned them out.

One of the tau swept up Apollonia's shock maul, and, as Jenna watched, another alien warrior lifted Dion's weapon. They began to spread out, intending to surround her, and though their features were alien and unnatural the hatred in their eyes was plain to see.

The odds were already against her taking out La'tyen, but with yet more tau against her, she was dead if she stayed to fight.

Jenna turned and ran from the chamber.

LA'TYEN WATCHED THE female torturer flee and made to pursue, but a restraining hand took hold of her arm.

Angrily, she turned to rebuke the owner of the hand, but the angry words died in her throat as she saw Aun'rai.

'Let her go,' said the Ethereal, and La'tyen immediately deactivated the blade she had taken from the shouting gue'la who had taken such relish in their humiliation and pain. 'Our first priority is escape, not vengeance. Revenge is pointless, and only serves to divert us from our service to the Greater Good.'

'Of course, revered Ethereal,' said La'tyen, bowing her head, 'for the Greater Good.'

Aun'rai turned to those tau who were free and said, 'Our captors will be back soon, and we must return to our comrades. Fetch my honour blades.'

Though none of their number were singled out by Aun'rai's command, a warrior named Shas'la'tero moved towards the room opposite the cells, all of them knowing without any words being spoken which of their number was singled out. A tau warrior gathered a set of keys from one of the dead torturers and began opening those cells that remained locked.

Within moments, fifteen tau were gathered in the chamber, and Shas'la'tero returned with a pair of short, caramel-coloured batons, each topped with a glinting blue gem. Aun'rai received the batons with a quick nod of the head.

Aun'rai twisted each of the gems and pressed them into the body of the batons. They began flashing in a regular pattern, before suddenly blinking urgently in an answering sequence.

'Secure that door,' said Aun'rai, indicating the chamber's entrance. 'Fellow servants of the Greater Good are on their way to us.'

'What do you require us to do with them?' asked La'tyen, pointing to where one of the mirror-helmeted captors lay next to the unconscious form of the shaven-headed torturer with the forked beard.

'Kill them,' said Aun'rai.

SEVENTY KILOMETRES NORTH, Captain Mederic ran for his life. Some preternatural sixth sense made him duck behind a tree trunk the instant before he heard the sharp, whining crack of a kroot rifle. A portion of the tree exploded next to his head, and only his goggles kept him from losing an eye as razor splinters of wood and sap sprayed his face.

He ducked down and checked the charge of his weapon. Half-full. Enough to give his pursuers cause to keep their heads down. Keeping low, Mederic rolled around the tree and let loose a series of shots. Aiming quickly towards the flashes of movement he saw in the long grasses and bushes of the hills, he didn't expect to hit much, but hopefully the threat of his weapon would give the aliens pause.

Men and women in the drab green scout uniforms of the 44th's Hounds darted through the hills and trees in their desperate bid to escape the trap the kroot hunters had set for them.

He should have known it was too good to be true, a forward observation post in the Owsen Hills that was strung just a little too far ahead of the advance forces to be safe.

After the warning from the Ultramarines that the tau were trying to hook around the hills north of Olzetyn, the 44th had rolled from Camp Torum to meet the threat head-on.

The heavy armour was some way behind the infantry, and Mederic's Hounds were first in the fight. The tau were moving swiftly, but the Hounds had blunted the thrust of their advance, lying in ambush for Pathfinder teams, and leaving cunningly hidden booby traps in their wake to target enemy tanks. Enemy squad leaders and commanders were singled out with deadly accurate sniper fire, and the tau advance slowed to a crawl as each potential ambush site had to be scouted thoroughly.

Pathfinders sent to engage them and bring them to battle were outmanoeuvred or ambushed and killed. The Hounds were like ghosts, moving through the mist-shrouded hills with all the skill and stealth learned the hard way on the battlefields of the Eastern Fringe. Mederic had trained his men well, and that sublime skill bred a confidence unmatched in any other soldier in the regiment.

That had been what had done for them, thought Mederic gloomily. Nothing could touch them, no force the tau had sent after them had come close to catching them, and no foe was beyond the reach of their weapons. How easy it was, he reflected, for confidence to slip into arrogance. Mederic knew they should have left the observation post unmolested, it had been too easy, too tempting.

Despite his misgivings, he had led the assault only to find themselves under attack.

Dropping from the trees and rising from concealed pits, the kroot were like feral barbarians or the forest itself coming to life. Raw, pink-fleshed monsters with savagely erect quills appeared from nowhere, smeared in mud and earth, and armed with bladed rifles.

Ten men had died in the first moments of the ambush, six more in the following seconds of stunned disbelief that the Hounds could have been tricked. Training and instinct kicked in after that, and, realising that standing and fighting was hopeless, Mederic had ordered his men to fight clear of the trap. Blood, bayonets and raw courage punched a hole in the kroot noose, and sixteen hours later they were still running.

Mederic scanned the undergrowth, remembering to keep one eye on the upper reaches of the trees. He saw movement ahead and swung his rifle to bear. A howling brute of a beast with a crest of vivid red quills vaulted from branch to branch, its ululating war cry taken up by a hundred other bestial throats. The creature halted, squatting easily on a high branch, and Mederic squeezed off a shot before it moved again.

His lasrifle cracked and spat a bolt of hard energy, but the kroot was already moving, its spring-like limbs pushing off the branch before his shot connected. More shots filled the air as his soldiers followed his example. Return fire splintered trees and ricocheted from rocks.

But the Hounds were too good not to have displaced after firing.

Mederic swung back around the tree as a trio of enormous creatures crested the hillside below him. Larger than the biggest grox he'd ever seen and looking like something an ogryn might ride into battle, the creatures were like thicker, quadruped versions of the kroot. Lumbering forwards on limbs as thick as Mederic's chest, they were enormous beasts of burden, though from the size of their fists and roaring, beaked maws, he didn't fancy his chances if it came to going toe to toe with such a monster.

A robed kroot stood tall on the back of each one, manning a heavy, long-barrelled gun fitted to the beast's enormous saddle arrangement. The kroot screeched and hollered as they moved with the motion of the enormous beast, and the others squawked frenziedly at the sight of them.

Mederic didn't need any specialised scout training to know these were bad news, and he bolted from cover as the red-quilled leader barked a shrill order.

'Down!' shouted Mederic, hurling himself flat.

The air split with booming cracks, like the rifles the kroot carried, but a hundred times louder. Flashing bolts of energy speared through the forest, turning the daylight blue. One beam struck a boulder and blasted it to fragments, each one a deadly bullet that cut down half a dozen of Mederic's men. Another struck a thick tree trunk and toppled a tree that had taken centuries to grow so tall and broad in an instant.

Mederic rolled as the tree crashed down, eating dirt and twigs as other soldiers were brought down by its fall. He didn't see where the third shot impacted. Another three shots banged and he heard the screams of Guardsmen in pain.

'Tylor, Deren, Minz!' he yelled, rolling to his feet. 'With me! Form a line on me and take out those gunners.'

Three of his scouts immediately turned and took up position with him, rifles going to their shoulders and scopes pressed tightly to their eyes. Minz took the first shot, her bolt punching one of the kroot gunners from its perch atop the muscular beast. Deren shot the kroot that attempted to climb up and take its place.

Tylor and Mederic both put las-bolts through the chest of the middle gunner, and the fire from the kroot's big guns slackened. They needed to displace, but even as he drew a bead on the kroot climbing to take his place, Mederic saw that it wouldn't matter. The red-quilled leader was moving his warriors around to flank them. There was nowhere to displace to, and he hoped that this last defiant stand had bought the rest of his men time to make good their getaway.

'Keep firing!' he ordered. 'We're only going to get a few shots, so make them count!'

He put down another kroot and turned to slam in a fresh clip. The trees to his right exploded, and Mederic was slammed into the ground. He tasted blood and dirt, and looked through the haze of smoke and dizziness to see Minz and Deren lying dead in a pulped mess of blood and shattered timber.

His rifle was useless, the stock shattered and the barrel warped beyond use. He reached for his pistol and knife, but his sidearm was gone, the holster empty.

Only his blade was exactly where it was meant to be.

Something moved through the haze of smoke, and he surged to his feet as he saw a crest of red quills go past him. Mederic staggered and lurched through the haze of gun-smoke, his blade bared and his heart thudding with the need to kill this enemy. He slashed his blade though the mist, screaming for the kroot to face him.

'Come on, you alien bastard!' he yelled. 'You wanted a fight, well fight me, damn you!'

There… a glimpse of mottled pink flesh and a flash of vibrant red. Mederic set off towards the sight, his blade held before him. He drew closer and prepared to strike. Then the mist cleared and he saw Tylor pinned to a tree with his combat knife. His chest was cut open and a fan of blood from his skull patterned the pale bark of the tree.

'Emperor's grace,' hissed Mederic, dropping to his knees. He could still hear the whooping squawks of the kroot, but they sounded distant and muted, as though coming from far away. Was that an acoustic trick of the hills' geography or had that last explosion damaged his hearing?

Then he heard another sound, a throaty rumble from over the hillside. It was deep and shook the earth, travelling along his bones and through his body like the beginnings of an earthquake. Mederic snatched up

Tylor's fallen rifle and marched uphill towards a sound he knew well.

As he reached the top of the hill, the mist and smoke thinned, and he emerged from the forest to see the most beautiful thing he could have imagined; scores of armoured vehicles in the livery of the 44th Lavrentian Hussars. The battered remnants of his Hounds clustered around the regiment's tanks, bloody and exhausted, but unbowed.

Leading the armoured convoy was the mighty form of *Father Time*, and riding high in the Baneblade's cupola was Lord Nathaniel Winterbourne. The colonel's arm was bandaged and his skin had the unhealthy pallor of a veteran tanker, but his uniform was immaculate, and shone with all the pride and honour it represented. The gold and green banner of the 44th, with its proud golden horseman reflected the sunlight, and Mederic felt tears pricking at the corners of his eyes at the sight of it.

'Captain Mederic?' called Winterbourne, and he straightened his spine. Mederic marched over to where the colossal tank idled, the bone-shaking rumble of its engine like a force of nature.

'Sir,' said Mederic, holding onto the skirts of the tank to stop from falling over. He noticed that someone had written *Meat Grinder* on the skirt, and smiled despite his utter exhaustion.

'Damn fine job you did here, captain,' said Winterbourne. 'Slowed them up long enough for us to get the heavy stuff over from Brandon Gate. The savants said you couldn't do it, but I told them to go to hell. If anyone was going to hold the tau back it would be Mederic's Hounds.'

'Thank you, my lord,' said Mederic.

'Now get your men some food and water, captain,' said Winterbourne. 'If the report from Sergeant

Learchus is right, we're going to see a lot more action here. These hills and forests aren't our kind of terrain, so I'm going to need your men sharp to keep the armour safe from those damn kroot and drone spotters. Are you up to the task?'

Mederic thought back to the red-quilled kroot leader and snapped off a salute.

'The Hounds don't leave a fight once it's started,' he said.

JENNA RACKED THE pump of her shotgun and nodded to the enforcers who waited at her back. She eased along a walkway that opened on one side, towards the door to the chamber in which the tau had barricaded themselves. Behind her, fifteen men in black body armour and mirror-visored helmets came similarly armed.

On the opposite side of the door, another ten armed men carefully edged forwards, knowing that a number of armed alien warriors were behind it. The tau had a few weapons at best, but after Apollonia's death, Jenna was in no mood to take chances. She knew in all likelihood that Culla and Dion were also dead. She cared nothing for Culla, but Enforcer Dion's death sat like a lead weight in her stomach, and she knew she would have to deal with the guilt later. But for now, she had to restore order.

She glanced down into the courtyard of the Glasshouse, empty of prisoners now that a lockdown had been declared. The tower in the centre, normally a symbol of Imperial justice, seemed to be staring at her, the polarised glass dome at its summit mocking her with its unblinking gaze.

Jenna had gathered her enforcers immediately after fleeing the detention block, and their response times had been admirably swift. In less than ten minutes, two strike teams were assembled and mustered for action. She waved a two-man team equipped with a breaching ram and shaped charges.

'Enough to take the door off in one blast,' she ordered. 'No mistakes.'

With the order given, she waited a frustrating minute while the charges were rigged on the hinges. At last, the charges were ready to go, and Jenna took up position next to the door.

She opened a channel to all the enforcers under her command.

'No survivors. These bastards killed Culla and two of our own,' she said, neglecting to mention that she bore a measure of responsibility for those deaths. 'I want them all dead. Understood?'

Her enforcers acknowledged the order, and Jenna flattened herself against the wall.

Seeing that the men on the other side of the door had done likewise, she cocked her elbow and pumped her fist down twice in quick succession.

Two things happened at once.

The door hinges blew out with a dull *whump* and a clang of metal.

And hot propellant fumes filled the courtyard as an Orca drop-ship blasted the full force of its jets downwards to arrest its screaming descent.

Jenna covered her eyes as grit and acrid exhaust gases billowed outwards. Through the haze and dust of the howling aircraft's engines she could see it rotating on its axis in midair, and hear the whine of a powerful motor spooling up.

'Oh hell,' she said, and dropped flat to the ground.

A sheeting storm of supersonic shells ripped along the length of the walkway, sawing through the waist-high barrier and turning its entire length into a hellstorm of explosions and death. Ten enforcers died in the opening second, cut apart and reduced to shredded mists of blood and pulped bone.

Jenna covered her ears, but the noise was too great to be blocked out. Shrieking detonations blew chunks of stone and rebar from the walls, and she felt a burning line across her back where a fragment of red-hot shell casing embedded itself in her shoulder. Something exploded behind her, and her leg spasmed as hot metal ripped into the meat of her thigh. Desperately, she pulled herself along the walkway, ignoring the pain in a frantic bid to escape the slaughter.

The cannons worked their way back and forth across the walkway until nothing was left alive. Bright lights flared in the smoke, and blazing darts of fire streaked away from the gunship, each swiftly followed by a booming explosion.

Guard towers. They're taking out the guard towers with rockets...

She thought the cannons stopped firing, but it was impossible to tell. The ringing echoes of the shooting and explosions were deafening. Jenna tore off her helmet and reached around to her shoulder, scrabbling for the hot shrapnel. She could feel its heat even through her gloves and gritted her teeth against the pain as she dug it from her flesh.

Gasping with effort and soaked in sweat, Jenna blinked away tears of pain and confusion. What was going on? Where had the tau gunship come from? She was sure the guns weren't firing anymore, and she tried to roll onto her side to see what was happening.

Thick clouds of smoke and dust obscured much of the walkway, but it was clear that there was nothing left alive. All of her enforcers were dead. Was this what mercy and notions of justice achieved? She screamed with frustration and looked around for a weapon. Her shotgun was lying a few metres away at the edge of a pool of glistening blood. The stabbing pain in her leg flared as she moved towards it, and she craned her neck to see how badly she was hurt.

The breath caught in her throat at the appalling mess. Spinning shrapnel had ploughed a wide furrow through her right thigh, leaving a gristly horror of rubbery-looking meat and exploded bone.

Her breath came in panicked hikes, but a cry of pain died in her throat as she saw the tau prisoners emerge onto the walkway. They had all looked the same to her before, but now it was abundantly clear which one was the leader. Nothing in their garb appeared to differentiate them, but the xenos she had instinctively known was not a warrior stood apart from the others. His bearing and stature were subtly different in ways that Jenna could not appreciate on a conscious level. She just *knew* that this one was special.

The drop-ship had stopped firing, and even the roar of its jets seemed to ease down in the presence of the tau leader. Jenna watched him move, her pain forgotten in the strange calm that enveloped her at the sight of so noble a being. It seemed strange she had not felt it in any of the others.

She crawled towards her shotgun, sweat running in rivers down her dust and tear-streaked face. Her skin felt cold and her vision was blurring. She guessed she was slipping into shock.

The instant the gunship opened fire, the dynamic between her and the tau shifted from prisoner and captor to enemies at war, and Jenna had no compunction about killing an enemy in battle.

Slowly Jenna pulled herself over to her weapon, determined to get one shot off at the murderous aliens. All her attention was fixed on the matt black finish of the shotgun's pistol grip, the gleam of reflected light on its trigger and the textured surface of the pump action. Her world shrank to the distance between her and the weapon. Only by focusing her entire will on this one task could she fight down the pain.

Her fingers brushed the stock of the shotgun, and she wept at this little victory. Galvanised by this success, she made one last effort and pulled the weapon towards her. Jenna knew that she would only get one shot, and her hand eased around the grip.

Before she could prop herself up to fire, a blue-skinned foot stepped onto the barrel.

She felt figures around her, and looked up through her tears to see the tau leader standing over her, staring down with an expression that might have been pity or regret. Beside the leader was the tau whose white top-knot she had cut. La'tyen. It was her foot that rested on the shotgun and prevented Jenna from shooting. In contrast to the leader's face, La'tyen's expression was all hate.

Jenna had failed, and the weight of that failure stole what little strength remained to her. Her head dropped to the concrete floor, and she could feel its coldness against her clammy skin.

The tau leader knelt beside her and placed a hand against her forehead. His skin felt smooth and warm to the touch. It was comforting and the pain retreated, yet Jenna wanted to pull away from the alien.

'My name is Aun'rai, and I can ease your suffering,' said the tau in flawless Imperial Gothic. His pronunciation was perfect, though there was a lilt common to dwellers on the Eastern Fringe.

'You have an accent,' said Jenna, her voice faint.

The tau looked puzzled. 'I do?'

'Yes,' nodded Jenna. 'Whoever you learned from had one, and now you do too.'

'That is likely,' agreed the tau with an amused glint in his eye, as though only just coming to the realisation. 'Raphael's pronunciation seemed often to not match his written words. Still, it is not important.'

'If you're going to kill me, do it and go,' hissed Jenna. 'Or just let me die.'

Aun'rai shook his head. 'Kill you? I am not going to kill you. I heard what you said to the gue'la who was intent on wreaking agonising pain upon me. I wish you to know that we are not what he thinks we are. I want you to know that we are not your enemies.'

'You killed my enforcers,' spat Jenna. 'That makes you my enemy.'

'That was regrettable,' agreed Aun'rai, 'but it was necessary. Now we must be away before your aerial forces respond to the presence of my drop-ship.'

Aun'rai spoke a few words in his own language to La'tyen, who looked surprised and almost offended by them, but knelt to obey the tau leader's command nonetheless.

'What are you doing?' gasped Jenna as La'tyen lifted her onto her shoulder. Unimaginable pain flared briefly in her leg, but once again Aun'rai's touch lessened the agony of her wound. As much as she was repulsed by his alien touch, Jenna was pathetically thankful for the absence of pain. Her eyes fluttered and she felt her consciousness fading.

'My healers are going to make you whole again, gue'la,' said Aun'rai, 'and then I am going to offer you a place within the Tau'va.'

℧
SEVENTEEN

FOR THREE MORE days, the defenders of Olzetyn endured punishing attacks against their lines, tau missiles falling like rain on their fortified positions and gradually breaking up the defences. After the first attacks had been beaten back, the alien commander quashed thoughts of rash heroics, and every assault was planned with a thoroughness that would have made Roboute Guilliman proud.

The front lines of battle became a meat grinder where men and machines were chewed up in the constant storm of fighting. 'Stratum, once the jewel in the Administratum's bureaucracy, was now little more than a shelled ruin. The dwelling places of the adepts were flattened by tau missiles, and the debris hauled to the front line to build barricades. On the third day of the fighting, the Tower of Adepts was brought down, the austere structure collapsing into the gorge, taking with it thousands of years worth of tax and work records.

Perversely, its destruction gave rise to a huge cheer from the ranks of the defenders, proving that even faced with alien invasion, there were few more hated individuals than those who levied taxes.

The tau continued to attack along the length of the defences, but the twin bastions protecting the end of the Imperator remained impervious. For all that the tau continued to send tanks and missiles against the bastions, the main thrusts were intended to take the Diacrian Bridge. It was clearly the weak point in the western defence, and drew the lion's share of tau attention.

By such logic are battles won, but what an attacker can reason, a defender can anticipate.

Tau aircraft attempted a bombing run along the length of the Imperator Bridge, but Uriel had foreseen such a manoeuvre, and staggered lines of interceptor guns blew them from the sky with their payloads undelivered.

A massed cadre of battlesuits launched an aerial drop on the Midden to seize the rear defences of the Diacrian Bridge and open the flank of the Imperator. Five hundred tau warriors armed with the latest and deadliest weapons their armourers could provide dropped from the night skies amid the reeking shanties of the Midden, only to find seven squads of the 4th Company waiting for them. Supported by Land Raiders and Thunderfires, the Ultramarines turned the landing zone into a killing ground. Lavrentian heavy mortars pinned the survivors in place while Imperial forces withdrew to allow the massed squadrons of Basilisks on the eastern banks of the river to fire.

As though a thunderstorm had been plucked from the heavens and dropped on the Midden, the Spur promontory vanished in a firestorm of such epic proportions that when the sun rose, it was as if the conurbation had never existed. Few bemoaned its demise, for it had long been evacuated and its cramped, over-populated streets had been rife with disease, poverty and crime.

Colonel Loic was proving to be a more than capable soldier, a man who fought with the heart of a warrior and the mind of a scholar. Even the battle-hardened soldiers of the 44th, men to whom the PDF were little more than dangerous amateurs, came to regard the stocky commander as a true comrade-in-arms.

The tau were having the worst of the battle, but each day saw the Imperial lines forced back towards the bridges. Casualties on both sides were horrific, with thousands wounded and hundreds dying every day. Neither force could break the other, yet neither could afford to pull back from the relentless killing. Both defenders and attackers were fighting bravely, but Uriel knew the outcome of the tau attack was as inescapable as it was inevitable.

The defences of Olzetyn were holding, but the defenders were at breaking point.

It would take only the tiniest reversal for the balance of the war to change.

URIEL WIPED A hand across his forehead, smearing the blood he hadn't had time to clean from his face. He saw Chaplain Clausel looking at him and shook his head.

'It is not mine,' Uriel said, marching through the controlled anarchy of the Imperator Bridge. Damaged tanks were drawn up to either side of the street, Lavrentian and PDF engineers working side by side to get them operational again. Supply clerks and lifter servitors thronged the thoroughfare, ferrying ammunition, food and water to the troops fighting to defend the bridges.

'I know,' replied the Chaplain, moving aside to allow a flatbed truck laden with Guard-stamped crates to pass. 'The colour is too dark. Where did it come from?'

Uriel thought back to the last attack on the rapidly shrinking defence lines, sorting through the strobing images of killing filed in his memory, the stuff of nightmares yet to come.

'I am not sure,' he said. 'Maybe the Guardsman whose head exploded next to me during the last assault on the trenches thrown out before the Diacrian Bridge? Or maybe the Fire Warrior I gutted when he leapt from a crippled Devilfish?'

Clausel nodded in understanding. 'Battles like this blur together into one seamless horror of blood and killing. It is war at its most brutal and mechanical, where the skill of a warrior counts for less than where he happens to be standing when a missile impacts.'

'I am bred for battle, Chaplain,' said Uriel. 'My every muscle, fibre and organ was crafted by the Master of Mankind for the express purpose of waging the most brutal war imaginable, yet this unrelenting, daily carnage is alien to me. We should not be here, yet we cannot abandon the men giving their lives to defend this place.'

'Look to the Codex Astartes and you will find your answer,' advised Clausel. 'We Astartes excel at the lightning strike, the dagger thrust to the heart and the decisive, battle-winning stratagem, not this prolonged, static slaughter. For us to leave Olzetyn will almost surely mean its fall, yet might we not be better employed elsewhere?'

'We must be able to do something that will serve this war better, but I do not yet know what it is,' said Uriel. 'All I know is that it sits ill with me to stay and die here, where a hero's life can be ended by something arbitrary. It is anathema to me.'

'Indeed,' agreed Clausel. 'Every Space Marine hopes for an honourable death in battle, one the Chapter's taletellers will speak of for centuries to come. To face death holds no fear for us, but to meet it without honour is something to be dreaded.'

'Then what do you suggest?'

'It is for you to say how we fight, not I,' said Clausel, 'but I suspect you already have a plan in mind, do you not?'

Uriel nodded. 'The beginnings of one, but our allies will not like it.'

'Their likes or dislikes are immaterial to us,' said Clausel. 'You are a captain of the Ultramarines, and the decision of how best to defend Olzetyn and Pavonis is yours to make.'

'I know,' said Uriel.

URIEL AND CLAUSEL emerged into the widest section of the Imperator Bridge, which currently served as the triage station for the Imperial wounded. Uriel could never get used to the scale of the bloodshed endured by the Imperial Guard. Row upon row of body bags covered in long tarpaulins awaited removal, and long pavilion tents were filled with screaming men and overworked medicae as they tried to keep the number of dead from growing even larger.

In the aftermath of battle, Space Marine dead could normally be counted on one hand, but the dead of the Guard ran to thousands. It was a scale of slaughter that horrified Uriel, and served, once again, to remind him of the mortal soldier's courage and the honour he earned just by standing before the enemy with a gun in his hand.

Colonel Loic and Captain Gerber were already here, and the two Astartes warriors marched towards them as they conferred over a series of makeshift maps chalked on the side of a ruined structure.

The two soldiers turned at the sound of their armoured steps, and Uriel was struck by how much they had changed in the last few days. He and Clausel were still functioning at the peak of their abilities, but for mortals the strain of battle was all too evident. Both men were exhausted and had slept little since the fighting began. Loic had shed weight, and looked like a solider now, not like an adept playing at being a soldier.

Uriel had only met Gerber briefly before the first attack, but the man's no-nonsense attitude and charismatic leadership had impressed him. Both officers had served their men faithfully, and Uriel was proud to have led them in battle.

'Uriel, Chaplain Clausel,' said Loic by way of a greeting, 'good to see you again.'

Uriel acknowledged the greeting with a short bow and turned to Captain Gerber. 'Any news from the other Commands?'

Gerber nodded, absentmindedly rubbing a fresh scar on his neck. 'Yeah, but they're patchy and hours old, so who knows how up to date they are. Captain Luzaine reports that Banner Command have Jotusburg under control, and that his forces are ready to ride out.'

'Excellent,' said Uriel, glad to hear some good news, 'and Magos Vaal? She claimed the supplies of weapons and ammunition would be flowing in three days, and that time has already passed.'

Loic looked uncomfortable and shrugged. 'She says they're still not ready,' he said, 'something about the machine-spirits of the forge hangars being difficult or being interfered with by some heretical tau wizardry, I'm not sure.'

'We need their ammunition and we need it now!' snapped Uriel. He took a deep breath to calm his rising anger. 'Does Vaal not realise that if she fails to get those supplies to us we may lose this world?'

'I rather think the Adeptus Mechanicus see that as secondary to offending the machine-spirits. Rest assured, Uriel, I have expressed our need in the most strenuous language.'

'Tell me of Sword Command,' said Uriel, nodding towards the maps. 'Tell me that Lord Winterbourne fares better than we do.'

Gerber pointed with the tip of his sword to one of the maps and said, 'Lord Winterbourne and Sword Command are currently engaged in the Owsen Hills. The tau have been halted for now, but they're pushing hard for a breakthrough.'

'Learchus took a great risk in breaking vox-silence behind enemy lines,' said Uriel.

'Good thing he did. His warning came just in time,' said Gerber. 'Thanks to him, our flanks are safe for the moment.'

'That's something at least,' said Uriel, looking at the map of Olzetyn the two men had been studying. 'Now to the matter of our own situation.'

'Of course, Captain Gerber and I have come up with a plan we believe is workable.'

'Tell me,' said Uriel.

'Of course,' said Loic. 'We believe that if we re-task men from the Imperator bastions, we can hold the Diacrian Bridge for at least another week.'

'It's possible,' allowed Uriel. 'Then what?'

'Then we think of some other way to stymie them,' put in Gerber. 'Do you have a better idea?'

Uriel decided there was no point in wasting breath and time with pointless softening of the blow, and said,

'We will not be re-tasking anyone from the Imperator bastions. The bastions will be reinforced and every other bridge will be destroyed. If we try and hold the southern bridge we will fail and the flank of the Imperator will be turned. The tau know the other bridges are the key to the defence of Olzetyn. Truth be told, we should have destroyed them as soon as the fighting started.'

'Destroy the bridges?' said Loic. 'But they have stood for centuries. We can't!'

'The decision has already been made, colonel,' said Uriel. 'I am not here to debate the point, merely to inform you of your new orders. We cannot continue fighting like this. We need this to happen now or we are lost.'

'But with the extra week we could buy, who knows what might happen,' protested Loic.

'The Ultramarines do not make war on the basis of what *might* happen,' said Clausel. 'Only on what *will* happen. If we continue this fight as it is, we will lose, and that is not acceptable.'

'Of course not,' said Loic, 'but there must be another way!'

'There is not,' said Uriel in a tone that brooked no disagreement.

Gerber glanced at the map chalked on the wall, and nodded. 'Honour has been satisfied, Adren, and we have shed enough blood for this city. The time to make the hard choice is here and we cannot be afraid to follow it through.'

Loic saw that he had no allies in his attempt to prevent the destruction of the bridges, and Uriel saw the resignation in his eyes.

'Very well,' said Loic. 'You're right, of course, it's just hard seeing great landmarks of your home world destroyed in order to save it.'

'We are like the surgeon who amputates an arm to save his patient,' said Clausel.

'I understand that,' said Loic, 'I just worry what will be left of any worth on Pavonis if we destroy it all to defeat the tau.'

Loic's words were like a light of revelation in Uriel's mind, and a plan that had been nothing more than half-formed ideas in his mind suddenly crystallised.

'What?' asked Loic, sensing that he had said something important.

'I know how we can win this war,' said Uriel.

THE CHASE WAS over.

Hot bolts of pulsing energy stitched a path towards Learchus, and he hurled himself behind a boulder as the two remaining scout skimmers streaked past and arced around on another strafing run. He rolled, and slammed his back against the boulder, bringing his bolter to bear in case the opportunity for a snap shot presented itself.

It had been a risk, sending the vox-signal bearing news of the tau flanking move, and Learchus only hoped that Uriel had made use of the information. Xenos electronic surveillance equipment had clearly detected their brief transmission, and criss-crossing teams of scout skimmers gradually tightened the net on Learchus, Issam and the scouts.

Their pursuers knew there was prey nearby, and had swiftly cut off all avenues of escape, hounding them towards the very edge of the coast. With Praxedes achingly close, it was galling to have to forsake their mission, but the time for stealth was over.

It was time to fight.

They had waited in ambush for their pursuers, and downed one of the skimmers with their first volley of bolter-fire. A second was blown from the air by a lethally accurate missile from Parmian's launcher. The remaining skimmers broke left and right, streaking up and around at amazing speed. They dived back down, pulsing energy weapons ripping through the scouts' position before they could find fresh cover.

Two of Issam's scouts were killed instantly. One died as his head vaporised in a superheated mist of blood and brains when the white heat of the skimmer's fire caught him full in the face. The second was cut in half at the waist by a rapid series of shots that sawed through his torso. Parmian took a hit on the shoulder, and cradled his mangled arm as he took shelter in a cleft in the rocks. Twisted molten metal was all that remained of the missile launcher, and now the last two skimmers dived back down to finish the kill.

'Why only two teams?' wondered Learchus as he watched them separate. An answer presented itself a second later. The tau obviously thought the transmission had come from a spotter team in their rear echelons, two or three men at most, and certainly nothing that required the attention of more than a handful of scout skimmers. Not for a moment had they suspected that the enemy in their midst was far more dangerous than that.

Once again, the tau had underestimated their foes, and they would pay for that mistake.

Behind Learchus, the ocean spread out like a dark mirror, while, to his right, the rocky landscape fell away in a series of graben-like shelves for three kilometres towards the ancient crater in which lay the port city of Praxedes. Learchus heard more shots and saw Sergeant Issam running for cover, firing from the hip as he went. He had no time to aim, and the scout skimmers were moving too fast for such hasty shots.

'Issam! Down!' shouted Learchus.

The Scout-sergeant dived to the side and darted between two tumbled columns of bleached rock as the second of the two skimmers streaked over his place of concealment. They were nimble vehicles, dart-shaped with what looked like a curving roll bar running from the engine nacelles at their prows to their tapered rears. Two tau warriors sat in the cockpit, only their shoulders and heads visible.

Learchus watched the first skimmer's velocity bleed off as it arced up on its turn, and dropped to one knee. He pulled his bolter in tight and sighted along the length of the weapon. A boltgun was no one's idea of a sniper weapon, but a Space Marine made do with whatever armaments were at his disposal. He let out a breath, and waited until the skimmer was at the apex of its turn, its speed greatly reduced.

He pulled the trigger, feeling the enormous kick of the weapon. The mass reactive projectile streaked through the air, its tiny rocket motor igniting as soon as it left the barrel. The shot was true, and no sooner had Learchus fired than he was running towards his target.

The pilot's head exploded as the bolt-round punched through his helmet and detonated within his skull. The skimmer dropped to the ground with a thump of metal on rock, and the co-pilot struggled to release his restraints as he saw Learchus bearing down on him.

A burst of blue bolts streaking past his head told Learchus that the last skimmer had seen him. He risked a glance over his shoulder and saw it arcing towards him. Stuttering blasts of gunfire fizzed through the air, and one struck him low on the hip. Learchus staggered, feeling the heat of the impact burning his skin, but kept running.

'Cover fire!' he yelled.

Issam broke from behind the fallen columns of rock and unleashed a hail of shots at the approaching skimmer. It broke off its attack run and heeled over as it pulled away from the lethal volley. The tightness of the turn bled speed, and the wounded Parmian fired his bolt pistol one-handed at the vehicle's exposed underside. The shot penetrated the lighter armour of its fuselage, and exploded upwards through the pilot's body, exiting in a spray of bone from his chest.

The co-pilot of the skimmer Learchus had brought down was free of his harness, but it was too late for escape. Learchus wrapped a hand around the tau's neck and dragged him from the vehicle. With the bare minimum of effort, he crushed the alien's neck and dropped him to the ground.

The second skimmer came down with a jolt, but surviving the death of his comrade only delayed the co-pilot's demise by moments. The alien expertly disembarked from the skimmer, and drew his sidearm, but it was a futile act of defiance. Issam put two expertly aimed shots through his chest, and he fell back.

Learchus let out a long shuddering breath as Issam jogged over to him, his bolter cradled close to his chest. Parmian followed him, and the last surviving scout, Daxian, formed up on their sergeant.

The battle had lasted seconds at most, but it felt like longer.

'We were lucky,' said Learchus. 'If they had come with the proper amount of force we would be dead.'

'This is simply a reprieve,' said Issam. 'These scouts will be missed soon, and future hunters will not come so ill-prepared.'

Learchus turned his gaze to the south, to where lines of smoke and a haze of energy hung over the horizon.

The gleam of the port city's towers was so close that he felt he could reach out and touch them.

'Praxedes is only three or four kilometres away,' he said. 'It is so close.'

'It might as well be on Macragge for all we can get near it,' said Parmian, pointing to where the sunlight glinted on what looked like leafless ceramic trees in the distance. 'There are ring upon ring of drone sentry towers guarding every approach, and our camo-capes won't fool them.'

Learchus looked down at the corpse of the tau co-pilot at his feet. Then he looked at the skimmer vehicle. An idea began to form in his mind.

'You are correct, Parmian,' said Learchus. 'We cannot get through as Space Marines, but the onboard systems of these skimmers are no doubt equipped with the correct identity codes to pass between the sentry towers unharmed.'

Parmian frowned. 'But how can you retrieve the codes? You don't know how these machines work.'

Learchus dropped to his knees and removed the tau warrior's helmet. The alien's features were twisted with the pain of his last moments of life. Learchus turned the head onto its side and took the combat blade a grim-faced Issam handed him.

He placed the long, serrated edge against the skin of the tau's temple and began sawing.

'Not yet I don't,' he said.

KOUDELKAR SHONAI POURED another glass of the warm tisane from the plain cylindrical pot his tau facilitator had provided him with that morning. The drink was sweet and had a deliciously fragrant aftertaste, about as far removed from the bitter taste of caffeine as it was possible to get. He set the pot down on a round tray, and settled back in the contoured plastic of his chair to read.

Like everything in his quarters, from the bed to the ablutions cubicle, the chair was simply and functionally designed, moulding its form to match his seated posture. It provided comfort that the most gifted human ergonomic designers could only dream of producing.

Koudelkar sipped his drink and returned to the device he had been studying all morning.

It was a flat rectangular plate, not unlike an Imperial data-slate, though it was far lighter and didn't keep shorting out every ten minutes. A wonderfully crisp display projected picter images of people at work and at play. They were ordinary men and women, and though there was nothing special about what they were doing, *where* they were doing it was quite remarkable.

Everyone in the moving images inhabited wondrous cities of clean lines, artfully designed boulevards, parks of vibrant green and russet brown, all set amid gleaming spires of silver and white. Aun'rai had told him that this was T'au, cardinal world of the empire and birthplace of the tau race. To see human beings in such a place was incredible, and although Koudelkar knew that images could be manipulated, this felt real and had a ring of truth to it that he felt was totally genuine.

Every man, woman or child in the films was dressed in more or less identical clothing that bore various insignia of the tau empire. Koudelkar had heard the rumours of defections to the tau empire; such stories were told in hushed whispers, for to entertain any notion of aliens as anything other than vile, baby-eating filth was punishable by death.

Everything Koudelkar had seen since his capture gave the lie to the idea of the tau as murderous aliens hostile to humanity. He had been treated with nothing but courtesy since his arrival, and his daily discussions of the Tau'va, the Greater Good, with Aun'rai had been most illuminating.

Each morning, Aun'rai would join Koudelkar in his quarters and they would speak of the tau, the Imperium and a hundred other topics. Much to his surprise, Koudelkar had warmed to the tau ambassador, discovering that they had much in common.

'The Greater Good is a fine idea in theory,' Koudelkar had said upon first hearing Aun'rai talk of it, 'but surely unworkable in practice?'

'Not at all,' said Aun'rai with a soft shake of his head.

'Surely selfish desires, individual wants and the like would get in the way.'

'They did once,' said Aun'rai, 'and it almost destroyed our race.'

'I don't understand.'

'I know you do not,' Aun'rai had said. 'So let me tell you of my race and how we came to embrace the Greater Good.'

Aun'rai had placed his staffs of office beside him and wove his hands together as he began to speak, his voice soft and melodic, laced with a wistful melancholy.

'When my race took its first steps, we were like humanity: barbarous, petty, and given to greedy and hedonistic impulses. Our society had branched into a number of tribes, what you might call castes, each with its own customs, laws and beliefs.'

'I'd heard that,' said Koudelkar, 'four castes, like the elements; fire, water and suchlike.'

Aun'rai smiled, though there was something behind the expression Koudelkar could not divine. Irritation or sadness, he couldn't tell.

'Those are labels humans have applied to us,' said Aun'rai at last. 'The true meanings of our caste names carry much complexity and subtle inferences lost in such prosaic terms.'

'I'm sorry,' said Koudelkar. 'It's what I've been told.'

'That does not surprise me. Humans have a need for definition, for yourselves and for the world around you. You struggle with concepts that do not easily sit within defined boxes. I know something of your race's history, and with everything I learn of you, I grow ever more thankful for the Greater Good.'

'Why?'

'Because without it, my race would be just like yours.'

'In what way?'

Aun'rai raised a hand. 'Listen well and you will learn why we are not so different, Koudelkar.'

'Sorry,' said Koudelkar, 'you were speaking of the castes.'

Aun'rai nodded and continued. 'The tau of the mountains soared on the air, while the plains dwellers became hunters and warriors of great skill. Others built great cities and raised high monuments to their craft, while those without such skills brokered trade between the different groups. For a time, we prospered, but as time passed and our race grew more numerous, the various tribes began to fight one another. We called this time the Mont'au, which in your language means the Terror.'

Aun'rai shuddered at the memory, though Koudelkar knew he could not have been there to see any of this. 'The plains dwellers allied with the tau of the mountains and took to raiding the settlements of the builders. Skirmishes became battles, battles became wars, and soon the tau race was tearing itself apart. The builders had long known how to fashion firearms, and the traders had sold them to almost all of the tribes. The bloodshed was appalling, and I weep to think of those days.'

'You're right, that does sound familiar.'

'We were on the verge of destruction. Our species was sliding towards a self-engineered extermination when we were saved on the mountain plateau of Fio'taun. An army of the air and fire castes had destroyed vast swathes of the land, and now laid siege to the mightiest city of the earth caste, the last bastion of freedom on T'au. For five seasons, the city held against the attacks until, at last, it was on the verge of defeat. This was the night the first of the Ethereals came.'

'The who?'

'I have not the words in this language to convey the true meaning of the concept, but suffice to say that these farsighted individuals were the most singular tau ever to walk amongst my people. All through the night, they spoke of what might be achieved if the skills and labours of all castes could be harnessed and directed towards the betterment of the race. By morning's light, they had brokered a lasting peace between the armies.'

'They must have been some speakers,' observed Koudelkar, 'to halt a war like that so quickly. How did they do it?'

'They spoke with an acuity that cut through the decades of bloodshed and hatred. They showed my people the inevitable result of continued war: species doom and a slow, moribund slide into extinction. None who heard them speak that night could doubt the truth of their words, and as more of the Ethereals began to emerge, the philosophy of the Greater Good was carried to every corner of the world.'

'And that was it?' asked Koudelkar. 'It just seems, well, a little too... easy.'

'We had a choice,' said Aun'rai, 'to live or die. In that respect, I suppose it was an easy decision to make. Your race has yet to face that moment, but in that one night, my people saw the truth of the Ethereals' words with total clarity. Almost overnight our society was changed from one of selfish individualism to one where everyone contributes towards our continued prosperity. Everyone is valued and everyone is honoured, for they work towards something greater than they could ever achieve alone. Does that not sound like what happened when your Emperor emerged and took the reins of humanity? Did he not attempt to steer your race's path from destruction to enlightenment? That he failed in no way diminishes the nobility of his intent. What he tried to do is what the tau have *managed* to do. Now, does that not sound worthwhile, my friend?'

'Put like that, I suppose it does,' agreed Koudelkar, 'and it really works?'

'It really does,' said Aun'rai, 'and you could be part of it.'

'I could?'

'Of course,' said Aun'rai. 'The Greater Good is open to all who embrace it.'

That thought was uppermost in Koudelkar's mind as he set the display unit down and sipped his tisane. The idea of renouncing the Imperium sent a chill down his spine and made his hands tingle. Men had suffered the torments of the damned in the dungeons of the Arbites for far less, and Koudelkar's mind recoiled from the thought, even as he relished the idea of a society where he was not constrained by petty bureaucrats and restrictive legislation: a society where he was valued for his contribution, not held back from advancing a better world for his people.

His good mood evaporated as the door to his quarters slid open and Lortuen Perjed entered. The adept wore a serious expression, and Koudelkar crossed his legs and folded his hands in his lap as he waited for him to speak.

'Good afternoon, Lortuen,' he said.

'I'll keep this brief,' said Lortuen.

'That will be a refreshing change,' replied Koudelkar.

Lortuen frowned, but pressed on. 'I have news of the progress of the war, and we need to talk about fighting the tau. The men are ready and we have a plan.'

Koudelkar sighed. 'Not this again. I told you before that you were wasting your time. There's nothing we can do, we cannot escape.'

'And I told *you* that it is not about escape. Damn it, Koudelkar, you have to listen to me!'

'No,' said Koudelkar, 'I don't. My eyes are open now, and I think I misjudged the tau. As matter of fact, I think we all did.'

'What are you talking about?'

'I mean that for all your fine talk of the Imperium, it is clear to me that it is a corrupt institution that no longer even remembers why it was created or the ideals for which it once stood.'

'You have gone mad,' said Lortuen. 'It's that Aun'rai! Every day he fills your head with lies. And you're falling for them.'

'Lies?' said Koudelkar. 'You were the one that told me the Imperium would not mourn our passing. We are already dead men, Lortuen, so what does it matter what we do?'

'It matters even more, Koudelkar,' said Lortuen. 'If we can abandon our beliefs in the face of adversity, then they're not beliefs at all. Now, more than ever, we have to fight these degenerate xenos!'

'I will tell you what is degenerate,' snapped Koudelkar, surging from his seat. 'Even as we face enemies from all sides, our race still fights amongst its own kind. We are told that the galaxy is a hostile place, and everywhere we turn there are foes, but does this unite us or bring us together? No, for we are so self-absorbed that we forget what it is to belong to something greater. Mykola was right, she knew that–'

'Mykola is dead,' said Lortuen.

Koudelkar felt like he'd been punched in the gut. He sank back into his chair and struggled to think of what to say.

'What? How do you know?'

'The same drop-ship that brought Aun'rai back also brought Jenna Sharben in.'

'The enforcer chief?'

'Yes. She was badly hurt, but the tau have treated her wounds and she's conscious again. She told me what happened.'

'Does my mother know?'

'No, I thought it would be best coming from you.'

Koudelkar nodded absently. 'How did my aunt die?'

'Does it matter?' asked Lortuen. 'She is dead. She paid the price for her treachery.'

'Tell me how she died,' demanded Koudelkar. 'I will find out, so you might as well tell me now.'

Lortuen sighed. 'Very well. She died in the Glasshouse. Prelate Culla beat her to death to learn what information she had given the tau.'

'Culla murdered her? I knew that bastard was insane!'

'If it's any consolation, Culla's probably dead too,' said Lortuen. 'The tau killed him before they escaped from the prison.'

'The Imperium killed Mykola,' said Koudelkar with an awful finality.

'No, her choices killed her,' said Lortuen.

'Get out!' roared Koudelkar. 'Get out and never speak to me again. I will have nothing more to do with you or your petty plans of resistance, and I will have nothing more to do with the Imperium!'

'That's the grief talking,' said Lortuen. 'You don't mean that.'

'I mean every word of it, Perjed!' shouted Koudelkar. 'I spit on the Imperium, and I curse the Emperor to the warp!'

♉
EIGHTEEN

Thunderous explosions lit up the dawn as the charges placed by the combat engineers went off one after the other in quick succession. Throughout the night, the centre spans and supports built into the gorges of the Aquila, Owsen, Spur and Diacrian Bridges had been rigged for destruction, and as sunlight threw the defenders' shadows out before them, the word was given to destroy the crossings.

The bridges had stood for hundreds of years, though there was little sense of history to them. They had not the pedigree of the Imperator, and the lost secrets built into its structure that made it virtually indestructible had no part in the construction of those around it.

Rock blew out as gigantic stone corbels were destroyed, and the supports built deep into the walls of the gorges blasted free. Spars of metal that had not seen sunlight for centuries tumbled to the rivers far below, trailing tank-sized chunks of reinforced plascrete and rebars.

The Owsen Bridge was the first to fall, the eastern end giving way and tearing from the rock. The roadway crazed and buckled as the metal beneath snapped, and the immense weight of it all ripped the supports from its other end. Within moments, the entire span was tumbling into the river. The Aquila soon followed it, its structure twisted and blackened by the explosions. When the dust cleared, the engineers saw that the thoroughness of their labours had not been wasted. Nothing remained of either bridge, and the route across the gorges through Barrack Town had been obliterated.

Unfortunately, the same could not be said of the charges laid upon the Diacrian and Spur Bridges. As the echoes of the northern bridges' destruction faded, it was clear that something had gone terribly wrong with the demolition of the southern bridges.

The correct rites of destruction were observed, the proper sequence of buttons pressed and levers pulled, but none of the charges positioned to destroy the crossings detonated. Frantic vox-traffic passed back and forth between the engineers and force commanders as each diagnostic test insisted that every charge was primed, the detonators were functional and the signal strength was optimal.

Even as the engineers and tech-priests struggled to divine what had gone wrong, the tau surged forwards and seized the western end of the Diacrian Bridge.

FOLLOWED BY THE warriors of squad Ventris, Uriel leapt from the assault ramp of *Spear of Calth*, the Land Raider that had carried Marneus Calgar into battle during the final storming of Corinth. Behind him, the smoke from the destruction of the northern bridges was blowing south, and a layer of dust coated everything from the roofs and sills of leaning hab-blocks to the roadway that led onto the Spur Bridge.

Shouting units of PDF scrambled to deploy from battered Chimeras as Colonel Loic positioned his men to hold the end of the bridge. Captain Gerber's Lavrentians were already in place, fire-teams setting up heavy weapons to repulse the assault that was sure to come.

Ultramarines debussed from their Rhinos, and moved into positions covering the approaches without needing any orders. Uriel climbed onto the parapet wall of the Imperator, and looked out over the gorge between the Midden and the southern edge of Tradetown. Information on the current state of battle was scarce, and the defenders needed to know what the tau were planning, although it wasn't hard to guess how the alien commander would exploit this shift in his army's favour.

The Midden was wreathed in flames and smoke, and the air crackled with what looked like miniature fireworks detonating every few seconds. Uriel had no idea what they were, but suspected the defenders would find out all too soon. From his vantage point on the parapet, he could see lancing beams of blue light stabbing out from the ruins at the northern edge of the Midden. Explosions rippled from Tradetown where those beams connected with targets.

From the location of the detonations, Uriel guessed the Imperial artillery positions were being attacked. Somehow, the tau had managed to deploy heavy weapons into the Midden without alerting the defenders, and the guns covering the approach to the Spur Bridge were being taken out.

Uriel dropped from the parapet and ran over to the PDF colonel. 'What have you got?'

Loic looked up, and the relief in his eyes at the sight of Uriel was plain.

'Tau tanks and infantry moving across the Diacrian Bridge. Lots of them.'

'How many?' pressed Uriel. 'And be more specific than "lots".'

'Hard to tell,' said Loic. 'Lots is the best I can do. Something's playing merry hell with our augurs and surveyor gear. The tech-priests say it's most likely some xenotech interference.'

'We don't have any eyes on the ground over there,' cursed Uriel. 'The Basilisks and Griffons are being taken out, so this will be an all-out assault.'

Captain Gerber emerged from a knot of Lavrentian soldiers, his helmet jammed in the crook of his arm as he wiped a dirty rag over his forehead. Commissar Vogel came with him, his uniform jacket dirty and torn.

'Damn pioneers,' said Gerber by way of a greeting. 'Why the hell didn't the charges blow?'

'I don't know, captain,' said Uriel, 'I suspect the same xenotech blocking Colonel Loic's surveyors prevented the charges from blowing.'

'But why just here? Why not the Aquila and Owsen bridges too? Doesn't make sense.'

'Who knows,' said Uriel. 'Perhaps their technology could not prevent all the bridges from being destroyed? In any case, the southern bridges are the ones that really matter.'

'True,' noted Gerber. 'We won't hold them long if they make a push along both bridges.'

'We'll damn well hold them here,' promised Loic.

'No we won't,' snapped Gerber. 'With this force, we can hold the end of the Spur for a time, but now that we're forced to fight on two fronts, it will probably be a very short time.'

'There's that defeatism again, captain,' said Vogel. 'It is becoming a habit.'

'Call it defeatism if you like, Vogel, and just shoot me,' responded Gerber, 'but Captain Ventris knows I'm right, don't you?'

'I am afraid Captain Gerber is correct,' said Uriel. 'A determined enemy will soon force us back, and the tau have shown themselves to be very determined.'

'Then what do you suggest?' demanded Vogel.

'Pull your men further back down the Imperator,' said Uriel. 'The Ultramarines will hold the bridge approaches until you are in position.'

'I thought you had someplace else to be,' said Gerber.

'We do, but it will avail us nothing if Olzetyn falls now,' replied Uriel. 'We will push the tau back, and then pull back to join you. Then your artillery will execute Fire Plan Eversor.'

'Eversor?' said Gerber. 'You can't be serious?'

'Deadly serious,' said Uriel.

FLAMES LICKED AT the clouds as Tradetown burned. Tau guns in the Midden pounded the Imperial positions, taking out any tank or artillery piece that dared unmask itself in a searing blast of blue fire. What had once been an unassailable position from which to rain down fire and ruin upon the tau was now a killing zone for alien gunners. Tau drones buzzed over the town, and Uriel just hoped the Lavrentian artillerymen were as good as Gerber claimed. There would be precious little room for error in the execution of Fire Plan Eversor.

The world was bathed in a hellish orange glow from the firestorm raging through the cratered eastern districts of Tradetown, and gritty ash blew in from the north.

Uriel felt as though Pavonis itself was ablaze.

He smiled grimly, hoping the tau were thinking the same.

The Ultramarines set off down the Spur Bridge at a rapid jog. The quicker they threw the enemy back the better.

The voice of Sergeant Aktis, leader of one of the 4th's Devastator squads, sounded in Uriel's helmet. 'Possible targets ahead. Two hundred metres from your position.'

Uriel acknowledged the warning, and his fighting squads fanned out.

Squads Theron, Lykon and Nestor swept out in an echelon to the left, with Dardanus, Sabas and Protus taking the right. Squad Ventris held the centre. Clausel stood with Sergeant Protus, and Uriel saw the pride in the posture of his squad at the Chaplain's presence.

The Ultramarines advanced with slow, steady strides. Bolters held before them, they marched in serried ranks of shimmering blue ceramite. The firelight glinted on the polished blue plates of their armour, and Uriel's green cloak billowed behind him in the hot air that swept over the bridge.

Uriel scanned the cratered and debris-choked length of the bridge. If Aktis was right, then the tau were almost on top of them.

'I don't see anything,' he said. 'Confirm enemy sighting, Aktis.'

'Possible false positive, captain,' said Aktis, an edge of self-reproach to his voice. 'The auspex picked up a reading, but I have no confirmation as yet.'

'But you think there is something there?'

Aktis hesitated. 'I believe so, but I can offer no corroboration, captain.'

'Understood,' said Uriel. Aktis was a good, steady leader of heavy gunners and if he suspected the enemy was close by, then that was good enough for Uriel. 'All squads, be advised of possible hostiles at close range to our front.'

No sooner was the warning articulated than a hail of shots ripped from the smoke and tore through Squad Theron. Two warriors went down, but both climbed to their feet as their squad-mates found cover. Chattering heavy bolter-fire from the covering Devastators slashed down the length of the bridge, which was closely followed by lascannon shots and missiles.

Uriel dived into the shelter of a smoking crater, rising to his knees at its forward lip. He scanned the ground before him, switching from one vision mode to the next as he tried to spot the tau. He saw nothing definite, just blurred disturbances in the smoke that seemed to bend the light around them.

'Stealth teams!' he shouted, raising his bolter to his shoulder. Even knowing what to look for, it was hard to draw a bead on the armoured tau. Just as he thought he had a fix on one, it would vanish or blur to the point where he might as well be firing blind.

Distance was the enemy in this engagement, and Uriel knew there was only one way to drive the tau from the bridge.

'All squads tactical assault!' he ordered. 'On me!'

The Devastators' covering fire ceased as Uriel scrambled from the crater and led his warriors forwards at battle pace. The Ultramarines' advance into combat was swift and sure, faster than a jog, yet slower than a run. It enabled a warrior to cover vast distances without tiring, and allowed him to close with enemy forces quickly while still shooting accurately. Where the Space Wolves charged with the fury of the berserker, and the Imperial Fists fought with a meticulously orchestrated precision, the Ultramarines took the fight to the enemy efficiently and directly.

As Uriel led his squads into battle, he heard the triggering of jump packs. Swooshing blurs of blue armour arced overhead as Squad Protus led the assault. At the forefront of Protus was Chaplain Clausel, a battle prayer bellowing from his helmet augmitters.

More gunfire snapped from the haze ahead, and Uriel saw more of the blurred silhouettes. He returned a hail of shots towards the closest, and one of the light-refracting shapes fell back, its armour punctured by the mass-reactive shells. As it fell, the concealing technology failed, and Uriel saw the tau warrior clearly.

Broader than a Space Marine, yet bulbous and with an insect-like carapace, the stealth battlesuits were unmistakably alien in their design. They carried long-barrelled rotary cannons on one arm and moved in almost complete silence.

The tau guns opened fire, a roaring burst of shots that tore into the ranks of the Ultramarines. An answering volley ripped into the tau, and for a few brief seconds the space between the two foes was filled with flying metal. A withering storm of gunfire shot back and forth, a no-man's-land where any but the most heavily armoured would perish in a second.

Uriel felt a trio of impacts, two on the chest and one on the shoulder. None penetrated the layered ceramite of his armour and he gave silent thanks to the soul of Brother Amadon for keeping him safe. The distance between the two forces was closing, and Uriel slung his bolter before drawing the sword of Idaeus. This was a chance to hone the skills he would need for the final part of his plan.

The Ultramarines fired a last volley, and the two forces clashed in a clatter of armour plates, short range gunfire and slashing blades. The assault warriors of Protus were first into the fight, dropping from above like a lightning strike. They hit like a hammer of the gods, unstoppable and invincible, their warriors fighting with the same implacable fervour of Chaplain Clausel.

A tau warrior stepped towards Uriel, its gun spinning up to fire. He dived forwards and rolled upright, slashing his sword in a sweeping arc as he rose to his feet. The blade clove through the bulbous carapace of a tau warrior, and Uriel relished the powerful surge of strength-enhancing stimms injected into his bloodstream. The enemy warrior dropped, and Uriel spun on his heel to hack the legs from another. This close, the tau stealth technology was useless, and Uriel pushed deeper into their ranks, his sword a blur of silver and gold.

As unequal a struggle as it was, the tau were warriors of courage and strength, and several Ultramarines were shredded by close-range cannon fire or clubbed to the ground by augmented limbs. Another tau fell before Uriel's blade, and the noose of the Ultramarines closed in on the surviving stealth warriors.

As the fighting continued, a towering mushroom cloud of fire and smoke suddenly erupted at the western edge of the Imperator. Seconds later, a thunderous booming explosion rolled over the landscape, and Uriel knew the bombs in the armoury of the western bastions had finally blown. While Uriel and the Ultramarines had advanced down the Spur Bridge, Lavrentian combat pioneers had been setting powerful explosives in the magazines of the Aquila and Imperator bastions.

Even from a distance of several kilometres, the collapse of the bastions was a spectacular sight, the cyclopean blocks of masonry tumbling down as though in slow motion. Anything unfortunate enough to be in the immediate vicinity of the bastions would be utterly destroyed, and though Uriel regretted their destruction, he knew there had been no choice. As though in reverence for the demise of so mighty a fortification, both forces paused in the struggle to watch their spectacular ending.

In the moment's respite, Uriel looked down the bridge, and he knew that this fight was over.

The tau were pushing out from the Midden and onto the Spur Bridge in force. A picket line of scout skimmers darted ahead of a wedge of Devilfish that were closely followed by a host of Hammerheads and Sky Rays.

'Chaplain!' called Uriel.

'I see them,' confirmed Clausel. 'Time to go?'

Uriel looked back at the smouldering ruins of the two bastions, and nodded.

'Time to go,' he said.

CAPTAIN MEDERIC AND his six-strong squad of Hounds dropped into a crater and pressed their backs against the forward slope. Lavrentian tanks in staggered formation boomed and roared to either side of them, firing into the hills where the sleek forms of tau armoured vehicles pressed home their assault.

This latest engagement was fought in the ruins of what must have once been an impressive estate. Ruined marble walls and stubs of fluted columns were all that remained, and soon even they would be crushed or blown apart by shellfire. Hundreds of hastily dug-in Guardsmen fired from the ruins in a bid to stall the latest tau attack. Somewhere behind him, a Lavrentian tank exploded, but Mederic couldn't see which one or what had killed it.

'Kaynon, watch our backs!' shouted Mederic over the din of battle cannon and heavy bolter-fire. 'I don't want to get rolled over by our own bloody vehicles!'

'Aye, sir,' called back the youngster. The fighting retreat through the Owsen Hills had made a man of Kaynon, and if they survived this battle, Mederic would see to it that the boy's courage was recognised.

'Reload!' he shouted. 'They're all over us, and I don't want anyone with an empty mag.'

The order was unnecessary, for the Hounds knew their trade and were already refreshing their power cartridges. Mederic slammed his power cell home, checking he had a full load before crawling to the lip of the crater.

The fight to halt the left hook of the tau advance was amongst the bloodiest and yet most clinical actions the 44th had fought in recent memory. Such was the strength of the tau forces that halting them was impossible, but the 44th were leaving nothing but ashes and blasted wasteland in their wake. Day after day, the tau pushed forwards, their advance relentless and coldly efficient in the face of the 44th's guns. Without the savagery of the greenskin or the terror of the devourer swarms, it gave the Lavrentians nothing to latch onto emotionally.

All Mederic saw in the faces around him was sterile dread, the fear that at any moment an unseen missile might end dreams of glory and service. The tau made war with such precision that it left precious little room for notions of honour or courage. To the tau, war was a science like any other: precise, empirical and a matter of cause and effect.

Mederic knew that was the fatal flaw in their reasoning, because war was never predictable. Unknown variables and random chance all played their part, and it was a foolish commander who fought with the belief he could foresee every eventuality.

A vast shadow eclipsed Mederic, and he looked up to see the skirts of an enormous armoured vehicle grind past their fragile cover. He smiled as he saw *Meat*

Grinder crudely scrawled on the vehicle's skirts, and knew it was Lord Winterbourne and *Father Time*.

A searing beam of energy slammed into the scarred glacis of the Baneblade, but so thick was the super-heavy tank's armour that it left barely a mark. *Father Time's* cannons roared in reply and an enemy tank exploded, pulverised by the mass of the enormous shell as much as the explosives.

'Support fire!' shouted Mederic, and his scouts joined him on the lip of the crater. Lethally accurate sniper-fire picked off tau squad leaders darting through the smoke, while Duken's missiles lanced out to disable enemy vehicles with relentless precision. It was risky, staying to shoot from one location, but settling smoke from the Baneblade's guns was helping to conceal their exact location. In any case, displacing in the middle of a tank battle was a sure-fire way to get crushed beneath sixty tonnes of metal.

Lord Winterbourne's command vehicle continued to wreak havoc amongst the tau armour, reaping a fear-some number of kills, while withstanding countless impacts that would have reduced most tanks to molten slag. Wherever *Father Time* fought, the tau advance would falter, and this latest engagement looked like being no exception.

Then Mederic heard a sound that chilled him to the bone, a high, ululating, squawking sound that could mean only one thing.

Kroot.

He looked up to see a host of the pink-skinned crea-tures crawling over *Father Time*. The kroot carried a device that Mederic knew was a bomb even before they bent to fix it to the honour-inscribed turret ring of Lord Winterbourne's Baneblade.

'Targets right!' he yelled, swinging his rifle to bear. His first shot punched one of the kroot from *Father Time's* upper deck, his second blew the arm off the creature attempting to affix the explosive charge.

Las-bolts whickered around the huge tank as the Hounds turned their fire upon it. A pair of kroot fell from the vehicle, though Mederic saw others taking cover behind the enormous turret. It felt unnatural and faintly heretical to be shooting at an Imperial tank, but Mederic knew they could not possibly do any damage to it.

'Unless we hit the charge...' he whispered, seeing a shot ricochet from the turret ring, no more than a few inches from the explosive device. Without thinking, Mederic pushed himself to his feet and ran towards *Father Time*, clambering up the rear crew ladder inset on the cliff-like sides of the Baneblade.

The Baneblade's turret was in motion, the autocannon blazing a stream of large-calibre shells at the enemy. Heavy bolter shells streamed from the guns mounted on the tank's frontal section, and Mederic tried not to think of how insanely dangerous it was to climb onto a moving, fighting tank.

A solid round spanked the metal beside him, and he threw himself onto the deck of the Baneblade. Something moved beside him and he rolled onto his back, firing his rifle. A kroot warrior fell back with its chest blown out, and Mederic scrambled to his feet as another alien fighter reared over him. A las-bolt from his right blew out the back of the kroot's head.

His Hounds were watching over him.

Keeping low, Mederic made his way towards the tau device, keeping clear of the discharging flares of actinic energy crackling around the one remaining lascannon sponson. He knelt by the turret, a hundred battles and campaign honours inscribed there in gold lettering. Mederic slung his rifle over his shoulder, and examined the device the kroot had fastened to the turret. The bomb was oblong, about the size of a fully-loaded Guardsman's pack, and Mederic had no doubt it would end *Father Time's* contribution to this battle. With no time for anything sophisticated, Mederic simply took hold of the device and hauled with all his might.

It didn't move so much as a millimetre.

Whatever technology held the bomb to the Baneblade was beyond his strength to defeat.

'Step away from the bomb, captain,' said a voice behind him.

Mederic turned to see a tall, hideously disfigured preacher in the black robes of a Mortifex standing above him on *Father Time's* rear deck. The man's face was burned, blackened and scarred with embedded fragments of coloured glass. Mederic had heard of the wounded preacher that had joined the fighting men of the 44th after the battle of Brandon Gate, but he had never laid eyes on him until now.

Campfire scuttlebutt had it that it was Gaetan Baltazar, the former Clericus Fabricae, but such was the horror of his injuries and permanent grimace of agony that it was impossible to tell who this wild-eyed preacher had once been. How could anyone have survived such dreadful wounds?

The Mortifex bore a giant eviscerator, the roaring blade throwing off smoke and sparks.

'Oh hell,' hissed Mederic as he realised what the Mortifex was about to do.

He rolled aside as the blade came down. Flaring light spilled from the device, but to Mederic's amazement it didn't explode. The tearing teeth of the eviscerator easily ripped through the metal and ceramic of the device until it fell from the turret ring in two halves.

He let out a shuddering breath as the Mortifex lowered his smoking blade.

'And lo the workings of the foes of mankind shall be rendered unto dust and memory,' said the preacher.

'Holy crap,' hissed Mederic, staring at the pile of inert material that was all that remained of the bomb. 'How the hell did you know it wasn't going to go off when you did that?'

'I did not,' said the Mortifex through a mouth burned lipless. 'In truth I did not care.'

'Well *I* bloody care, and I won't have some madman taking me with him,' said Mederic. 'So just keep the hell away from–'

Mederic's words were cut off as a hand-span of serrated steel erupted from the Mortifex's chest. Blood squirted, and, as the long blade tore out the preacher's heart in a flood of crimson, Mederic saw the man's expression change from one of agony to one of peace.

'My life is a prison and death shall be my release,' said the Mortifex as he toppled from *Father Time's* deck.

Mederic didn't watch the Mortifex fall.

His attention was fixed on the monstrous kroot with vivid red quills that had killed him.

ENERGY BLASTS HISSED past Uriel's head as he backed onto the ruined thoroughfare of the Imperator towards the collapsed buildings where their transport vehicles awaited them. His bolter kicked in his grip, and as each magazine clicked empty, he smoothly replaced it without taking his eyes from the approaching tau. Flames licked at the plates of his armour from fires the debris from the flaming bastions had touched off. Once again he gave thanks to the ancient builders of the bridge that they had thought to make it so strong.

The Ultramarines retreated in good order from the Spur Bridge, falling back by combat squads, firing into the tau as they went. Missiles streaked from launch tubes and lascannons pulverised anything that might serve the enemy as cover. The Space Marines were retreating, but they were leaving nothing but destruction behind them.

Missiles from the Lavrentian support teams further down the bridge slashed overhead, punching spiral contrails through the smoke. The blooms of their detonations echoed distantly down the span of the bridge.

Fire Warriors and battlesuits darted through the flames and smoke, firing at the retreating Ultramarines as they abandoned the crossing to the Midden, but their pursuit was half-hearted, and Uriel could sense their dismay at the devastation.

'This world will burn before we let you have it,' whispered Uriel as he looked around to ensure that all his warriors had escaped. Chaplain Clausel was to his right, his Crozius Arcanum held high while he bellowed the Battle Prayer of the Righteous.

More rockets and gunfire filled the air above them, and Uriel heard the furious revving of engines over the destruction raging all around him. Brothers Speritas and Zethus, the company's Dreadnoughts, marched backwards along with their battle-brothers, the boom of their weapons punctuating the din of battle.

Uriel looked over his shoulder, seeing plumes of exhaust smoke billowing over the escarpment of a fallen hab structure.

'Fall back by squads to transports!' he ordered. 'Withdrawal pattern Sigma Evens.'

The Ultramarines moved smoothly into formation, Squads Theron, Lykon and Nestor taking up covering positions, while Dardanus, Sabas and Protus turned and ran for their previously designated lines of retreat. Punishing volleys of bolter-fire filled the ground before the Ultramarines with explosive death as more missiles arced overhead, curving up into the air before slashing down like hunting raptors to explode amongst their prey.

'Aktis, Boros, suppressive fire!'

As the order was given, the covering squads pulled back from their positions as a deafening crescendo of fire bloomed from the Devastator squads behind.

'Captain Gerber,' said Uriel, walking backwards alongside his warriors, 'commence Fire Plan Eversor.'

'Understood, Captain Ventris,' replied Gerber. 'Sending rounds down now.'

Uriel heard the solitary boom of a basilisk artillery piece, which was quickly followed by another and then another. Soon, the sound of the guns was a continuous, thudding drumbeat.

'Everyone back, now!' shouted Uriel, turning and running to where the 4th Company's vehicles awaited them. He leapt broken spars of adamantium and ducked down through a gap torn in an angled slab of rockcrete. Ahead, he could see four Rhinos and a pair of Land Raiders, their engines coughing exhaust smoke and their assault doors open. Space Marines clambered on board while the vehicles' auto-systems fired their machine-guided weapons down the length of the bridge.

Arcing streaks of dazzling light flashed overhead, and Uriel felt the first of the artillery shells detonate on the bridge behind him. Pounding hammer-blows struck the structure again and again, the percussive impacts shaking the very foundations of the bridge, until it felt as though the heavens themselves had fallen.

'Emperor bless you, Gerber!' cried Uriel as he saw that virtually every shell was landing exactly where it was needed. The Lavrentian gunners were justifying their captain's faith in them.

Uriel stumbled and fell to his knees as the titanic forces pounded the Spur Bridge to ruins. The noise was deafening, even through the protective dampening of his armour's auto-senses. Those hab-blocks that had not already been destroyed in the fighting vanished in the searing detonations, whole districts wiped out in an instant as hundreds of shells landed on target. Nothing could live under such a thunderous bombardment, and the tau pursuit was annihilated in moments.

High explosives and incendiaries bathed the entire span of the bridge in a living typhoon of flames and debris. The point where the Spur and Imperator were joined suffered worst under the sustained bombardment, the steel connections of the newer bridge obliterated and tearing loose. Shells with armour piercing warheads penetrated deep into the roadway junction of the Imperator and Spur Bridges, before exploding with unimaginable force to leave thirty metre craters in their wake.

Following shells impacted in those craters, burrowing ever deeper and further weakening the connection, until the weight of the Spur Bridge completed the job begun by the barrage of explosives. Buckling and shearing under loads it was never built to endure, the Spur tore from the Imperator, falling away and twisting like wet paper.

Thousands of tonnes of stone and steel dropped into the gorge, and those few Fire Warriors that had survived the bombardment fell with it. Infantry and armour tumbled downwards, and, although a few skimmer tanks were able to control their descent, they were smashed to ruins by the crushing torrent of debris.

The route from the Midden onto the Imperator was utterly destroyed, and, as the last shells fell, little remained to indicate that there had ever been a bridge between them. Billowing clouds of dust and smoke rolled towards the Ultramarines position, and Uriel picked himself up as the cataclysmic echoes of the massed artillery bombardment faded.

Clausel awaited him by the forward ramp of the nearest Land Raider and waved him over. Uriel ran towards the Chaplain and hammered the door closing mechanism once he was inside.

The red-lit interior of the battle tank reeked of oils and incense smoke, and Uriel pressed a fist to the black and white cog symbol of the Adeptus Mechanicus etched into the wall beside him.

'And the Emperor shall smite the iniquitous and the xenos from his sight,' said Clausel, slapping a palm on Uriel's shoulder-guard. The destruction of the Spur and the tau pursuit force had put the Chaplain in good spirits.

'With a little help from the hammer of the Imperial Guard,' said Uriel.

He opened a channel to Gerber once more. 'Captain, the Spur is down. Pass your compliments to your gunners, their fire was dead on.'

'Will do,' answered Gerber. 'We ran through damn near our entire stockpile of shells to lay down that barrage.'

'It will be worth it, I assure you, captain,' promised Uriel.

'It had better be,' said Gerber. 'When they come at us again, all we've got left to throw at them are rocks.'

'Understood,' said Uriel, 'but I do not believe it will come to that.'

Uriel shut off the vox and turned to Clausel. 'What news from Tiberius and the *Vae Victus*, admiral?'

'He can do as you ask,' said the Chaplain, his skull-faced helmet the very image of death, 'though it will be very dangerous. If we are delayed so much as a minute, we will miss our launch window.'

'Then we had best not be late,' said Uriel.

'And Learchus?' asked Clausel. 'Has he responded to your communication?'

'No,' said Uriel, 'but he might not be able to.'

'He might be dead.'

'That is possible, but if anyone can do what must be done, then it is Learchus.'

'There's truth in that,' agreed Clausel. 'You are sure this is the only way?'

'I am,' said Uriel. 'You said it yourself, Chaplain, this isn't our kind of fight.'

Clausel nodded, and Uriel saw that the prospect of taking the fight to the enemy appealed to the venerable warrior.

'We will show the tau *exactly* what kind of fight we were built for,' promised Uriel.

Ʊ
NINETEEN

THE RED-QUILLED KROOT lunged at Mederic with its knife outstretched, the Mortifex's blood whipping from the blade as it slashed for his neck. Instinctively, he threw up his rifle to block the blow. The knife, a sword more like, smashed into the stock of Mederic's weapon, and he fought to hold the creature at bay. The kroot's strength was incredible, and, with a savage twist of the blade, it wrenched the rifle from Mederic's grip.

He slid to one side, and the kroot's fist slammed down on *Father Time's* battle-scarred topside. He wondered if anyone inside knew of the life and death struggle being played out above them.

Mederic kicked out at the kroot, his boot connecting solidly with its shin. The beast went down on one knee, and Mederic seized the opportunity to push himself backwards along the upper deck of the Baneblade.

Father Time's main guns fired, and the crash of displaced air plunged Mederic into a world of silence as the deafening sound of the Baneblade's cannons reverberated in his skull.

He scrabbled for his knife, knowing it would probably do him no good, but finding reassurance in having the edged steel in his hand. A las-bolt flashed past the kroot, but the clouds of acrid propellant smoke obscured his Hound's aim.

Mederic got his feet beneath him, still dazed by the violence of the Baneblade's firing. The kroot loped towards him with its oddly spring-like gait. Its milky, pupilless eyes bored into him with an expression that Mederic couldn't read, but which looked like feral hunger.

The beast stood to its full height, which was at least a head higher than him, and the bulging cables of its muscles were taut and sharply defined. A bandolier, hung with all manner of grotesque trophies, was looped diagonally across its chest, and Mederic saw that human ears and eyes hung there on thin metal hooks. Its bright red crest seemed to pulse with an inner blood-beat, and a loathsomely moist tongue licked the toothy edge of its beaked maw.

The kroot took a step forwards, its quills flaring in challenge as it cocked its head to one side. It hammered the hilt of its knife against its chest, and said, 'Radkwaal.'

Mederic thought the sound was simply animal noise, but, as the creature repeated the word, he realised it was saying its name.

'Redquill?'

The creature nodded and screeched its name once again. 'Radkwaal!'

'Come on then, Redquill!' yelled Mederic, brandishing his combat knife. 'Come and get me if you want me!'

Redquill sprang forwards without apparent effort, and Mederic was almost gutted before he even knew he was under attack. More by luck than skill, he threw up his knife and deflected the kroot's blade. Sparks scraped from the knives, and Mederic doubled up as the kroot's fist slammed into his stomach. Knowing a killing stroke wouldn't be far behind, Mederic threw himself to the side. He landed on the Baneblade's co-axial mounted autocannon and spilled over it onto the track-guard beside the heavy bolter.

Heavy calibre shells pumped from the stubby barrels, each noise a harsh bang followed by the whoosh of a tiny rocket motor. Redquill vaulted the turret guns and landed lightly beside him, its blade slashing for his head.

Mederic deflected the blow, and twisted his knife around Redquill's, slicing the blade down the kroot's arm. The beast snapped back in pain, and Mederic didn't give it a second chance. He rolled over the bucking heavy bolter and slashed his blade at Redquill's guts. It was a poor strike, and it left him off balance, but he was out of options.

Redquill's clawed hand snapped down on his wrist, Mederic's blade a hair's-breadth from burying itself in the kroot's belly. Redquill's knife stabbed towards him, and Mederic knew he couldn't block it. Instead, he gripped Redquill's bandolier and hauled the kroot towards him. Off-balance and perched precariously on the track-guard, the two fighters rolled over the heavy bolter's housing, and landed on the buckled metal of the enormous tank's leading edge.

Mederic hit hard, the weight of the kroot driving the breath from him and sending the combat knife tumbling away. Redquill reared up, holding its knife in two hands, ready to drive it down into Mederic's heart. And there wasn't a damn thing he could do to stop it.

Then the heavy bolter fired again, and the top half of Redquill's body disintegrated.

Mederic was drenched in blood, spitting and coughing mouthfuls of the stuff as the shredded remains of the kroot war leader fell across him before slipping from the Baneblade.

He lay unmoving for some moments until he realised that the battle tank was no longer firing any of its guns. Slowly, he rolled onto his front, keeping clear of any of *Father Time's* myriad weapons systems and wiping as much of Redquill's blood from his face as he could.

Guardsmen were emerging from foxholes and ad-hoc dugouts, their faces bloody and grimy with las-burns. They were elated at having survived the latest engagement. The hillsides were thick with smoke from burning vehicles and tau corpses. Mederic smiled in weary triumph. Once again, *Father Time* had steadied the line and held the tau at bay. Would that they had an army of Baneblades!

He heard the sound of a hatch opening behind him, and climbed to his feet, using the warm barrel of the demolisher cannon to pull his battered frame upright. Mederic turned and saluted a bemused Nathaniel Winterbourne, who stood tall in the turret.

'Is there some reason you're on my tank, captain?' asked Winterbourne.

Mederic laughed, an edge of hysteria to the sound. 'You'd never believe me,' he said.

THE COASTAL CITY of Praxedes was laid out before them, and Learchus could barely credit that they had reached their destination. To have come so far through enemy territory was nothing short of miraculous, tau territory even more so, but Learchus knew of no finer scouts in the Imperium than those of the Ultramarines.

Taking care to expose only a fraction of his head, Learchus scanned the enemy activity in the city below. He and his fellow warriors were concealed in a warehouse perched on the cliffs above the landing platforms, and, while Issam changed a field dressing on Parmian's arm, Daxian kept watch on the building's only entrance.

The cavernous structure was stacked high with crates stamped with tau markings, and the Ultramarines had been thorough in searching for anything of use. Most of the crates were filled with tau ration packs, none of which the Space Marines deigned to eat, though Issam found fresh dressings and sterile counterseptic to treat Parmian's wound.

The two skimmers they had taken from the Pathfinders lay in one corner, and Learchus tried to block the memory of how they had come to make use of them. Impossible, he knew, for the genetic imprint of the xenos warrior that had crewed it was now part of him.

Even after armour-administered emetics and purgatives, he could still feel nebulous alien emotions and thoughts scratching in his mind. The rank, oily taste and rubbery texture of the tau's brain was repulsive, but it held the information they needed to safely negotiate the drone sentry towers scattered around Praxedes. Learchus had been able to access that information, thanks to a highly specialised organ, implanted between the cervical and thoracic vertebrae, known as the omophagea.

Though situated within the spinal cord, the omophagea eventually meshed with a Space Marine's brain and effectively allowed him to learn by eating. Nerve sheaths implanted between the spine and the preomnoral stomach wall allowed the omophagea to absorb genetic material generated in animal tissue as a function of memory, experience or innate ability.

Few Chapters of Space Marines could still successfully culture such a rarefied piece of biological hardware, but the Apothecaries of the Ultramarines maintained their battle-brothers' gene-seed legacy with the utmost care and purity. Mutations had crept into other Chapters' genetic repositories, resulting in unwholesome appetites and myriad flesh-eating and blood-drinking rituals. To think that he had indulged in flesh eating in the manner of barbarous Chapters like the Flesh Tearers and Blood Drinkers was abhorrent to Learchus, and he had confessed his fears to Issam as the moon rose on the night they reached Praxedes.

'We had no choice,' said Issam.

'I know,' said Learchus. 'That does not make it any easier to stomach.'

'When we get back to Macragge the Apothecaries will swap your blood out and cleanse it of any taint. You'll be yourself soon enough, don't worry.'

'I will not be tainted,' said Learchus angrily. 'I will not stand for it. Look what happened to Pasanius, stripped of rank and disbarred from the company for a hundred days!'

'Pasanius kept his… affliction from his superior officer,' said Issam. '*That* is why he was punished. Listen to me, you need to be calm, brother.'

'Calm? How can I be calm?' cried Learchus. 'You are not the one who ate an alien brain.'

At first, he had thought the tau brain too alien, too far removed from humanity to allow him to absorb anything of value, but, within moments of swallowing his first bite of the moist chewy meat, Learchus had felt the first stirrings of the alien's thoughts. Not memories as such, but impressions and inherited understanding, as though he had always known the abhorrent things that crowded his mind.

Though he could not read the symbols on the control panel of the scout skimmers, Learchus had known their function and instinctively accessed the inner workings of their cogitators. The others had watched as he tentatively piloted the tau skimmer around the rocks, taking note of how to control it without crashing or activating unknown systems.

Within the hour, they had been on their way, travelling across the rocks towards Praxedes on the scout skimmers, and no sooner had they dropped down into a rocky canyon than a pair of the slender remote sentry towers confronted them. The drones telescoped upwards upon detecting them, but without thinking, Learchus pressed a series of buttons on a side panel and the domed tops of the towers sank back into their housings.

The skimmers were swift, and the Ultramarines had soon reached the outskirts of the coastal city. The towers were more thickly gathered around Praxedes, but, armed with the correct access codes, the Ultramarines penetrated the screen of remote sentries and secreted themselves within the warehouse without alerting their enemies to their presence.

Issam joined him at the window, and Learchus acknowledged the sergeant with a curt nod of the head. Since eating the tau's brain, he had found himself needlessly prickly and prone to a sharpness of tongue. More so than usual, he reflected with uncharacteristic honesty.

You should rest,' said the scout sergeant. 'You've been staring out of that window for nearly ten hours. Daxian or I can watch for enemy activity.'

'I cannot rest. Not now. Captain Ventris is depending on us.'

'I know, but he asks a lot of us,' said Issam. 'Perhaps more than we can give.'

'Do not say that. We are Ultramarines. Nothing is beyond us.'

'We are four warriors, Learchus,' pointed out Issam, 'and one of us is badly wounded.'

'With four warriors, Chapter Master Dacian took the pass at Gorgen against five hundred.'

'Aye, that he did,' agreed Issam. 'All 1st Company veterans in Terminator armour.'

'You do not think we can do it?'

Issam shrugged. 'As you say, we are Ultramarines. Anything is possible.'

Learchus grunted and turned his attention back to surveying the city below. He had seen little activity to suggest that Praxedes was anything other than a garrison town, which meant that most of the tau's strength was probably deployed in theatre. The presence of so many remote sensor towers around Praxedes seemed to support that conclusion. No matter the sophistication of automated surveyor gear, nothing could surpass eyes-on intelligence from a living being.

Learchus estimated the tau presence in Praxedes to be around five hundred infantry, with perhaps fifty battle-suits. He had seen a few Hammerheads parked in the shadow of the loader derricks clustered at the water's edge, but few other armoured vehicles. More importantly, a thousand or so Lavrentian Guardsmen were being held prisoner on one of the vacant landing platforms jutting out to sea.

That was the key, and if Uriel's plan was to work, Learchus and his warriors had to prepare the way by sowing confusion and mayhem. During a brief communications window, Uriel had outlined his plan to Learchus in Battle Cant, impressing upon Learchus the importance of his part in its success. This was all or nothing, and though Uriel's plan was incredibly risky, Learchus could find no fault in his captain's reasoning in regards to the Codex Astartes.

Learchus and the scouts were in position, but with zero hour for the assault into Praxedes imminent, they could not report their readiness for fear of giving away their position once more.

'Look,' said Issam, nodding towards the prison facility. 'Is that who I think it is?'

Learchus followed the direction of Issam's nod, and smiled. 'Indeed it is. We might get to fulfil our original mission brief after all.'

His enhanced eyes easily picked out Governor Shonai, strolling through the prison in the company of a tau, robed in cream and red and gold. Learchus's expression darkened the more he watched the tau and Koudelkar Shonai. Their body language spoke of an easy rapport, like two old friends out for a morning constitutional.

'Who's the governor's companion?' asked Issam.

The tau all looked the same to Learchus, but this one had a hint of familiarity to his features.

'Guilliman's blood,' exclaimed Learchus as he realised the tau's identity. 'That's the bastard we captured at Lake Masura. How in the name of the warp did he get here? We stuck him in the Glasshouse with the enforcers!'

'However he did it, he must be important, judging by the number of guards he has.'

'Captain Ventris said he was one of their leader caste, a noble or something.'

'Most likely,' said Issam. 'What do you suppose he and the governor have to talk about?'

'I'll be sure to ask him before I break his damned neck,' said Learchus.

THE IMPERIAL COMMANDERS of Olzetyn gathered beneath the great triumphal arch at the eastern end of the Imperator Bridge. The destruction of the Spur Bridge had bought the Lavrentian Pioneers time to construct the eastern defences thoroughly, and they had not wasted the time the Ultramarines had bought them. Coils of razor wire, stoutly-walled redoubts and armoured bunkers were efficiently and cunningly constructed before the archway, a defence in depth that would exact a fearsome toll in attackers' blood.

A cold wind whipped along the length of the bridge and over the defences. In the bunker serving as the Imperial command post, Colonel Loic shivered in his cream greatcoat as he poured himself a measure of *Uskavar* from a silver flask. The flask was emblazoned with the white rose of Pavonis, and had been a gift from the men under his command.

Emperor alone knew where they'd sourced such a thing in the midst of all this fighting, but wherever they had found it the gesture had touched him deeply.

'Chilly today,' he noted, offering the flask to Lieutenant Poldara.

Poldara was gracious enough to accept, and took a polite sip of the potent liquor. 'Thank you, colonel. If you are cold I can fetch you a cloak.'

'No need,' replied Loic. 'I expect the tau will make it hot enough for us in due course.'

The first time he had met Gerber's lieutenant, he remembered thinking that he looked absurdly young to be a soldier. The fighting at Olzetyn had changed that. Poldara now looked as weathered as any seasoned infantryman.

'War ages us,' said Loic, wondering how worn out *he* must look to the young lieutenant.

'Sir?'

'Nothing, don't mind me,' said Loic, realising he'd spoken aloud.

He was so tired he couldn't tell what he was saying.

He took a deep breath to gather his thoughts. The defence of Olzetyn was in its final stages, that much was obvious to everyone. All stratagems were exhausted, and all war-tricks had been employed. The Ultramarines were gone, and all that stood between the tau and Brandon Gate were the courageous soldiers of the Pavonis PDF and the Lavrentian Imperial Guard.

Watching the Space Marines embarking on their gunships, Loic had felt a dreadful sense of loss. He knew Uriel and his warriors had a vital, potentially war-winning mission to attempt, but he couldn't shake the feeling that, with their departure, something fundamental had been lost from the hearts of the defenders of Olzetyn.

He'd heard that a single Astartes warrior was worth a hundred mortal soldiers, but Loic knew their real worth could not be measured by simple arithmetic. Space Marines were inspirational figures, warriors that every man dug deep into his soul to emulate. Their courage and honour was immeasurable, and to fight with them was to fight with the gods of battle themselves.

It would be a shame to die without such companions at his side.

Loic shook off gloomy thoughts of death and returned his attention to the present. Captain Gerber and Commissar Vogel pored over a series of consoles embedded in the forward wall of the bunker, the screens illuminating them with a soft green glow. Both men were examining schematics of the defences, pointing at various features along the length of the ruined bridge.

Loic joined Gerber and Vogel at the sandbagged loopholes of the bunker.

'You're wasting your time,' he said. 'Everything that needs to be done is already done. Supplies are in place throughout our position. Caches of ammunition, food and water are set up, medicae triage stations are ready to receive wounded. All that's left to do now is wait.'

'There's always something left to do,' said Gerber, 'something we should anticipate.'

'Maybe so, but if there is I don't think it will make much of a difference.'

Loic took out the silver flask and offered it to his fellow officers. '*Uskavar*? It's a good blend, nice and smooth, and I think we deserve it, eh?'

Gerber nodded. 'Might as well. We're on our own now, so where's the harm?'

'Commissar?'

Vogel accepted the flask and took a hit, his eyes widening at the strength of the drink.

'Told you it was a good blend,' said Loic, taking the flask back.

The three officers shared a companionable silence as they looked over the bridge. Many of the teetering structures were gone and the bridge was carpeted with ruins of hab-blocks and temples, battered down by tau missiles or pulverised by Imperial shelling.

'Any word from Captain Luzaine and Banner Command?'

'They're on the march from Jotusburg, but they won't get here for at least another six hours,' said Gerber.

'Too late for us then?'

'Except to avenge us,' said Gerber, and this time Vogel said nothing.

'Look!' said Gerber, pointing down the bridge. 'Here they come.'

At the far end of the bridge, Loic saw the sleek shapes of tau vehicles moving through the ruins. Devilfish and Hammerheads slid over the rubble of the destroyed habs, and Loic blanched at the sight of so many armoured vehicles. Battlesuits and darting Stingwings arced through the air above the host.

'Emperor's mercy,' whispered Vogel. 'There are so many.'

'Now who's being defeatist?' chuckled Gerber.

A line of light lit up the horizon as a hundred streaking missile launches painted the sky with bright contrails. Loic watched them arc upwards, as though on a ballistic trajectory.

'Incoming!' shouted Gerber as the missiles streaked down towards the defences.

Loic finished the last of the *Uskavar*.

'To victory,' he said.

URIEL AND CHAPLAIN Clausel stepped from the Thunderhawk and onto the steel-grille embarkation deck of the *Vae Victus*. Beside them, a long line of gunships growled as servitors and crew chained them to locking spars while ordnance officers rearmed them. Fuel lines were connected and lifter cranes swung out with fresh loads of missiles and shells for their guns. Flashing lights spun above recently closed airlocks, and the air was redolent with the actinic charge of integrity fields and void chill.

Admiral Tiberius was waiting for them, and clasped Uriel's hand in the warrior's grip.

The commander of the *Vae Victus* was a giant Space Marine of nearly four hundred years with skin the colour of dark leather. A golden laurel encircled a shaven scalp that bore scars earned during the Battle of Circe, and the moulded breastplate of his blue armour was adorned with a host of bronze honour badges.

'Uriel, Clausel,' said Tiberius, 'by the primarch, it's good to see you both.'

'And you, admiral, but we have no time to waste,' said Uriel, jogging towards the far end of the embarkation deck. 'Is everything prepared?'

'Of course,' said Tiberius, though Uriel already knew that the venerable admiral would not let him down. 'Now get your men locked in so we can launch. Those tau vessels are closing fast, and, if you're not gone inside of five minutes, you'll be looking for a new battle-barge for the 4th Company!'

'Understood,' said Uriel.

Ultramarines moved rapidly through the embarkation deck to their assigned rally points, where armoury serfs passed out fresh bolter ammunition and power-cells for chainswords. Uriel and Clausel made their way along the deck, ensuring that their warriors were ready for the fight of their lives.

Chaplain Clausel stood beside him and said, 'You are once more on the path of the Codex Astartes, Captain Ventris. It is good to see.'

'Thank you, Brother-Chaplain,' he said. 'It means a lot to hear you say that.'

Clausel nodded curtly, and made his way to his designated position without another word.

A series of green lights lit up along the embarkation deck. They were ready.

With no time for inspiring words or the proper rites of battle, Uriel simply raised the sword of Idaeus for every warrior to see.

'Courage and honour!' he roared.

* * *

KOUDELKAR SHONAI STOOD in the doorway of his quarters, looking out over the dark waters of Crater Bay and sipping his tisane. The morning sunlight glinted from the dark expanse of ocean, and a bitter wind whipped cold salt spray into the prison facility. Koudelkar had thought it beautiful, but today it seemed like a thing of menace.

He looked over his shoulder to where Aun'rai sat inside, accompanied by three armed Fire Warriors. Mostly, they ignored him, but a female tau with a scarred face and the beginnings of a white topknot glared with undisguised hatred. He didn't know what he'd done to offend her, and didn't feel much like asking for fear of what the answer might be.

'Will I ever see Pavonis again?' he asked.

'Perhaps in time,' answered Aun'rai. 'Though given your past association with this world, it might be better if you did not. Will that be a problem for you?'

Koudelkar thought about that question for a moment, looking at the hostile faces of the soldiers milling around the prison compound. 'No. I thought it would, but the notion of seeing new horizons, new seas and new worlds appeals to me immensely.'

'Good,' said Aun'rai, sounding genuinely pleased.

'Of course there will be things I'll miss,' he said, 'but I expect I'll get over that.'

'You will,' promised Aun'rai. 'You will want for nothing in your new life as a valued citizen of the Tau Empire. With everyone working towards the Greater Good, no one goes hungry, no one lacks shelter and everyone is afforded the opportunity to contribute.'

'It almost sounds too good to be true,' said Koudelkar, only half joking.

'It is not,' said Aun'rai. 'You will be welcomed into our empire, valued for the skills you possess and honoured for your contribution to the Greater Good.'

Koudelkar took one last look at the bay before heading back into his quarters. He set down his glass on the plain oval table next to his bed and sat on the chair opposite Aun'rai.

'But what exactly will I do?'

'You will work with others of your kind to spread the word of the Greater Good,' said Aun'rai. 'You will be a shining example of what we can offer your people, a bridge to cross the gulf of misunderstanding that exists between your race and mine.'

'You mean I'd be an ambassador?' asked Koudelkar.

'Of sorts, yes,' agreed Aun'rai. 'With your help, we can avoid bloodshed when the Third Expansion reaches other human worlds. If humanity will accept the teachings of the Ethereals and become part of our empire, there is no limit to what we might achieve.'

'You know, before talking with you I would have been repulsed by thoughts of working with an alien race,' said Koudelkar.

'And now?'

'Now I look forward to it, though I wonder if the same can be said for your followers.'

Aun'rai followed his gaze and nodded in understanding.

'La'tyen was taken prisoner and suffered greatly at the hands of her captors. She was tortured and beaten, as I would have been had we not escaped.'

'I'm sorry to hear that,' said Koudelkar, hiding his sudden fear of the warrior, knowing that she had been tortured on his orders. He looked away from her scars to hide the guilt that he felt sure was written all over his face.

'It is of no consequence,' said Aun'rai, and Koudelkar wondered if La'tyen felt the same. Somehow he doubted it.

He saw a sudden stiffening in the posture of Aun'rai's guards, and turned his chair to see Lortuen Perjed standing in the doorway. Koudelkar's mother stood beside him, and an ashen-faced Jenna Sharben supported herself on a set of metal crutches. Koudelkar felt a rush of unease at the sight of the Chief of Enforcers, suddenly remembering that she was, first and foremost, a judge of the Adeptus Arbites.

'Adept Perjed,' said Aun'rai smoothly, 'would you care to join us? There is enough tisane to go around. I am told it is quite pleasant to human tastes.'

'I have nothing to say to you, xenos,' said Perjed.

'What are you doing here, Lortuen?' demanded Koudelkar. 'I have nothing to say to you.'

'Then listen,' snapped Sharben, her voice a mix of controlled fury and pain as she awkwardly limped on her crutches into the centre of the room. 'Koudelkar Shonai, by the authority of the Immortal God-Emperor, I hereby relieve you of Imperial command of Pavonis and all its domains. This I do with the full support of this world's senior Administratum adept. From this moment onwards, you pass from the protection of the Imperium, and are numbered amongst its enemies.'

Koudelkar shrank before Sharben's steely glare, her words like a knife in his guts, until he remembered that he had already forsaken this world for a new life amongst the tau.

'You think I care about that?' he asked, rising to his feet as a simmering anger swelled within him. 'The Imperium gave up on Pavonis long ago and I welcome your censure. It only proves I have made the right decision.'

'Oh, Koudelkar,' said his mother, tears running freely down her cheeks. 'What have they done to you to make you say these things?'

Koudelkar pushed past Sharben and embraced his mother.

'Don't cry,' he said, 'please. You need to trust me, Mother. I know what I am doing.'

'No,' she said, 'you don't. They've used some sort of mind control on you or something.'

'That's absurd,' he said.

'Please,' she begged, holding him tightly to her. 'You have to come with us. Now.'

'What are you talking about?'

'You know what she's talking about,' said Perjed, and Koudelkar looked over his mother's shoulder to see a group of Lavrentian soldiers gathering outside. It was impossible to miss the threat of violence they wore, and Koudelkar felt a hot flush of fear as he realised that Adept Perjed's threatened uprising was at hand.

'It is time to fight,' said Perjed, 'and you had your chance to stand with us.'

Koudelkar turned to shout a warning to Aun'rai, but before the words could leave his mouth, the noise of an explosion sounded from somewhere nearby. From his position at the door, Koudelkar saw pillars of flame and smoke rising from the towers on either side of the prison gates. A deafening boom sounded an instant later as crackling lightning ripped around the circumference of the camp and fizzing sparks fountained from the pylons of the perimeter force barrier.

Alarm klaxons sounded, and Koudelkar heard the bark of gunfire.

He rounded on Perjed. 'What have you done? You have killed us all!'

But as the sounds of fighting grew more intense, Koudelkar saw that Adept Perjed was just as surprised.

ʊ
TWENTY

LEARCHUS SHOT A Fire Warrior through the chest, and then ran from the wreckage of the burning guard tower towards a low structure that might have been a power generator. Its sides were cream coloured and marked with a number of tau symbols. Issam covered him with a series of well-aimed bolter shots into a knot of assembling Fire Warriors, and they scattered, leaving two dead in their wake.

Learchus hammered into the structure, and leaned out to fire into the tau warriors reacting to the sudden invasion of the prison. He put one down with a snap shot and blew the leg off another who was too slow to find cover.

Daxian fanned out to the other side of the smashed gate as Parmian fired his bolt pistol from behind the second skimmer. The remains of the first skimmer burned just beyond the gateway in the midst of a pile of tau corpses.

The opening moments of their assault had been more devastating than Learchus could have hoped, and he knew they had to maintain their momentum and keep the tau off-balance. The shock and awe of their sudden assault was forcing the tau to dance to their tune, but as soon as they realised just how few in number were their attackers and fought back...

Using the scout skimmers to speed through the streets of Praxedes, they had swiftly made their way to the landing jibs, and Learchus had felt his fingers moving across the vehicle's armaments panel of their own volition. He had no idea what he was doing, yet a targeting matrix had projected onto the canopy of the skimmer and seemed to acquire targets one after another. He expected the front-mounted rifles to shoot, and had been disappointed when they stubbornly refused to open fire at their targets. That disappointment had been short-lived as he heard rapid *whoosh, whoosh, whoosh* sounds from behind, and a series of streaking missiles leapt from a tall sentry turret.

The missiles impacted on the guard towers on either side of the prison entrance and they exploded in blistering fireballs. Both collapsed into piles of twisted metal, taking out the tau guards and a number of the humming pylons surrounding the camp. Bolts of jade lightning arced between the pylons, and a thunderclap of electrical discharge boomed like an enormous whip-crack.

The skimmers plunged through the smoke of the destroyed gateway, but the tau were quick to recover from their surprise, and a hail of gunfire shot out of the skimmer carrying Learchus and Daxian. Both warriors leapt from the stricken vehicle as it tumbled end over end and exploded, showering the Fire Warriors who had shot it down with whickering fragments of red-hot metal.

Issam and Parmian skidded their vehicle to a halt, azure bolts of energy spitting from their skimmer's weapons. Before the prison guards could react, Issam leapt from the pilot's seat, and began firing his bolter as he ran towards cover. Parmian clambered from the vehicle, and took up position behind it, sniping at enemy soldiers from behind the hovering skimmer.

'Issam!' shouted Learchus. 'We need to keep pushing on!'

'Understood,' replied the scout sergeant. 'Going to be tough though.'

That was an understatement. The structure Learchus was sheltering behind was rapidly disintegrating under repeated impacts, and, despite Parmian's covering fire, there was no way Learchus could move without being cut down. A firing line of Fire Warriors was systematically destroying his cover, and there was nothing he could do to stop them.

Then Learchus heard a roaring howl of rage, and the fire pounding his cover slackened. He risked a glance around the structure, and saw something that filled him with exultation. Unarmed prisoners were swarming from their barrack buildings to attack their guards, dragging them down with their sheer weight of numbers and fury. Dozens were dead, for they had no weapons save their fists, but these men were hungry to expunge the stain of their earlier humiliation, and nothing was going to keep them from their vengeance.

All across the camp, the Imperial prisoners were rising up and attacking their captors. Mobs of imprisoned Guardsmen hurled themselves at the tau, tearing them apart with their bare hands or clubbing them to death with whatever blunt objects came to hand. Others tore the weapons from the dead Fire Warriors and turned them on their captors with savage glee.

Learchus had seldom seen a more inspiring sight, and, though he wanted to punch the air in triumph, the very gaucheness of the gesture restrained him. He spun from cover, and surged forwards into the melee, seeing Issam break from cover at the same instant.

Daxian moved out to join his sergeant, and the three Space Marines were a wedge of fighting fury that plunged deep into the tau. Learchus felt a savage sense of release as he shot another Fire Warrior in the chest. After so long avoiding contact with the enemy, to release the controlled aggression of the Astartes in close-quarters battle was as cathartic as it was exhilarating.

He turned to wave Parmian forwards with them, to join in the slaughter, but the joy of battle drained from him as he saw that the tau forces beyond the camp were finally reacting to the enemy in their midst.

At least two dozen battlesuits were jetting through the air towards the prison, closely followed by three Hammerheads, moving swiftly towards the burning gateway. Learchus's assault was pushing deep into the camp, and the inmates were rising up, but a rabble of prisoners with a handful of rifles and four Space Marines could not hope to face such a force and live.

Seeing the tau reaction force, Parmian tried to find cover, but he was spotted by the lead battlesuit team and had nowhere to run. The first battlesuit landed just behind Parmian and unleashed a searing blast of fiery plasma at point-blank range. The wounded scout had no time to scream as he was instantly incinerated, leaving nothing but the blackened shreds of a corpse.

Learchus and his fellow warriors ducked into the cover of one of the barrack buildings. A flurry of shells shredded the ground where they had been standing.

'COME ON, URIEL,' he hissed. 'Where are you?'

At the sound of the first explosion, Jenna Sharben leapt into action. Her burst of movement caught

Koudelkar's eye, and he watched in horror as she spun her crutch around and stabbed it into the belly of one of Aun'rai's bodyguards. Only then did he notice that the bottom of each crutch had been sharpened to a lethal point.

The Fire Warrior screamed foully and collapsed, blood pouring down his legs from the terrible wound. Clearly the chief of enforcers was not as debilitated by her wounds as she had led the tau to believe.

Sharben swung her other crutch around in a short, brutal arc, the heavy end hammering into another bodyguard's helmet with a solid crunch. The warrior went down heavily as Sharben turned to face the last of Aun'rai's protectors.

Koudelkar made to go to Aun'rai's aid, but his mother gripped his tunic tightly. Her eyes pleaded with him not to go, but, for better or worse, Koudelkar had made his choice, and he had to live up to his end of the bargain.

He threw off her grip, though it broke his heart to hear her despairing cry.

'Koudelkar, no!' shouted Perjed. 'Don't.'

Though Sharben had fooled them with her display of weakness, the element of surprise could only see her so far, and La'tyen leapt on her with an anguished cry of hatred. Arbites Judge and Fire Warrior rolled on the ground, punching and clawing at one another.

The chief enforcer's elbow slammed into La'tyen's midriff, but the Fire Warrior's flexible body armour bore the brunt of the blow. La'tyen hooked her arm around Sharben's throat and dug her fingers into her neck. Sharben slammed her head backwards into La'tyen's face, and Koudelkar heard the crack of a cheekbone breaking. Sharben rolled from her opponent with a grunt of pain, scrabbling for a weapon as La'tyen drew a glittering knife from her belt.

Koudelkar had heard that they were called honour blades, and were ceremonial weapons used to symbolise fraternity amongst the tau, though there was nothing ceremonial about its viciously sharp edge. The blade slashed towards Sharben, who leapt back to avoid being gutted. She cried out in pain as her weight came down on her injured leg. The Arbites Judge was not as badly hurt as she had made out, but she was still hurt.

Koudelkar wanted to intervene, but knew La'tyen would as likely gut him as Sharben. The bleeding Fire Warrior continued to cry out in pain as his blood spilled from his wound, but his dazed compatriot was rising unsteadily to his feet with a rifle held before him.

La'tyen feinted with her honour blade, and Sharben fell to one knee as her wounded leg gave out beneath her. It was the opening that La'tyen needed, and she plunged the blade of her knife into Sharben's chest.

The combatants crashed to the floor, and La'tyen stabbed the mortally wounded enforcer again and again in a frenzy of grief, anger and hatred. Blood spurted, and sprayed the walls in spattering arcs as La'tyen let the horror of her torture in the Glasshouse pour from her in a frenzy of savage violence.

Koudelkar recoiled from the awfulness of Sharben's death, horrified at the animal savagery of the killing. La'tyen looked up, and through the mask of blood coating her twisted features, Koudelkar saw the true nature of the tau race, the darkness they kept hidden behind their veneer of civilisation and fantastical notions of the Greater Good.

Lortuen Perjed ran forwards as Sharben died, desperation lending his aged limbs strength. He bent to retrieve the short-barrelled weapon dropped by the Fire Warrior Sharben had first attacked, and fumbled with the firing mechanism.

'Don't be an idiot, Lortuen! Put the gun down!' shouted Koudelkar, having no wish to see Lortuen killed in this terrible folly. The adept was not to be dissuaded from his course, however, and he and the dazed Fire Warrior pulled the triggers in the same moment. Koudelkar flinched as volleys of searing blue energy beams sprayed the room.

The Fire Warrior went down in a crumpled heap, his chest a cratered ruin, but he had taken his killer with him. Lortuen Perjed was punched from his feet, his fragile body torn virtually in two by the flurry of high energy bolts.

As terrible as was Lortuen's fate, the true horror was behind the murdered adept.

Koudelkar's mother slid down the pristine walls of his quarters, leaving a bloody smear behind her. Pawluk Shonai's eyes were wide with pain, and her prison-issue tunic was soaked with an expanding red stain.

'No!' cried Koudelkar, running over to his mother. He gathered her up in his arms as tears blurred his vision. He put his hand on her stomach, trying in vain to stem the flow of blood from her body.

'Emperor save her, please, oh please no!' wailed Koudelkar, desperately pleading with the only god he knew to save his mother. 'Oh God-Emperor, no, don't let this happen!'

Koudelkar watched the life drain from his mother's eyes, and gave a terrible, aching cry of loss. His eyes filled with tears, and he sobbed as he held her lifeless body tight.

'I'm sorry, I'm sorry,' he wept. 'It's all my fault. I betrayed you, oh Emperor forgive me, please forgive me...'

Koudelkar felt a presence near him, and looked up from his grief to see Aun'rai standing over him, his expression one of profound disappointment.

'You call to your Emperor for aid?' asked Aun'rai. 'After all we have discussed, you still turn to your distant Emperor for solace? No matter what your intellect might say, you look to gods and spirits in times of trouble. How pathetically human of you.'

'She's dead!' wailed Koudelkar. 'Don't you understand? She's dead.'

'I understand all too well,' said Aun'rai coldly, as La'tyen appeared at his side, her face and armour drenched in Sharben's blood.

Koudelkar fought to cling onto his sanity in the face of this horrific bloodshed. In a matter of seconds, his bright future of importance and luxury had turned to horror and grief. He shook his head, and gently laid his mother down on the cold, hard floor of his quarters.

He stood and faced the two tau. One desperately wanted to kill him, the other to enslave him, and Koudelkar wasn't sure which fate he dreaded more.

'It does not have to end here,' said Aun'rai. 'You can still be part of the Greater Good.'

'I think not,' replied Koudelkar, backing out of the doorway, through which the crack of gunfire and the boom of explosions could be heard. 'I want nothing from you or your race. If I am to die, then I will die among my own kind.'

Koudelkar turned and walked down the steps to the landing platform. He could taste the smoke in the air and the crackling electric charge of the downed security fences. Shouting soldiers and the bark of weapons' fire surrounded him, but Koudelkar had never felt more at ease with himself.

He remembered a conversation he'd had with Lortuen Perjed not long after they had arrived at the prison camp.

'We are prisoners of war,' Koudelkar had said. 'What honour do we have?'

'Only what we bring with us,' was Perjed's reply, and only now did Koudelkar understand what the adept had meant. He lifted his head and looked into the achingly blue sky, taking a deep breath of the ocean-scented air.

Koudelkar frowned, and raised a hand to shield his eyes from the sun as he saw a number of falling objects that looked out of place in the heavens. He smiled as he recognised them for what they were.

Aun'rai appeared in the doorway of his quarters, seemingly unconcerned with the fighting that raged through the prison complex.

'This foolish uprising will be quashed,' spat the tau. 'And nothing will have changed.'

'You know, I think you're wrong about that,' said Koudelkar, pointing towards the sky where a host of Space Marine drop-pods streaked towards the ground on blazing lines of fire.

Uriel's drop-pod hammered down in a blazing flare of rockets and pulverised metal decking. Explosive bolts blew out the heat-shielded doors, and the locking harnesses securing the Space Marines within snapped upright. What had been a hermetically sealed environment for travel through the cold of space and the heat of re-entry was now open to the elements and the reek of propellant and scorched metal filled the air.

'Go! Everyone out!' shouted Uriel, and the warriors who had endured the thunderous ride from the embarkation deck of the *Vae Victus* with him leapt instantly to obey. Uriel led them from the drop-pod, taking in the ebb and flow of the battle in a moment.

Learchus had done his work well.

The Praxedes detention camp was in uproar, with desperate Fire Warriors in combat with hordes of equally desperate prisoners. The fighting was ferocious, but it was clear that the tau had the upper hand. Though considerably outnumbered by their captives, the Fire Warriors were highly-trained and had no give in them.

Numbers and courage could carry any assault far, but against disciplined soldiers armed with powerful weapons, it was never going to be enough, and the Lavrentian prisoners were being slaughtered. Uriel saw Learchus and two scouts firing on a battlesuit squad from the cover of a barrack building. While the weight of fire kept Learchus pinned in place, two other battlesuits were moving to encircle him.

Chaplain Clausel's voice sounded in his helmet. 'Our arrival is most timely.'

'So it would appear,' said Uriel, quickly identifying the key points of resistance. 'Secure the gate. I will link with Learchus.'

'Understood.'

The tau forces were reacting swiftly to the arrival of the Astartes, turning their guns on the new threat in their midst. Flurries of blue energy beams slashed towards the Space Marines, but they were answered by a weight of fire greater than isolated bands of infantry could hope to muster.

Landing seconds before the main assault, drop-pods equipped with automated heavy weapon systems instead of troops unleashed furious barrages of missiles upon the tau. Following preset logic parameters, they engaged targets with merciless precision, and explosions ripped through the greatest concentrations of Fire Warriors.

The tau reeled from the shock of the sudden violence of the assault, but Uriel knew from past experience that they would recover quickly. To win this fight, the Ultramarines would need to keep the tau on the back foot, never allowing them to regain the initiative.

Two further drop-pods slammed down, buckling the metal of the landing jib's deck and scorching it black with the fire of their retros. Sequential bangs sounded like a string of firecrackers, and the wider doors of these drop-pods fell open to reveal the ancient and revered Dreadnoughts of the 4th Company.

Brother Speritas stepped into the battle with his assault cannon roaring, and a string of missiles leaping from the armoured rack mounted at his shoulder. Zethus followed his brother Dreadnought's example, opening fire on the tau the instant his fiery chariot's doors were opened. Twin beams of incandescent laser energy blew the turret from a Hammerhead as it turned to face the Dreadnoughts, and a tongue of blazing promethium jetted from beneath his monstrous crackling fist.

The tau fell back from the two Dreadnoughts in disarray, leaving dozens afire behind them. Powerful though the Fire Warriors' guns were, they could not hope to defeat the armour of such mighty war engines.

Clausel's squads arced on fiery jump packs towards the entrance of the prison complex, gunning down those Fire Warriors that had disembarked from their Devilfish transports. Hammerhead battle tanks floated gracefully through the fires of battle, their enormous guns tracking around to unleash their fury upon the Space Marines.

Chattering cannons and blisteringly bright spears of high energy tore into the Space Marines alongside Clausel, and Uriel saw that not all would be getting to their feet. He grieved for the fallen, but the assault had always carried the risk that many of the 4th Company would be returning to Macragge as honoured dead.

A drop-pod exploded behind Uriel, the Ultramarines it had carried swatted to the deck by the blast. Most climbed swiftly to their feet, but three remained on the ground. Barely seconds had passed since the thunderous arrival of the Ultramarines, yet the tau had already realigned their defences to meet the threat.

A warrior in brilliant blue armour emblazoned with a glittering golden eagle, and who wore a white-winged helmet, stood next to Uriel. His cloak billowed in the thermals of the drop-pods' descent, and he carried a long pole of black adamantium topped with a crimson crosspiece.

Ancient Peleus unfurled the banner of the 4th Company, and the power of its magnificence was akin to the sight of a hundred other Space Marines. The gold leaf and silver threading of the clenched gauntlet glittered in the sun, and its sacred fabric was a beacon to every warrior of courage and honour who beheld it.

'The banner of the 4th flies above us!' shouted Uriel. 'Let no warrior falter in his duty to the Chapter!'

His warriors answered with a cheer of pride and love, their devotion and faith in the power of the banner pushing them to new heights of courage. To fight beneath the company standard was an honour, and every warrior knew that the heroes of the past were watching them, standing in judgement of their courage. The Lavrentian prisoners had been on the verge of breaking when the tide had turned against them, but, with the arrival of the Ultramarines, they surged from their boltholes to once again attack the tau. Though the standard of the 4th was not their own, it represented centuries of courage that spoke to the heart of every warrior who beheld it.

Uriel led squad Ventris and the standard towards the barrack building where Learchus and his warriors fought. He fired as he ran, for there was no shortage of targets. Fire Warriors dropped with every volley, as shots flashed past Uriel's head and skidded from the deck around him. Running battles between prisoners and Fire Warriors filled the compound, and Uriel was forced to weave a path through the struggling combatants.

Hot air blasted downwards, and Uriel looked up to see a tau aircraft roar overhead. Bulky and oblong, he recognised it as an Orca, and he knew exactly why its pilot dared risk flying over such a hostile environment.

The craft was soon lost to sight, and Uriel pounded onwards through the warzone of the camp. Learchus looked up as Squad Ventris drew close, and Uriel saw the swell of pride in his sergeant as he caught sight of the banner they carried.

'Squad Ventris!' shouted Uriel. 'Combat squads. Hold and engage left!'

His warriors smoothly split into two units, one bracing and opening fire on the battlesuits pinning Learchus and the scouts in place. Rippling volleys of bolter-fire hammered the battlesuits, a pumping barrage of shells that detonated within the armoured chest cavity of the first enemy warrior and sent the other into cover.

The second combat squad followed Uriel to join Learchus and his ragtag scouts, but there was no time for greetings, for the two flanking battlesuits roared over the roof of the barrack building. They landed in a flurry of exhaust gases and gunfire. One of the scouts screamed and went down, his kneecap a pulped mess. Another, a sergeant, dropped as a shell clipped his shoulder and spun him around.

A white-hot lance of plasma bored through the chest of an Ultramarine, and the warrior fell, dead before he

hit the ground. Uriel and Learchus charged the battlesuits as the second unleashed a seething torrent of fire
from its weapons. Uriel felt the heat of the fire wash
over his armour, and red warning icons flashed up on
his visor. Coolant gases vented from his armour's backpack as it fought to counteract the heat, and Uriel heard
cries of pain behind him as the lightly armoured scouts
scrambled back from the killing flames.

Uriel emerged from the inferno, his cloak a blazing
ruin, and the eagle of his armour blackened as tiny
flames guttered and died on his chest. The battlesuits
braced to meet their charge as bolter shells sparked and
ricocheted from their armoured hulls.

Learchus ducked beneath a roaring cannon and
shoulder-charged the nearest battlesuit. Its legs crumpled under the sheer mass of Learchus's frame, and it
fell backwards into a crumpled, helpless heap. Uriel
swung the sword of Idaeus at a descending fist the size
of his head, and hacked the limb from the battlesuit facing him. Hydraulic fluids sprayed from the neatly
severed machinery, and the battlesuit reared away from
his deadly blade.

Uriel leapt forwards, and took hold of the battlesuit's
armoured carapace as it activated its jets and powered
upwards. The ground spun away, but Uriel wasn't about
to let his foe escape so easily. He rammed his sword
through the battlesuit's chest, and its jets cut out almost
immediately. The battlesuit dropped through the roof
of the barrack building, and Uriel kicked himself away
from the dying Fire Warrior.

He twisted in the air as he fell to land on his feet with
a slamming thud.

Learchus stood with one boot resting on the chest of
the downed battlesuit as he ripped his chainsword from
its body. Torn metal and blood came with it, and the

armoured suit convulsed as its occupant died. Learchus spun his sword and brought the blade down across the battlesuit's neck like an executioner's axe.

'Nicely done,' commented Uriel. 'A bit over the top though, don't you think?'

'Says the man who killed his foe in midair,' grunted Learchus, though Uriel heard the amusement behind the sergeant's brusqueness.

'It is good to see you, my friend,' said Uriel.

'Aye, good indeed,' agreed Learchus, 'but save your heartfelt gratitude for later, we're on the hunt!'

'He is here?'

'He is here,' confirmed Learchus, pointing through the maze of barrack buildings.

Uriel ducked his head around the corner of the building in time to see Koudelkar Shonai being dragged towards the Orca drop-ship he had seen earlier. A bloody-faced Fire Warrior held a knife to the governor's throat, and hurrying alongside him was a figure Uriel recognised immediately.

The tau noble they had captured after the battle at the Shonai estates.

The tau *leader* whose Orca drop-ship the *Vae Victus* had tracked to Praxedes after his escape from the Glasshouse.

'Let's go,' said Uriel.

♉
TWENTY-ONE

Colonel Loic blinked away the afterimages of the missile's explosion, and coughed up a mouthful of blood and dust. His ears were still ringing from the deafening bang, and he felt warm wetness on his face. He rolled onto his side, dislodging the timber, stone and flakboard that covered him in a mini avalanche. Dust and smoke obscured his view, but sparks fizzed from broken cables. The solitary data-screen that remained unbroken hissed with glowing static.

He groaned in pain, feeling as though he'd been run over by Lord Winterbourne's Baneblade. He coughed another mouthful of blood, and felt a twitch of concern as he noted its brightness. Had he punctured a lung or nicked an artery somewhere inside?

It didn't feel like he'd been too badly hurt, but you never knew with combat injuries.

He looked around, waving a hand in front of his face to clear some of the dust. Ahead was a wall of bright daylight, which was odd considering there had been a solid barrier there only moments ago. What little that remained of the roof groaned ominously, and dust drifted down from cracks in the ceiling.

The rest of the bunker was a slaughterhouse, the remaining walls coated in blood from the ruptured corpses that lay in mangled piles of shredded limbs. Data-servitors still sat at their posts, or at least pieces of them did. Bloody flesh and cybernetic augmentations were scattered around the bunker's wrecked interior like torn rags.

'Oh Emperor's mercy,' he hissed, seeing Captain Gerber and Commissar Vogel buried in a pile of cracked rockcrete and roof timbers. The sound of explosions and gunfire still came from beyond the bunker, but it was muted, as though coming from the bottom of a deep chasm, and Loic wondered if his eardrums had burst. Probably not, he surmised, thinking that he'd be in a lot more pain if they had.

Strange what random thoughts were coming to him now. Was it shock? Some post-traumatic reaction to a near-death experience?

'Pull yourself together, man,' he chided himself, clambering over piles of debris to reach the fallen Lavrentian captain. He stumbled over a collapsed roof spar and fell onto all fours. His hands landed on something soft and warm that gave way beneath his weight. Loic recoiled, horrified as he realised that his hands had landed in the ruptured stomach cavity of Lieutenant Poldara. The young man's face was peaceful and serene, youthful again, and Loic felt a terrible, wrenching grief. Poldara was dead, and he would never have to worry about the ravages of war and time.

'Age shall not weary you, nor the years condemn,' he whispered, the words clearly audible even over the far-away crackle and boom of gunfire and explosions. He wiped his hands on his greatcoat, leaving long crimson smears on the cream fabric. Watching for any more gory pitfalls, he finally reached the two Lavrentian officers.

Vogel was clearly dead, half his skull missing and his brains leaking out over the debris-strewn floor. Loic reached out and placed his fingers on Gerber's neck, and was rewarded with a pulse, weak and thready, but indicative of life.

Carefully, he removed the debris covering the captain, tossing chunks of smashed stone and sandbags to the floor. Gerber coughed and groaned in pain, his eyelids flickering open as he felt Loic's ministrations.

'What... what happened?' asked Gerber.

'I'm not entirely sure, captain,' said Loic, 'but I think we were the target of a well-aimed missile barrage.'

Gerber tried to push himself onto his elbow, but he fell back with a yelp of pain.

'Don't move,' advised Loic. 'I think your arm's broken.'

'I've had worse,' said Gerber. 'Help me up.'

Loic helped Gerber into a sitting position, both men struggling with pain and the sight of so many dead comrades around them. They had thought themselves secure in the bunker, but within moments of the initial tau barrage, the world had exploded in noise and fire.

'Are we still in the fight?' gasped Gerber, his eyes clenched shut with pain.

'I don't know,' said Loic, looking out into the hellish maelstrom of battle beyond.

Gerber took a moment to get his breath, wiping dust and blood from his face with his free hand. A fresh rain of dust and rubble fell from the ruined ceiling as an explosion rocked the Imperator Bridge nearby.

'We need to get out of here,' said Loic. 'Re-establish command and control of what's left.'

'Agreed,' hissed Gerber through gritted teeth as he tried to stand.

Loic bent to help him, and hooked Gerber's arm over his shoulder.

The rear door of the bunker was blocked with tangled steel beams and slabs of fallen masonry, so the two soldiers limped and hobbled towards the open front of the bunker. The dust was settling, but the view from outside was not encouraging.

The tau were all over the defenders, Fire Warriors swarming the outer defences and pushing hard for the second line as heavy tanks provided covering fire and destroyed the redoubts and bunkers one by one. The Imperial lines were bending backwards, and it was clear to both men that they would break in moments.

'It's over,' said Gerber.

'Surely not,' protested Loic. 'We can still win this!'

No sooner were the words out of his mouth than a towering battlesuit slammed down on the rubble before them. Its armour plates were scarred and its head unit was pale blue with a striped pattern on its left side.

A flaming sphere was painted in the centre of its chest panel and upon one shoulder-guard. Two other battlesuits landed a second later as the first raised its weapons, a huge cannon with multiple barrels and a thick tubular device with a hemispherical muzzle.

'It's over,' repeated Gerber.

URIEL BOLTED FROM cover with Learchus right behind him. The scout sergeant, whose name Uriel remembered was Issam, ran alongside Learchus, coagulated blood patterning his shoulder where a shell had clipped him. Their quarry was making a swift retreat to the Orca drop-ship, and Uriel cursed as he saw that they would probably make it before the Ultramarines could catch them.

Koudelkar Shonai was being dragged without cere-
mony by a single Fire Warrior, while the tau noble
jogged alongside him.

'Hurry,' said Uriel. 'All this is for nothing if that noble
gets away.'

'You think I don't know that?' hissed Learchus.

A flurry of shots engulfed the three Space Marines as
a group of eight Fire Warriors ran from between one of
the barrack houses and opened up with a volley of close
range fire. Uriel felt the impacts, and pain flared in his
midriff as the coolant coils below his breastplate ruptured. He dropped to one knee as howling gales of sonic
energy and a swirling blast of light erupted before him.
His auto-senses fought to filter out the aural and sonic
assault, but it was impossible to filter out the hash of
interference completely.

Something smashed into his helmet, and he felt a
sharp object stab into his side. The blow didn't penetrate, but Uriel rolled away and came to his feet in one
motion, sliding his sword from its sheath as his vision
began to clear. The tau warriors threw themselves into
the Ultramarines, attacking in a frenzy of clubbing
blows and point-blank shots of their stubby carbines.
Uriel killed the first with a powerful lunge, dragging his
blade back and decapitating another as he came at his
flank. Another alien ran at him, and Uriel saw that these
tau wore a lighter armour variant to the others.

These warriors were Pathfinders, and it was a measure
of the tau's desperation to protect their leader that such
lightly armoured warriors were being sent to stop them.

Learchus killed an enemy soldier with his fist, and
smashed another's face with the butt of his boltgun.
Issam slid between the enemy warriors with his combat
knife, opening bellies and throats with every deft and
deadly slash.

The fight was brutal, but one-sided. The tau fought with frenzied courage, but they could not hope to best three such professional killers.

'No stomach for a real fight, you said,' said Uriel, cutting down a screaming Fire Warrior as he ran at him with his weapon held like a club.

'I thought the tau preferred not to engage in close combat,' said Issam, gutting another.

'They *really* do not want us to capture their leader,' said Learchus, putting the last Fire Warrior down with a brutal chop from the edge of his fist.

'Damn it,' said Issam, setting off after the tau once again. 'They're just trying to delay us.'

'And it has worked,' cursed Uriel, heading after the Scout-sergeant. He glanced over his shoulder as he ran, seeing Learchus lifting one of the tau carbines. 'Come on, sergeant!'

Uriel ran as fast he was able, but there was no way he or Issam were going to reach the tau noble before he boarded his transport and escaped. Uriel's gamble had failed, and he had probably doomed the defenders of Olzetyn for nothing.

The rear ramp of the Orca cycled open, and a pair of slender tau in flight-suits emerged, beckoning hurriedly to the running noble and his Fire Warrior escort.

Suddenly, a slashing shape came out of nowhere, and Uriel ducked as a missile blazed a path overhead. It streaked towards the Orca, and, in the fraction of a second before it impacted, Uriel was shocked to see that it was a tau missile. It slammed into the side of the Orca's hull, and punched through the lightly armoured skin of the drop-ship before exploding. A jet of fire erupted from the rear of the Orca, and it cracked at its middle as the blast split the aircraft's spine.

Secondary explosions ripped along the hull of the drop-ship as the weapons and ammunition carried inside cooked off. Thick smoke boiled from the stricken craft, and sudden hope flared in Uriel as he saw their targets sprawled on the ground before the blazing wreck.

Issam looked back at Uriel. 'Where in the name of the primarch did that come from?'

Uriel suspected he knew the answer, and looked back the way they had come to see Learchus holding one of the tau carbines at his shoulder. The weapon looked tiny in his hands, yet it had undoubtedly saved their mission.

'How did you know how to use the Valkyrie's Mark?' shouted Uriel as Learchus tossed the weapon aside.

'I will tell you later,' said Learchus. 'Now let's get that bastard.'

The tau were beginning to pick themselves up from the ground, and Uriel could almost feel their dismay at the sight of the wrecked drop-ship. The Fire Warrior with the knife turned, saw the Ultramarines bearing down on them, and dragged Koudelkar Shonai to his feet. As Uriel closed, he saw the remains of a white topknot, and realised that he recognised her.

She was the warrior he and his brothers had captured in the ruins of the de Valtos estate.

Her name was La'tyen, and Uriel felt the hand of synchronicity at work.

She shouted something at the noble, who was climbing unsteadily to his feet, but it was already too late for him. Issam reached the tau leader and hauled him upright. Issam's combat blade pricked the skin of his captive's neck, and Uriel held up his hand as Issam looked to him for the killing word.

Learchus marched up with his bolter aimed at La'tyen, and Uriel held his breath, recognising the brittle nature of this moment. He could see the hate in La'tyen's eyes, and he knew that Koudelkar Shonai's life hung by a thread. Uriel reached up and removed his helmet, the sounds of the battle raging through the camp surging in volume.

'Uriel!' cried Koudelkar. 'Don't let her kill me! Please.'

Uriel nodded and turned to the tau noble. 'Do you understand my language?'

The tau hesitated, and then nodded. 'I do, yes.'

'I am Uriel Ventris of the Ultramarines. Tell me your name.'

'I am Aun'rai,' said the tau.

'And you are the leader of this invasion force?'

'I am the Ethereal of the Burning Star Hunter Coalition.'

'Then you will end this war,' said Uriel, stepping close and looming over Aun'rai. 'Now.'

'Why would I do such a thing?' said Aun'rai. 'My forces are on the verge of overrunning Olzetyn and there is little left to stop us from taking this world.'

'You will do it because I will kill you if you do not.'

'My death matters little,' said Aun'rai, but Uriel saw the first chink in the tau's outward cool. Uriel was no interrogator, but he knew the tau noble was lying.

'Let me tell you what I know,' said Uriel, conscious of the fact that the longer this confrontation went on without resolution, the more men and women would die. 'I know this invasion was a gamble for you and that you needed to defeat us quickly. I know that you have not the resources in place to defend this world against a counterattack, a counterattack that I assure you *will* happen. I know that even if Olzetyn has already fallen, the rest of this world will be ashes before we let you have it. You will have to kill every single human on this planet to hold it, and even then the Imperium will not let you keep it. Forces from neighbouring systems are already en route to Pavonis, and you won't have a strong enough grip on this world by then to keep them at bay.'

La'tyen shouted something angry, but Uriel ignored her.

Aun'rai's eyes flickered towards La'tyen, but Uriel waved a hand before the Ethereal's face. 'Do not look at her. Look at me, and listen to what I am saying. You have fought well, Aun'rai. Your warriors have earned themselves much honour, but you will gain nothing by continuing this fight.'

'And why is that?' asked Aun'rai, a hint of arrogance in his tone, the same arrogance Uriel had recognised in all his encounters with the tau in this war.

'Because my starship carries weapons that can reduce a world to a barren airless rock in moments,' said Uriel, 'and if you do not order an immediate withdrawal, I will order those weapons deployed.'

'You are lying, Uriel Ventris of the Ultramarines,' sneered Aun'rai. 'Just to prevent us from taking this world, you would see it burned to ash?'

'In a heartbeat,' said Uriel, surprised to find he actually meant it.

How far he had come since his last time on Pavonis...

Aun'rai saw the truth of his words, and the moment stretched as the sheer bravura of Uriel's demand sank in.

'You are a barbarous race, you humans,' said the Ethereal. 'To think we were once like you fills me with shame.'

'Then you agree to end the fighting?' asked Uriel.

'If I order a withdrawal, you guarantee the safety of my warriors?'

'Every one of them,' said Uriel. 'I am a man of honour and I do not lie.'

Once again, La'tyen shouted something at her leader, and Aun'rai closed his eyes. Uriel could feel his despair, yet took no pleasure in the Ethereal's defeat. What he had said was true. The tau had fought with honour, and were a foe worthy of recognition.

Uriel nodded to Issam.

'Release him,' he said.

'You sure, captain?' said Issam. 'I don't like the look of that one with the governor.'

'Do it.'

Issam removed his blade from around Aun'rai's throat, and stepped back with his weapon raised. The Ethereal rubbed his neck, shaking his head sadly as his fingers came away sticky with red droplets.

'Captain!' shouted Learchus, and Uriel turned in time to see La'tyen's anguished face twist with rage and hatred. Whether it was the agreement her leader had made, or the sight of the Ethereal's blood, Uriel couldn't say, but, even as Aun'rai started to speak, it was too late to stop the inevitable.

La'tyen's honour blade sliced across Koudelkar Shonai's throat at the same time as Learchus shot her in the head. The Fire Warrior pitched backwards, the top of her skull blown away, but it was too late for Koudelkar. Arterial blood sprayed, and Uriel rushed to the governor's side.

He knelt beside Koudelkar, pressing his gauntlet to the ghastly wound, though he saw that it would do no good. The governor tried to speak, his eyes desperate with the need for a valediction, but La'tyen had cut deep and his life slipped away before he could form any words.

Issam took Aun'rai by the throat once again, but Uriel shook his head.

'Let him go, Issam,' said Uriel. 'This changes nothing. Aun'rai and I have made peace.'

The Scout-sergeant reluctantly released the Ethereal, and Uriel saw that he was itching to avenge the death of the Planetary Governor.

'I did not mean for that to happen,' said Aun'rai. 'Truly.'

'I know,' said Uriel.

'La'tyen suffered terribly while she was held prisoner.'

'I do not doubt it,' said Uriel without apology.

Aun'rai shook his head at Uriel's apparent indifference. 'You are a doomed culture, Uriel Ventris of the Ultramarines. You thirst for personal gain and glorification while your Imperium rots from within. Such a society cannot, ultimately, survive.'

'It has survived for ten thousand years since its inception,' pointed out Uriel.

Aun'rai shook his head. 'What you have is not survival, it is merely a slow extinction.'

'Not while warriors of courage and honour stand to defend it.'

'No such warriors exist amongst your race,' snapped Aun'rai. 'You are gue'la barbarians, and you delay the inevitable, nothing more. The frontier of our empire moves with the turning of the planets, and it will push you before it until there is nowhere left for you. Then your race will be no more. The frontier is for those unafraid to face the future, not for those who cling to a forgotten past. I am done speaking with you, Uriel Ventris of the Ultramarines, and if this war is over, then let me go.'

'When you order your forces to stand down,' said Uriel.

'It is already done,' replied Aun'rai.

THE TOWERING BATTLESUIT stood immobile before them, its weapons poised to destroy them. Colonel Adren Loic stood tall in the face of the alien war machine, ready to face death with a comrade-in-arms and with his head held high. A crackling nimbus of plasma played over the muzzle of the long tubular weapon, and Loic hoped his end would be swift.

'What the hell are you waiting for?' shouted Gerber. 'Do it!'

'Shut up, Gerber,' hissed Loic.

The battlesuit didn't move, and only then did Loic notice that the sounds of battle had ceased.

The sky was empty of the continual rain of missiles, and the high-pitched electrical noise of their battle tanks' main guns was strangely absent.

Loic shared a sidelong glance with Captain Gerber.

'What the hell's going on?' he asked.

'Damned if I know.'

The silence enveloping the battlefield was unnerving and unnatural. Loic had lived with the continuously droning rumble of war for so long that he had forgotten what silence was like. He heard the soft sound of the wind passing through the bridge's suspension cables, the distant rush of the rivers in the gorges below them, and the eerie sound of a silent battlefield.

Guardsmen and PDF troopers were emerging from their dugouts and bunkers, shock and confusion at the sight of the unmoving tau army overcoming their natural caution.

Then the scarred battlesuit with the blue helmet and flaming sphere emblazoned on its chest took a step forwards, its weapons powering down with a diminishing hum.

Loic flinched, and Gerber reached for a sidearm that wasn't there.

The red lens of its head-unit whirred as it focused on them, like the microscope of an inquisitive magos closing in on a specimen dish.

'I am Shas'El Sa'cea Esaven,' said the battlesuit, 'Fire Warrior of the Burning Star Hunter Coalition.'

Captain Gerber made as if to say something hostile, but Loic shook his head. 'Allow me, captain.'

Loic pulled his bloody and torn greatcoat tighter, attempting to straighten it and make himself more presentable.

'I am Colonel Adren Loic of the Pavonis Planetary Defence Force.'

'You command these warriors?'

'I am one of their commanders, yes,' said Loic, turning to face his fellow officer, 'and this is Captain... er... I'm sorry I don't know your first name, Gerber.'

'It's Stefan.'

'And this is Captain Stefan Gerber of the 44th Lavrentian Hussars,' said Loic, smoothly returning his attention to the tau. 'What's happening? Why have you stopped attacking?'

'My forces are standing down and leaving this world,' said the tau commander.

'Why?' asked Gerber. 'You had us beaten.'

'I am withdrawing because I have been ordered to withdraw by Aun'rai of the Ethereal caste, and warriors from Sa'cea do not disobey orders,' said the battlesuit, turning and marching away.

'You mean that's it?' demanded Gerber. 'All this killing and you're just walking away as if it never happened?'

'The Ethereals have spoken, and for the Greater Good, I must comply,' said the battlesuit, though Loic could sense the deep frustration in its voice. Like any warrior, the tau commander wanted to see the job done. As the battlesuit commander reached the edge of the ruins, he turned to face them once more.

'You were correct, Captain Stefan Gerber of the 44th Lavrentian Hussars,' said the tau warrior. 'You *were* beaten, and when the tau return to Pavonis, we will beat you again.'

IN THE LAST undulant slopes of the Owsen Hills, Lord Winterbourne watched through the vision blocks as the line of Hammerheads and Devilfish pulled back behind the ridge above his forces. The ferocity of the fighting had raged undimmed through the hills for days, and now, with Winterbourne on the verge of ordering a full retreat to Brandon Gate, the tau had ceased their assault.

'What the hell?' he muttered as the last of the tau spearhead vanished from the threat board.

'Sir!' cried Jenko. 'Vox-net has just cleared. I've got the captains of every Command on the horn trying to get hold of you! Every frequency that was jammed has just come back online!'

Winterbourne wiped a hand across his forehead, hardly daring to believe that the fighting might be over or that Uriel's plan could have succeeded.

'Any hostile contacts?' he asked. 'This could be a ploy.'

'None, sir,' confirmed Jenko, his voice rising with excitement. 'All tau forces are withdrawing further into the hills. They're going home! We saw the bastards off!'

Determined to see for himself, Winterbourne hit the hatch release and spun the locking wheel, opening *Father Time's* turret. He pushed his body upright, standing on his commander's chair as he looked along the line of dug-in tanks and fighting men of Lavrentia.

His fellow tank commanders had popped their hatches, and were watching in disbelief at the empty, shell-cratered wasteland ahead of them. Smoke from burning Leman Russ tanks and Chimeras drifted across the battlefield, and Winterbourne smelled the reek of scorched metal. Guardsmen in their foxholes were looking over to him to confirm what they were all hoping, that the fighting was over.

Captain Mederic of the Hounds, *Father Time's* guardian angel since the attack of the kroot, slung his rifle and said, 'So that's it then?'

Winterbourne was at a loss. 'So it would appear, Mederic.'

Mederic nodded. 'Good. Maybe I can get some sleep now.'

As Winterbourne watched the man turn from the hills, he felt incredibly proud of what his soldiers had achieved. They had fought courageously, and had done everything he had asked of them. Once more, the honour of the regiment had been tested, and, once more, the men and women of Lavrentia had risen to the challenge.

To think that he had been about to order the retreat...

'Contact all Commands,' said Winterbourne. 'Tell them that the war is over.'

ᘜ
AFTERMATH

WITHIN TEN HOURS of the truce being brokered between tau and Imperial forces, an armada of Mantas was rising into the air above Praxedes. Cheering Lavrentian Guardsmen watched them go, and Pavonis heaved a sigh of relief at its reprieve from invasion. Under the watchful gaze of the *Vae Victus*, the Mantas were recovered by their fleet, which turned and departed for the Tau Empire.

The aftermath of any fighting is always costly, and, though the tau had been defeated, the price of victory had been high. Thousands were dead, and many thousands more would forever bear the horror of their wounds. Scars, both mental and physical, would be borne by every man and woman who had resisted the alien invaders.

Much of Pavonis was in ruins, and yet again the loyalty of its leader had been found wanting. No longer could the people of Pavonis be trusted to guide their destiny, and though the yoke of alien overlords would not descend, the full might of the Imperium was sure to take Pavonis in an unshakeable iron grip.

In years to come, many would believe that the wrong army had won.

URIEL WATCHED AS the lifter servitors collapsed the last of the structures that had made up Fortress Idaeus, and loaded them into steel-skinned containers on the backs of heavy flatbed crawlers. Three Thunderhawk transporters sat on the wasteland of Belahon Park on the edge of the stagnant lake, ready to clamp the containers to their bellies and carry them to the hold of the *Vae Victus*. Warships from nearby systems, and a rapid strike cruiser from Macragge, had translated from the warp at the system jump point an hour ago, and were even now drawing near. Their might was no longer needed, but the threat of their arrival had won the day for the Imperial forces.

The Ultramarines presence on Pavonis was almost at an end, and, as the last of the containers was sealed, the time had come to return to Macragge.

The honoured dead and wounded were already ensconced within the Apothecarion at the *Vae Victus*, including the terribly wounded Techmarine Harkus, whose tenacity had kept him alive throughout the fighting.

Seventy-one members of the 4th Company, all those fit for duty, stood in ordered ranks before their captain and their Chaplain. Ancient Peleus stood at the centre of the warriors, the standard of the 4th Company flapping in a stiff wind blowing in from the south. Just beyond the Ultramarines, a deputation from the senior commanders of Pavonis waited a respectful distance from the Astartes ritual of closure.

Ancient Peleus lowered the standard towards Uriel, and he dropped to one knee before it. The fabric of the standard was blackened and tattered around its edges from the fighting at Praxedes, though Uriel would swear it was nowhere near as damaged as it had been when he had last seen it.

He took the heavy cloth in his hands, and touched it to his forehead before rising to his feet. Chaplain Clausel also knelt and touched the standard to his forehead before taking up position beside him once more.

Ancient Peleus lifted the standard, and reverently rolled the fabric around the banner pole before securing it with a soft rope of blue and gold velvet.

With the lowering of the banner, the Ultramarines were no longer on a war footing, and the sergeants turned and marched their squads away to their transports.

Chaplain Clausel said, 'It is done,' and Uriel felt a curious blend of sadness and relief wash over him.

'Yes,' agreed Uriel, 'although I cannot help but feel that we leave with a job half-done.'

'What do you mean?' asked Clausel.

'We drove the tau from Pavonis, but I fear we will have to fight those same warriors again.'

'If the Emperor wills it.'

Uriel nodded, knowing that there was no more to be said. As he made to follow his men to their transports, Clausel said, 'I meant what I said before we launched the drop assault. I truly believe you have paid the price for your transgressions against the Codex Astartes.'

The Chaplain paused, and Uriel could see that the skull-faced warrior was struggling for words, something he had never expected to see.

'It seemed impossible that a man who had abandoned the teachings of the primarch could ever find his way again, but you have proved me wrong,' said Clausel.

'Thank you, Chaplain.'

'I shall be sure to tell the Chapter Master upon our return home,' said Clausel, 'and any who doubt your loyalty or fidelity to the Ultramarines shall answer to me.'

Clausel hammered his fist against his breastplate, and bowed to Uriel before turning and following the rest of the Ultramarines.

Uriel watched him go, feeling a wholeness in his heart that came from knowing that he was truly home. Though he had felt welcome upon his return to the Fortress of Hera, only now did he feel fully accepted once more.

He heard footsteps approaching, and smiled at the sight of Lord Winterbourne and Colonel Loic. Both men wore their finest dress uniforms, a vivid panoply of gold and green, cream and bronze. The three-legged vorehound padded alongside the Lavrentian colonel, and Uriel saw a glittering medal hanging from its collar.

Winterbourne saw his glance and said, 'Old Fynlae deserved a medal as much as anyone. Saved my life back in Deep Canyon Six, after all.'

'I could not agree more,' said Uriel, shaking hands with Winterbourne. 'He is a credit to your regiment.'

'Farewell, Uriel,' said Winterbourne. 'If you ever find yourself in Segmentum Solar, you'll be assured a place of honour at the regimental mess on Lavrentia.'

'Thank you, Lord Winterbourne,' said Uriel with a short bow.

Winterbourne turned to Loic. 'I keep telling him to call me Nathaniel, but he never listens.'

'It was an honour to fight alongside you, Captain Ventris,' said Colonel Loic as Winterbourne led Fynlae away. 'I'm sure my lads will be speaking of this campaign for decades. That's twice you've saved this world.'

'I hope there will not be a third time,' said Uriel, and Lòic chuckled.

'You and me both, but I think we'll be fine from here.'

Uriel nodded. 'I hope so. You have come a long way since we first met, Colonel Loic. You and your soldiers have proved to be warriors of courage and honour, let no man tell you otherwise.'

Loic beamed at Uriel's words and gave him a crisp salute. 'Farewell, Uriel. Courage and honour!'

Uriel smiled and made his way towards the waiting gunships.

Courage and honour indeed.

ADMIRAL TIBERIUS WAS waiting for Uriel when he stepped from the ramp of the Thunderhawk that had brought him from Pavonis.

Straight away Uriel saw that something was terribly wrong.

The embarkation deck was strangely quiet, the crew standing with their heads bowed, as though in mourning. An atmosphere of anger and loss pervaded the ship, and Uriel marched straight over to the venerable Tiberius.

'Admiral? What has happened?'

'News from Macragge,' said Tiberius. 'It's Tarsis Ultra.'

'Tarsis Ultra? Where we fought the Great Devourer? What of it?'

'It's gone, Uriel,' said Tiberius. 'Destroyed.'

ABOUT THE AUTHOR

Hailing from Scotland, Graham McNeill worked for over six years as a Games Developer in Games Workshop's Design Studio before taking the plunge to become a full-time writer. In addition to many novels for the Black Library, Graham's written a host of SF and Fantasy stories and comics, as well as a number of side projects that keep him busy and (mostly) out of trouble. Graham lives and works in Nottingham and you can keep up to date with where he'll be and what he's working on by visiting his website.

Join the ranks of the 4th Company at
www.graham-mcneill.com

THE ULTRAMARINES SERIES

ISBN 978-1-84416-403-5

UK ISBN 978-1-84416-724-1

UK ISBN 978-1-84416-722-4
US ISBN 978-1-84416-723-2

UK ISBN 978-1-84416-860-6